*St. Martin's Paperbacks titles
by Marianne Willman*

THE MERMAID'S SONG
THE LOST BRIDE

The Mermaid's Song

MARIANNE WILLMAN

St. Martin's Paperbacks

THE MERMAID'S SONG

Copyright © 1997 by Marianne Willman.

ISBN: 0-312-96256-8

Printed in the United States of America

St. Martin's Paperbacks edition/July 1997

St. Martin's Paperbacks are published by St. Martin's Press, 175 Fifth Avenue, New York, NY 10010.

10 9 8 7 6 5 4 3 2

This is (as the Irish would say) a wonderfully long dedication, because I have so many wonderful people to thank.

To Jennifer Enderlin, my marvelous editor, who is every writer's dream of what an editor should be.

To Karen Solem, not just my terrific agent, but my friend.

To Margaret Singleterry, Sharon Hlavacek, Veronica Wilson, Chevelle Austin, Donna Bradshaw, and Laura Gilles, without whom this book would never have been written.

Also, to our "roommates" Janice and Richard Compton. To Terry and Judy Phillips, Jim Cobb, Jim Bender, Don and Karen House, Mark Hale, Mike McCall, Dan and Florence Crowell, Joe White, Kathy Mathis, Harold and Scott Morris, Scott Bernard, Bob Ramsey, Steve Fountain, Neil Bucholtz, Bruce Lanzer, and all the wonderful guys from Mueller Pipeliners and from Plumbers and Pipefitters Local 190—and in fond memory of Jeff White and Don Mathis, whose friendship meant so much. Thanks for your love and support during the year from hell.

To Barb McKinley, Patty Zuba, Donna Estes, Sandy Dunham, Kathleen Reed, Amy and Nancy from PT, Myrtle and Patty, and the staff at U of M for their caring and commitment.

And finally to those goddesses of cyberspace, the fabulous, the beautiful, the unique Ladies of the Lounge, for their generosity, encouragement, and boundless love.

. . . and of course, to Ky, my love and my inspiration.

The Mermaid's Song

Prologue

Strange things happen in the British Isles at certain times of the year, such as Midsummer's Eve and the winter solstice, when a net of invisible enchantment covers the entire land. This mystical web is most evident at sites sacred to the ancients: rings of standing stones or artesian springs similar to the great henge on Salisbury Plain or the numerous St. Bridey's wells that dot the countryside.

It is said that if you are of Celtic blood or pure of heart—and look very closely—you might catch glimmers of the magical net here and there in the gloaming. Of course, it is also said, you will mistake them for fireflies . . .

Flora O'Donnell looked up from the folklore book she'd been reading and listened intently. Her bedchamber, like that of the other teachers at the Hawthorne Academy for Young Ladies, was a spartan cubbyhole below the servants' attic. Hot in summer, cold in winter, its only benefit was its customary quiet—but a faint sound had broken her concentration.

Footsteps, perhaps? Reading after hours was a vice strictly forbidden by the headmistress. So was possession of a candle stub: while the students of well-to-do families were provided with beeswax tapers, the headmistress considered simple rushlights as adequate for her staff.

There were no further sounds, and Flora tried to relax. Her nerves were on edge—and had been since yesterday's newspaper had arrived. *Madman Escapes from Broadmoor* was not a headline conducive to a quiet night's rest. Especially when one happened to be only too well acquainted with the madman in question.

But she wouldn't think of that now. *Mustn't* think of that now. This was a new life with a new name. As far as the world at large was concerned, Katherine McCall had vanished into the fogs of London minutes ahead of the police, never to be seen again. Who would connect the missing woman with Miss O'Donnell of Hawthorne Academy?

She glanced down at the thick volume on her lap. In retrospect, a book about ghosts and pixies and things-that-go-bump-in-the-night was a poor choice for reading in the dark hours. However, it was the only book she'd had ready to hand.

Her thoughts jerked back to the sounds she'd heard earlier. There it was again—a low, insistent tapping, as of someone softly demanding entrance. Sliding the book inside her nightstand drawer, she blew out the candle, then tiptoed to the door. As she opened it an icy draft pushed past her and danced into her chamber. Flora realized that the casement window on the landing had blown open yet again.

A stark breeze tugged at strands of her auburn hair as she hurried to the far end of the hallway and reached up for the faulty latch. Her breath was snatched away by something more than the cold, shivery air. A brilliant, starry sky swept down to the far horizon, except to the north, where it was half obscured by the ominous black bulk of Swarthern Wood. Everything else was covered by a glittery crystal frost. She paused, struck by the wild beauty of the night. The winter solstice. According to folklore, this was one of the nights when pagan spirits roamed the land, and doors opened between the real world and the invisible realm of faerie. And if she were not a grown woman and an educated one, Flora thought she might very well believe it.

A breeze murmured through the ivy outside the window in a cryptic, ancient tongue, and the restless rustling of the vines came like an answering chorus of whispers. The primal voices filled her with strange, unspoken yearnings. A sudden conviction came over Flora that the window now framed a world no longer hers. On such a night, in such a setting, it seemed that almost anything—no matter how implausible by light of day—might occur.

On the heels of her thought, she saw tiny flickers of light from within the black heart of Swarthern Wood. They darted in and out of the trees, weaving their way among the dark branches from east to west. Their glimmering reminded her of fireflies, but it was too late in the year—and, of course, these lights were much too large.

Laughter drifted on the wind, like faint, silvery bells. Curiosity overwhelmed Flora's caution, and she opened the casement wide for a better look. It took her a moment to figure out their cause. Not fireflies at all, but white-gowned figures moving purposefully through the screen of brambles and branches. Her breath caught in her throat. She knew the Old Religion was still very much alive in rural areas throughout the British Isles. Could this be a procession of worshipers performing some arcane ritual from the dawn of time?

A door opened behind her and she jumped. Miss Melbourne, the librarian and mathematics teacher, exited her own room in a flannel gown and robe. Her sleeping cap was askew and her thin, pointed face etched with distress. "Thank goodness, you've seen them, too! What . . . what do you intend to do?"

"Do?" Flora pulled the casement shut and turned the latch firmly. "I intend to return to bed and bury my head beneath the covers until morning!"

"You will have your little joke, Miss O'Donnell," her colleague whispered earnestly. "I know how brave you are, after the way you rescued little Sarah Lipton when she fell into the pond. And, you know, we really cannot let the senior girls go wandering about in their nightshifts, unchaperoned."

Eva glanced back at Swarthern Wood, where the white-garbed figures were quickly disappearing into the deepest shadows. Of course. She'd fallen for a silly student prank. A last, girlish gasp of defiance from those who were leaving

the academy in the morning, to enter society as marriage-
able young ladies.

Her heart was still racing but she tried not to show it. It
would be a shame to disillusion timid Miss Melbourne, who
had invested her younger colleague with a wealth of what
Flora felt to be nonexistent virtues.

"I am more concerned by their lack of cloaks than their
lack of decorum. And why *are* the senior girls stealing
abroad at midnight, in this cold and frost?"

"Why, it's the winter solstice, you know. I imagine they
are on their way to St. Piska's Well to make a wish. It's
strictly forbidden. If Miss Pemberly discovers what they're
about, there will be trouble."

Flora grimaced. "In other words, you and I shall be
blamed for it." The headmistress of the academy was a
stern woman, and although she couldn't take her displeasure out upon the daughters of the wealthy families that
patronized her academy, she had no compunction where her
subordinates were concerned. She could usually keep the
girls in line by threatening to withhold their privileges.

"We're on the third floor, but Miss Pemberly's chamber
is on the second floor with the students' rooms. I wonder
that they would risk her wrath for such a foolish escapade!"

Miss Melbourne looked surprised at Flora's comment,
and more than a little wistful. "Why, they're hoping to
discover the identities of their own true loves." Surely a
risk worth taking, her tremulous voice implied. "Have you
never heard the legend of St. Piska's Well?"

"No, nor do I recollect having heard of a saint with such
an outlandish name." Flora was growing tired and cold,
and more than a little irritated with her students. Very likely
something would have to be done—and *she* was the one
who would have to do it.

But Miss Melbourne had become sidetracked by the romantic legend. "Piska was a beautiful young Briton, living
under Roman rule. She was a Christian and had taken a
vow of virginity. A centurion saw her bathing one day, and
became . . . er . . . demanded . . . Well, suffice it to say that
she leapt into a well rather than surrender to his lust, and
was transformed into a fish."

"A poor reward for her piety," Flora said. "Had *I* the power, I should have turned the centurion into a fish, instead."

Her levity shocked her companion. "I know you are funning, but you must not say such things, you know." Ignoring Flora's shrug, Miss Melbourne continued with her story. "To this very day the villagers believe that a mystical fish dwells in the Swarthern Woods, at the bottom of St. Piska's Well. They say that a young woman who goes to the well in her shift at the winter solstice, and throws a silver coin into the waters, will see the face of her one true love in her dreams. And, if that same young maid has a gold coin to part with as well, she may make a wish that is *certain* to come true."

Flora was torn between a laugh and a sigh. She was young enough to remember when such nonsensical stories would have captured her own fancy—and old enough to recognize the folly of it.

"I can imagine how uneducated young women might be taken with the legend. Piska, I'm sure, was neither a saint nor a Christian, but likely a minor Celtic goddess, adopted into the Christian faith just as the goddess Brigantia became Saint Bridget, and Lugh became Saint Michael."

Miss Melbourne was offended by her friend's dismissive tone. "Scoff if you like: I know you have a great interest in such studies." Her fingers clutched Flora's arm. "But there *is* something very strange about the well. There have been documented reports by clergymen and others of good repute of an intense glow that sometimes lights up Swarthern Wood. The source of this astonishing light has never been found, and all attempts to solve the mystery have met with utter defeat."

The little teacher's voice sounded rather wistful to Flora's ears—as if she hoped, in her heart of hearts, that such things were indeed possible. Flora tried to imagine the fearful Miss Melbourne tiptoeing out upon a dark midnight to cast her hard-earned coins into St. Piska's Well, and failed.

As they watched, the flickers among the distant trees grew less frequent, and finally coalesced in the spur of wood where Piska's Well was located. Within half a minute

they were already starting back. One by one the white of
the girls' nightrails vanished as they covered themselves
with their cloaks.

"Go back to bed, Miss Melbourne, you're shivering.
And look, the girls are already heading home through the
woods. They'll be in their beds in no time. I'll keep an eye
upon them until they're back, safe and sound."

Miss Melbourne's fears were eased. She let Flora persuade her, for her lungs were delicate and she suffered from
the effects of the night air. "If you are sure, then . . . ?"

Flora nodded and watched until her friend's door closed
softly and she was alone. She was quite fond of Miss Melbourne. In the year since she had joined the faculty as
French and history instructor, she had made no other
friends among her peers. The others were at least ten years
older than Flora, and the anxious and suspicious atmosphere fostered by the academy's headmistress did not pro-
mote fellowship among the staff. They survived her iron
rule under the theory that the best method of having their
own imperfections go unnoticed, was to point out the short-
comings of others.

Nor, to be truthful, would Flora have encouraged any
friendly overtures. Lonely women, isolated from the outside
world, tended to dig out information from one another with
the fervor of young boys searching for buried treasure.
Flora wasn't interested in such exchanges: the fewer lies
she had to tell, the better.

She turned her attention back to the window, where the
lights bobbed and danced like will-o'-the-wisps. Flora wondered if the students had more than a scant handful of cop-
per and silver coins left to share; and she sincerely doubted
that there was a single gold sovereign among them, with
which to test the second part of the legend. Most of her
pampered charges had squandered their monthly pin money
allowances on ribbons and lotions and all the things they
felt would make them desirable to the opposite sex.

She shook her head. Poor things, so young and eager for
love. So sure that it would solve their every problem and
turn their humdrum schoolgirl lives into sheer delight. A
few years ago she surely would have joined them in their
midnight pilgrimage if she'd had the chance, laughing and

giggling all the way. Dreaming of handsome and charming strangers, and a thoroughly romantic future. The more fool she!

It was because she'd fallen under the spell of handsome and deceptively charming Robin Harding that she was trapped in her present circumstances, living a lie under an assumed name. The only remnant of her past she'd kept was her middle name, an inheritance from her beloved mother, and one common enough that it would raise no comment.

Flora was lost in bitter memories. So much time had passed since she'd thought of Robin that she'd felt she'd successfully blotted him out of her mind, and put it all firmly behind her. But the pain was still there, festering anew after learning of his escape from Broadmoor. She willed it away, concentrating instead on the errant students.

There were a dozen or more of them, racing away from Swarthern Wood, across the old stone bridge toward the school. Saint Piska's legend would surely grow after this night's work: any villager seeing the students abroad in their nightgowns might be forgiven for mistaking them for phantoms. Perhaps that was how the woods had gotten their haunted reputation.

She waited at the window to make sure they all negotiated the old bridge safely. The last stragglers caught up with the rest and they rounded the corner to the side door, then vanished from her view. She wasn't able to make out any faces, but she would have been surprised if Johanna Cheney was not their ringleader.

Johanna's determined and rebellious nature would have gotten her sent home months ago, if not for the fact that her guardian was extremely wealthy, and willing to pay whatever it took to keep her at Hawthorne Academy. Flora had heard that Mr. Cheney paid double the usual fees, and wondered if it were true. If so, the teachers should be given a salary increase for having to put up with her. Johanna was a rare handful. She had intelligence, beauty, and money. Everything a girl on the verge of womanhood could want—except a loving family, and a guardian who did more than pay her fees and grant a generous allowance of pin money. For all that the other students envied her, Flora felt a deep pity for Johanna Cheney. She knew herself how difficult—how very painful—it was to be alone.

The wind turned icy, and Flora reached up to close the casement. As she was about to turn away, her gaze was arrested by something peculiar. She strained her eyes. Was that a white shape lying still among the trees? A pale hand waving? Impossible to tell at such distance. Had one of the students stumbled and injured herself?

How thoughtless of the others not to have noticed one of their number was missing! Why, if Flora hadn't stolen a few hours to read in bed, and the fallen girl were one of the few with a private room, her absence might not have been noticed till breakfast. Poor child, whoever she was, she must be terrified to find herself deserted and alone. Especially at midnight, in what was reputed to be a haunted wood! She hoped the injured girl wouldn't catch her death from lying on the frigid ground.

Regretfully, she tiptoed past Miss Melbourne's room. There was no one else to whom she could turn. She ducked into her own chamber, slipped into her boots, and hastily threw on her hooded wool cloak. Pausing only to grab up her spare blanket, she hurried quietly down the stairs. She had to pass Miss Pemberly's door, and was reassured by the rasp and buzz of heavy snoring that issued forth.

She hurried down the circling stone steps to the ground floor, along a corridor thick with shadow, and out through the side door—which, she noticed, no longer squealed like a *ban sídhe* as it opened and shut. One of the taller girls must have secretly cleaned and oiled the iron hinges.

As she crossed the bridge, the wind whipped at her cloak, almost wrenching it off. She realized that the button had come loose and was hanging by a mere thread. Fortunately, she had a bowknot brooch pinned to the shoulder of the garment, a gift from happier days. Flora unfastened it and used it to secure the neck of the cloak.

It seemed to take an inordinately long time to reach the outskirts of the wood. If she cut through that jutting tongue of trees, she could reach the injured girl more quickly. Something primitive and frightened inside of her protested, but she pushed it away and plunged into the mysteries of

Swarthern Wood. The smell of dank leaf mold and earth filled her nostrils. For several minutes she lost sight of the crumpled white figure, but after a few twists and turns she quickly spotted it amid the gloom. But surely it had been closer to the edge of the trees? Her shortcut seemed like a poor idea now.

She made her way over the wet, slippery ground cover and past mossy trees. Brambles clutched at her hem and snagged against her bare ankles, leaving streaks of fiery pain. No matter how far Flora went into the heart of the wood, it seemed like the white figure remained just a few more fearful yards ahead. Tripping over a fallen limb, she skinned her knuckles. Although the pain brought tears to her eyes, she stumbled to her feet once more. There was nothing to show her the direction, only darkness and the blacker columns of the trees. She turned hastily around.

A tall form loomed out of the shadows and Flora exclaimed aloud. Her imagination had immediately molded it into the shape of the escaped madman. Reason asserted itself as her vision adjusted. She had almost run into a standing stone as tall as a man. Its rough shape vaguely suggested a hooded head and shoulders, and it seemed to radiate an eerie, pagan menace. Reason was no match for fears born of primal instinct.

In sudden fright she plunged deeper into the woods, until the need to catch her breath made her stop to get her bearings. She forced herself to act sensibly. There was no use in blundering about like a half-witted calf in a bramble patch. Cold moonlight speared down through a gap in the trees. Ah, yes. She knew where she was now—and there was that motionless patch of white dead ahead. *A poor choice of words*, she thought to herself.

She crashed noisily through the brush and the figure moved. "Don't be alarmed. It is Miss O'Donnell and I've come to help."

Flora bent back the branches and found herself in a small clearing. It was very bright in the open moonlight, and the hollow sound of dripping water was louder than the wind soughing through the treetops. She saw the white form amid a tumble of rocks and recognized it as she drew close. Not the figure of some fallen student, but Johanna Cheney's expensive white wool shawl, snagged from an overhanging branch. Flora ground her teeth. She felt a complete and utter fool. All this way in the frosty air, well after midnight, on a wild-goose chase.

Her own predicament struck her. She'd had no fear for herself when starting out on a supposed mission of mercy; what possible explanation could she have now, if she were spotted returning from the wood at midnight, like a silly schoolgirl? Miss Pemberly's punishment of such a transgression by a faculty member would be certain dismissal.

Flora shivered. It would not be the first time she'd been set adrift without an oar, but each time it became more difficult to bring herself about. This time she didn't think she would have the strength to even try. No, the Hawthorne Academy was her last hope and refuge.

A blast of wind stirred the branches overhead until they groaned in protest. Every weird tale she'd heard of Swarthern Wood flooded back to chill her blood. Wisdom warned her to flee, but curiosity drew her closer. So this was the legendary St. Piska's Well. Why, it wasn't a proper well at all, as she'd imagined, only a small pool formed amid the rocky outcropping. Certainly not anything that would conjure up magic and mystery in the minds of the locals.

If there were any credence to the story, Flora thought, the poor saint would have had to be a minnow. No, a tadpole at best!

A drop of pure, burning cold fell upon Flora's hand, silencing her inner laughter. She gasped and birds flew up in alarm, blacker than the deep night sky. She seemed frozen to the spot. Another splash of fire on her hand made her look up. The drops of cold water dripped from the lip of a high ledge, each one as round and white in the moon's pale glow as a shimmering pearl.

Or a bright and fishy eye.

Flora drew back abruptly, and the spell was broken. Her arm brushed against something solid hidden in the thicker shadows. What she had mistaken for a flat, black rock was actually the yawning mouth of a wide cistern. As she reached up to detach Johanna's expensive shawl, Flora's cloak swirled and tangled around her like a living thing. Grabbing at the low edge of the cistern for balance, she caught her hair on the twigs of an overhanging branch. Flora didn't know whether to laugh or cry. No matter where she went, it seemed that she brought her own contrary luck with her.

Patience had never been one of her better qualities. The more she struggled the more entangled she got. Something skittered down the rocks and a sudden atavistic terror seized her. She jerked violently back, wrenching several hairs from her scalp. The pain brought tears to her eyes. Shrugging off her cloak, she managed to extricate herself. As she yanked at the garment to free it, she heard something small and metallic plink away. Oh, no! Flora reached for her slipping cloak and muttered a Gaelic oath. She'd lost her brooch.

Her brief search was futile. She had no idea in which direction the brooch had gone. She could try all night and never hope to find it. With the lack of light and the rapidly falling temperature, the only solution was to come back by day.

Still muttering, she hurried back the way she'd come, wanting to throttle the spoiled schoolgirl who'd left her shawl and given her such a fright. She and Miss Johanna Cheney would have to have a little chat in the morning. Flora clutched her cloak more tightly against the chill. *Magic wells and mystical fish, indeed!*

A short time later she was safe and sound, in the small, undistinguished room that was both haven and prison. She sighed as she hung her cloak from its peg and readied herself for sleep. Climbing into bed, she pulled the quilt up to her chin. Starlight frosted the window, but a cozy warmth seeped into her body. It was likely that she would live out her days beneath the brooding rooflines of the Hawthorne Academy. A dreary fate, but far better than anything she might have expected a few years ago. Certainly better than Newgate Prison.

Unlike her students, Flora knew she must be contented with her fate, no matter how much it rubbed against the grain. Not that she could truly fault their girlish longings. Dreams and wishes nourished the hungry soul and stirred the feminine heart. Reality, in the form of Robin Harding, had cured her of such foolishness—God rot his black soul!

But Flora's passionate nature and longing for love existed quite independent of her intellect, although she fought to subdue them. There was no use crying over the past. But if life *were* a fairy tale, what would she wish for herself? A new life. Adventure. Freedom. The ease that wealth can bring. All the things that were impossible to a woman of her circumstances, except perhaps through marriage. But after Robin Harding, it would take a most unusual man to ever again tempt her into such romantic folly. It was extremely unlikely such a paragon should ever come her way.

But the wish was there, as real as a thought or prayer, when she closed her eyes and drifted into sleep.

And that wish, having taken form out of Flora's hopes and longings, drifted out toward Swarthern Woods just as the rising wind sent the branches dancing around the stones of St. Piska's Well.

A twig reached out like a fairy hand and caught at the bow-shaped gold brooch that had fallen from Flora's cloak onto the rock. The dancing breeze bent the twig and, as it sprang free, the brooch went flying over the well's dripping edge. It bounced against the sides of the cistern, like the chiming of elfin bells. A gentle *plip!* announced the moment that it struck the dark water far below. The golden brooch sank without a ripple. At first the water's surface remained a smooth black mirror, reflecting a tangle of silvered branches and dappled starlight.

The disturbance came a few seconds later, stirred by Flora's heartfelt wish and her unwitting gift of gold. For a few long moments the woods were wrapped in a profound silence, as if the Earth held her breath. Then something immense and sleek rolled over in the depths of St. Piska's Well, sending wide ripples lapping and sighing against the ancient stone sides. It broke the water's surface, leaping joyously up toward the pearly moon, then fell back in a glitter of milky, iridescent scales.

The great splash produced a flare of blinding white light that lit up half of Swarthern Wood for several seconds. The phenomenon was seen for miles around by amateur astronomers, insomniacs, poachers, and the few desperate lovers who were abroad at such an ungodly hour, and passed from pub talk to local legend in the wink of an eye.

Although several adventurous boys thoroughly searched the woods hoping to find a meteorite in the following weeks, nothing was found of one.

Nor, though its owner searched just as diligently, did Flora O'Donnell find any trace of a certain small, golden pin fashioned in the shape of a bow.

Chapter One

$\mathcal{F}$lora's intuition failed her the next day, when Blaise Cheney entered her life. There were no waking premonitions, no warnings of the unusual events about to surround and enfold her. It was only later that she recalled vivid, tangled dreams: warm sun, brisk wind; armies of ancient standing stones; voices like golden bells, singing; granite cliffs and rock-strewn bays defending the land from a restless, foam-lashed sea.

The morning dawned rosy and bright over the little village of Hawthorne, but she was dull and heavy-eyed as she dressed. Splashing cold water into the chipped china basin, she shivered in her thin chemise. She hoped her senior students felt the worse for wear after their midnight adventure—and that it would be worth the pain of conjugating irregular French verbs after losing so much sleep.

Then she heard sound of early activity, and remembered that there were no classes scheduled. Of course! The students, except for the few year-round boarders, would be leaving to return to their scattered homes for the Christmas holidays. As for the senior girls, the majority of them were leaving for good, in preparation for the coming Season, when they would make their official debuts.

Flora smiled. It was no wonder they'd been so daring the previous night. It had been their last girlish gasp: in a matter of weeks they would go from schoolroom misses, ineligible for parties and balls and scarcely permitted to utter a "yes" or "no" in public, to fashionable young ladies thoroughly immersed in the serious business of en-snaring eligible husbands.

Ordinarily the girls would have departed the previous week, but heavy winter rains had turned the roads to quagmires. Now, with three days of penetrating frost, the general exodus was to begin. It seemed she would have to postpone her chat with Johanna Cheney until the following day, if she meant to pursue the topic. That seemed unkind, since Johanna would be left behind while the other girls went home to families gathered together for the holidays.

Flora sighed. Poor Johanna. Perhaps she could speak to the girl as an interested and well-meaning mentor, not as an exasperated faculty member. There had been times when she'd felt a rapport building between them, but too often Johanna would retreat without notice into prickly aloofness, like a hermit crab pulling back into its shell.

As she descended the stairs a short time later, she was still thinking of Johanna and what she might do to help her. Flora knew, all too well, what it was like to be alone in the world. Her irritation had turned from Johanna's thoughtlessness to her mysterious guardian, who spent a fortune on his ward's physical upkeep, but not a penny's worth of effort on any other aspect of her life. Little wonder the girl was so sulky and ill-tempered. How must she feel today, with most of her friends leaving, never to return?

Halfway down the staircase she saw a group of senior girls milling about in the great hall below, in positive fevers of excitement. Movement from the corridor above caught her eye. She looked up in time to see Johanna turn and slip away from the second-floor railing, pale and forlorn.

Flora burned with indignation on the girl's behalf. If Monsieur Blaise Cheney ever crossed her path, she would give him a rare earful!

From a window high up in the attics of Hawthorne Academy, a lone figure watched the parade of arriving and departing carriages. Sunlight winked and sparked off the polished fittings. Inside the various vehicles, excited students looked forward to holiday reunions with friends and family.

For some, there would be weeks of happy indulgence before returning to school; for others this was the final departure. They had left the schoolroom forever, exchanging it for the adult pleasures of the drawing room and ballroom. Their schoolroom days were as dead and gone as last summer's scattered leaves. Not a single girl looked back as the carriages rolled out through the gates.

Johanna Cheney leaned her forehead against the cool windowpanes and watched, too numb for envy. Her particular friends, Lottie Lewis and the Honorable Alice Granville, were among those leaving to enter society. For all their promises of frequent letters and invitations to town, Johanna knew their friendships were irrevocably lost to her. Their paths would not cross again.

Turning away, she went silently past the trunks and boxes that were the detritus of generations past. She moved like a ghost through the shadows. This forgotten corner beneath the eaves was her secret place. She had discovered it years ago, during one of the long summers when school was not in session and the other children gone. At first she had enjoyed those times alone. For a bold and curious child, the winding corridors and interconnecting rooms beneath the jumble of roofs and gables had been a mysterious kingdom to explore.

Then one day she had slipped behind a large traveling trunk and found a hidden door. It hadn't been intentional, but the opening had been obstructed so long that no one had remembered its existence. The chamber ran along the sheltered side of one wing. It walls were paneled, the floor covered with woven mats, and the two dormer windows hung with worn velvet curtains. In winter, the heat from the kitchens radiated from the massive chimney that formed the end wall. Johanna suspected the room had once been a priest's hole. Other times, brooding times, she imagined it was where Mr. Rochester's mad wife had been locked up in *Jane Eyre*.

She had made herself a hideaway in her corner attic. Inside it, she'd found a treasure trove of discarded furniture and enough ancient finery to outfit an elaborate costume drama: farthingales and panniered gowns of damask and silk; cavaliers' wide-brimmed hats with crumpled plumes attached; velvet capes and dressing gowns with tasseled sashes; dark dresses that resembled Puritan garments; long-sleeved muslin tunics, whose purpose she could not fathom, and colorful shawls from the earth's four corners.

It was her Aladdin's cave, her sanctuary, where she could read undisturbed or while away her boredom with day-dreams of fairy palaces and handsome princes, and magical islands that rose from the sea every hundred years. Lately it had begun to look like what it really was: a shabby, abandoned room filled with abandoned goods. *And I have fitted right in,* she thought disconsolately.

She had pretended that she didn't mind her strange status at Hawthorne. Indeed, she had convinced her friends that she felt fortunate to be unique among her peers. That had been a lie. She cared bitterly. But she had grown adept at hiding her innermost feelings. Sometimes they churned so violently they were hard to rein in. More so in these past few weeks, when everything was changing and out of her control.

She went back to the window and looked out beyond the busy courtyard. The roofs of Hawthorne Village were off to her right. Beyond it lay the tidy estate of Squire and Lady Hawkins and the sprawling stone farmhouse and pros-perous acres belonging to William Black's father.

Johanna had seen the Black family at church every Sun-day she could recall. A thin, birdlike widow accompanied by her eight strapping, red-haired sons. Every lusty village girl—and more than a few more tenderly raised students at Hawthorne Academy—daydreamed of being courted by William, the most handsome and charming of all. Not so short a time ago, she had been one of them.

Movement attracted her eye. In the far distance an ele-gant carriage bowled along the main road. Closer at hand a fusty wagon pulled up before the vicarage: Miss Tomp-kins, the vicar's spinster sister, returning from Oxford no doubt. Life went on as always.

Johanna left the little room, closing the door behind her. She knew, as she did so, that she would not return again. Like her friends, she had passed over the line from school-girl to adulthood, and must put away the things of her child-hood. But, oh! how she envied them.

*   *   *

It was long after noon when Blaise Cheney expertly tooled his carriage through the ornate entrance gates of Hawthorne Academy, and reined in near the front door. He took up a parcel from the seat beside him, dismounted, and turned his vehicle over to a waiting groom.

The groom eyed the newcomer warily. A well set-up fellow, black as a gypsy from some foreign sun, and with a dangerous glint in his eyes. Not the kind of man you'd want to meet of a night on some dark moor. But when the man nodded and threw him a coin, the groom decided it was just the way the foreigner's dark brows knit together that gave him such a fierce appearance.

Blaise frowned up at the gloomy brick walls and turrets. His recollection of the place was faulty. The grounds were well kept, but more modest than he recalled, and the gray stone buildings looked damp and sorry in the pale winter sunshine. Perhaps, he decided, it was only that the scene suffered in contrast to Egypt, and the golden lands where he'd spent the past several years.

He wished he were there now: he would never have left Cairo if urgent business had not necessitated this abrupt visit to Britain. Blaise felt no affinity for England. The last time he'd set foot on English soil had been to escort his niece to boarding school a few years before.

It was only as he'd prepared for bed, late the previous night, that he'd realized his travels had brought him within thirty miles of Hawthorne. And, once so close to the academy, he'd felt that he would be remiss in not paying a visit to his ward. He doubted that Johanna would even remember him, but he supposed that he owed it to her late parents.

To Eve.

Mounting the steps in easy strides, he stepped inside the academy's great hall, and stopped short in surprise. It was colorful and noisy as an aviary of tropical birds. A dozen young ladies, modishly dressed for traveling, laughed and chattered among mounds of luggage and bandboxes. More trunks were being hauled from the upper floor by a beleaguered stable hand. He stumbled and a leather traveling case went cartwheeling down the stairs in a series of thumps, adding to the din.

Cheney looked around for someone in authority, and his glance fell on an auburn-haired woman. At first he'd thought her to be one of the older students, but then heard her addressed as Miss O'Donnell. She stood in the center of all the commotion like the calm in the eye of a storm, answering questions, solving problems, and issuing orders. Although she was fighting valiantly to keep from being overwhelmed, she appeared to be in imminent danger of losing the battle.

O'Donnell. He recalled that name from the annual summary he received on Johanna's progress from the academy. Blaise was surprised to find her so young and comely. From the astringent tone of her report on his ward's progress in history and French, he'd envisioned a much older woman. Someone all starch and vinegar, with steel gray hair skinned tightly back in an uncompromising bun. Someone, in fact, exactly like Miss Pemberly.

A housemaid in a print dress backed into him and muttered beneath her breath in exasperation. When she turned about and saw the dark stranger with his elegant clothes, she goggled as if he'd fallen from the moon. "Begging your pardon, sir, I didn't see you standing there."

"I would like to speak with the headmistress."

"She's not available sir, begging your pardon."

"I can see that affairs are hectic at the moment. I am prepared to wait until she is free to speak with me."

The maid gaped at him. "She's not here," she blurted out, having exhausted her store of known responses. "Been called away to visit the sickbed of her poor old auntie, she has."

He took pity on the panic in her eyes. "Then I wish to speak with whomever is in charge."

The maid knew the voice of authority when she heard it. She decided to put him in Miss Pemberly's private parlor, and wash her hands of the matter. "This way, sir."

He followed her down a short corridor to a fussy, overfull parlor crowded with a suite of brown horsehair furniture interspersed with side chairs, small tables, and whatnots. One wall held rigidly posed sepia photographs of students in their academy sports uniforms. A row of larger and unpleasantly stern photographic portraits hinted at Miss

Pemberly's forebears. He was amused. There was a tangible smothering sense of bourgeois respectability in the room, obviously aimed at reassuring anxious parents.

The maid waved vaguely in the direction of the sofa, muttered something inarticulate, and fled to report his presence. Cheney smiled wryly at her departure. He knew that he was no gothic hero, but was just as certain he hadn't grown fangs and wolves' ears since entering the grounds, as the woman's flight might suggest.

Flames danced in the hearth, adding a mellow sheen to the gold-painted walls. He set his parcel down on a side table and warmed himself before the fire. Even in summer, England always seemed to hold a chill. Without warning, his thoughts took a sharp turn, and he was assaulted by terrible memories. It was on just such a sunny and cool day, although in the springtime, that his life had been irretrievably shattered.

Blaise felt his throat tighten at the memories he thought he'd conquered long ago: he remembered how happy his brother and sister-in-law had been to leave as they'd set sail for Pont du Mor aboard his yacht, with their young daughter in tow. Hilliard had never been more happy, nor Eve more beautiful. His chest constricted as he remembered her then, hazel eyes reflecting the sun and rippling blue seas, her golden hair braided into a coronet.

They had set sail in a fair breeze, but as they passed the lle d'Ouessant, a fearsome storm had come whipping up out of the north without warning. He had never, before or since, seen clouds move in so fast, nor seas swell so high, so suddenly. It was still there in his mind's eye: sheer walls of glistening, gray-green water towering to the sky, while the yacht was tossed between them like a walnut shell. They had swamped the craft quickly, taking it—and his brother—to the bottom of the sea. The violent storm had become the stuff of legends along the Breton coast.

Blaise had managed to keep Eve and her daughter afloat on the mast until they were rescued by the brave men of Isle d'Ouessant in their lifeboats. Safe upon land and seemingly out of danger, Eve had succumbed to a lung fever. Less than two weeks later, after enjoining Blaise to see to her child and arrange for her to be reared in England, Eve had turned her face away, given a tiny gasp, and died. That had been his blackest hour.

He was left with nothing but emptiness, and a young girl who never asked after her parents, and played quietly in a corner as if nothing untoward had happened. The doctors had said it was a not uncommon reaction in a child to a devastating catastrophe, and she had seemed to recover uneventfully. Blaise could not say the same for himself.

He shivered and held his hands out to the fire in Miss Pemberly's study. For months after the yacht's sinking, he'd spent every waking moment wishing he could turn back time. Shaking his head, he forced the horror of the memories, and the bitter guilt they represented, into the shadows of the past once more.

There was nothing he wanted of England but to see the last of it.

Flora waved to the last of the departing students and the final parade of carriages wound through the school gates and out to the road beyond. As the clatter of iron wheels on cobblestone faded away, blessed peace descended. She heaved a sigh of relief. The past hours had been a mad scramble. Everyone had come at once for the last group of girls, leading to much loud and frenzied activity.

As the boot of the last vehicle vanished from sight, Flora sighed. What an incredibly hectic day it had been—and it was far from over! The headmistress had been called away to the bedside of a great-aunt, who was not only in danger of dying, but said to be as rich as Croesus. Which, Flora thought with cynical humor, explained the haste with which Miss Pemberly had hied herself off to the wilds of Yorkshire.

Adding to that, Miss Melbourne was prostrated with the migraine, and three of the other teachers were suffering from the effects of tainted cream buns they'd eaten on an outing to the village the previous day, leaving Flora with all the responsibility. She had thought the headmistress's role to be an easy one, with all the real work delegated to subordinates. Having to fill Miss Pemberly's shoes for the past hours had been a great eye-opener. Flora had an overwhelming desire to go upstairs and fall facedown on her bed for half an hour. Providing, of course, that there was no new crisis erupting.

The chances of that were doubtful, since she was still responsible for the other teachers, the household staff of twentysome—and Miss Johanna Cheney, who spent every holiday at Hawthorne. Small wonder, she thought, that the girl was increasingly bored, resentful, and moody.

The gong sounded, signaling time for the second meal of the day. The few students left behind turned wistfully away from the door and straggled toward the main dining room, where a cold collation had been set out. One was missing: Johanna Cheney, who was now the only senior student left in residence. No doubt she had gone off somewhere to brood. *Poor, forsaken thing,* Flora thought. She understood how difficult it was to be alone and isolated. She was determined to spend more time with the unhappy girl.

Not that Johanna would welcome any show of pity, of course, so it must be tactfully done. *When,* was the question. Flora hadn't had a free moment to herself since coming downstairs this morning. She was desperate to discover if Miss Pemberly had taken the London newspaper with her in the carriage, or left it behind. She had to learn more of Robin Harding's escape from Broadmoor, and see if there was any mention of herself in the article.

But first there was the meal to be gotten through. She turned and found one of the maids hovering nearby, looking ready to burst with news. "There's a visitor asking for you, Miss O'Donnell. A gentleman. I put him in Miss Pemberly's private parlor."

"For *me?*"

Flora's heart jumped in alarm. She took a deep breath around the sudden constriction in her throat. No one knew where she was. When she'd disappeared from London, she'd been careful to leave no traces as to her intended destination. Indeed, when she'd departed so precipitously she'd had no clear idea of where to go and what to do—only to cover her tracks carefully. "This gentleman . . . did he ask for me by name?"

"No, ma'am. He asked for Miss Pemberly." The maid wrung her apron. "Was it all right to put him in the private parlor? I didn't know, with Herself being gone and all.''

Flora smiled in relief. "Yes, Maisie. That was the proper thing to do.''

Now that her fears were allayed, she was able to enter the parlor with assurance. A stranger stood with his back to the fireplace, drawing a pair of gray driving gloves through his hands. A curious ring, some sort of signet with a carved sapphire stone adorned one finger. It caught the light, seeming to glow with its own cold fire. She saw that he was dark, with aquiline features and black eyes beneath slashing brows. Every line of his body radiated impatience and restless energy. The small room, with its fussy furniture and antimacassars and Staffordshire dogs was overwhelmed by his commanding presence.

He might be handsome in an unconventional way, Flora thought, except for that forbidding frown. Then he turned and she saw the puckered, star-shaped scar that marred his left cheek. It must have been caused by a savage wound.

He eyed her coldly. A warm flush rose from Flora's throat to cover her face. She was embarrassed enough that she hadn't noticed his arrival, and even more so now that he had caught her staring. He turned his face slightly so that the scarred cheek was in shadow.

"You're much younger than I expected.'' He came toward her, frowning.

Flora's flush deepened. "I am not the headmistress. Miss Pemberly was called away by grave illness in her family.''

That made his frown deepen. He was, she thought, either a man not used to making mistakes, or one not used to having them corrected. "I am aware of that. You are Miss O'Donnell.''

His abrupt way of speaking threw Flora off stride, and left her uncharacteristically irritable. "You have the advantage of me, sir. Maisie did not tell me your name, or what business you might have.''

"I am Blaise Cheney, Johanna Cheney's guardian.'' Kicking his heels for the past half hour had done nothing for his temper. "It's evident that the place is at sixes and sevens today. I trust my unheralded arrival hasn't caused you any inconvenience.''

A light flared in Flora's eyes. So, this was the elusive Mr. Cheney. And he was incensed at being left to cool his heels while she attended to the academy's affairs. While it was not her place to chide him for his neglect of his ward, she could not resist the opportunity: hadn't her grandfather always said she'd tweak the devil's tail, just for the tweaking of it? She purposely pretended to misunderstand.

"Oh, dear! I'm afraid your arrival has thrown me into disorder, Mr. Cheney. You see, we always pack up the students' trunks well ahead of their departure day. Unfortunately, Miss Pemberly didn't leave word that you had plans to entertain Johanna over the holidays this year, and I fear she isn't ready to accompany you."

He was clearly taken aback. "You mistake the matter. I have no such plans for my ward. I am in England on personal business. Since I was so near to Hawthorne, I thought I would take the opportunity to look in upon her and see how she gets on."

Flora lowered her eyes so he wouldn't see her opinion of him reflected there. Arrogant, unfeeling man! As usual, when her temper was riled, it ran away with her tongue.

"How fortuitous that you happened to be passing by the academy," she said tartly. "I am sure Johanna will be happy, after all these years, to see her . . . *uncle,* is it?"

His complexion darkened in anger. How dare this snip of a schoolmistress chide him in such an impertinent manner? "I am both her uncle and guardian," he said shortly. "But I am sure I need not bore you with the intricacies of my family relationships."

She felt a spurt of triumph. He didn't look the sort of man who could be goaded into such a sharp snub. Pricked his pride a bit, had she? Well, he deserved it. She ignored his carefully couched rudeness.

"Johanna is one of the senior students under my care. I take great interest in her studies. You will be glad to know that she has a keen intellect and ready understanding."

Blaise felt his annoyance grow. He couldn't remember when a woman had so aggravated him at such short acquaintance. And a mere schoolteacher, at that. "I am delighted to hear your praise," he retorted, "and I hope to judge for myself, very shortly."

Flora was weary of the game. "Very well. I will fetch her for you. Meanwhile, I shall order some refreshments."

"You needn't bother. I can only . . ." He saw the trap and stopped himself just in time. He could just imagine her smirk if he'd announced that he didn't mean to stay long. Devil take the woman! "Thank you."

He wanted a diversion to gather his thoughts. "If you are going to her room . . ." As he picked up the parcel, firelight glinted from his ring. It was quite unusual. A shield-shaped heraldic device with a mermaid holding an oval sapphire, and it appeared to be quite ancient.

Removing the lid, he handed the box to Flora. "I bought this for Johanna in town."

"It is very beautiful," she said genuinely. Whatever the man was, he had exquisite taste.

The box held a doll of marvelous workmanship. It was dressed in blue velvet edged with ermine, and held a tiny ermine muff in its lovely china hands. The heart-shaped face was lifelike and enchanting, framed by golden hair and complete with blue glass eyes that opened and closed. Flora judged that it had cost Mr. Cheney an amount equal to half her yearly wage. And, of course, it was totally inappropriate for a girl of an age to make her debut. She wondered exactly how old he imagined his ward to be.

She handed it back to him. "Perhaps you would prefer to give it to her yourself. I wouldn't wish to deprive you of seeing her face when she opens it."

She left Mr. Cheney with a guileless smile that made him feel uneasy and somehow at a distinct disadvantage.

Maisie hovered in the hall. "Begging your pardon, miss, but the special biscuits are all eaten up. The only ones left are the regular ones for the students' tea."

Flora's smile widened. "They will do quite well."

After searching for several minutes, Flora finally found her quarry. Johanna was in the wide window seat of the winter parlor, staring out through the wavy glass panes. An open book lay beside her. From the crease between her winged brows—so very like her uncle's—her thoughts were not happy ones. Flora could not tell if the girl's hazel eyes glittered with anger, or with tears. She imagined that perhaps it was a little bit of both.

Johanna scowled when she noticed Flora enter. "One would think that in this great empty pile of stones, there would be one place I could go to be alone."

Flora smiled. "Why, if you wish to be alone, I shall be happy to oblige you, Johanna. However, I think I should tell you that you have a visitor."

"If it is Mrs. Feeney, I do not wish to be measured for my gown today. She may return another time."

It seemed certain that Johanna had inherited her guardian's manners, along with the physical resemblance. Her rudeness annoyed Flora. "Yes," she answered crisply. "I am sure it would be nothing to send a forty-year-old woman trudging back two miles to the village on foot, on a cold winter afternoon, at the whim of a cross schoolgirl."

Johanna merely turned her face away and stared out the window. "The assembly is a month away, and I am not in the mood for visitors."

"Oh? That is really too bad," Flora said quietly. "The gentleman will be disappointed to hear it."

"Gentleman!" Johanna jumped and the book tumbled to the floor. Her complexion went from white to red to white in as many seconds.

Flora took pity on her. "Yes. Mr. Blaise Cheney, your guardian, is waiting for you in Miss Pemberly's parlor. I told him I would fetch you."

The girl knelt down to retrieve the fallen book and took so long doing so that Flora realized she was buying time to collect herself. No matter how much Johanna had secretly longed for family, it must be a shock to finally have her uncle appear in the flesh.

"Perhaps you would like to go to your room first and freshen up?" she suggested. "I'll tell him you'll be down shortly."

"Th-thank you!"

"Shall I come back for you?"

"No! I . . . no, thank you. I'll be down presently." Stumbling to her feet, Johanna flew from the winter parlor.

Flora went back down to the great hall, a frown between her brows. Seeing the reaction that the news had upon the girl, she felt even less in charity with Mr. Cheney. How thoughtless of him to ignore his ward's existence for so many years, and then descend upon her out of the blue, like some Olympian god! Not that she expected Johanna to fall on his neck with expressions of affectionate gratitude for his sudden visit. Johanna was a passionate little creature, and was quite capable of reacting with an outburst of some sort. And Flora wouldn't miss it for the world!

At the foot of the stairs she saw Maisie enter Miss Pemberly's parlor with a tray of refreshments. Flora entered in her wake. Mr. Cheney was clearly not impressed by the offering of dry, floury biscuits and tea. "I am afraid the only refreshments left are those normally reserved for the students."

That made him scowl. "Miss Pemberly runs a spartan establishment."

Flora coughed to stifle a laugh. She hadn't been so entertained in months. So, Mr. Cheney was ill-pleased to learn that the lavish fees he paid for Johanna's upkeep didn't provide her with much in the way of creature comforts.

"The academy's philosophy is that rich foods are not only unnecessary, but detrimental to the constitutions of growing children."

He paced from the fireplace to the window. "I shall have something to say about this to the trustees, you may be sure."

Flora's high spirits were punctured like a balloon. She'd meant to expose his neglect, and had instead exposed Miss Pemberly's miserliness. It might cost her her teaching position. Something in her face must have betrayed her flutter of alarm.

"You needn't be concerned," he said in his brusque way. "I'll not betray you. Any comments I may make will come from my own observations."

She was chagrined that he'd read her so easily, and mortified by her quick spurt of relief. Flora despised herself for it. She saw it as proof that her precarious situation had made her into a moral coward: another debt to chalk to Robin Harding's account.

Before she could say anything in return, Johanna arrived. She was pale and a little breathless as she entered and stood just inside the threshold. Although her face was defiant, Flora was glad to see that she had put on her best Sunday

dress of deep rose worsted, with neatly starched white collar and cuffs. It showed off the girl's blond beauty to good
effect, and at the same time endowed her with a measure
of dignity.

Cheney heard her, and picked up the gift he'd brought,
holding it before him as he turned, as if it were a shield.
The sight of his niece had a profound effect on him.

"Eve!"

He took a quick stride across the carpet, then stopped
dead in his tracks. All the blood had drained from his face,
leaving it white and haggard.

Flora looked from one to the other. Her intuitions stirred
uneasily. She felt a strange current swirl through the room,
filled with the ghosts of long-buried emotions. Cheney was
visibly shaken, but tried to recover his composure.

"Forgive me. You are Johanna, of course. I was startled.
You are the very image of your mother at the same age!"

An odd expression flitted over the girl's face. "Am I?
I've never seen a portrait of her."

He appeared confounded by her revelation. Dark color
flooded his face. "I believe there is a miniature of her at
the château. I shall arrange to have it sent to you."

He sent Flora a sharp glance, then looked down at the
boxed doll in his hands. "I am sure that you would prefer
it to this. Time seems to have flown by without my being
aware of it."

Johanna came forward and took the box from him, her
face white with strain. "Thank you," she said stiffly. "It
is exactly the kind of doll I should have wished to have
when I was younger. It was very kind of you to think of
me."

The unintended poignancy of her words smote Flora to
the heart. Evidently Cheney felt it as well. "Apparently,"
he said roughly, "I have not thought of you enough."

There was anger in his eyes, but Flora realized it was
directed at himself. "I suppose," he continued, "that I
imagined time had stood still for you, and that you were
the same child I used to take for pony rides along the
strand."

His niece flashed a look at him. "Did you really? I don't
remember. But then, I know so little about you."

He grimaced. "Every word you speak is another knife in my flesh. The more so because they are unintentional."

Johanna flinched and Flora stepped in adroitly. "I am sure you have much to talk over. I will leave you to visit privately. Johanna, you must tell your uncle about your triumphs at the local assemblies." She nodded graciously to Cheney. "Miss Pemberly subscribes to them as a way of introducing the girls to a bit of society, while under her protection. You will be gratified to know that Johanna dances, quite prettily, and that her dance card is always filled."

Blaise scowled. "Your point is well taken, madame. I see that my niece is a young lady on the verge of adulthood. You needn't beat me over the head with the knowledge."

Flora shrugged. "You will forgive me for thinking otherwise."

Her arrow found its target. To her surprise, there was a glint of appreciation in his dark eyes. "If your wits are anywhere near as razor-edged as your tongue, Miss O'Donnell, you could flay an unsuspecting man to death with a single thought."

Johanna bristled. "You must not judge Miss O'Donnell so harshly. Indeed, she has been kinder to me than anyone!"

Once again her innocent words took her guardian aback. Flora intervened. "Thank you for your defense of me, Johanna. Although I rather believe Mr. Cheney meant his words as a compliment."

"I did indeed." He sketched a mocking bow. "And once again I am indicted by the response."

She was so patently startled that he smiled. It wrought a sea change in him. With the smile he looked engagingly handsome, and younger than she'd imagined him to be. It vanished as quickly as it had come, like a flash of summer lightning.

She wondered cynically if he could put on and off this cloak of charm in the same way Robin Harding could. She wished she could intuit his intentions; but her instincts, so excellent in other areas, always betrayed her where men were concerned.

"I will leave you to your visit," Flora said. Although there was still awkwardness between uncle and niece, she saw that her continuing presence would be more of a hindrance to them. "Ring for the maid if you should require more tea."

"I imagine our visit will be short," Johanna said with a coolness she didn't really feel. "I doubt that we have much to discuss."

Flora read her charge's emotions well: the girl's initial shock was giving way to her more heated resentments. "You will give your uncle reason to believe he has wasted his substance on your schooling," she said severely, "if you show him so little evidence of your breeding."

"Oh, very well!"

As Flora left the room she was aware of the heavy silence behind her. She noticed both Maisie and Gladys hovering near the parlor door, and shut it firmly. Uncle and niece had much to discuss. In private.

As she left them and went off to see how the invalids were faring, Flora felt a weight lift from her shoulders. She'd been more worried about Johanna's increasing moodiness than she'd realized.

In her early years, Flora had trained herself with the intention of becoming a governess, partially as a means to escape her grandfather's house. She had also been drawn to it by her love of learning, and by Yeats's observation that a student's mind was not an empty bucket to fill, but a fire to light. Unfortunately, she'd discovered that the average student at Hawthorne was the mental equivalent of waterlogged kindling. Their main preoccupations seemed to be how to dress their hair to advantage, what colors best suited them, and which of the young men from St. John's School would be likely to sign their dance cards at the next assembly.

Johanna, though, was not as entranced with such matters. She had a quick intelligence that needed only the proper spark to illuminate it. Flora had begun to despair of ever kindling that spark. She'd long decided that the girl's chief problems were boredom, and a growing sense of isolation. It was no wonder that her childish mischievousness had curdled to sullen rebellion.

As Flora went up to check on the teachers who had fallen ill, she hoped that Mr. Cheney would conclude that his ward had outgrown the academy, and was ready to leave and make her entry into society. If not, she would point it out to him in no uncertain terms. Flora judged him to be the kind of man who took care of his obligations—once they were brought to his attention. It was time—and past time—that Johanna was returned to the bosom of her family. No matter how inconvenient that might prove for Mr. Cheney personally.

A half hour later Maisie accosted her outside Miss Melbourne's room. "If you please, miss, the gentleman and Miss Cheney have requested to speak with you."

"Thank you, Maisie." Flora headed down the stairs and toward the parlor, spirits rising.

She found Cheney staring into the fire, just as before; but he turned quickly when she entered. Johanna sat in an armchair across the room, looking uncharacteristically subdued. She was occupied in the inelegant task of picking at a rough cuticle on her thumb. Flora's first impression was that they had quarreled. His next words disabused her of the notion.

"I must make amends to my niece for my unwitting neglect, Miss O'Donnell. I have decided to remain in England for a few weeks longer, and to take Johanna to London for a little holiday, if there is no objection on your part. She is very eager to see something more of the world. A few days of shopping and dining out, and visits to the theater, seem to be long overdue."

Flora didn't hide her satisfaction. "I have no reason to object. You are Johanna's guardian, and she would certainly benefit from acquiring a little town polish. She will be ready tomorrow at any time you name."

Cheney held up a hand. "We leave at once. I have an appointment in London to conclude some urgent business. It cannot be put off."

His high-handed manner set her teeth on edge, but she had no choice. "Very well. I'll set the maids to packing immediately." She glanced at Johanna, expecting to find her ecstatic. Instead the girl looked dismayed. "That is," Flora continued, "if your niece is in agreement?"

Johanna rose. ''I should like to leave as soon as may be possible. I shall help pack up my things.'' She left the room with awkward grace, like a fawn taking its first tentative steps into the unknown world.

And so it was that the Cheneys, uncle and niece, drove away from Hawthorne Academy late that afternoon, on the first leg of their journey to London. As she watched their carriage pull out of the courtyard, Flora had a strong feeling that they were driving out of her life and that she would never see either of them again.

Which was the second time that day that her intuition grievously failed her.

Chapter Two

Flora walked briskly down a street of shops of Tunbridge Wells in the mild January sunshine. Pausing outside a confectioner's shop, she pretended to examine the display of sweets in the window, while anxiously studying the reflection of the street behind her.

She had the uncanny feeling that she was being followed. She had first noticed it after leaving the lending library, and it had grown stronger by the minute. Perhaps it was her imagination. No one from her past knew where she was. No one from the present knew *who* she was. But she still had nightmares of Robin finding her; and if it were someone else following her now, the alternative was equally bad: the Bow Street runners were after her.

Her heart skipped in her chest as the images in the windowpanes vanished, replaced by terrifying memories. She had been young and foolishly romantic when she'd met Robin. So eager to be loved. To belong to someone.

Robin had been so charming and sophisticated, so much the very model of a storybook hero with his shining fair hair and green eyes flecked with gold, that she'd endowed him with every splendid virtue. Flora, blinded by infatuation and his flashing smile, had blithely stepped into his web.

She wondered now how she had been so gullible; but he had seemed as perfect as he looked. Robin was a marvelously convincing actor. The stories he'd woven of his past and glowing future were the practiced lies of a man who earned his keep preying on lonely old women. Miss Hansen, the spinster who had hired Flora as companion, had begun to see through Robin's veil of lies, but hadn't shared her suspicions. That had proved to be a fatal error.

Flora fought back a sudden sting of tears. Robin dazzled her with declarations of love, seduced her with dreams of happily-ever-after. Luring her out of the house with plans of an elopement, he had instead robbed Miss Hansen of her father's extremely valuable collection of jeweled jade ornaments. The old woman had caught him in the act, and paid for it with her life. And Flora, fleeing in panic after discovering the crime, had been named by the police as Robin's accomplice.

Without benefit of trial, her guilt had been pronounced. She had been convicted by scandalous speculation in the London papers, and Robin's own statements at his trial. She had nothing but the truth on her side, and no one wanted to hear it. Especially since the only witness to the crime was dead.

Her fingers went to her throat involuntarily, as if she felt the hangman's rough noose biting into her flesh. She realized her hand was shaking.

She was jolted back to the present as rapid movement caught the corner of her eye. Glancing up quickly, she saw a man in blue livery coming along the street. Only a footman, bent on some urgent errand. Perhaps she'd imagined the whole thing. After all, she'd taken great care to cover her tracks.

Flora moved farther down the pavement and pretended to survey a fetching green bonnet in a milliner's shop. Perhaps the sense of being stalked was only a figment of her anxiety. She examined the reflected scene and her heart caught in her throat.

No. It was all too true. There he was, a nondescript man in a brown frieze coat. She remembered seeing him outside the stationer's, and there he was at the apothecary shop. He stood in the shade of the apothecary's sign, scanning the strollers intently. There were several carriages passing between them, and he seemed to have lost track of her when she'd crossed the street. He had only to turn her way, however, and the game would be up. Flora was furious with herself. Oh, if only she'd gone into the shop instead of standing outside like a ninny!

There must be some way to escape his notice again. Her agile mind went to work. Just ahead two young girls strolled arm in arm, talking and laughing, while their maids followed a dozen steps or so behind them. From their clothing and mannerisms, she judged them to be fresh from the country. The daughters of a newly prosperous merchant or a rustic squire as excited to see as to be seen.

They appeared to have no notion that this wasn't the high season for visitors, nor that the town had passed its prime as a fashionable destination. Except for the cathedral, there was little to fascinate.

The maids, one young and apple-cheeked, the other auburn-haired, were as smitten with their change in fortune, but hiding it more discreetly. The elder of the abigails, in a plain bonnet and navy cloak similar to Flora's, dropped her coin purse. A few shillings spilled and rolled along the pavement. She tsked and waved her companion on, then stooped to retrieve her coins. Without breaking stride, Flora neatly stepped into her place beside the younger servant.

"Could you be so kind as to tell me the way to the Church of St. Mary Magdalene?" she said, as the little group continued down the street. "I was told that it is well worth a visit. I believed it to be just around the corner when I left my hotel, but now I cannot find it to save my life!"

"St. Mary Magdalene?" The maid, being of good Calvinist stock, was taken aback. Her round pink cheeks flushed to crimson. "I wouldn't know, to be sure, miss. But then, we're new to Tunbridge Wells, we are."

Flora was relieved. In the stress of the moment she hadn't been able to think of a single church in town, and had used the first name that came into her mind. "I am new to town, also, and have become hopelessly lost. Perhaps I might walk along with you for a little way until I get my bearings."

A London maid would have been chary of Flora from the start, but this country girl hadn't learned to be suspicious of friendly strangers yet. Before they'd gone more than a short way, Flora and the talkative servant were chatting like old friends. She learned that the maid was employed by the Winslows, who had just hired a house in town for the season. They had come in hopes that a change in location would help the family matriarch recover from an attack of the rheumatics. And, Flora deduced from the overly casual mention of a coming ball, in hopes of successfully marrying off the Winslow daughters.

As they rounded the corner, Flora thanked her companion, wished her a good stay in town, and whisked inside the first shop they passed. A small bell tinkled to announce her arrival. Holding her breath, she waited until the second maid, the one in the navy cloak like hers, hurried by. She was soon followed by the man in the brown frieze coat. He wore a look of determined triumph.

Flora sighed in relief. Despite her agitation she was relieved that the other woman could give her a good twenty years. There was no chance of the Winslows' older servant being mistaken for Flora and hauled off before a magistrate as a wanted fugitive.

Keeping her back to the door, she moved to the far side of a display, blind to the rose and gold opulence of her surroundings. She was still in shock that the runners had tracked her as far as Tunbridge Wells. Perhaps they had merely spotted her by chance. After two years of successfully eluding them, Flora stopped watching over her shoulder. She should have never dropped her guard.

She couldn't believe how complaisant and careless she'd become. A chance to see the shops and visit the lending library had seemed like a safe and proper reward for all the months she'd been immured at the academy. Existing quietly at Hawthorne, like a mouse in its burrow, she'd forgotten that the cats were always on the loose. Oh, why had she ever let Miss Melbourne talk her into a trip to town?

Her heart was hammering so loudly it drowned out the voice of the very superior young woman addressing her. Flora hadn't even noticed her come out of the back. "I . . . I beg your pardon?"

The saleswoman, who'd greeted Flora in the cool voice reserved for discouraging impecunious shopgirls from wasting her valuable time, changed tactics when she saw Flora's face and heard her cultured tones: this was no tearoompourer or parlormaid on her half-day out.

The saleswoman put on her second-best smile. Once a wealthy eccentric had come in, dressed like a scullery girl, and bought up half the place. This auburn-tressed woman in the plain navy cloak might prove to be another such windfall in disguise.

"Good Afternoon, madame. I am Miss Henry, Madame DuValle's special assistant, at your service. Is there anything in particular I might show you?"

Flora took in her surroundings. She was in the shop of a fashionable modiste—and an expensive one. Any of the frothy tea gowns and tailored walking costumes would have paid the wages of the academy's entire faculty for a year.

"This morning dress in Pomona-green silk? Or perhaps the ombré velvet?" The saleswoman caressed one of the more expensive works with reverent fingers. "With Madame's coloring, this ivory tea gown with Venice lace would be exquisite!"

Her flattery was wasted.

Flora needed time to think. The looking glass on the far wall had shown her a glimpse of the man in the brown frieze coat, slowly retracing his steps. He hadn't given up; but neither had he spotted her thus far. And even if he did, the runner wouldn't accost her in the modiste shop because he couldn't be sure of her identity yet. Another man crossed the street to join him, and they stood talking together. Sharp panic stabbed at her. If there were two of them, she was in terrible trouble. She had to buy time.

In fact, it would be even wiser if she bought something else. Flora was thinking fast, and a plan was forming in her agile mind. Slipping off her cloak, she reached a hand inside her pocket, and touched the flat packet pinned into the seam. Its bulk reassured her. It was all the money Flora had in the world, except for the few coins in her reticule, and was intended to pay her traveling expenses if flight became necessary again.

She couldn't bear to part with it; yet, it would be useless if she were taken into custody. Better to be safe now, and make good her escape. She tried to guess at which of the lovely garments would be least dear. Her gaze fell on a display. "I should like to try on the . . . the bronze faille walking cloak."

"Ah, yes. Elegant. But rather ah, *mature* . . . ?" And not nearly as costly as the tea gown. The saleswoman tried to hide her disappointment.

Glancing around the shop, Flora spied a pelisse of russet velvet, with gold braiding at the collar and sleeves. There was even a matching hat, complete with curling plumes to coquettishly obscure half the wearer's face. Some instinct told her that it had been ordered made up and then not purchased.

"You are right, of course. I would look positively dowdy in the bronze. What, if you please, is the cost of the russet ensemble?"

The saleswoman told her, and waited for a betraying gasp. Flora kept her head. She knew the little games of mutual reward that wealthy woman and shopkeepers played: it was only the poor and middle class who paid full price for anything. Status and continued patronage were everything.

"That is too dear. I could find something far more suitable in London for two-thirds the price." She gave the saleswoman a shrewd look. "This is a predicament. My bedchamber sustained damage from a chimney fire early this morning, necessitating the replacement of my *entire* wardrobe. I sent my maid to take care of certain tasks, but cannot charge her with the responsibility of choosing my clothing." She indicated her dress and the cloak slung over her arm. "Naturally, I do not want to go about town in this shabby, borrowed garment."

Since MadameDuValle's special assistant was actually the fictitious Madame DuValle herself, Flora's words had fallen on delighted ears. Replace an entire wardrobe? And for a woman with such an elegant figure and the good taste and pocketbook to match? She made a few rapid calculations. With the low wages she paid her seamstresses and apprentices, she could make a small fortune. She toted the possible expenditures up in her mind, until it fairly whirled with visions of profit.

As she was doing so, Flora pulled out the packet of money in its velvet pouch. "I prefer not to have bills sent to my home," she said with what was almost a wink. "You see, I have my own income and rather extravagant tastes.

My husband is a proud man . . . touchy about such things. You will understand what I am saying."

Miss Henry did, indeed. There were quite a few dashing matrons of independent means, who also didn't wish their husbands to become aware of the great sums they spent on clothing.

This time it was her voice that lowered. "Madame DuValle's policy has always been to offer certain, ah, benefits to her outstanding customers. I am sure that it would apply to this instance."

"I see we understand one another," Flora said dulcetly.

A quarter hour later an elegant young woman in russet velvet stepped out of Madame DuValle's shop, and into a waiting hansom. The curling plume of her chic bonnet hid her face from view as the beaming shopkeeper handed the driver a bandbox and several parcels. Although Flora had purchased only a hat and pelisse, the woman was certain there would be many more profitable sales to her new customer, in the very near future.

The door closed and Flora leaned back against the seat. If the Bow Street runners entered the shop in search of her, they would learn that the only customer had been a Mrs. Winston, a wealthy merchant's wife, currently residing in a hired town house. She almost laughed aloud, thinking of the tongue-lashing the respectable merchant's wife would give to any Bow Street runner bold enough to confront her in her home.

She watched their reflections in the polished glass of the side lamps. The man in the frieze coat and his companion had paid no attention to the departure of the lady in russet velvet. The wind was cold, their quarry obviously gone to ground. They shrugged and went along the street, disappearing behind the brass-fitted door of the Acorn and Ivy.

Flora was giddy with relief for the few minutes it took to reach the inn where she was to meet Miss Melbourne and pick up the school trap. She would repack the russet outfit in the box with silver paper and don her worn navy cloak once the cab drove away from the inn.

She wondered what on earth she'd do with her elegant new clothes, when she returned to Hawthorne Academy and became plain Flora O'Donnell once more.

Not that it would be for long. It was, Flora thought with sinking heart, time to make another abrupt departure.

The sun had started its downward slide toward the west as Flora and Miss Melbourne headed back toward the academy in the school's trap. The chill wind blew through the leafless trees of the windbreaks, and she longed for the warmth of the new outfit, stowed safely away. She'd managed to hide the boxes under the piles of supplies and drapery fabric samples they'd brought back for Miss Pemberly. She'd worry about smuggling them up to her room later.

She had pulled the trick off, and should feel some satisfaction from eluding her pursuers, yet Flora was deeply dismayed at her capacity to deceive. The loss of her entire savings was devastating, but she gladly made the sacrifice for her freedom. The loss of her integrity was equally severe. She envisioned her path in life to come as a series of interludes, linked only by the change of seasons and a crooked path strewn with lies.

Her grandfather had warned her repeatedly of her nature. *"You are your mother's child, willful, disobedient, and deceitful! Mend your ways, or you will follow her in the same downward path to perdition!"*

He would, Flora thought glumly, certainly be pleased if he could know that his dire predictions for her were coming true.

While she plotted her next move, she must be very, very careful about where she went and what she did. There was the private assembly next week, and she saw no way of avoiding going to chaperone her charges. Although, she mused wryly, it didn't seem likely that a Bow Street runner would be genteel enough to join the select list of invitees for the subscription dances.

"You are very quiet," Miss Melbourne said, as the trap turned at the corner near the village's square-towered Norman church. She could hear the ivy rustle in the sharpening breeze. "I do hope you have not taken a chill."

Flora collected herself. "Not at all. I am merely thinking of tomorrow's history lesson."

"*Dear* Miss O'Donnell!" The fading light reflected from the round lenses of Miss Melbourne's spectacles. "So de-

voted to promoting the education of young women! I wish
I had *half* your dedication.''

Fortunately Flora's bonnet hid her blush. She was
ashamed of how glibly the lies came to her lips. The ne-
cessities of survival were changing her, she thought, and
not for the better.

Another quarter mile and they overtook a handsome and
muscular young man on a farmer's cob. The wind tugged
at his thick red hair and the open throat of his smock. He
tugged his forelock and grinned cheekily as they passed by.
''Good afternoon to you,'' he called out in a mellow bar-
itone.

There was something about the appreciative way he
looked at a woman of any age, Flora thought, that made
her feel both flattered and flustered. William Black was
nineteen, and radiated a powerful masculine energy. *Every
maiden's young dream,* she mused, *and every father's
worst nightmare.*

''Young Will Black has a high opinion of himself,'' Miss
Melbourne sniffed indignantly. ''I believe he was trying to
catch a glimpse of our ankles!''

The teacher's face was flushed, but whether with gratification or embarrassment, Flora couldn't decide. ''He's a
handsome scamp, but I don't believe there's any harm in
him.''

''That is because you're so innocent of the world,'' Miss
Melbourne said primly. ''But he almost caused a dreadful
scandal at the academy. It was before your time. Miss Pemberly hired him to turn over the academy's kitchen garden
one fine morning, and sent him packing by noon. He was
found with a senior girl walking in the shrubbery.'' She
lowered her voice. *''They were quite alone.''*

''Scandalous,'' Flora murmured, already losing interest
in the conversation. Suddenly she longed to be out of the
trap. She was tired of small minds and petty concerns. Not
that her thoughts were lofty, she conceded, but she required
something more than gossip and schoolgirl chatter to feed
her mind. Privacy was a luxury at Hawthorne Academy.

They were almost at the public footpath that skirted the
village proper and wound over meadow and dale. She
reined in on a sudden whim. ''I believe I'll take the foot-

path and let you drive on alone, Miss Melbourne. I need a walk to clear my head.''

"But . . . are you certain? The wind is sharp."

Flora got down. ''It is exactly what I need to blow away the cobwebs.''

She knew that she could walk the distance in the same time it would take Miss Melbourne to drive through the village and up the secondary road. It would give her a chance to review her options in case she had to make a hasty departure.

Miss Melbourne watched her colleague start off. Dear Miss O'Donnell. *So* conscientious. It was obvious that she was in the grip of the muse, and needed time to plan out her lesson without the distractions of friendly conversation. She started the trap and drove off, determined to model herself even more strongly upon Miss O'Donnell, who had become her heroine in every way.

Flora struck off along the footpath with the wind at her back. She had been country-bred, and loved the out-of-doors. The season didn't matter much, although spring and summer were her favorites. The times when flowers came into bloom, covering the greening earth like an embroidered quilt. The very first caning she'd ever received had been for slipping out the back door of her grandfather's dark house, to admire the climbing roses just bursting into bloom in the arbor, when she was supposed to be memorizing the Book of Job. She had taken Job and his tribulations in acute dislike ever since.

Her opinion of her grandfather had been formed long before that incident, however.

Suddenly she stopped. The young vicar and his older sister rounded a turn ahead on the footpath, as if her thinking of the Bible had conjured them up. They were an odd pair. The younger Reverend Tompkins tall, fair, and as good-looking as Will Black, in a rather faded, anemic way. Certainly he had none of the younger man's animal magnetism. Poor Miss Tompkins was squat and dark and as homely as a bloodhound. Deeply devoted to one another, they were vague yet amiable, with interests in classical language, literature, and lands.

Reverend Tompkins was famous locally for drifting off into deep thought in the middle of a sermon, carried away to loftier heights than any mere mortal could understand. Or so his sister claimed. A few of the less respectful locals put it down to a nip or two of the communion wine.

They were coming Flora's way, and the vicar doffed his hat to her, revealing a head of perfect golden curls for which many an aspiring beauty would have given her soul. She was sure that half of the students cast him as the hero of their most romantic daydreams. He favored her with his sweet, sad smile.

"A fine, brisk afternoon for a walk, Miss O'Donnell, is it not?"

"Yes, indeed. I thought I might take some exercise before supper."

Miss Tompkins was pleased by their chance encounter. "This is our first time abroad in some days. I have been laid low with the ague this past sennight. If not for our good parishioners, and the ministrations of my dear brother, I don't know how we should have gotten on."

Flora made all the proper polite responses, but encouraged no further conversation. The vicar's sister, even on a bad day, could talk the ears off an elephant, and Flora was anxious to arrive at Hawthorne at the same time as Miss Melbourne did, so she could unload her hidden parcels. Miss Tompkins didn't take the hint.

"It is fortuitous that we met by chance this way. I have been meaning to pay a call at the academy and inquire after dear Miss Cheney. She hasn't paid us a visit since well before the school holiday. I do hope that she is well, and intends to continue her lessons in Greek with us?"

Flora was nonplussed. "But I thought you knew. She has gone off with her uncle, who is her guardian."

The vicar's sister was astonished. "Why, I cannot believe that Miss Cheney went off without a word to us. It is quite unlike her."

"There must have been a mix-up," Flora responded. "I distinctly remember Johanna saying she left a letter to be sent to the vicarage before she departed. It's very strange that it never reached you."

Reverend Tompkins looked grave. "How unfortunate, when she was making such excellent progress. When does Miss Cheney mean to return?"

"To be truthful, I doubt that she will. Johanna is ready to take her place in the world, and I believe that Mr. Cheney has come to realize his responsibilities to seeing her safely settled."

"Well," Miss Tompkins said, "that's as it should be. I must admit that I shall miss her. We were quite fond of the girl. She has a lively mind, and Henry always said that she was one of his best pupils."

She looked to her brother for confirmation, but the vicar was checking the time on his pocket watch. "We must turn back toward the village, Dorothea. Dr. Hardy gave me strict instructions that you must not overdo."

Flora flashed him a look of gratitude that held more warmth than she'd intended, and was rewarded by a startled expression, followed by a beatific smile.

As they went their separate ways, Flora was still thinking of that smile. Although her life was secluded, she couldn't always keep her imagination from spinning foolish, romantic fantasies. Fortunately, the Reverend Tompkins didn't have the charm and presence to match his golden looks and sterling intellect, so her heart wasn't in the least jeopardy.

Leaving the path to cut through Swarthern Wood— which was still rather eerie in the light of day—she entered the grounds through the wicket gate, and managed to arrive precisely at the moment that Miss Melbourne pulled the trap into the yard. It was only then that Flora realized how great a strain the past hours had been: for once, she was delighted to find herself surrounded by the walls of the academy. Most times she felt it to be less a sanctuary than a prison.

"If you would be so kind as to take the drapery samples to the headmistress, Miss Melbourne, I shall fetch the rest."

"Of course." The little mathematics teacher scurried away, glad to be out of the rising wind.

Once inside the hall, Flora unloaded the other goods and hurried up to her room with her own parcels. She would have to hide them away before one of the maids decided to investigate their contents. There was no way any of them could resist the temptation to discover exactly what an ill-paid teacher could have purchased from one of the town's most elegant modistes. She settled on the low built-in cupboard where her warm-weather clothes were stored. Maisie and Gladys would never guess what was nestled beneath her worn and faded dresses.

It was almost time for supper, and she had barely changed her shirtwaist and smoothed her hair when she heard the first gong. Miss Pemberly was a stickler for punctuality, and expected her staff to set the proper example for the students. Flora quickly put on her silver locket, tucked a clean handkerchief in her pocket, and hurried down the stairs.

As she reached the first landing she could hear the voices of the girls as they lined up in the corridor. It was suddenly good to be back in her familiar place. Should she be able to stay at Hawthorne, many students would pass through her classroom. Among the numbers, surely there would be a few eager minds ready to catch Yeats's fire of learning. That would justify her existence on this earth, and perhaps make some amends for the damage she had caused. That proposition seemed all the more attractive now, when circumstances were turning against it.

Flora started toward the dining room, but her progress was abruptly arrested by a sharp voice. She turned quickly. Miss Pemberly stood in the doorway of her private parlor at the far end of the hall, a pinched look upon her face as if she'd sniffed an offensive odor. She stepped back to allow Flora's entry and motioned for her to take a chair. The door clicked shut behind them.

"I hope you enjoyed your outing, Miss O'Donnell?"

"Yes, thank you. The day was fine and I was able to conduct all my errands."

"And I am certain you enjoyed the company, as well?"

Miss Pemberly smiled, a chilly exercise that stretched her features sideways. Miss Melbourne had described that look, saying it made her feel like a trapped field mouse, helplessly watching a snake disarticulate its jaws, to swallow her whole.

But, Flora reminded herself, *I* am not a mouse. And as long as I have my wits about me, I am not helpless.

"Miss Melbourne is always a pleasant companion."

A spark of anger flared in the headmistress's eye. Miss O'Donnell was not reacting with the expected—indeed, the *anticipated* meekness. "I am referring to the Reverend Tompkins. I happened to look out the window at the end of the third-floor corridor, and saw you speaking privately with him."

"You are mistaken. I took the footpath from the village and came upon Mr. Tompkins escorting his sister on an airing. Possibly your view was obstructed."

The headmistress pursed her mouth in disappointment. For a few satisfying moments, she'd thought that she had something to hold over Miss O'Donnell's head. It bothered Miss Pemberly greatly that Miss O'Donnell never seemed afraid or ruffled by her presence. It was unnatural, and made her feel oddly off center.

Flora O'Donnell had an odd way of making her feel that way. There was something unusual about the younger woman . . . something that the headmistress couldn't quite put her finger upon. Given time, she would solve the puzzle.

"You will remember our rules at all times, Miss O'Donnell. The reputations of the teachers at the academy must be beyond reproach. Any infraction of these rules will lead to instant dismissal!"

"I understand fully."

"Very well. You may go."

Later that evening when Flora reached her small chamber, the altercation with Miss Pemberly was forgotten. The episode in town was her main concern, responsible for a growing sense of panic. If the Bow Street runners tracked her to the school, she was lost: she had no funds left with which to flee and reestablish herself anew.

Flora packed her few belongings up as insurance against the growing fear that she would be forced to flee within a matter of days. Perhaps she was foolish to wait. To hope. Tomorrow was market day, and if she could catch a ride at first light with a farmer's cart as far as Little Berrington, she might make her way to a larger town by evening, where it would be more difficult to trace her. And from there . . . *where?*

That night, while the others lay fast asleep, she tossed and turned, hoping she could find some way to avert disaster.

Flora was dreaming. She knew it, but couldn't wake herself. But this time it was not the gallows dream, where she mounted the steps and felt the weight of the rough noose about her neck. This was different . . .

Instead she found herself a child again, wandering into the parlor where her father always sat in the evening, a crystal decanter of rich amber liquid at his side. Tonight the lovely bottle was almost empty. Reaching out, she ran her small fingertip over the deeply incised lines that turned the firelight to rainbows. "What is in here, Papa?"

"Dreams," he answered softly. "Dreams of what might have been."

Turning toward his voice, she saw his favorite wing chair was empty. Dark stains streaked the soft tan leather and left a spattered trail into the shadows. Shaking with fear, she followed that beloved voice. Papa would keep her safe.

But when she reached the window alcove she found herself in his bedchamber instead. Her mother on her knees, weeping and clinging to Papa's hand. Mamie, their maid of all work, at the foot of the bed, blocking the rest of the view with her wide hips and crumpled apron.

"Never you worry," she said. "I'll make him presentable for the child. She'll want to see him."

"No! I don't! Don't make me look!"

Rough hands dragged her forward. She fought and fought with all her might and . . .

Flora bolted upright out of her sleep. The bed linens were tangled around her like a shroud. The terrifying dream clung to her as she tried to calm her erratically beating heart. At first she was completely disoriented. The outlines of her bedchamber gradually took solid form as the nightmare dissolved into the thin blue morning light.

She was safe. For now.

Leaning back against the pillow, she stared at the shadows on the ceiling. It had been years since she'd had that recurring dream. At least this time she'd awakened before she'd seen her father laid out upon the bed, his mangled head wrapped in bloodied towels.

Not that she'd actually seen him that way in real life. No, when her mother had brought her to his side, his dear face was in profile, carefully propped against a cushion. There was nothing of the fatal wound visible to her in the carefully contrived dimness. He'd had a black eye. Other than that, and the terrible stillness, he had seemed to be asleep. But his hand, when she touched it, had been cold and stiff as wood.

It was years before she learned it was not a regrettable hunting accident that had caused his death, but suicide.

That had been the beginning of the downward spiral that began with debts and bankruptcy and culminated in her mother's eventual downfall and shameful end. And it all could have been averted, if only her grandfather—that cold, hateful, self-righteous man—had unbent toward his late son's wife. He had never forgiven his son for marrying beneath his station, but he agreed to take in Flora. With one condition: that her mother never try to see or contact her young daughter again.

Her mother's final words echoed in her head now: *"Don't hate me, darling. I am doing it for you. So that you may have the good and happy life you deserve!"*

Flora's mouth twisted wryly as she considered her present situation. She doubted Mama had envisioned anything like this! She tossed back the covers as if unburdening herself of the weight of memories. The quilt slid to the floor and she retrieved it, sighing.

Dashing cold water from her pitcher into the china basin, she bathed her throbbing temples. Flora ran through her options again. They were pitifully few. A gentlewoman alone, with no money, no friends, and no references, could not hope to escape and survive in the world beyond these walls. Perhaps she could forge references, if only she could learn of a position in some obscure household, where no one had heard of the infamous Katherine McCall. *If* there was such a place in the whole of England. But even if fate offered a second chance to flee her problems, there was no way she could outrun her conscience.

There was little hope of seeking work as a common domestic. Her accent and clothes, her well-kept hands, would be enough to make a tavernkeeper suspicious that she was, at the very least, a ladies' maid turned out of some genteel house for stealing or harlotry. No one would hire her even as a scullery girl or tavern wench. Except, perhaps, at one of the rough taverns frequented by scoundrels, where the serving girls were also required to act as house doxies.

Despair came over her like a caul. There was no place to go but down. She had seen at first hand what happened to women who stumbled from the tidy ranks of middle-class respectability, into the gutters of society. They stood on street corners with ruined faces, gin-raddled bodies, and dulled horror in their eyes. Or, like her own mother, they were passed from one protector to another, each one worse than the one before, until they died alone, in squalor. Victims of fate, cruelty, or their own faulty judgment.

Flora pulled back the threadbare curtain at her window and looked out across the grounds. It was a peaceful country scene. The distant treetops of Swarthern Wood were glazed with golden light from the rising sun, but it was still a place of secrets and mystery. A few weeks earlier the sum of her troubles was worrying over the antics of foolish schoolgirls. She wished the same were true today. But if the Bow Street runners were on her trail, her days—perhaps hours—of freedom were numbered. She had done everything she could to avoid it, and it had not been enough.

Her grandfather's stern parting words echoed through her mind like a discordant tune: *"Only God, or the Devil himself, can help you now!"*

Flora was in her classroom, reading aloud to the students from a book of French folktales, when a hesitant tap sounded at her door. It opened a crack to reveal Miss Melbourne. Her usually pale face was suffused with unbecoming color as she signaled to her colleague. Flora joined her in the corridor.

"There's a visitor to see you. A *man*."

Flora's heart stopped for a beat, then began to pound. She was sure she'd covered her tracks back to the academy yesterday. She was sick with fright.

"A man you say? Not a gentleman?"

Miss Melbourne was aghast at her gaffe. "How inexcusable of me. Yes, most certainly a gentleman! And of the first stare! He says it is urgent that he speaks with you. Privately." Her complexion turned from puce to the dull red of a radish skin. "I hardly knew what to reply to *that,* you may be sure!"

It was plain from her agitation that Flora's friend thought she was assisting with a romantic rendezvous of some sort. She lowered her voice to a whisper. "I put him in the faculty parlor where Miss Pemberly wouldn't see him. The others are with their students, and *she* never goes in there this time of year because of the chill drafts. I hope you are not angry with me for presuming . . . ?"

"Not at all." Flora relaxed a little. By no stretch of the imagination would Miss Melbourne have called a Bow Street runner a gentleman. She smiled at her colleague reassuringly. "You did the right thing, Miss Melbourne."

"Well, then! Hurry along. If Miss Pemberly finds out she will be quite displeased."

"Thank you. I shall go at once."

Flora gave her students an assignment to write out, then headed briskly for the tiny back parlor the teachers sometimes used, thoughts churning. She was puzzled to know who her mysterious visitor was. Robin Harding, clever as he was, would surely not have tracked her here. He would be in hiding somewhere in the north—or, hopefully, back in custody of the police.

That left only her grandfather, who had refused to help her, and had cast her off after the scandal.

Then who?

Stepping inside the faculty room, she caught the familiar odor of damp and mildew that pervaded the room. Wind rattled the window sash and a draft stirred the limp draperies. One look at the man starting a fire in the hearth, and she had her answer. "Mr. Cheney!"

"Ah, Miss O'Donnell. I will be with you shortly."

He must have asked one of the servants to bring the wood and kindling: such niceties were not normally allowed in the faculty parlor except on the very coldest days of the year. Flora had spent many a miserable afternoon there with her colleagues, all dressed in layers of shawls and fingerless woolen mittens.

He plied the bellows expertly. In moments bright flames leapt merrily, chasing the chill from the small room. Cheney rose and faced Flora. He looked thinner than she recalled, but the same slight frown was there between his brows as he considered her for a moment with a connoisseur's eye.

He was slightly taken aback by her fresh-faced appearance. In memory's view he'd painted her slightly older—and a good deal plainer. Even in her severe gray gown with her auburn hair pulled tightly back, she was attractive. In the right clothes, with her hair done up, she would be stunning. Not that it mattered a whit to him personally.

Flora found his silence disconcerting. "How is Miss Cheney? I hope she is well?"

"Yes. She sends you volumes of her best wishes, none of which need repeating, I am sure. Please close the door. What I wish to say to you must be said in private."

His request startled her. It was most improper. She closed the door nonetheless. Something in his voice told her it was the wisest course of action. "I understood that Miss Cheney is making her home with you, and will not be returning to Hawthorne?"

"That is correct. I have come on another matter. However, it does have bearing on my niece." His dark eyes were opaque, his tone severe. "I understand that, in her time as a student here, you were very strict with Johanna. In fact, that you did everything in your power to make her toe the line when she showed her obstinate tendencies."

Flora drew herself up. "Yes, although it is a little late for you to bring the matter to my attention. You mustn't fault me for it. Johanna has a restless nature, and needed the discipline. At times she was angry with me; however, I would have been failing both the academy and your ward, Mr. Cheney, if I had not carried out my responsibilities."

Her indignation had a strange result. Laughter danced in his eyes and tugged at the corners of his firm mouth, transforming him completely. "What a vehement creature you are, Miss O'Donnell! But you misunderstand. I am not complaining. Rather, I am commending your fortitude in withstanding her when she flies into her tempers. My niece is woefully headstrong.

"Yes, a family failing," he added quickly, correctly interpreting the look that flitted across her face. He indicated the couch. "Perhaps you would care to sit, Miss O'Donnell. Like my niece, I am restless by nature. I prefer to prowl about the room when I have something upon my mind."

Flora sat and folded her hands in her lap. "You and Johanna are having difficulties in adjusting to one another."

"I salute your superior understanding!"

A wry smile again twisted his mouth and changed his appearance. He suddenly looked almost handsome, Flora thought. And rather dangerous.

Mr. Cheney, she decided, was a man not easily crossed. She could well imagine that he and his niece had butted heads. "It does not take genius to come to that conclusion, sir. You have already stated how very like you Johanna is."

He turned and eyed her beneath lowered brows. "I'd forgotten how sharp a tongue you have, Miss O'Donnell. It is not becoming in a woman."

Flora had had enough. Her nerves were already on edge, and she didn't need his sarcasm to abrade them further. She rose and started for the door. "If you are *quite* sure you have finished insulting me, Mr. Cheney, I will take my leave."

"Wait!" He stepped between Flora and the door. She went rigid with anger.

"Stay, if you please," he said with quiet urgency. "I did not come here to quarrel with you. Indeed, I had every intention of currying your favor. You see, I've come to ask for your help. I have been wracking my brains as to how to cope with Johanna, and I believe that you may hold the key."

Curiosity, and something in his voice, inclined Flora to give him another chance. Or perhaps it was only curiosity to see his smile again. And she was fond of that lonely, prickly girl who was his niece. She paused near the door. "Very well. I will listen and offer what advice I can, Mr. Cheney, but you must be brief. I have a class in progress."

Cheney ignored her words. Instead he paced to the fire and leaned his arm along the mantel. Firelight burnished his cheekbones, giving his face a masklike quality. "I imagined Johanna growing up contentedly here, as her mother did before her. Yes, Eve Norville was a boarding student at Hawthorne in her day. She always spoke of her time here with great fondness."

He watched the emotions march across her features. He could almost read her thoughts. "You dislike me, Miss O'Donnell, and feel that I have neglected my ward. No," he said, as she started to speak. "Make me no polite protests. It is written in your face. I admit my guilt. But you must acquit me of active malice. I did not do so intentionally.

"My business takes me to the earth's four corners, and letters may take months to reach me. Instead I had arranged for my aunt in France to keep in touch with the details of Johanna's schooling. To correspond with Miss Pemberly—and of course, Johanna—and see to her comfort. My responsibility, as far as I saw it, was to provide for her financially."

His eyes grew shadowed. "I make no excuses for myself. I should have kept in closer touch with Johanna. And I should have realized that she was no longer a child. When she appeared, fully grown, I was shocked."

Flora had seen it herself. Perhaps she had misjudged him. "It is surprising how suddenly a child can bloom from girlhood into a young woman."

He looked up and smiled. "Thank you. You are kinder than I deserve. Not only has Johanna grown into a young woman, she has grown into a rare handful. Despite the fact that you were strict with her, it may surprise you to know that she holds you in great affection. Indeed, she has spoken of you with the warmth and trust another girl would use in regard to a fond aunt or mother. For that I thank you, and more. Anyone who can influence Johanna has my complete admiration."

Flora was astonished. She hadn't expected compliments from him. Yes, she had known that Johanna had a high regard for her, and was touched to realize how desperate the girl had been for her approval; yet there was something in Blaise Cheney's manner that put her on alert. She had the strangest feeling that everything was off kilter, as if she'd stepped back into a very realistic dream.

"Johanna was my favorite among the students. I suppose I regard her in the same light that I would a favorite niece."

She was gratified to see the flush that spread over his tanned cheekbones. "I am quite fond of her, and will do anything that is in my power to help, although I do not see what I can possibly do. So, now we come to the crux of the matter," she said briskly. "How may I be of assistance to Johanna?"

He regarded her in silence a moment before speaking. "I would like to transform your former relationship with her into a permanent one. If you agree, I should like to implement the plan immediately."

"I beg your pardon!"

"I realize how precipitate this is. You may think me mad. Perhaps I am, but since I returned to England my life has been at sixes and sevens. Undoubtedly your circumstances would be changed dramatically; but I cannot think that becoming a member of our little family would be to your disadvantage." He eyed the damp patch in the corner of the faded brown wallpaper, the uncomfortable wooden chairs.

"Only consider, Miss O'Donnell. There would be some travel involved, of course, but your surroundings would be far more comfortable. You would be given a generous allowance. You would have servants to wait upon you, carriages at your disposal, all the fashions and furbelows that are supposed to brighten a woman's life."

She leveled a look at him from across the room. "You will forgive me, Mr. Cheney, if I point out that your generosity seems quite extraordinary."

An odd, reluctant smile tugged at the corner of his mouth. Once again she felt the force of that elusive charm. "I am a desperate man, Miss O'Donnell. But you have spent enough time with Johanna to understand my predicament."

He frowned then, rubbing his index finger along his scarred cheek, and chose his words with care. "This is rather difficult . . . let me assure you that, if you accept my offer, I would not interfere in your, ah . . . private life, shall we say—in any way. As long as you remain discreet. You have been in the world long enough to understand my meaning.''

Flora was on her feet again. The man *was* mad. ''You are certainly lenient where your household is concerned, if I *do* understand you correctly. You are offering me carte blanche to carry out romantic entanglements while under your roof, as long as I do not cause a scandal in the process?''

Her boldness surprised him. ''I had not expected such frankness from an Englishwoman. Your assumption, however, is correct.''

Flora felt her face flame with mortification. ''I do not know what I may have said or done to give you such a false impression of my character, sir! I would not consider becoming a governess in such a disorderly household under the most dire of circumstances—nor do I feel such an environment would be in Johanna's best interests. If your establishment is so . . . so . . . .''

Words failed her and she gave up. ''It is my opinion that Johanna should return to the academy until such a time as she can be placed under the protection of another relation. You are no more fit to oversee her care than she is. Less so, in fact, given the state of your morals!''

Once more Cheney interposed himself between Flora and the door. He had looked shocked initially, but was now increasingly amused at her response. ''I fear we've been talking at cross-purposes, Miss O'Donnell.'' Those dark eyes fixed on hers. ''I am not asking you to become Johanna's governess . . . I am asking you to be my wife.''

Flora felt the color drain from her face along with her blood. ''You are mocking me, sir. Either that or you are insane. The interview is ended.''

She swung about so precipitously she collided with a pedestal. The Roman bust wobbled on its stand and she automatically reached out to steady it. Cheney was there first, catching the statuary in one strong hand, and Flora's arm in the other. He steadied the statue, then put his other arm against the door, effectively pinning her there. He was so close that she could almost sense the warmth of his body.

Flora found herself unable to move, paralyzed, like a hare in a hawk's talons.

"I am perfectly sane, Miss O'Donnell, and my proposal is genuine." He gestured toward the cast-off furniture with sagging springs, the smoky ceiling of the small room which gave evidence of poor chimney draft. "You are surely a woman used to finer surroundings. I am offering you a way out of this meager, menial existence. A completely new and infinitely more comfortable way of life."

That caught her attention, snapping her out of the present moment and back into her earlier panic. Thoughts of the Bow Street runners flooded Flora's mind, drowning out everything else. He was offering her more than he knew. A way out. A new identity. A chance to outrun the past and put it behind her forever.

Cheney released her arm gently. He did not know what he'd said to create such a change in her, only that it was to his advantage. "Consider the circumstances, Miss O'Donnell. As you are aware, I am a man involved in his own interests. I am a businessman and scholar, with no experience of children, and am currently in the midst of intensive research. Suddenly I find myself saddled with a young girl who has never been broken to bridle, and is suffering all the vapors of her age. As for Johanna, she is as desperate as I. We very much need your help."

"Yes." Flora lifted her chin and eyed him straightly. "But you do not need a wife."

"You are wrong there. As a teacher, you have only so much say over my niece's behavior. As Mrs. Blaise Cheney, you would have considerably more. I have come to know Johanna's mind. While she rebels against outside restraint, family relationships are very crucial to her well-being."

Flora laughed cynically. "And you see the noble sacrifice of offering yourself up in marriage as a means to provide it?"

He gestured impatiently. "Do not fence with me, Miss O'Donnell. You must understand that I am proposing a marriage in name only." His hand went up to his scarred cheek again, in the same unconscious gesture. "I am conscious that I am no prize specimen; however, I have much in the way of material things to offer you."

"It chills me to hear you speak of it in such a cold-blooded way, sir."

"Let the thought of my wealth warm you, then! I am speaking of a term of two years only. Johanna will make her official come-out to society next year, during the little season. She is a remarkably pretty girl, and has quite a substantial dowry. I doubt that it will take long for some young swain to fall head over heels and press for an early marriage. Once my niece is established, I intend to go abroad for good."

"And what of your 'wife'?"

"You need not fear that I would cast you off, penniless, or divorce you and ruin your standing in society. An annulment can be easily arranged, or an official separation, if you prefer. You would have a generous marriage settlement, a separate allowance for household expenses, as well as one for your personal expenditures, and the use of any of my properties during your lifetime. To put it baldly, you would have all the benefits of my name and wealth, with none of the drawbacks of my person."

Flora shook her head. "You are reacting too strongly. It is merely that you are unused to the role of parent, and are making too much of a young girl's high spirits. I realize that you travel extensively. It might do Johanna a deal of good to go abroad with you. An older woman as suitable companion could be easily arranged. A few days' contemplation will show you how unnecessary this marriage charade would be."

"You are wrong. Unforeseen circumstances will take me home for an extended period. And therein lies the problem.

"The Cheney estate consists almost wholly of land in Brittany. Pont du Mor, where my home is located, is a small fishing village. The culture is Breton to the core; the remnants of the ancient Celtic influence have been merely glazed over with that of France. A milieu, I need not add, completely foreign to my niece.

"Johanna and I will necessarily be thrown into each other's company for many months until her debut next year.

It would be a miracle if one of us did not strangle the other, during that time.''

At his words a horrible picture flashed into Flora's mind: Miss Hansen lying dead on her parlor rug, in a bloody pool, a brass letter opener protruding from her wounded throat.

Instantly Cheney was at Flora's side, holding her by the elbow. He led her back to the chair. ''You are overcome. Forgive me for throwing so much at your head all at once. No doubt I have shocked you with my manner of speaking. Another failing common to the Cheneys.'' He lifted her chin with his fingertip. ''Despite my rough speech you need not worry: I assure you that Johanna will come to no further harm under my guardianship.''

Flora's mind was spinning like a wheel. ''I still cannot see, sir, why you are intent on taking a wife, when it seems that a governess-companion is what you require.''

''Do you not?'' He favored her with one of his rare smiles. ''Good God, I fear that you have a very exotic view of Breton morals! The prevailing mores of the countryside are quite different from those tolerated in Paris, you know. Or London, for that matter.

''You are a very personable young woman, Miss O'Donnell. Can you imagine the scandal that would ensue if I brought you into my home and introduced you to the neighborhood as a sort of companion-governess? I doubt it would be believed for one moment!''

''And what is Johanna's opinion of your scheme?''

He flushed beneath his tan. ''I did not take her into my confidence. I thought it best. After all, you will have more influence upon her if she considers you her aunt by marriage, than as a temporary chaperon. Afterward we shall say we did not suit.''

Flora didn't know what to do. A short time ago she faced a bleak and terrifying future. Now this odd and decidedly dangerous man was offering her the perfect avenue of escape. The protection of his name, the freedom of traveling to another country on his passport, with no questions asked. The devil of it was that she had to act immediately. And there would be no going back once the die was cast.

He sensed the change in her. "You will not regret the bargain, Miss O'Donnell. I swear it. But I must know your answer today. Now."

Flora looked away, unable to meet his eyes. In France she would no longer have to look over her shoulder for Bow Street runners, or Robin Harding. Perhaps, in time, she would be able to put the past to rest and turn toward the future. But at the present moment she had to deal with Blaise Cheney. She was painfully aware of him. The scent of his cologne, the fine wool of his coat, the restless masculine energy he radiated, like heat from the fire roaring in the grate. Her instinct warned of dangerous complications, but was overruled by her intellect. His offer, bizarre as it might be, was the answer to her prayers. Why did she feel as if she were about to step blindfolded off a cliff, and into an abyss?

"Your offer is such that any woman in my circumstances would find difficult to refuse." She took a deep breath. "Very well, Mr. Cheney."

"Excellent. Ring for the maid to pack your things. Johanna is waiting for you at the Green Man with her maid. I have already made arrangements for us to marry before the Channel crossing."

She stared at him then. "You were very sure of yourself."

"No. Very desperate." He flashed his abrupt smile again, took her hand and pressed it lightly. "Now I am very relieved."

His actions sent a sharp tingle up her arm, like a shock of static electricity. For a moment their eyes locked. He released her far too abruptly, as if he'd felt the same jolt. He frowned and turned away.

Something sent alarms ringing through her. Although she saw no other choice, it seemed that she had made a dangerous agreement. He had been frank and open with her regarding their proposed alliance. He was a gentleman. She did not doubt his promise that the marriage would be one in name only, nor that he would provide handsomely for her future; and yet, intuition warned, something was not what it should be.

But then, Flora mused, thinking of her own dark secrets—neither was she.

Chapter Three

"*I* hope you are not making a serious mistake," Miss Pemberly said stiffly. "Since I must fill your position, I cannot take you back, should you regret your hasty action."

Flora nodded. She had convinced the headmistress that she had been offered a position as companion to an elderly relation living in Devon. The lie seemed more believable than the truth, and would further serve to disguise her trail. The episode with the Bow Street runner had shaken her. Not until she was safely in France would she stop looking over her shoulder.

Miss Pemberly's small mouth pursed. "You may live to regret this day's work, Miss O'Donnell. You would not be the first to be taken in by an elderly relative, promising to leave you property in exchange for your services."

Flora wondered if the older woman was thinking of the way she'd heighed off herself off to Yorkshire to attend the "deathbed" of a wealthy and cantankerous relation, only to find herself cut out of the will entirely. If possible, the event had soured Miss Pemberly even more.

"I do understand your position," Flora replied quietly, although inside her heart was pounding like a miller's wheel. "However, I must take the opportunity fate has offered."

Johanna's guardian had given her only an hour to gather up her belongings, fearing, no doubt, that she might back out of their agreement, given time to think it over. It was both exhilarating and frightening. This time she was truly cutting off all ties with the past. Flora O'Donnell would soon cease to exist.

And, sooner than seemed possible, "Madame Blaise Cheney" would appear in France, an entirely new entity. Flora anticipated her new identity with great uneasiness. The annihilation of one's history—one's true self—was not something to undertake lightly. It didn't matter that this was the second time she had done so.

While she had her final interview, Cheney waited impatiently in the closed carriage in the courtyard. At Flora's insistence he had kept himself from view. This only reinforced the impression his investigators had formed: although they could find no hint of problems, Miss Flora O'Donnell was something other than what she appeared to be. Perhaps the daughter of a poor clerk, or even of upper servants, trying to raise her status in the world by pretending to a better background than that from which she sprang. It didn't matter. The important things were that she was genteel enough to pass for his wife—and that she was willing.

Indeed, he couldn't have found a more suitable candidate if he had placed an advertisement in the London papers. She was perfect for the task at hand: educated, well mannered. Worldly enough to want to be better herself.

And unlikely to interfere with his plans.

The door of the hall opened and Flora descended the shallow stairs. She paused on the cobbles, hesitant to take the last few steps that would lead her out of Hawthorne Academy and into a strange new life.

Cheney was also given pause. He'd been expecting her to look exactly as she had before: neat and prim and in subdued clothing. Instead he saw her flooded with light from the afternoon sun, her fair skin and auburn hair glided with light. She looked totally changed, glowing like an ember against the dull stone walls in her russet velvet ensemble. Lush and exotic as a Chinese peony in a simple kitchen garden.

Even as his masculine interest stirred, his resolution wavered. He hadn't counted on this. It might prove a complication. But, he reminded himself, it was too late to turn back now. The die was cast, the game begun.

The waiting groom handed her up into the vehicle. Cheney helped her inside, and felt the tremor of her gloved hand in his. The door shut firmly and the carriage shifted as the groom placed her trunk in the boot and then jumped up into his perch. She was suddenly pale. Her husband-to-be smiled at her encouragingly.

"Apprehensive, Miss O'Donnell? You need not be. I have pledged you the word of a Cheney."

She didn't reply. Her mouth was too dry to speak. She wished very much that he had brought Johanna with him.

Inside she found a hot brick for her feet, and a luxurious fur rug and matching muff to keep her warm on their travels. His thoughtfulness eased her worries somewhat, but when he knocked on the window and the coachman snapped his whip her stomach fluttered and her spine was rigid with tension.

Soon they were bowling out through the academy gates and heading down the lane for the high road. He seemed disinclined to speak further, turning his face to look at the window, apparently watching the passing countryside.

Flora leaned back against the cushioned squabs and closed her eyes. She had burned her bridges behind her before, and sincerely hoped that this was her final offering on the altar of desperation.

Not that the bargain was so bad on her side. In the usual arranged marriage, prevalent in the middle and upper classes, the groom's wealth and position were bartered for the bride's dowry and innocence. Theirs was a one-sided bargain, since she brought nothing to the marriage but her interest in his niece's welfare. With that being his only requirement of her, they would avoid the pitfalls inherent to alliances between virtual strangers.

Best of all, the charade would be maintained for two years only. *Why, before I know it, I shall be free to establish my independence.* She had no fear at all of Johanna, with her lovely face and splendid inheritance, remaining a spinster.

Cheney eyed Flora's reflection in the window thoughtfully. He'd hired a prime team to pull their carriage. They had a long drive ahead of them and he wanted to cover a good many miles before stopping to change horses.

The carriage skirted the village of Hawthorne, then swept past the church and turned onto the highway. Two figures stood on the steps of the vicarage. Flora had a brief glimpse of the vicar and his sister staring in wonder as she passed them in a fine coach-and-four. She was just wishing that she'd kept her face hidden from view when the groom sprung the horses and she was thrown back against the squabs. "Good God!"

"Forgive me, Miss O'Donnell, for not warning you that I'd ordered the driver to proceed with all due speed. We have many miles to cover before we reach our destination."

Flora was so flustered at being seen and so surprised at their spanking pace, that it was some time before she realized that the carriage was going in quite the opposite direction from what she'd expected. "I believed that we were bound for Portsmouth," she said. "If so, the coachman has taken a wrong turning!"

He cursed beneath his breath. She was too perceptive. "No, Miss O'Donnell. We're on our way to Dover."

The coach careened around a corner and she grasped at the hanging strap to keep from being flung against the side. She was nervous now. "Why Dover, if your home is in Brittany? It is not at all on the way."

He gave a bark of laughter. "Do you fear this is an abduction after all? I am not nearly so romantic a figure as you seem to believe. I have business in Paris first. I also have a home there. The thought occurred to me that you might wish to 'honeymoon' in comfortable surroundings while we get to know one another, before setting off for the wild Breton shores. Come, I am convinced you will enjoy our sojourn in Paris."

Flora fixed him with her direct blue gaze. "I didn't realize that 'knowing one another better' formed any part of our bargain, sir."

He scowled. "Your suspicious attitude does you no credit. Think, Miss O'Donnell. After our 'whirlwind' courtship, it would certainly look very odd if we seem scarcely acquainted with each other. The lack of intimacy between us will be less noticeable in Paris, among the company and activities. It would stand out glaringly in the isolation of Château Morgaine."

She relaxed. "I suppose you are right."

"Remarkable! You have actually agreed with me, for once."

"More than once, Mr. Cheney, else I would still be back at Hawthorne."

He favored her with one of his dazzling smiles. "I knew I could not be wrong: you are a woman of great good sense."

Flora looked down at the skirt of her worn and unfashionable dress peeking out from beneath her elegant new pelisse. "Enough to belatedly realize that my wardrobe is singularly unsuited to society in general—and Paris in particular. I shall cause you acute embarrassment when I am taken for a scullery maid!"

"Not at all. I had the forethought to make some purchases. You will find a few things waiting for you in your chamber at the Dover inn. I hope they will meet with your approval. The rest you can obtain when we are settled in France."

She frowned, reacting to something he'd said earlier. "A moment ago you referred to a château. I was under the impression that your home was a comfortable one, of course, but in a small fishing village?"

"Have you visions of moats and crenellated towers? Or perhaps some gilded baroque fantasy of the Bourbons? If so, you may forget them." He looked mildly amused, and dismissed the subject with a wave of his elegantly gloved hand. "Tell me something of your girlhood and family. I understand you are an orphan? Have you any living relatives?"

"Only one, from whom my parents were estranged. I have no wish to discuss the matter further." That was the last kernel of truth she fed him on the long ride.

Flora knew that to make up a history of whole cloth would put her in danger of forgetting what she had said and tripping herself up later; so she adopted the life and family background of one of her former friends, tailoring it to fit her present circumstances.

He listened to her rattle on, a small smile playing about his mobile mouth from time to time. Every now and then he asked a question. Although he seemed amused at times, and slightly bored at others, she had the impression that he was testing her.

They stopped only to change horses at the posting inns the first several hours, where he ordered mulled wine to warm them, and a packet of sandwiches to eat along the way. "I shall go on horseback from here," he told her outside the Lance and Dragon. "In general I don't care to ride inside."

Flora was relieved. The strain of his presence was wearing on her nerves. Despite this—or perhaps because of it—she dozed off afterward, awakening to a world gone dark and very much colder. The air smelled of the sea. She was disoriented for a moment, and frightened as the carriage slowed and reined in to a stop. Then she spied the lights of the inn ahead.

Dover. It all came tumbling back to her. She was with a man who was almost a stranger, yet soon to be her husband, and she was fleeing England and her past for French shores and new adventure—exactly like the heroine in one of the more lurid Gothic adventures.

A sudden urge to laugh hysterically bubbled up inside her, and was firmly suppressed as Blaise Cheney dismounted and came to assist her to alight. The sharp contrast of light and shadows cast his features into high relief. His eyes were hidden and the star-shaped scar on his cheek looked more prominent in the lampglow, giving his face a stern and almost frightening appearance. Flora shivered.

Whatever else Blaise Cheney might be, he was no storybook hero. And this wild adventure was no laughing matter.

The sound of carriage wheels and hooves roused Johanna. She had been abed several hours, but hadn't slept a wink. She rose from her bed, hurrying past the truckle bed and Malin's blissfully snoring form. Nothing short of Judgment Day would wake her maid once she fell into slumber.

She touched the cool glass of the windowpanes and looked out. A traveling coach had swung through the gate and into the cobbled yard below. Holding her breath, she waited to see if there were any passengers. The door was on the far side, and the rambling roofline partially obscured her view.

Her feelings at that moment were tangled into knots. She wanted so much for Miss O'Donnell to come to her, yet knew how difficult it must be for her to leave everything familiar behind. It was the same for Johanna. Although she had lived her first six years in France, she had only vague recollections of it. England and Hawthorne Academy were the only home she knew.

But she did remember Malin. Thank God Uncle Blaise had arranged for Malin to come over and accompany them back. Perhaps she would recall more once they reached the château. She was dreading it.

Opening the casement, she leaned out into the night. The tang of the sea was overwhelming, and she could hear the sigh of the waves at the foot of the cliffs. A woman came around the back of the equipage and Johanna's heart sank. The modish hat and elegant russet pelisse were far too expensive to belong to her former teacher. She should have known that her uncle would be unable to persuade Miss O'Donnell to agree to his scheme.

She hadn't realized until that moment how much she had hoped against hope that he would prevail. Tears welled in her eyes and she started to turn away. Then the woman looked up and her face was illumined by warm lamplight from the open inn door. It *was* Miss O'Donnell. *Oh, thank God!*

The sight of that familiar and much-loved face loosened all the emotions that she had held in check so long. Uncle Blaise had said he would fetch her away from Hawthorne, and he had somehow accomplished it. If he could do that, he could accomplish anything! Johanna blinked away the tears of relief, but more came in their place until she was sobbing like a child.

She wanted to throw on her robe, go and fling herself into Miss O'Donnell's arms in gratitude. Instead she climbed back into bed, and wept into her pillow until it was damp and she was all cried out. Everything would be all right now. She was sure of it. Then, with a child's trust in the future, she turned her pillow over and gave herself up to the luxury of sleep.

* * *

The murmur of waves carried in the clear, cool air as Flora stepped away from the traveling coach. A sign creaked overhead in the wind, displaying a battered design, which she couldn't make out in the lantern light; but the inn, with great bow windows and shining brass lamps, was a substantial one, far grander than any she had stayed in before.

"You are registered as Mrs. Cheney," he told Flora in a low voice as he escorted her inside. She went rigid and tried to pull her arm away from his, but he restrained her. "Don't be missish," he said sharply. "It ill suits a woman of your intelligence. I've arranged for you to have your own chamber, next to that of Johanna and her maid. My own room is next to yours, but has no connecting door."

Flora was chagrined at her reaction, but lifted her chin to glance up at him. "Thank you. I shall sleep the better for knowing it."

A spark that might be either laughter or anger shone in the depths of his dark eyes. "If it's rape you fear, lodge a chair-back beneath your door handle. Even such a hardened rake as you appear to think I am, would hesitate to wake the entire household by battering down your door in the midnight hours."

She knew she was being ridiculed. "Forgive me if I have offended you; but I'm weary and hungry and longing for my bed."

"I'll see that a tray is sent up to your chamber immediately. I gave orders for a fire to be lit early, and the bed to be warmed the moment we pulled into the yard."

"Thank you. I am most grateful." And Flora was. Mr. Cheney might travel as though the devil were after him, but he was liberal with his purse. No creature comforts would be found wanting on their journey. He knew how to travel in style.

The landlord bowed them into the inn with an obsequiousness she had never seen equaled. At least, not directed toward herself. As she followed the chambermaid up to her room, she was tired and edgy. The chamber was spacious, with thick curtains to shut out the chill and a warm fire in the hearth. The bed was piled high with feather comforters, and decked in embroidered Irish linen scented with lavender.

Almost immediately another maid entered, bearing a tray with hot food and a mug of mulled wine. At the moment they were more welcome than gold, and Flora polished off the refreshments in a winking. Within the hour she was snug in the comfortable bed, with the light of the banked fire glowing in the dimness. After the privation of her cold and drafty room at Hawthorne, it was luxury indeed. She drifted to sleep on the thought that she could very soon become accustomed to it.

The next thing Flora knew, someone was stirring in her room. Pushing herself up on one elbow, she looked around. A fresh-faced chambermaid was pulling back the curtains to a pearly gray sky. A line of pink showed above the waves at the distant horizon. Somewhere in that direction lay France, and the beginning of her brave new life.

The hour seemed ungodly early, but there was a tray with a teapot and a covered dish on the side table. The maid, seeing that she was awake, dropped a curtsy. "Good morning, ma'am. Monsoor Cheney says, as soon as you're dressed and ready, he would like for you to join him in the private parlor."

"Good morning." Flora sat up and the maid plumped up her pillows and then set the tray over her knees. Oh, yes, she could get very used to this!

The tea was rich and fragrant, the toast—wonder of wonders—hot beneath its cover. As she sipped the tea, in a delicate porcelain cup finer than any to which she had lately been accustomed, the maid began laying out her clothing. The door opened and a second maid entered, carrying several garments carefully over her arm. She dipped a curtsy and spread them out over the wing chair.

"Monsoor Cheney thought as how you might like to put on your new traveling dress for the Channel crossing, ma'am."

Flora eyed the embroidered peach silk underdress and the other finery. She could find no fault with her affianced husband's taste. The traveling outfit made the velvet pelisse she'd bought look like a cheap rag in comparison. The color was a forest-green faille, with subtle shadings. Collar, bodice, and cuffs were lightly embellished with bronze cording, and there was a fur-lined, hooded cloak to match. The perfect ensemble for a woman of wealth and distinction who didn't wish to draw undue attention to herself.

Once she had bathed and dressed, Flora stood before the mirror and evaluated her reflection. With the new garments and her hair arranged in a more fashionable coif, the transformation was complete. If she walked past Miss Pemberly now, the headmistress herself would fail to recognize her erstwhile employee.

Flora adjusted her cuffs. She had to credit Blaise Cheney with exquisite taste, but was chagrined at how accurately he'd predicted her dimensions. Even the half-boots fitted. If the waist of the traveling dress was a trifle large and the bust a trifle tight, it must be blamed on the imperfectly fitted garments she'd worn in her role of schoolteacher. It seemed that he wasn't a novice at buying clothes for the female of the species, which gave her a little insight into his character.

More daunting was the realization that he was a man who noticed minute details, and could recall them accurately at a later date. She would have to watch her step most carefully in the coming months. One mistake and she might yet see it all unravel.

The maid escorted her down to the private parlor. They passed the empty taproom, which carried the rich aroma of grape and grain. A glimpse in another parlor revealed a runny-nosed girl cleaning the cold ashes from the grate. Flora was led down a second corridor. Although the inn was still quiet, people were starting to stir overhead. The maid stopped outside a paneled door. "In here, ma'am, if you please. Breakfast is set out on the sideboard."

Flora entered a nicely appointed room with polished chestnut paneling and casement windows studded with clear rounds of bull's-eye glass. She stopped inside the threshold in surprise. She'd been expecting to find Johanna with her uncle, but there was no sign of the girl. Blaise Cheney was facing the window, his arms folded. A sleepy-eyed cleric, who had been polishing off scrambled eggs and a thick slice of country ham, shot to his feet. Cheney turned.

Once again he was surprised at her appearance. It was more than the traveling dress he'd purchased for her in London, in anticipation of her acceptance of his bargain. It was more than the way the muted shade of green brought out her own peach-bloom coloring, or even the way the fine tailoring accented her figure—a really marvelous figure, he must admit to himself. Overnight she seemed to have taken on the persona of a wellborn lady, used to all the elegancies of a fashionable life.

Was this a return to her origin, he wondered, or the adaptation of a chameleon to its new background? It both intrigued and puzzled him. Perhaps he hadn't been as clever as he'd thought. He showed nothing at all of his thoughts as he greeted Flora.

"Ah, there you are, my dear. This is Mr. Overton, who will officiate over our wedding vows."

Flora started, and felt a warm blush rise up her throat. Not since she was a young schoolgirl, receiving admiring glances from the squire's son, had she been prey to such fluctuations in her color. But she hadn't been prepared for this. Not so soon. It seemed so . . . so irrevocable!

Swallowing her nervousness, she nodded coolly to the minister. "How do you do, sir? It is very kind of you to accommodate us at such an unusual hour."

"Upon my first meeting with Mr. Overton," Cheney went on, "I explained that a grave family calamity impels us to such hasty measures, instead of waiting to wed this spring, as we had originally planned. He perfectly understands your hesitance at embarking for France under my care, without benefit of banns, and is ready to unite us and avoid any taint of impropriety."

The cleric flushed at this speech. Indeed, he had been thinking that this affair had more than a taint of impropriety. Until setting eyes on the prospective bride, he'd suffered from the fear that he'd been called to officiate at a runaway match. The thought of refusing Mr. Cheney had entered his head, only to be exchanged for another plan, of bolting when the gentleman's back was turned. There was something about the Frenchman that made Mr. Overton hesitant to cross him directly.

But Miss O'Donnell's age and elegance and calm sensibility reassured him completely. Since everything seemed in order, he was prepared to go through with the ceremony. "If you will assemble your witnesses, monsieur, we can begin."

A smile lit Cheney's eyes. "Anxious as I am to make Miss O'Donnell my wife, Mr. Overton, I suggest we allow her to break her fast with something more substantial than the tea and toast she had earlier."

Although Flora thought she couldn't manage a single morsel, due to the butterflies dancing in her stomach, she found that biscuits and ham went down quite easily. In fact, she had a second helping. Evidently she lacked the delicate female sensibilities that the heroines of romantic novels had in such abundance.

As she was finishing up, her intended went to the door and spoke to a servant loitering in the corridor. In less than a minute the innkeeper appeared with his wife. The man was dressed in his usual garments, but his spouse had gone to quite a bit of trouble to dignify the occasion. She wore an old-fashioned gown of black wool, which smelled slightly of camphor, and a necklace of cameos at her throat.

The cleric looked from the bride to the groom. "Your papers . . . ?"

Flora was panicked. She had no papers. How could she have been so foolish? Everything would fall apart now!

"All here." Cheney removed a thin leather packet from his pocket. He peeled off several papers and set them on the table: the special license, a letter from a bishop, and his birth certificate. He withdrew another folded paper and glanced at Flora. "I took the liberty of obtaining a notarized copy of your birth certificate while I was in London, my dear."

"His dear" was at a complete standstill. The date was correct, but the rest a complete surprise. As Flora examined the document, she saw that the name "Flora O'Donnell" was entered in a neat copperplate, along with "London" as her place of birth. It appeared to be authentic in every way: except that it officially recorded the birth of a woman who had never existed.

But London was a large city, she told herself. It *was* possible that there had actually been a Flora O'Donnell, born in London within a year of herself and whose birth was duly recorded at Somerset House.

She managed a smile. "How fortunate that you thought of it, as such a contingency had completely escaped my mind."

Cheney smiled and reached out to her. His touch was strong and warm, and she was mortified to find her hand trembling in his. "Then we are ready to seal our troth." His grip tightened and he gave her an encouraging smile.

"But . . . what of Johanna?"

"She is recovering from an indisposition. I thought it best to let her sleep in."

But just as he finished speaking, the door opened once more and Johanna stepped in, accompanied by a sloe-eyed ladies maid. She entered shyly, but appeared to gain confidence when she spied Flora hand and hand with her uncle.

"I had to come down," she said simply. "It wouldn't be right for you to be alone among strangers on this important day."

"I am very happy that you did."

Johanna came to her side. Her pale eyes searched Flora's countenance. "And you shall be much happier as Madame Cheney, than as Miss O'Donnell of Hawthorne Academy."

It was a statement, but there was such a question in the girl's expression that Flora felt compelled to allay her fears. "Can you doubt it?"

Blaise lifted Flora's hand to his lips and kissed it. "You relieve my mind, my dear. How humbling it would be to have my fiancée cry off at the last minute."

The landlord gave a short laugh and the tension eased. Satisfied, Johanna stepped back. Flora wished that the girl hadn't mentioned the academy by name. But surely her remark had gone unnoticed by the others.

Mr. Overton, who had a long ride after the ceremonies were over, took that as the signal to proceed. Clearing his throat loudly, he opened his book to the wedding vows, and the room fell silent. Flora had the odd sensation that everyone present could hear the frantic beating of her heart. It was so loud in her own ears that it muffled the cleric's words to a low hum. She was caught off guard when she found everyone staring at her, Blaise Cheney with a frown between his slashing brows.

A heavy sapphire ring seemed to have materialized on her left hand, and she realized that she had missed her cue. Flora took a deep breath. "I will," she said in a voice that was strong and clear.

And so, within a very few moments, she found herself receiving the congratulations of the innkeeper and his wife. Johanna kissed Flora's cheek. "I wish you very happy," she said, with an undertone of doubt in her voice. Blaise took Flora's hand in his and raised it to his lips. "I shall do everything in my power to make her so."

The light touch of his mouth against her skin sent shivers up her arm. She withdrew her hand as soon as she could properly do so, hoping he wouldn't feel called upon to offer many such gallantries.

A little spark gleamed in his eyes, as if he'd read her thoughts and been amused. "I am sorry that we must spend our wedding day in travel," he told her, for all to hear.

Flora's back was to the company. She gave her new husband a wry smile. "I have not the least objection to it."

He tipped her chin up and leaned close to her ear, as if to whisper a sweet nothing into it. "Touché, Miss . . . ah, *Madame Cheney*. But you must not show your teeth to me when others are present. It might give them a very odd notion of our marriage, you understand? Something, I am sure, that neither of us wants."

For the benefit of the others, he stood back and said more loudly: "I shall make it all up to you in Paris, my dear. It is truly the most romantic city in the world."

Yes, Flora thought wryly, *the most romantic city in the world, but under the most unromantic of circumstances: as the wife of a man who had no interest at all in having a wife.*

In reality she was little more to Blaise Cheney than a servant, hired to keep him from being inconvenienced by his niece. Then she caught sight of her reflection in the mirror above the mantelpiece, rather splendid in her fine new garments. Light caught the sapphire on her finger. *A very highly paid servant,* she amended. Well, she was ready to keep her part of their unorthodox bargain.

She only hoped that he intended to keep his.

The sky was a dome of azure crystal, unmarred by a wisp of cloud as they prepared to embark on the private yacht Blaise had hired to take them across the Channel. The trunks had been loaded and the crew were ready to cast off, but Johanna hung back at the gangway. "What is it?" Flora asked. "Have you forgotten something?"

The girl's eyes were troubled. "No," she replied quietly. "I have *remembered* something." The breeze ruffled the girl's fair hair against the brim of her bonnet. "I wonder if I am making a mistake."

And you are not alone in that, Flora thought. She covered Johanna's gloved hand with her own. "You are feeling anxious about leaving England. Even though you were unhappy at the academy at times, its familiar routine was known, and therefore comforting. But we can't turn back the clock. Whether you left this term or stayed, the time would have inevitably come for you to leave the nest, and go out into the larger world." She tried to make a joke of it. "At least we are facing it together."

Johanna looked down at her gloved hands. "You are right, of course." Squaring her shoulders, she went up the short gangway and onto the yacht.

As they weighed anchor, Flora stayed at the rail to watch the shining white cliffs diminish with distance. When they melded with the glare off the water, she turned her back on England and her face toward France.

The journey from Dover to Calais took twice as long as anticipated. Although they set sail beneath clear skies and the promise of fine weather, a black squall blew up out of the north without warning. Flora had gone down below earlier, to tend to Malin, who was dreadfully seasick; but she came topside as the yacht began to lurch with the heaving seas.

The blue skies had vanished behind banks of dark clouds, and the Channel waters were inky black. Their experienced crew seemed totally caught off guard. Amidst their shouts and the lowering of canvas, Johanna stood at the rail as if mesmerized. Flora picked her way across the deck with difficulty.

"Johanna!"

The howling wind snatched her voice away, but carried Johanna's to her. Flora thought she heard her call out a prayer to Saint Mary. Were the Cheneys Catholic? It seemed highly likely, although the girl had attended services with the rest of the students. How odd that it hadn't occurred to her to inquire before. But then, there was so very much she hadn't stopped to think through before committing herself to this rash adventure.

Blaise came along the rail from the bow and pried his niece's fingers from it. "You must both go down below, at once. A wave could sweep you off your feet and wash you overboard."

The girl didn't seem to hear him. Flora frowned. Johanna wasn't praying, but singing beneath her breath. The haunting melody sent chills racing up her spine. "Come, Johanna. Let us seek shelter below deck."

The girl looked at her, but didn't seem to see her; yet she didn't resist when Blaise forced her away from the rail. Flora saw that Malin had followed her up. She was huddling among the pile of luggage tied down on the aft deck. "Come below. It is not safe here, Malin."

"Ah, no. I am even more vilely ill, madame. To go below would only make it worse."

She refused to listen to reason, and Flora called to her "husband." Cheney finally scooped the maid up and carried her down the gangway, with Flora and his niece following. He handed Flora a silver flask. "Brandy. Give them both sips of it. And take some yourself."

"Aren't you going to stay with us?"

"No. I must go back. Every man is needed, and I am an experienced sailor." He cupped her chin in his hand and examined her face. "You are white as snow. Don't worry. You will be safe enough, I promise you."

"It is not my own safety that concerns me at the moment, Mr. Cheney."

"You must practice calling me something other than 'Monsieur Cheney' when you speak to me, or people will begin to wonder.'' He smiled down at her. "Say my name, Flora.''

She bit her lower lip. A simple request. Yet it seemed to move their relationship to a more intimate level. "Very well . . . Blaise.''

"Good girl. You see, it was not so difficult.'' He touched her mouth with his fingertip. "It will get easier to say with time.''

Then he was gone, leaving her robbed of breath and feeling weak in the knees from more than the rolling deck.

Flora spent the next few hours below, fortified by brandy from his engraved silver flask and every prayer she could recollect. Malin was ill from the tossing waves, but Johanna's plight was even worse. She had withdrawn into a speechless state of near catatonia, and barely managed to fling out an arm when the yacht lurched violently, to keep herself from being thrown across the cabin.

Above deck Blaise was too busy to feel any fear. He had grown up along Brittany's Atlantic coast and was, as he'd told Flora, an experienced seaman. He worked alongside the crew. With every pitch and yaw the shouts of the sailors were overpowered by the groaning wood of the beleaguered vessel.

Although he was athletic and fit, his muscles were tired and aching with fatigue when the battering eased. If fear had kept some of the crew going, it was anger that had fueled his own energy. At the height of the storm's fury he had shaken his fist at the waves and cursed: *"You will not have me this time, either!"*

As the storm blew itself out he went below, exhausted and exhilarated. He'd expected some degree of hysteria to greet him, but saw that he'd underestimated his bride. Flora had the situation well in hand. She'd tucked his niece into the lower berth and cushioned her all about with pillows. She had even dragged a small trunk across the cabin to keep Malin from falling out with every lurch of the boat. As for herself, she was perched on the bottom edge of the mattress, holding a support beam for balance.

The wind was dropping but still made hearing difficult. He went to her side and spoke into her ear. "You had my gratitude earlier, *chérie*. Now you have my admiration as well.''

''You need not use endearments when we are alone,'' Flora said sharply.

The floor tilted beneath them and Johanna groaned. All the fears that Flora had been holding in check burst out, transformed to anger. ''I cannot understand why you let us leave Dover with such bad weather in the offing.''

''The weather gave no sign of turning violent,'' he replied, ''or I should certainly never have set sail.'' His long fingers turned the ring he wore on his right hand as he spoke, almost as if he were unaware of their actions. ''I came to inform you that the sky is clearing, and we are in sight of land.''

''Thank God!''

At her exclamation, Johanna roused from her stupor and murmured something. Flora could only pick out the name Mary, and someone perhaps called Morgan. Flora remembered her whispering those names when the squall had first hit them. She leaned toward the girl. ''Who is it you are calling for?''

''She is merely rambling,'' Blaise said curtly, and held the flask of brandy to his niece's lips. Flora wondered why she didn't quite believe him.

Johanna was white with exhaustion as Flora bundled her ashore at Calais. She had never thought to be so grateful to feel solid land beneath her feet. Within minutes of their docking the storm was over, as if it had never been. The last of the clouds scudded away, revealing a pallid sun in a washed-out blue sky.

While Blaise saw to the removal of their baggage, Flora steered her charge over to a stone ledge.

''Sit here a moment and recover yourself.'' Flora looked around for Malin, and saw her standing to one side, looking relieved but much the worse for wear.

Nearby, and within the women's earshot, two sailors were exclaiming that they had never seen the like in all their years upon the waters. ''Not blowing up out o' nowhere, as it did, with nary a warning.''

"Aye, 'tis lost I thought we were, that last nasty bit. Thought the bloody sides would be stove in, so I did!"

Flora sent them an indignant glance and they lowered their voices, moving away toward the wharf. "Will you be all right, Johanna? I don't carry smelling salts in my reticule, but I'm sure I could obtain some."

The girl only shuddered and turned her head. Blaise joined them, looking grim. He chafed his niece's hands between his. "There is a coach awaiting us at quayside. I had hoped to press on to Amiens, but that is now out of the question. We might still reach Abbeville tonight, but if you are all in, I will obtain lodgings here in Calais, instead."

Johanna stared out at the ruffled waves, her eyes wide and dark. "No. I should like to go on. Away from the sea."

His eyes met Flora's over the girl's head. She nodded. "I think it would be best."

Later, when Johanna was safely bestowed in the luxurious traveling carriage with Malin, Flora watched their trunks and traveling cases being loaded. After being confined so long at sea, she was unwilling to get inside until they were ready to depart. Blaise approached her.

"No doubt you are shocked at the severity of Johanna's reaction at sea."

"Not in the least! I, myself, was frightened near out of my wits."

He gave her a long, straight look. "Were you? You certainly hid it well."

Flora wondered if she'd blundered into making an error. He mustn't guess what an accomplished actress she had become. "You forget I was a schoolmistress. It would never do to let the students think me unsure or afraid. Had I been so foolish, they would have run over me roughshod."

"Yes. Of course." He glanced at the carriage. "Perhaps you know that Johanna's parents were lost at sea when she was a child."

"Yes. I had heard that."

"And did you know that Johanna was with them?"

Flora was appalled. "No. Poor girl, it's no wonder she was in such a state of shock."

"Yes. She has a great fear of being out on the open sea. You must see that Malin does nothing to encourage it." He frowned and his eyes were as dark as the storm just past. "Brittany is full of legends, some of them dire. Malin was my niece's nursemaid, and used to tell her the old stories."

"She seems scarcely old enough to have cared for Johanna then!"

"Indeed, she was only twelve or so when she joined the nursery. Malin's mother is our housekeeper at the château, so it was only natural. The Kerjeans are very loyal to the family. Our histories go back together many years."

He handed Flora up into the waiting carriage, and shut the door. She was glad that he chose to ride once again, rather than be forced into close quarters together for the next several hours. Johanna was asleep against a pile of pillows beside her, while Malin was opposite, eyes closed. In the afternoon light she looked older than Flora had thought, taut lines around her eyes and mouth and the strain of their crossing visible in her pallor.

The coachman gave a blast of his horn, startling Johanna briefly out of her sleep.

"Eh, eh, *chèrie*," Malin said, reaching out to pat her charge's hand. "Sleep you a while." She nodded to Flora. "I have given her a headache powder. She will be well by the time we reach Abbeyville." The maid closed her eyes once more.

The driver gave the team their office and they started out on the land leg of their journey in a clatter of hooves and wheels and jingling harness. Blaise rode ahead, mastering the fractious horse as easily as he seemed to manage everything else. He was a magnificent horseman.

Now that there was no going back, the realization of their continued relationship intimidated Flora. In her panic to escape England, she had neglected to think past setting sail for France. Somewhere along the line there were bound to be moments when she and Blaise Cheney were alone, husband and wife united by law and their common desire to see Johanna comfortably established.

But not by anything else in the whole wide world. Flora didn't look forward to it. She reminded herself that the awkwardness would pass with time, and that one could become used to almost any circumstances if there were no other option. Certainly she was living proof of that.

Although the carriage was well sprung and the road well maintained, Flora was far too distracted to relax. They traveled through a rough section of road, where the jouncing awakened her companions once more.

Johanna sat up in stark terror, her pupils widely dilated. "Mary Morgan!" she exclaimed breathlessly, turning her head from side to side. Flora put her arm around the girl's shoulders. "It is all right. You were dreaming again."

Gradually Johanna's fear eased and she leaned back again. It was evident, at least to Flora, that she was fighting to stay awake. Malin's headache powder proved too strong for her will and she was back in a deep slumber within minutes. Her maid seemed wide-eyed and refreshed by the short nap.

Flora addressed her. "Who is this woman, this Mary Morgan, of whom Johanna is so frightened?"

Malin was watching her peculiarly. "Ah, you do not know, then. It was wrong of Monsieur not to tell you." She pursed her lips, but a sly smile lurked in her eyes.

"A *mari morgan* is not a human woman, madame, but a merwoman. A mermaid, as you English have it. They live in pearly caverns in the deep waters off Brittany's coast."

"Surely you do not believe that!"

Malin gave a short laugh at Flora's disbelief. "But I do, madame. And so will you, when you come to the château. You may hear them calling when the seas run high before a storm. Then the *mari morgans* sing their pretty songs and comb their hair with coral branches upon the rocks, to lure unwary sailors to their deaths."

Flora was angry. "If these are the kind of tales which you told to Johanna in her childhood, it is no wonder that she has nightmares."

Malin shrugged. "Whether you believe or not, you cannot change what is, madame. There are *mari morgans* in the waters of Brittany. And every generation they claim the life of a Cheney as their tribute." She leaned forward, dark eyes serious. "It is a curse upon his line."

"It is pure *poppycock*!"

Flora was upset. No wonder that Johanna was in such a sorry state. "I do not want to hear any more such folly in my presence; and I must forbid you to speak of such things to Johanna again."

"As you will, madame." Malin gave her a humorless smile that sent a chill through Flora. "But remember this, I beseech you: if you are wise you will be very careful near the sea . . . for *you* are also a Cheney, now!"

Chapter Four

All Paris was aglow by lamp and candlelight, when the weary travelers at last arrived in the city. The season was in full swing. Fine carriages thronged the Avenue des Champs-Elysées and Place de la Concorde, where the needle of the Luxor Obelisk faded up into the starry sky. It all seemed like a dream to Flora.

Johanna stared out the window, by turns apprehensive and excited, asking questions and talking sixteen to the dozen. Country-bred Malin was struck dumb by the noise and the grandeur. She had come directly from her Breton homeland to England to join Johanna, and even the sights of ancient St. Malo had left her unprepared.

Only Blaise, who had joined them in their vehicle some hours past, was completely at ease. This was his world. "Paris, the most beautiful city in the world," he said with quiet satisfaction. "It is good to be back home again."

Home. There was a time when that had meant the Château Morgaine. When he had drawn his strength and comfort from the towering granite rocks and foaming sea of his birthplace. But that was long ago, and he brushed the thought away. "The house may not be in perfect order for your arrival, Flora. I did not give the servants sufficient notice to ready everything for a new mistress; however, it will all be set to rights shortly."

Flora hid her unease. She was as ill-equipped to be the mistress of the Cheney mansion as Johanna: perhaps even more so. And a new mistress would be closely observed. She was a complete foreigner here, not merely in the sense of being an Englishwoman in France, but in being thrust into a level of society far above the circles she had formerly known.

The vehicle turned up the rue de Rivoli past the Tuileries gardens, then along the rue de Castiliogne to the Place Vendôme. Warm light spilled through the windows of the elegant square. Glimpses of silk hangings and crystal chandeliers merely hinted at the elegance of the interiors. Flora knew that the ladies and gentlemen had finished dining and would soon be leaving for the opera, the theater, or private balls and receptions. A woman peered out of an upper window as they passed, the jewels at her throat blazing with reflected candlelight.

Blaise watched Flora's face but couldn't read her thoughts. This new wife of his was a study in emotional contrasts, either transparent or opaque as stone. It intrigued him against his will. He must not think of her as a woman, with all the complications that could entail. He must remember that, despite her legal role, she was merely a superior sort of employee. One whose tenure would be brief.

The carriage rolled to a stop and the groom got down to lower the steps for the passengers. Johanna's face was solemn as she gazed up at the façade of the house. The last time she had seen it she had been a child, and she had no recollection of it.

Blaise leaned forward, looking from Flora to his niece. "Welcome to your new home."

Flora tensed with apprehension. She felt like an actor about to take the stage on opening night, in an unrehearsed play. It would be difficult portraying a dewy-eyed bride when the man she'd married was almost a total stranger. She hoped that she could keep up their deception of intimacy under the eagle-eyed scrutiny of the servants within, and any friends of the Cheneys' she might be forced to meet during her stay here. She would be happier once they left Paris for the wild shores of the Breton countryside.

No sooner had Blaise alighted and begun to assist the ladies, than the door at the top of the steps opened wide. Someone called his name. He turned and looked up. A woman was silhouetted in the doorway, behind her a glimpse of a hall ablaze with light. "*Mon Dieu!* It is Claudine."

A man appeared in the doorway by her side. "I tried to stop her, Blaise, indeed I did! But you know how Claudine is, when she gets an idea into her head. And she was adamant that she must be here when you arrived."

The woman laughed and ran gracefully down the stairs. "Yes, you impossible man," she said in rapid Parisian French. "But did you expect me to wait until you had decided to bring your bride on a formal visit to me? Nicolas and I, we must meet this paragon who has melted the stony heart of such a confirmed bachelor. She must be as clever as she is beautiful!"

Inside the carriage, Flora flushed in the dimness. The woman was in for a disappointment, she feared.

Blaise laughed warmly, then put his hand on Claudine's shoulder and ushered her back toward the steps. "You will catch your death in that shockingly indiscreet gown, *ma petite*. Do go inside, and I shall bring my bride to you."

She laughed girlishly, and did as he requested. Flora let Blaise hand her down from the carriage, wondering at his relationship with his cousin. They seemed to be on intimate terms, and he certainly revealed a different side of his personality from any that she had seen so far.

Blaise leaned down and whispered in her ear. "My *cousine*, Claudine, and her husband, Nicolas Le Vec. I should have prepared you for this."

There was no time for further talk, as they were bustled into the house where two footmen and a majordomo waited to take their wraps. The older man's face was filled with satisfaction as Blaise greeted him: Monsieur Cheney was home at last, where he belonged. After taking Flora's cloak, the butler spoke a word in Malin's ear, and she immediately went through to the back of the house.

Flora was staggered by her first impressions. The foyer was all white and gold, with saffron silk on the walls and at the windows. The crystal chandelier spattered darts of light, like loose diamonds, over the inlaid marble floor. The far wall held a marvelously carved staircase that swept up toward the upper stories in lovely, curving lines. Beneath a long mirror, a gilt console held a porcelain vase with a lush bouquet, and a cut-glass bowl to receive visitors' cards. Everything visible spoke of exquisite taste, and the wealth to indulge it.

Flora found herself guided into a superb drawing room, all done up in shades of emerald, ruby, and gold, where crystal lamps shone and glittered, and a fire leapt in the hearth.

This first glimpse of the world in which her new husband moved, stunned Flora. The perfect proportions, the fabulous furnishings, were more beautiful than anything her active fantasy could have imagined. To be told that someone owned great wealth was one thing; to experience it at first-hand was quite another. There was so much to take in she was blinded by the splendor, like a mole that had stumbled out into the sunlight.

Flora realized that she had been horribly misled. From her conversations with Blaise, she had thought him to be firmly established in the upper middle class. She'd imagined that launching Johanna would involve a few dinners and parties. Nothing that would put her in the spotlight. Now she realized that he moved in the first circles of society as easily as she had trod the drab corridors of Hawthorne Academy.

Her hopes of living in genteel obscurity vanished, while the odds of her running into her own countrymen and women had increased dramatically. Would any of them recognize her from the artist's rendering that had been published in the London newspapers?

"Ah, a perfect English rose!" Claudine exclaimed, eyeing Flora with approval. "I see why Blaise fell head over heels. What man would not, Nicolas?"

Her husband laughed. "Now you have put me on the spot! If I agree, I have slighted you. If I disagree I am rude to Blaise's bride. Let me declare there are no finer women in all of Paris than the two here with me now."

Their raillery set Flora at ease, and gave her time to examine them more closely. Blaise's cousin and her husband looked as if they had stepped out of a colored fashion plate of fairy-tale royalty. Nicolas was tall, with a hint of military bearing and a pleased, welcoming smile. His light brown hair was generously streaked with gold, accenting light blue eyes in a tanned, aquiline face.

Claudine, Flora decided, was simply the most beautiful woman that she had ever seen. Prettily plump in the accepted mode, yet with the perfect hourglass shape that fashion required. Flora felt like a stick beside her.

Blaise's cousin had hair as dark as his, elegantly arranged to show off her heart-shaped face. Her magnificent eyes were the deep golden color of fine brandy. She had a child's mischievous expression, a ready smile, and wore a scandalously low-cut dinner gown of topaz velvet and crêpe de chine that had surely come from the House of Worth. The blaze of white and canary-yellow diamonds at her throat, ears, and wrists were worthy of a queen.

It was only upon closer examination that Flora realized Claudine wasn't beautiful in the classical sense. But her expressive features and vivacious personality combined with her enchanting mannerisms to project a glamorous image. She was the kind of woman who would draw people to her side from across a crowded room. Together, husband and wife were a stunning couple, radiating charm and distinction in equal measure.

"Welcome to Paris, my dear new cousin!" Flora found herself enveloped in a cloud of perfume and those scandalously bared, alabaster arms. "I have been so very eager to meet you! We must have a comfortable coze as soon as may be, and you shall tell me everything of how you met Blaise and made him fall in love with you, *hein*?"

Flora groaned inwardly but thanked her, hoping her accent was as impeccable as she'd always thought it to be. Claudine clapped her hands together in delight.

"*C'est merveilleux!* You speak the language like a Frenchwoman. Oh, clever, clever Blaise to have found you!" She slipped her hand through Flora's arm. "Come, I will take you to your chambers. I could not let you arrive to a house all set on end, and came to make sure everything was in readiness."

But then Blaise stepped aside and Claudine spied Johanna standing just inside the threshold. She went completely white. *"Mon Dieu! Eve!"*

At her words Nicolas spun around and stopped dead. He, too, looked pale and shaken. Then he smiled and placed his hand on his wife's arm. "Not Eve, *chèrie*, but certainly made in her image. I apprehend that this is Eve's daughter."

He crossed the floor to Johanna's side, guiding Claudine along. "You will not remember us, but we remember you well. Welcome home."

Johanna looked from one to the other and her cheeks pinked with pleasure. "But I do remember you. Both of you. You, *Oncle* Nicolas, used to tell me stories and whittle little dolls of poplar wood for me—and *Tante* Claudine would dress them in scraps of velvet and satin and lace from her old gowns."

"Oh, pauvre petite!" Claudine enveloped the girl and hugged her to her scented bosom. Flora saw tears in both their eyes, and realized her own were suddenly full. Johanna was not so alone in the world as she had thought, and was only now discovering it.

Something niggled at the back of Flora's mind. At the moment, the reunion between the family members occupied the forefront of her thoughts. Even the precariousness of her own position was pushed to the back.

The butler coughed discreetly in the background. Claudine laughed and relinquished her young cousin. "Ah, we are reminded that a light supper has been set out on the buffet in the small dining parlor."

She whirled around to Blaise and stood on tiptoe and planted a kiss upon his cheek as he leaned down to her height. "You see, I have thought of everything! Food and fresh flowers, the finest sheets. Everything for the comfort of you and your bride. And Johanna, of course."

The butler looked so offended by this that Flora almost burst out laughing. Nicolas had noticed, also. "Come, Claudine, admit that you knew very well that Pierre would have all as it should be. Your primary reason for being here tonight was to satisfy your own uncontrollable curiosity."

"Ah, beast that you are, to expose my motives," she laughed, giving him both her gloved hands to hold. He kissed her fingers.

Flora watched their loving interplay and felt even more an outsider than before. Merry, generous Claudine was so ready to take her into the family fold that she couldn't help but deplore the deception she was practicing. She would dearly love to have the friendship of so gay and charming a creature, but it could never be. She must keep the Frenchwoman at arms' length or she would give herself away.

Blaise went to Flora's side. "You are weary from traveling. We'll have our refreshments and make an early night of it."

"So speaks the eager bridegroom," Nicolas whispered into his wife's shell-like ear.

Unfortunately the words carried clearly in the sudden silence. Flora's face flamed. "Can you blame me?" Blaise said smoothly, smiling down at his embarrassed bride. "After all, we set out immediately after the ceremony."

"Then," Claudine laughed, "we are considerably *de trop,* and shall be on our way at once."

Flora realized that the role of hostess had shifted to herself. "Not at all. Please . . . do stay!"

Claudine seemed to waver. "Alas," Nicolas said, taking her cloak from the footman, "we cannot. We are pledged to old General Robier and his wife, for a night at the opera."

His wife made a moue of disappointment. "But I shall pay you a visit tomorrow. That is a promise, my new cousin."

The footman opened the carved front door and they went out. Malin came out of the back, and Johanna relaxed. "I am too weary to dine," she told her uncle. "If I may, I would prefer a tray to be brought up to my room."

"Of course. Go with Malin, and everything will be seen to."

Flora wished Johanna a good night's sleep, and promised to look in upon her. "Thank you, but I would rather you did not." The girl's cheeks grew red. "I don't mean to be ungracious, but I am so very tired. I will surely be asleep before you've come upstairs at all."

"As you will." The two young women left together.

Flora took a deep breath. They were alone. Blaise folded his arms and regarded her. "I thought for a moment you were going to bolt the door so that Claudine and Nicolas could not leave."

She was alarmed. "I hope I wasn't that obvious."

His mouth curved up in a wry smile. "Only to me, my dear Flora. Only to me."

Blaise escorted her to a cozy room with thick apricot draperies drawn over the long windows. She had a vague impression of polished wood and gold-framed paintings on the walls, but her attention was claimed by the sight of chafing dishes set out along the wide sideboard. She'd expected a cold collation. Instead everything was freshly prepared and piping hot.

"How is this?" she exclaimed in amazement. "Your servants had no way of knowing what time of day we would arrive."

"I have not the slightest idea," he responded indifferently. He lifted an eyebrow at the man responsible for the orderly running of his establishment. "Unlike myself, Madame Cheney is naturally interested in such domestic details."

Pierre bowed. "It is very simple, madame. Appropriate meals have been prepared around the clock these past two days, so that they might be ready upon your arrival."

Flora tried to hide her astonishment at such unnecessary expense and effort. "I hope the food was shared among the servants and not merely gone to waste?"

The man looked appalled. "No, madame. However, if that is your wish in future . . . ?" He sent his master a glance of helpless appeal.

Blaise shrugged indifferently. "Madame Cheney will speak to the housekeeper about whatever arrangements she feels necessary."

Flora took her place at table, feeling foolishly encroaching. After they had been served, Blaise dismissed the butler with a gesture. He withdrew, shutting the door silently behind him.

After the fuss and bustle of the journey from Hawthorne to Dover, the Channel crossing, the journey through France and arrival in Paris, Flora was suddenly completely alone with the stranger who was her husband. He picked up the decanter of brandy from the sideboard and carried it toward the table.

"Forgive me if I spoke out of turn. I do not mean to turn your household all topsy-turvy."

"As the mistress of this house, you must do as you see fit."

She set her ornate silver fork down. "It would be highly presumptuous of me to—"

He replaced the decanter and caught her wrist. She looked up startled, and he sent a warning glance toward the closed door. "Now that you are my wife, my dear, you may do as your heart desires. You will know best as to the running of the household."

He lowered his voice to just above a whisper and spoke in English. "Be careful what you say. If you must be private with me, wait until we are alone."

"I thought we were!" she hissed and pulled her hand away. His fingers had left a red imprint on her skin.

"As my bride, you must expect the staff to be very curious about you. Use your native tongue if you insist on being indiscreet. The servants will not understand."

Raising his voice, for benefit of any eavesdroppers, he lifted a glass and proposed a toast to Flora. "To my lovely bride! May this be the first of many happy days together."

She took up her wine glass, sending him an arctic glance across the crystal rim, and drank.

When the silent meal was over, he escorted her upstairs. The turns in the landings were marked by alabaster lamps the color of honey, on pedestals shaped like torch-bearing, nymphs. Their amber glow lent an intimate atmosphere that unnerved Flora.

They continued on to the bedroom floor, which was lit by a succession of wall sconces in the same warm alabaster. At the far end of the hall and flanking wide double doors, two more nymphs bore their glowing lamps aloft. More than ever Flora felt as if she'd stumbled into a bizarre fairy tale. It wouldn't surprise her to find Scheherazade, even a djinn or two, waiting behind that elaborately carved mahogany. Light-headed with wine and weariness, she wondered if she were still in the carriage, asleep and dreaming all this.

But Blaise's hand upon her back, as he opened the right-hand door, was real enough. So was the room beyond. It ran across the width of the house and was dominated by a wonderful mural between the long windows, and by the great bed centered there. The bedchamber managed an air that was both highly masculine and intensely sensual. It was rather a shock to see her own nightshift laid out upon the bed.

The hairs on Flora's arms stood up when she heard the door close behind her, and realized that Blaise was still in the room. Before she could demand an explanation, he was at her side, pressing his finger against her lips. "Do not be alarmed. You see, there is no adjoining suite here for husband and wife, as there is at Château Morgaine. You must admit that it would seem quite odd for us to begin our wedded life with you in my bed, and I in a guest chamber."

She jerked away. "If you think for a moment—"

His hands clamped down upon her shoulders. "Lower your voice, if you please. I do not think *whatever* it is that you have in mind, *chèrie*. I have given you the word of a Cheney."

"I am *not* your *chèrie*!"

"Ah, but you are." His dark eyes showed a glint of mocking laughter. "At least in the eyes of the world. However, if you wish, I shall merely call you Flora . . . *chèrie*.

"Now, ring for the maid and ready yourself for bed. And try to do so with the demeanor of a bride anticipating a night of lovemaking with her eager bridegroom—not that of a woman on the way to the guillotine."

"You are abominable!"

"We have already agreed upon that." He gave her a smile that had her blood fizzing in her head like champagne. "Calm yourself, Flora. Such theatricalities do you no credit. I shall sleep in the dressing room off this chamber. But no one must know of it save you and I . . . if our little charade is to be maintained."

"Very well. I only hope there may be a bolt upon the dressing room door."

He made her an elaborate bow. "If you wish, you may nail it shut. But not tonight, or you will rouse the house."

"Now you are being ridiculous."

"No, Flora," he said sternly. "You are the one being ridiculous. We made a bargain, you and I, and I shall certainly keep it. I have given you the word of a Cheney. You, madame, are the only one with the power to change those terms."

While she was still pondering those cryptic words, he walked to the dressing room and opened the door. "*Bonne nuit,* Flora. Sleep well."

His valet was waiting to undress him. "You may go, Georges. I shall not be needing you tonight." The valet withdrew, discreet as a shadow, and Blaise shut the dressing room door. He quickly stripped off his shirt. Tiredness came over him in a wave. A good thing he wasn't the eager bridegroom that he pretended to be, he told himself wryly.

Pouring heated water into the china basin, he thought of Flora in his bed and felt an unwelcome tug of desire. He cursed the tightness in his loins. Nothing must sidetrack him from his ultimate goal.

At least they had passed the first hurdle, tonight's meeting with Claudine and Nicolas. Yes, he had chosen well. She was quick-witted, well-bred, and educated; pretty, sensuous, and yet so amusingly serious at times. And her figure was superb. The image of Flora, naked in his arms, rose unbidden.

Physical desire slammed into him so hard it caught him unprepared. Blaise gripped the sides of his shaving stand. He fought the sensation off, laughing at himself. Habit was a terrible thing. It was merely that this was the first time he'd had a desirable woman in his bed, and no intention of sleeping with her. What he needed was a woman to ease his needs.

Splashing warm water over his face, he wondered if Odile de Broceliand was in town. And if her husband was out of it.

Flora listened to the sounds of Blaise moving about his dressing room. A few minutes and all was quiet. She was alone in the welcome dark, beneath the luxurious down quilts of his bed. Sure she would fall asleep instantly, she was dismayed to find herself overtired and wakeful. She wondered if he were asleep already, and felt a pang of guilt that he had to take a cot while she had his bed.

She pictured him there beside her suddenly, reaching out to her in the dark. A wave of heat washed over her. Her breasts tingled and she imagined him touching them, caressing them, as Robin had. *It must be the wine,* she told herself, pushing the image away.

Flora tried to distract herself by thinking of something else. Anything else! But the fine linen sheets were softer than velvet against her skin, and carried a faint aura of Blaise's physical presence. An intriguing blend of cool citron and warm spice—mysterious, subtle, and complex. Like the man himself, she thought.

She was still thinking of him when she finally drifted off into dreams. His scent followed her even there.

Flora found herself in a castle of gleaming white marble. She was looking for Blaise. It seemed urgent that she find him. Making her way along corridors, up curving staircases and down secret passages, she discovered that she was back where she had started.

No matter which way she turned, her footsteps always led back to a single door, carved with the figure of a nymph. It seemed imperative that she open the door, but it was locked fast. Her sense of dread grew.

Finding a ring of keys at her side, the dream-Flora tried one after another, to no avail. Each time that she thought she had come to the last key, one more would materialize on the ring. There were soon dozens of them, each more worn and ancient than the last. Again and again she fumbled to select yet another, her fingers made awkward by her haste. She could have wept in frustration, but there was no time. No time.

At last she found the key. Shaking with relief, she fitted it into the keyhole and unlocked the door. She groaned aloud. Behind was another door. A most formidable one. Black as ebony and cold as death to her touch. Her heart hammered painfully. She was terrified of what she might find behind it, yet even more fearful of what terrible things would happen if she failed to reach the other side.

Footsteps echoed behind her. Slow. Menacing. Coming ever closer. Flora tried to cry out for help. Panic filled her mouth and throat and she was unable to utter a sound. The thing that stalked her was just around the turn of the corridor now. Mere seconds separated her from doom. Once more Flora began to work her way desperately through the ring of keys, in hopes of reaching safety.

But none of them would so much as fit into the lock.

In the morning Flora recalled nothing of her dream. She did remember waking once, thinking that someone was beside the bed looking down at her; but the room had been empty. The pillow beside her was rumpled, and the linens were wildly disarranged. One of her legs was bared to the thigh. No doubt she'd been restless in her sleep, after the excitement and travails of the past few days.

The light had a watery quality that made her think of a dim mermaid's grotto. Her gaze rested on the ceiling. She blinked. The wall mural was a companion to the painted medallion overhead, which she had neglected to notice last evening. At first it seemed to be a clever copy of Botticelli's Venus, rising from a green, foam-splashed sea.

Careful scrutiny showed the central figure to be a regal mermaid, riding the crest of the waves on a scallop shell, drawn by a pair of crabs in gilded harness. The scenes along the walls, above the wainscoting, showed the undersea world filled with starfish and coral, gracefully waving strands of seaweed—and several mermen, passionately entwined with the seductively beautiful mermaids.

Flora knew she should be shocked, but the murals were so beautifully rendered she had to admire them for their artistry. If these were the dreaded *mari morgans* of Brittany; there was nothing so terrible about them or their doings. Unless, she thought wryly, one were a parish priest. She wondered what romantic Miss Melbourne would have thought upon awakening to such a sight. Most likely, she decided, her timid friend would have suffered a fatal attack of apoplexy.

The clock on the mantelpiece chimed, and she saw that it was past ten of the clock. She couldn't remember ever having lain abed so long. Snuggling beneath the warm down coverlet, Flora enjoyed the luxury of the bed and the late hour. And the blessed privacy, after four days on the road, with Johanna and Malin her constant companions.

Suddenly she noticed the warm and flickering glow from the fireplace, and realized that a fresh fire had been laid in the grate, and was burning brightly. Someone had been in the room with her, after all.

She sat up and looked around. The door to the dressing room was open and a large mirror on the bedroom wall reflected Blaise at his shaving stand. He was shirtless, and she found herself oddly compelled to watch. She had never seen a naked male back before. Although his well-tailored clothes had displayed his physique to advantage, she hadn't expected him to have the body of an athlete. The interplay of muscle and sinew was mesmerizing.

He'd whetted the razor on the strop, and was applying foam to his jaw with a brush when he stopped in mid-action. Setting the brush back down, he took up the damp towel and blotted the foam away. He leaned forward, resting his hands on either side of the stand, and regarded himself in the mirror. Had he cut himself? Then he turned around. The look of surprise on his face was almost comical.

It occurred to Flora, belatedly, that if she could see his reflection, he could also see hers. Dear God, how long had she been staring? She had always blushed readily; now, as the heat rose up her cheeks, she feared her face was flaming like a beacon.

He vanished from sight, only to appear in the doorway a moment later, belting his red jacquard dressing gown. "Good morning. I trust you slept well?"

"Yes, thank you." She couldn't meet his eyes.

"Ring for the maid. She'll bring your breakfast to you in bed." A slow smile lingered on his lips. "I informed the servants last night that neither of us would be down for breakfast this morning. They understood of course."

Flora grabbed the tasseled end of the bellpull as if it were a lifeline, and yanked too strongly. Myriad gold threads came loose in her fingers. A maid appeared instantly, as if she had been hovering in the corridor, waiting.

Blaise smiled down at Flora. "I will see that it is repaired."

The maid dropped a curtsy, delighted to be the first to see Monsieur and Madame together in so intimate a setting, and even more delighted to see the groom's smiles, the pretty bride's blushes, and the rumpled bedclothes. When she spotted Madame's silk negligee on the floor at the foot of the bed, she was ecstatic.

As she lifted the gossamer garment and placed it tenderly across the foot of the bed, she was anticipating her coming triumph in the servant's hall. They would listen when she spoke at the next meal, even the unbending majordomo, and hang upon her every word.

She would have been less sanguine had she still been in the room when Flora noticed the negligee a bit later. "Where on earth did this come from? It is not mine!"

Blaise stood brooding at the window. He didn't turn to answer. "I thought it wise to provide it," he said in English. "A prop for our little play, like the pillow I flattened earlier, and the mussed bedclothes."

Flora was taken aback. So her vague recollection of someone in the room with her in the early hours had been true. She felt a flush rise up from her throat. "Your mastery of the telling detail is evident. So, too, is a rather dismaying talent for calculation and duplicity."

He turned and cocked his eyebrow. "You do not approve? Strange, I was sure that you would."

The maid returned with a tray for her mistress, and there was no chance for Flora to reply. Before Blaise went back to the dressing room, he paused at the foot of the bed. "Claudine has been busy spreading the news of our nuptials. Several notes have already arrived for you this morning. They are on the table in the sitting room, and I will leave them for you to answer."

Flora finished her chocolate and put on the traveling dress, which a maid had brushed and pressed out for her. It looked as good as new. Before going downstairs, she peeked in upon Johanna. Pleading fatigue from their travels, Johanna was propped up in bed, reading a note on heavy lavender paper.

"Do not call me lazybones, I beg. I am still fatigued from our travels and I want to be rested, for Claudine has made all sort of plans for us." She glanced down at the note: "Visits to the Tuileries gardens and the museums and the theater and to see Monsieur Eiffel's strange tower, which I quite forgot to look for when we arrived so late at night! And we are to dine with Claudine and Nicolas tomorrow, and perhaps see a play next week, and oh! Many, many more things."

While she was glad to see the roses returned to Johanna's cheeks, this was the first Flora had heard of any of it. She groaned. "If even half of this is to be accomplished, I believe that I should go back to bed myself!"

Hurrying down the stairs, she noticed now that the nymph torchères at the landings were actually mermaids. Sensual creatures with seductively bared breasts and sleekly rounded bellies above; intricately carved scales tapering down over slender hips to end in gracefully curving fins below. The face of each one was different, as if carved from life; yet all shared an eerie perfection. A cold, inhuman beauty. Flora wondered if Johanna had seen them in childhood, and if they were as much the source of her nightmares as Malin's folktales.

As she walked along the lower corridor, the maids dropped her their best curtsys. Flora almost wished that she could retreat to her bedchamber. There must be great speculation about her first night as the new bride and mistress, and the servants were greatly interested in the success or failure of the previous night's events.

From the sly or shy smiles she encountered, Flora guessed that they took her abstracted state of mind for the contented daydreams of a satisfied bride; actually, she was wondering how she could possibly avoid Claudine's planned activities. It was all too possible that her path might cross with that of some English visitors to Paris, which would bring everything to ruin. Flora wished they could have gone directly to Brittany, where such an event was much less likely.

As she took her place in the breakfast room, she heard Claudine's velvet voice in the foyer. A moment later she swept in with Blaise in tow. She was chic in a tightly fitted walking dress of finest merino wool. The deep burgundy color, picked out with gold and black cording, brought out the beauty of her dark eyes and the red highlights in her brunette hair. Flora thought she had never seen a more glamorous woman, or a more sophisticated ensemble.

Claudine was filled with energy and good spirits. *"Bonjour, bonjour, ma cousine!* Are you still breaking your fast? But I have come to carry you away with me for a drive. I have instructed the groom to walk the horses until you are ready."

Blaise laughed. "Let my poor wife have something to eat, if you mean to drag her through the Paris shops today." He turned to Flora. "I sent Claudine a note this morning to tell her your trunks vanished from the vehicle conveying our baggage to Paris yesterday. She has taken on the enormous task of seeing you completely reoutfitted."

"Mon cher Blaise, I am delighted to be charged with such an enjoyable commission. What a splendid time we shall have, Flora! I know all the very best shops."

"You might have mentioned it to me," Flora said to Blaise. She knew it was just his way of explaining why Flora had none of the fashionable garments as befitted her present status, but his high-handedness set her back up.

Blaise frowned at Flora. "What an unusual woman I have married, so reluctant to add to her wardrobe!"

Claudine put a hand to her lips. "But how very bad of you, Blaise! Flora, I thought this plan met with your approval, or I should never have come!"

Flora felt Blaise's hand press down firmly on her shoulder. "I am sure that my wife will be glad to have the assistance of the most exquisitely dressed woman in all Paris. You will have the dressing of her from the inside out, Claudine. Naturally, you have carte blanche to outfit her at all the premier houses. I only hope you are up to the task."

"Foolish man! But I shall merely introduce Flora to the finest that Paris has to offer, and let her choose from among their wares."

Her diplomatic words were immediately followed by a torrent of plans: ideas, events, colors, couturiers, lists of required apparel tripped from her tongue until Blaise held up his hands in mock protest. "Enough. My head is whirl-ing."

"And mine," Flora said. "Really, it is kind of you, Claudine, but I don't think I should leave Johanna today."

Blaise frowned. "Nonsense. I am here, as well as Malin and a houseful of servants to look after her. And you cannot continue to wear the same costume day after day."

Flora gave in. Not for the promise of refurbishing her wardrobe, but to see something of Paris. "Very well. I'll make myself ready."

He started to turn away. "I had almost forgotten. Stop by my study on your way out, if you will. There are certain papers I wish you to sign before you go off."

Claudine threw up her hands in despair. She gave Flora a roguish look. "Men! Well, if it is business you must talk of, then we shall not depart for hours. I know just how it is, for Nicolas, he is the same. Blaise, cannot these affairs be put off until this afternoon?"

"I suppose so." He smiled at his cousin. "There, you see how marriage has already had a mellowing influence on my personality." He seemed to remember that some-thing more was called for: bending down, he gave Flora a chaste kiss upon her cheek. "Enjoy your excursion. I can think of no one more suitable to show you Paris's most expensive shops than my cousin."

Before Flora had time to protest further, she was hustled out of the house and into the Le Vecs' elegant carriage. Blaise watched them drive away, a slight smile at the cor-ners of his mouth. Claudine waved to him, then turned to Flora.

"Indeed, you have had a good effect upon him. The change is quite noticeable. Even Nicolas remarked upon it. I can see in him now remnants of the Blaise I remember of old. Oh, it does my heart good!

"He has been so cold and aloof since . . ." Her dark eyes sparkled with unshed tears. "Since his younger days. *Vrai dire*, in our childhood, he was always the best of good companions. And it is you who has wrought this change in him. I salute you with all my heart."

Her tears made Flora feel ashamed of her imposture. How could she possibly keep up this charade without causing great grief to all? She should never have let her fears entangle her in the lives of the Cheneys. Nothing but disaster was sure to come of it.

Her cheeks were hot with mortification. Fortunately, the Frenchwoman mistook Flora's hectic flush for the blushes of a bride receiving compliments. "La, how I go on," she said, blinking away the moisture in her eyes. "Let us talk of happier things. Tell me of how you met my cousin and won his heart: for indeed, I thought he was long past praying for!"

"It is nothing as romantic as you think," Flora said, sifting through the truth for a few palatable facts. Best to be frank. "I was one of Johanna's schoolmistresses at the academy. We met when her uncle came to pay her a visit."

The expression on the other woman's face would have been comical under other circumstances. Not, however, for the reasons that Flora expected. Claudine clapped her gloved hands. "Yes, so Blaise said. It is delightful! Quite like a storybook. Not Cinderella, *hein*? More like Beauty and the Beast?" Her dimples peeked out. "Oh, how angry Blaise would be to hear me say so."

She sent her companion a brilliant smile. "If you can tame my fierce cousin, *ma chère*, you will have all of Paris at your feet. I predict that you shall become all the rage."

As she rattled merrily on, Flora sank back against the upholstery. Even when she told the truth, it only served to mire her deeper in lies.

Claudine's hand covered Flora's. "I expect it was your courage, as well as your beauty, that conquered him. So brave you are, *ma chère*. But of course you had to make your way in the world, after you were thrown out of your home without a sou to your name!"

Flora gave a start and felt the blood drain from her head. "How did . . . what exactly did Blaise tell you?"

Her companion made a moue of dismay. "*Mon Dieu*, how my tongue runs away with me. You must not be angry with him, Flora. He told me all. That your father's estate was entailed, since he had no sons, and that the cruel cousin who inherited it threw you out when you refused his advances. So resourceful you were, under the circumstances!"

Now Flora took a deep breath. For a horrible moment she'd thought that Blaise and Claudine knew the truth. But the Frenchwoman's last words filled her with equal parts relief and chagrin. If Claudine indeed knew the truth, she would shrink away in horror, not offer congratulations on Flora's "resourceful" behavior.

"He sounds a veritable monster!" Claudine continued. "I do not understand the way you English leave your estates entailed to the eldest male in the family descent. It is barbaric. But it was quick thinking of you to bash this horrid cousin with the soup tureen, before escaping with nothing but your mother's jewelry. You are well rid of such relations!"

Flora's nerves were still quivering but she almost laughed aloud. Good God! Blaise had concocted a bizarre fantasy, wherein she had been an orphaned heroine fleeing the improper advances of a knavish relative, to placate Claudine's curiosity. How well he knew his cousin! It was just the thing to appeal to her extravagantly romantic nature. But, Flora thought darkly, he should have warned me of it in advance!

"I know what you are thinking," Claudine said, startling Flora once more. "It was wrong of me to bring it up. I should not have said anything to you. Indeed, Blaise told me that I must never mention it to you, because the memory of it still caused you great distress. And I see he was right! Never fear, Flora. I shall not refer to it again. Your secrets are safe from discovery."

Flora bit her lip. She certainly hoped so.

Claudine was a whirlwind of energy and advice as they visited the Paris shops. Most were as elegantly outfitted as fine drawing rooms, with swooping draperies, lush carpets, and tasteful accessories. Flora knew that she was in over her head, and let Blaise's cousin take charge. The Frenchwoman knew exactly where to go, just as she knew exactly what would suit Flora to the best effect. An airy wave of her gloved hand and unsuitable items were whisked away almost before Flora had a glimpse of them.

At one establishment, so fine and elegant it might have once housed royalty, Claudine sniffed disdainfully at a sampling of various walking dresses in shades of pale, watery greens, deep purplish reds, and ripe yellows. "Do not waste our time or yours with those garish *vegetable* hues which are all the rage. Madame Cheney's exquisite coloring requires certain tones, you comprehend. Think of jewels in candlelight, or the rich, muted palette of a Titian or a Rembrandt."

The shrewd Paris modistes, sensing the potential for a profitable and continuing patronage, sent their shopgirls and seamstresses scurrying to please Madame Cheney and her companion.

By four o'clock they had shopped, stopped for a marvelous midday meal, and were on their way back to Blaise's town house. Flora was exhausted and the carriage filled with bandboxes and parcels tied up with fancy ribbons. Four times as many items were to be delivered directly to the house. She was amazed that, on nothing more than a name and a reputation, so many expensive garments could be bought. Day dresses, morning gowns, walking ensembles, tea gowns, and evening ensembles had been selected, along with myriad gloves and bonnets and feathered adornments. There were warm shawls of challis and wool, and spangled silks for evening wear; jackets and cloaks, hats and muffs, shoes and boots and evening slippers, gloves and stockings and all manner of lacy lingerie.

Claudine had even charmed and sweetly bullied the modiste into altering a dress to have ready for Flora to pick up on their way home. It was of tissue silk in the soft color of apricot tea roses, something Flora would never have thought to wear. But Claudine's taste was exquisite; the delicate peachy-rose set off Flora's hair and skin to perfection. They carried it away with them like a trophy, wrapped in a box lined with silver paper and tied with an enormous silver bow.

"There," Claudine said as they left Madame Valois' fashionable salon, "at least you will have something suitable to change into for dinner at home tonight. La! How I should like to see Blaise's face when he sets eyes upon you in it. But for evening wear we shall go to Worth or to the Callicot sisters tomorrow. Nothing less will do."

Flora's head was reeling, but Claudine could have gone on for hours more. "I have not had such fun since I bought my trousseau," she assured her as they headed back for the Place Vendôme. "It is exactly like dressing my baby dolls when I was younger."

Her face grew pensive and she fell silent. It was as if a light had been quenched, turning a bright window dark. The change was startling. Watching her, Flora sensed the Frenchwoman's secret sorrow: Claudine desperately wanted children, and had none.

As suddenly as it had appeared, the mood vanished and she was her vibrant self again. "Ah, here we are." She smiled impishly. "You must tell Blaise that we have only just begun to replace your wardrobe. That way he will become used to receiving so many modistes' bills. Although when he sees you in that ivory peignoir with the sapphire ribbons, he will not care in the least!"

Laughing at Flora's blushes, Claudine pressed a quick kiss on her cheek. "I cannot come in with you, for we have an engagement this evening. So tiresome, when I am dying to spend more time getting to know you."

Flora looked up at the mansion and sighed. Although she'd gotten glimpses of wide boulevards framed by arching chestnut trees and famous landmarks of which she'd read, she had mainly seen the insides of the city's most fashionable shops. She felt oddly let down. For a few short hours she had enjoyed herself tremendously, letting herself get caught up in Claudine's enthusiasms. But, like Blaise this morning, she had only been playing a role.

And a very expensive one, at that, she thought as she descended the carriage and entered the town house. Flora still felt guilt over her extravagance. She was filled with even more guilt at deceiving Claudine regarding her marriage, as well. Blaise's cousin was an amiable and generous creature. She had taken Flora to her warm heart, treating her with the affection of a sister, and vowing that they would be the very best of friends from that day forth. Under other circumstances, Flora would have gladly pursued the friendship. Instead she felt shamed and unworthy to be on the receiving end of so much good will. She would be relieved when Blaise's affairs took them away to Brittany.

The case clock at the foot of the stairs chimed out the hour, and Flora was astonished to see how late it was. As he took her cloak, the majordomo informed her that Johanna was out in the square, taking the air with her maid, adding: ''Monsieur Cheney will be in his study, awaiting Madame's pleasure.''

She had completely forgotten that Blaise had wanted her to sign some documents. ''Please inform Monsieur that I have returned, and will be with him shortly.''

Within half an hour she was costumed in her new dress, and Geneviève had managed to arrange her hair in a fetching new style. Flora eyed her reflection. At least she now looked the part of the role she was playing. Madame Blaise Cheney, the fashionable wife of a wealthy aristocrat. She rose from the padded bench with an air of new confidence.

Her husband's study was on the first floor, beyond the main dining room. It had a rich, masculine aura created partly by the warm chestnut paneling, the deep burgundy leather chairs, and the bronze lamps and sconces here and there. Two walls had open cupboards built into them, and the shelves were filled with books and objets d'art from around the world. She wished that she could be alone in this room for an hour or two: surely it would reveal something more of the man whose name she had taken.

Blaise was replacing a book when she entered. He paused, the book in midair as he gazed at her. His eyebrows rose. ''Turn around.''

Flora felt acutely self-conscious. She knew that she did him credit in her new finery, and hoped he would say something complimentary. Instead he frowned. ''You need pearls with that gown. I shall have to buy you a set.''

Disappointment sharpened her tongue. ''You need not buy me anything further. In fact, when you receive the receipts for my expedition with your cousin, you will be filled with regret for your generosity.''

His frown deepened. ''I did not ask you here to quarrel.'' He came around his desk and escorted her to the chair beside it. ''There are several papers for you to sign.''

''But what are these?''

"The marriage settlement, for one. And your will, leaving everything to me, should you meet an untimely demise. Which, I may add, is extremely unlikely."

"And extremely unnecessary! As you know, I have nothing to leave to anyone. Unless," she said witheringly, "you are referring to the fortune's worth of clothing which your cousin selected for me today."

Instead of answering, he removed a lacquered chest from his desk. "There are these." Blaise eyed his bride keenly. He touched one of the drawers. "Open them."

One by one she pulled out the four drawers. The first held an exquisite suite of iridescent opals and diamonds: necklace, brooch, jeweled hairpins, bracelet, earbobs, and several rings. The second drawer held sapphires and the third magnificently cut topaz squares, mounted in heavy gold. The last suite of jewels appeared to be quite old: enameled medallions rimmed with diamonds, and studded with rubies, sapphires, and emeralds in an intricate floral design. They winked and shone in the dancing light from the fireplace, evoking images of the *ancien régime,* and fine ladies in powdered wigs. They were exquisite examples of the jeweler's art.

"I cannot accept these," Flora said stiffly. "They are obviously family heirlooms,"

Blaise muttered an exasperated oath. "Why must you balk me at every turn? Of course they are heirlooms. They are part of the Cheney Jewels; and, I might add, it would look rather singular if my bride was never seen to wear any of them. And I must furnish you with a few others if we wish to avoid comment."

Her dismay was genuine. "I didn't imagine there would be any opportunity for wearing such priceless jewels! I thought we were to spend merely a few weeks in Paris, before removing to the country?"

His mouth quirked up at one corner. "You speak of the château as if it were a fisherman's cottage, where you would spend your time gutting fish for the family supper. I assure you there will be many occasions when you will wear them in Brittany. You may consider them in the nature of a loan, if it makes you contented. I will keep the jewels in the vault until they are needed."

"I would much prefer it."

But she realized that wasn't strictly true. She wanted to touch them, and try them on, and hold the stones up to the light and watch them burn with colored fire. Not because they were worth a fortune, but because they were so beautiful.

Blaise appeared to read her mind, in that disconcerting way he had. "It would please me very much if you were to wear them. The opals would look well with that gown."

How could she resist when he asked her so politely? "Very well." Quickly picking up the topmost document, she scanned the page. It was her will, and the provisions were exactly as he had stated them. Flora took up the pen from the standish, dipped it in the inkwell, and signed it.

He handed her the other papers. "The provisions of the settlement are stated clearly." A gleam came into his eyes. "Even you, madame, with your penchant for argument, should find nothing there to annoy you. And you will understand why a will is necessary."

Flora started to scan the contract. She stopped, went back to the start, and read through the first two pages slowly. "I cannot sign this settlement! You cannot be serious," she exclaimed, stopping again. "This is a fortune!"

He came beside her and stood frowning down at her angrily. "I am very serious. You have placed yourself in my hands, by taking me as your husband. An act of trust. It is only fair that you are offered some security in return."

"My little role in your affairs is scarcely worthy of such wages."

He gave her one of his darkly opaque looks. "Believe me, Flora, when I say that you shall earn every penny of it."

A frisson of fear danced up her spine. She searched his face, but his eyes hid far more than they revealed. His features looked chiseled from stone. The thought came to her that, had she known him better before embarking on their strange marriage, she would have been less easily swayed. Blaise Cheney was a complicated and dangerous man.

She fought the urge to shrink back in her chair. "Perhaps you will explain what you mean?"

He shot her an impatient glance. "Do you fear you've wandered into a Bluebeard's castle? Allow me to disabuse you of any such notion. You are not a servant in my home, madame, but the mistress of my household. Sign the papers and be done with it."

She dropped her lashes and read through the short contract again. It was hard to concentrate, knowing that he was watching her so intensely. Flora realized that she hadn't retained a single word, and went back to the beginning. The main provision was simple: under the terms, the equivalent of fifty thousand pounds was to be invested in funds in the name of Flora Cheney, espoused wife of Blaise Yvon Cheney.

At first she might draw upon the interest for her pin money and everyday expenses, although her husband had agreed to supply her with everything else that she might need, including setting up her own horses and carriage should she so desire. And, if the other stipulations were met, in time Flora would receive the principal sum, outright. Free and clear and in her own name. She could not credit it.

"You see," he said softly, "you have an out, madame. Read on."

Flora read. The principal would come to her, utterly and irrevocably, after two years of marriage, or the birth of an heir—whichever might come first.

"An heir! What is this?"

He smiled wryly at her dismay. "That last was put in by my man at law. Naturally, he is unaware of the true nature of our marriage. Monsieur Bernard is both cautious and prudent. I am sure you cannot fault him for that."

"N . . . no."

Yet Flora could scarcely believe the evidence of her eyes. Blaise was a man of his word, seeing that she would be free to set up her own establishment after Johanna was married and his guardianship ended. She would be a woman of independent means, able to afford not only the elegancies of life, but all the luxuries. Her future was secure. And yet . . .

Everything seemed in order, but a sense of alarm ran through her blood. Perhaps it was only that she couldn't believe her good fortune. Or perhaps it was the intensity in the way Blaise was looking at her, like a hawk about to swoop down upon an unwary creature.

Flora was no lawyer, but she had a good mind. There was nothing hidden or wrong that she could see. Drawing in a shaky breath, she dipped the pen in ink once more. She signed the contract, all three copies, and Blaise sanded it to dry the ink. His posture, so tense before, was more relaxed. Almost relieved.

When the ink was dried, he put his copy into his desk drawer and locked it. "You will wish to retain yours," he told her.

The timbre of his voice echoed satisfaction, even triumph. *Now I have you, Flora. Now you are mine!* He hadn't realized that, right to the end, he was afraid she would find an out. But she had snapped up the lure he dangled before her. He understood that it was not greed, but the desperate desire for independence that had won her over. No matter. His plan would succeed. He was sure of it!

Blaise slipped her copy of the settlement into a thick envelope and handed it to her. The room was filled with a sort of static electricity that ran up and down Flora's spine. "If you are through with me . . ."

"Ah, no, madame. I am just beginning."

Their hands brushed, and she jumped like a scalded cat. The envelope fell to the floor. They both ignored it.

He put his hands upon her shoulders, and she felt the heat of them searing through the fragile silk to her skin beneath. It robbed her of breath. Flora tried to move away. His grip tightened and his eyes were sparked with mystery.

"Why do you fear me, Flora?"

She wanted to say she was not in the least afraid of him. Instead she blurted out the truth: "I don't know."

Blaise laughed, a low sound that left her more confused. "Honesty in a wife is a rare virtue."

She couldn't move away. His breath whispered through her hair. Tipping her chin up, he scrutinized her features. His own face was unreadable. He stood looking down at her while Flora struggled with her reactions. And then he smiled.

"I will have to teach you not to bolt from me, *ma chère.* If your aversion to me was noted, it would cause comment."

He lifted his hand and ran the back of it along her cheek. Heat bloomed in the pit of her stomach. Flora felt as if the wind had been knocked out of her. They faced each other in a room suddenly charged with tension. The very air hummed with it. It was like that moment at sea, just before the storm had boiled up out of nowhere and swept over them. She waited for him to say something, anything.

He seemed, in turn, to be expecting something from her. He touched her lips with his fingertip. They tingled as if he had kissed them. His mouth was mere inches from hers.

"Why do you fight me, Flora? What do you fear? Something in me . . . or in you?"

She felt herself sway toward him. A pulse throbbed at her throat and a tide of panic swept through her. She stiffened and pulled back abruptly. This time he let her go.

Turning swiftly, she fled the room.

Flora flew along the corridor blindly and almost collided with one of the footmen. She didn't stay to hear his apologies.

Eventually she found herself at the back of the house, without knowing quite how she'd gotten there. She took sanctuary in a small parlor, then realized it was the antechamber to a formal reception room. The draperies were closed but she made out two great chandeliers, glinting like black ice in the shadows. Flora entered and sat down on a damask settee. Hiding, yet not knowing why.

Dusk was closing in and she heard the sounds of Johanna's voice in the corridor, but didn't go out to her. Her heart was still pounding and her breath came in a quick, jerky rhythm. Blaise had a potent effect up on her. Yet, try as she might, Flora couldn't define why that was. She only knew that, in his presence, she couldn't think clearly. Logic and wisdom were paralyzed, and caution totally suspended.

Which, she decided, was half the reason she'd agreed to fall in with his mad scheme. She mustn't let him see it. What in God's name was wrong with her? It was like Robin all over again, that swell of yearning, that terrible longing to be held, to be swept away on the winds of passion, and caution be damned!

And she didn't imagine herself in love with Blaise, as she had with Robin. In fact, she was quite sure she didn't even like him. There, she'd finally put it into words in her mind. She was strongly attracted to a man she hardly knew and whom she doubted she would care to know any better.

Grandfather was right, she thought in despair. *I am my mother's child!*

Once before she had fallen under a powerful spell spun by a man, and it had led her to disaster. Her unease grew until it threatened to choke her. Flora pressed her hands to her temples and fought for a calm that wouldn't come.

She had the unnerving sensation that she'd stepped into the path of a fragile cobweb, and attempted to brush past—only to have it wind around her like a cocoon of woven, steel strands.

Chapter Five

$\mathcal{A}$s her maid tucked in the last pin, Claudine inspected
her image in the triple mirror on her dressing table—one
of Nicolas's extravagant gifts, it had belonged to a queen
of France. Everything must be perfect tonight, herself in-
cluded. This was an important evening—Flora's debut in
Parisian society.

She wished she'd had enough notice to throw an elaborate ball in their honor, but it would be weeks before she
could pull it off. Instead there would be an intimate dinner,
just the four of them, followed by a night at the opera. It
didn't matter. She was sure the appearance of Blaise and
his English bride would create a sensation.

Nicolas came out of his dressing room and stopped to
admire her. " 'Painting the lily,' my dear?''

Claudine smiled at her husband's reflection in the looking glass. The way his face lit up when he saw her, after
all these years, still made her heart turn over with joy. Few
married women she knew were engaged in love affairs with
their own husbands.

She dismissed her maid with the dazzling smile that
charmed her servants as much as her friends. "*Très bien,
Marie.* You have outdone yourself! You may go now.''

As her dresser withdrew, Nicolas crossed to his wife's
side and put his hands gently upon her bare shoulders. A
spark leapt between them and their glances locked in the
mirror. He leaned down. "Every day you are more beautiful than the day before.''

She turned her face up to receive his kiss. "Do you not know that love makes all women beautiful? And I am very much in love with my husband."

"And I with you. Six years, *mon coeur,* and I am more besotted with you than the day I proposed."

She dimpled. "Now, what should I reply to that? If I admit to the same, I shall be giving away all my secrets, and you will grow tired of me."

"Never. 'Age cannot wither her beauty, nor custom stale her charms.'"

His quote pleased her and she pretended to preen excessively. "La, you are full of flattery tonight. I shall be the most conceited woman in France." The china clock on the mantelpiece chimed the quarter hour. "And the most tardy hostess, as well. Blaise and Flora will be here shortly."

Claudine cast one more appraising glance in the mirror and opened her jewel case. Removing a regal emerald ring from her right hand, she selected a sparkling diamond cluster instead. "Speak truth, Nicolas. What do you think of them?"

Nicolas was admiring her rosy shoulders. He pressed a kiss against her nape. "Your taste is always exquisite. Chose whichever you like."

She laughed at that. "My handsome and absurd one! I am speaking of Blaise and Flora. Is not the whole thing surprising? For so many years he is a dedicated bachelor, traveling the world and taking his pleasure where he finds it, but loving no woman as he loved Eve."

"Then, *voilà!* We learn that he is returning to France, that he is bringing Johanna back with him—and that he has acquired a wife! To think that it would be quiet, sensible Flora, so unlike his usual taste in women!"

"Yes." Nicolas frowned. "I find it very surprising."

"Do you? I find it *fort amusant.*" Claudine rose and smoothed the skirt of her gold mousseline gown. "I like her very much. She has a good understanding that one. And, I believe, a good heart to match."

"She must, to put up with his vile humors," Nicolas remarked.

Claudine sighed. "Perhaps Flora will banish his dark moods forever. I think she will be good for him. And I hope that Blaise will have the sense to appreciate her as he should, and not hurt her in any way.''

That startled her husband. "You make him sound a veritable Bluebeard. Since he thought enough of Flora to make her his wife, surely he has no plans to treat her ill?''

For a moment Claudine was silent, struggling to put her conflicted emotions into speech. "I have loved Blaise deeply my entire life. He was my first hero, you know.'' She saw the rueful look in his eye and a smile played at the corners of her mouth. "Of course, I had not seen you then, or I should never have looked his way twice!''

Nicolas laughed and she went on: "But he had imagination and boldness, yet was very kind to me and let me tag along with him like one of his puppies. But . . . since Eve's and Hilliard's deaths, he has been so different. So cold and remote at times, that he seems almost a stranger, and not the same Blaise with whom I grew up.''

A little shiver ran up the backs of her arms and she reached for the shawl her maid had left draped across the bed covering. "Loic Kersaudy—you remember him from Pont du Mor—he said that the villagers whispered that Blaise had lost his soul. That the *mari morgans* took it when they took Eve and Hilliard to their home beneath the waves.''

Nicolas scowled. "Young Kersaudy is a fool, encouraging the villagers to keep the Breton superstitions alive, under pretense of studying the legends. Fairies and dancing dwarves and standing stones that uproot themselves at midnight and lumber down to the sea to drink! Pah!''

Unconsciously, his wife had made a small sign to ward off evil. Sophisticated as she was, Claudine had spent her youthful summers at Château Morgaine, absorbing the local tales along with Breton cider and pancakes. A fundamental part of her believed that the magical *fées* and the corrigans, dwarves who entrapped unwary travelers in their dances, still haunted the countryside of Brittany. It did not do to antagonize them, even at a distance.

She sighed. "All the same, I am concerned for Blaise. He sometimes frightens me a little. Even now his eyes can change, become black and empty like the night sea below the cliffs. And at such times I think . . . I fear . . . that perhaps Loic is right.''

She fell into a brooding silence. Nicolas cursed Loic Kersaudy to the devil. The son of the local schoolmaster, Loic had inherited a small independence from his maternal grandfather, and devoted his time now to antiquarian conceits, particularly the lore and legends of the Breton peninsula. He seemed, as far as Nicolas was concerned, to take an unwholesome delight in stirring up the old superstitions.

Well, the next time they went to the château, Nicolas decided, he would warn Loic not to fill Claudine's ears with any of his foolish tales. Or Flora's and Johanna's either, for that matter. Château Morgaine was eerie enough as it was!

He drew his wife into his arms. "Lift your spirits, *chérie*. Surely Blaise's bride will work the same magic you have done with me: no man married to the woman he loves can remain in gloom. It is against nature.''

He'd expected a smile, but was doomed to disappointment. Claudine's face was still pensive. "I have been hesitant to speak of it before, but . . . at first I thought it was a love match. That Blaise had met Flora and been captivated against his will.''

She looked up at her husband. "I admit to being worried, a little. After being with them so much these past few days, I have begun to wonder. They do not touch hands, or even exchange glances as you and I do. It is as if they share the same space, yet are totally separate.''

He lifted her chin and smiled into her troubled eyes. "You forget the natural reserve of the English. And there are other factors. Blaise and Flora have known each other only a short time. They have been married less than a month, and have not had a honeymoon and the chance to be alone together. There is Johanna almost always with them. She is a very volatile girl, either in alt or in gloom— much like Blaise, may I point out. Flora has her hands full with the two of them. It is not an ordinary situation.''

That relieved some of Claudine's unease. Her dazzling smile burst forth like the sun through the clouds of her concern. "You are very wise. I had begun to imagine all sorts of things: that they had quarreled or regretted their hasty contract; or perhaps even that she had only married him for his fortune . . . but I could not decide why *he* had married *her* then, you see.''

"The Cheneys take great pride in their line,'' Nicolas said unthinkingly. "Blaise is the last in direct descent. Perhaps he decided it was time and more that he thought of begetting an heir.''

A tiny gasp of dismay caught him up short. Claudine's lower lip quivered and she bit it with her sharp, white teeth. Nicolas cursed himself this time. He knew how tender a topic such things were with her, what a burden her continued barrenness was to his wife. He couldn't bear to be the one to hurt her.

As always she was sensitive to his every change of mood. She was determined to be always gay and charming in his presence, never to let him know the despair she felt at not producing the children they both so wanted. So much lay unspoken between them, an invisible burden of sorrows and concerns that each wanted to spare the other. It had become a silent game. No shadows were allowed to come between their joy at being together.

"Ah, yes. That might explain it.'' She lifted her chin and looked away, and he recognized that she didn't want him to acknowledge the sheen of tears in her eyes.

Pretending not to notice that anything was wrong, he slipped his arm through hers and led her toward the door. "Not that Blaise wants for Cheneys, you understand, with those numerous cousins in Canada. Do you know,'' he continued lightly, "I believe there are dozens of them. Steely-eyed Québecois fishmongers and bakers, rubbing their hands and dreaming of inheriting that great pile of rock and the haunted château, with all its dire legends attached. Perhaps with an eye to turning it into a hostelry for Gothic-loving English tourists, complete with candlelit tours of the donjons and oubliette.''

Her smile and quicksilver change of mood were his reward. "Foolish man, you know there are no donjons and there is no oubliette at Château Morgaine. Only the tower and, of course, Madame Morceau, whom I admit can be *far* more alarming.''

"So she is ! A veritable dragon of a woman, is Blaise's stern relative. My knees knock together at the very thought of her."

Claudine laughed aloud at that. Nicolas smiled in relief. The dangerous moment averted, they went down the stairs arm in arm, to face the imminent arrival of their guests.

Flora's heart sank when she entered the foyer of the Le Vecs' exquisite mansion, in Paris's most fashionable district. Claudine's faultless taste was evident in the fine statues and paintings that graced the domed, circular chamber. Flora had been raised to believe that a pure heart and a well-informed mind could take one anywhere with confidence. It wasn't true. Surrounded by such splendor, she felt gauche as a schoolgirl at her first ball.

Was her gown of sapphire silk too daring? Could she carry off wearing a fortune in jewels without betraying how foreign it was to her experience? She felt as if the word "imposter" were emblazoned across her forehead.

Blaise leaned down to whisper in her ear: "Try to look more like a woman expecting an evening of pleasure, and less like a victim led to the guillotine."

She laughed at that. "Am I so transparent, then?"

He caught her chin in his hand and smiled down at her. "Transparent and very, very lovely."

Flora's heart skipped a beat. When he stood so near, with that peculiar, dazzling light in his eyes, he robbed her of breath. She couldn't look away.

Claudine, resplendent in deep gold satin and diamonds, watched them unobserved from the head of the stairs. How foolish she had even been to question their relationship. They were the very portrait of a happy, newlywed couple.

Blaise didn't give away, by so much as a glance, that he knew his cousin was on the landing above. *That ought to ease Claudine's qualms!* Her worries had been easier to see through than Flora's.

Their host and hostess greeted them warmly. Claudine approved that Flora had chosen to wear the antique necklace with the jeweled medallions. "The perfect touch! You look quite splendid," she said, holding Flora's hands as the men exchanged comments. "There is not a fault to be found with your toilette. Not even Madame Morceau could find cause for complaint.''

"I beg your pardon?''

"Gaelle Morceau.'' Claudine made a face. "Blaise's cousin, who has acted as chatelaine of the château since his mother's death. She raised him from childhood.''

"But . . .'' Flora was thunderstruck. He hadn't mentioned that his aunt lived at his chateau. In fact, he'd given the distinct impression that he had no female relatives capable of looking after his niece. Why on earth hadn't Johanna been placed in charge of this Madame Morceau?

Claudine misunderstood her reaction. "A good woman, you understand. She is rather a recluse, content with her rosaries and devotions and overseeing the household there. I have always thought that Gaelle would have been happier had she joined a convent. She rarely leaves the château except to visit the church in Pont du Mor, or attend the *pardons*, the religious festivals of Brittany. But you must form your own opinion of her. I will say no more.''

Flora's nervousness increased. There was so much she didn't know about Blaise. While her time had been spent in shopping and settling in, Blaise had been occupied with his research—whatever *that* might entail. Her curiosity was aroused but she hadn't been able to satisfy it. He'd been closeted in his library, poring through crates of books sent by publishers and prominent booksellers, as well as letters from around the globe. From their shopping and visits, she knew more about Claudine than she did of her own husband.

There was worse in store for her at the opera house. Flora had expected to blend anonymously with the crowd. From the moment they entered the Le Vecs' private box, she was aware of heads turning her way. A stir went through the audience. Whispers skirled through like a rising breeze, and curious faces turned their way. Several women focused their lorgnettes and a few bold young men trained their opera glasses on Flora. She was unnerved to find herself the center of attention.

A distinguished gentleman in one of the private boxes bowed to her, and another murmur ran through the bejeweled throng. Blaise leaned down to her. "That is Monsieur

Ronceneau, current arbiter of what—and who—is fashionable." He raised her hand to his lips. "Congratulations, *chèrie*. You have conquered Paris."

Hot blood rushed to her cheeks. She was horrified by the attention she'd drawn to herself; even more, she was confused by the seductive warmth of his glance, the ardent caress of his lips on her skin.

"Charming!" a high-pitched voice said from the next box. "I see now that Cheney is as head over heels as I have been told."

Flora's blush deepened.

Claudine smothered a laugh behind her fan. "That shrill announcement came from Madame d'Aubry, one of the reigning queens of Parisian society. Her manners are peculiar, but her heart is good—and her approval, with that of Monsieur Ronceneau, will make you acceptable to all."

Two gentlemen entered the box directly opposite them. The older of the pair had dark hair liberally streaked with silver. While not conventionally handsome, he had interesting features, and the slightly world-weary air so devastatingly attractive to women. Flora couldn't help but notice him: he lifted his eyeglass and examined her through it, then favored her with a low bow. His nod to Blaise was rather curt, she thought.

"Ah," Blaise said sardonically. "The comte has deigned to sanction your debut in Parisian society. A signal honor!"

"A count?" Flora was surprised. "I thought all titles were abolished at the founding of the New Republic."

"Officially, yes. However, the scions of the *ancien régime*, those who escaped the revolts, continue to live as their ancestors did. The de Broceliand family is among the oldest and most noble in Brittany. He is planning to hire a scholar to undertake a study of his family's history."

"There is nothing unusual in that," Flora said. "It is quite common for noble families to underwrite such research into their past, so that it won't be lost to future generations."

Blaise's mouth twisted wryly. "To inflate their background and lie about their peasant origins, you mean. You may not know that Bretons believe King Arthur and Camelot belong to them, and not to England at all. Since arriving in Paris, I have heard a story making the rounds, that the de Brocelands are descended from a bastard born of the legendary King Arthur and a fair Breton maid. You may guess who is behind it. Although he may be plain 'Monsieur' now, on his estates Guy de Broceliand is very much the feudal prince.''

His tone surprised her. ''You dislike him.''

Blaise leaned forward, teeth gleaming as he covered her gloved hand with his. ''How can I not, when he is publicly ogling my wife?''

Flora blushed. It was true. De Broceliand was eyeing her like a man about to purchase a horse. She wished he would look the other way!

''In addition to being a rogue and roué, De Broceliand is a minister in the foreign office. Or so I have heard. What his actual function is, I do not know.''

Although Blaise tried to block the view of her with his shoulder, De Broceliand looked Flora over with frank admiration. Lovely. That hair! That creamy skin. It would feel like satin. His practiced eyes stripped away her clinging garments. She would be magnificent nude. Cheney was a fortunate man.

Meanwhile, De Broceliand himself was the object of interest from a man in the pit below. He was young, blond, and dressed with quiet distinction. Unremarkable unless one noticed his deep-set, piercing eyes. The eyes, Flora thought unexpectedly, of a saint. Or a fanatic. He turned away and spoke to his companion and she lost interest as the orchestra struck the first notes of the overture.

When the curtains swept back, Flora was plunged into a world of color and music more wonderful than anything she had ever imagined. The rich, rippling notes filled the great chamber, soaring and dipping like swallows in flight, and her soul flew with them. When the lights came up at the intermission, she was left dazzled.

The foreign minister had made his way to their box to pay his respects. De Broceliand swept Flora an elegant bow as introductions were made. Interesting lines bracketed his mouth and fanned out from his eyes, which were a curious blend of brown and green. The warm appraisal in them was flattering, and bolstered her confidence.

"You are very fond of music, Madame Cheney?"

"Passionately!"

His sensual mouth turned up at the corners. "It is said that those who are passionate about music are passionate about life."

Blaise was annoyed. "I have heard the same thing said about those who are overly fond of their supper."

De Broceliand laughed. "And who can say they are wrong?" His gaze roved over Flora appreciatively. "*Le Bon Dieu*, he gave us the senses so that we might enjoy them, is that not so? And who am I, an insignificant mortal, to deny His plans?"

While Flora wasn't used to such sophisticated flirtation, her wit served her well. "You are quite the philosopher, Monsieur. Perhaps you should have entered the church, rather than the government," she said, and was rewarded with a laugh.

Blaise gave a snort of derision. "Every morning De Broceliand prays for the gift of humility: his enemies pray that someone will teach him it."

The flash of irritation in her husband's eyes surprised Flora. Under other circumstances she might think he was jealous. De Broceliand turned away the insult with a roguish lift of his eyebrow.

"Perhaps one day I shall find a man equal to the task."

Blaise's eyes narrowed. "Perhaps, monsieur, you already have."

The air crackled with tension between the two men. Nicolas stepped hastily into the breach. "Ah, there is Madame d'Aubry beckoning to you, Guy. You must stop by her box before the curtain rises for the second act, or she will be greatly offended."

"As you say." De Broceliand shot Blaise a look filled with malice, then turned to Flora. "I hope we shall all meet in Pont du Mor this year, for the *pardon*, Madame Cheney. My wife looks forward to making your acquaintance."

Flora heard Claudine give a tiny gasp. De Broceliand made his bows to the ladies and took himself off. Blaise was greatly annoyed. He had forgotten his satisfaction in seeing how Flora was admired earlier. He and De Broceliand went back a long way, but though they moved in the same circles and exchanged visits in Paris and Brittany, their relationship had never been cordial.

Claudine tapped Flora's arm with her fan. "La! You have made your first conquest, *chère*. And Guy is quite a connoisseur of women, if you can judge from his current mistress. Do not look now, but that is she, Madame Beauvoir—the elegant redhead in the second box across the way."

Flora was all too human, and couldn't keep her gaze from sweeping across the audience to the private box on the other side of the opera house. Madame Beauvoir was indeed elegant, like a haughty princess in emerald-green satin, with a necklace of stones to match. The woman smiled at Guy de Broceliand and inclined her head graciously. He returned her recognition with a suave bow that had half the ladies in the opera house whispering to one another behind their fans.

Claudine was indignant. "Poor Odile de Broceliand! How fortunate that she is not here to be humiliated. I thank *le Bon Dieu* that Nicolas is not the kind of man to flaunt his mistresses publicly."

She had lowered her voice, but not enough to keep her husband and Blaise from overhearing. The expression on Nicolas's face registered amused dismay.

"My dear, you are scandalizing Flora! She will think I have a mistress or two hidden away somewhere!"

"I understood what she meant," Flora said, between gasps of laughter.

"It is nothing to laugh at," Claudine protested, stifling her own smiles. "Indeed, I do not know what I would do if I were Odile."

"No," Flora said, sobering instantly. "To be deceived by one's husband would be unforgivable!"

Blaise frowned. "You are very vehement."

"If there is not trust—and truth—between a man and wife, then there is nothing." A blush rose over Flora's throat and cheeks and she turned to look out over the audience again. Her face burned as if it were on fire. Who was she to be lecturing on truth and trust? She, whose entire existence was woven on a loom of lies!

The lights dimmed, the curtain rose, and the opera resumed. Flora was glad to be in relative darkness, aware that Blaise was still looking at her thoughtfully. She was overwhelmingly conscious of his scrutiny. What was he thinking? Had she given herself away in some manner? The music, which had engrossed her completely before, faded into the background. She spent the rest of the evening aware of her husband's nearness, the brush of his sleeve against her bare arm, the tilt of his head that told her he was watching her while she pretended to watch the stage below.

She was afraid for the evening to end, when she would be left alone with him in their carriage. And she had never wanted anything more.

The new opera was an outstanding success, the glittering patrons bubbling with comment as they made their way from the opera house. It was as Flora and Claudine were waiting for their carriage with Nicolas, that an altercation erupted. One moment there was an orderly line of carriages moving forward to pick up the waiting passengers, the next a voice was shouting: *"Death to all traitors!"*

The crowd jostled and scattered as gunshots shattered the crisp night air. Two, in rapid succession, and shockingly close at hand. A woman screamed, eerie and high-pitched. *"Assassin!"* a hoarse, masculine voice cried out.

Amid the shrieks and resulting chaos the horses began rearing and plunging in alarm. The crowd churned like a maelstrom. *"Stop him,"* someone shouted hoarsely. *"Stop that man!"*

In the press of bodies Flora was suddenly separated from the rest of her party, trapped between a lamppost and a portly man. It had happened in an instant. There was no sign of her companions. She wriggled her way free but found herself worse off, wedged beside a wheel with no place to go. The struggling mass surged forward. The danger of being trampled was very real.

"Get down!" a familiar voice shouted in her ear. Another shot rang and Flora was shoved out of the way. Something whistled past. She didn't realize it was a bullet until the loud report sounded. She had only the barest glimpse of Blaise's shoulder before the crowd lifted her off her feet.

It was like being caught in an undertow, swept helplessly away by the crush of fleeing bodies. Flora was helplessly borne with the tide. There was a small clear patch near the street, where a carriage was caught in the surging throng. A stout man with an ebony walking stick slashed out to clear a path, and struck one of the horses viciously. The frightened beast screamed in pain and tried to rise up between the shafts.

The line of carriages parted and Flora was thrust into the opening. At that same moment the forward vehicle rolled back into the sudden gap. She was frozen with horror, unable to dislodge herself from the press of bodies, watching the flailing hooves catch the light as they came down at her.

"Nicolas! Help her!"

She heard Claudine's shriek and was struck by a great force and sent flying into the street. The next moment Flora lay sprawled on the ground, her hands dirty and scraped. But she was miraculously clear of danger.

"Monsieur de Broceliand . . ." someone cried out.

"Mon Dieu, he has killed him!"

Amid the shouts and bedlam, an elderly bystander came to Flora's aid and helped her out of the street. Shaken and trembling with relief, she was found by an ashen Claudine and led away.

"Mon Dieu, Flora! If not for Nicolas's quick action you would be dead! Are you injured? Come, sit here on this bench. Where is Blaise in all this? He should be attending to you!" Her last words were spoken with mingled fear and anger. Then she embraced Flora and burst into tears.

Nicolas found them shortly after. He was as white and smudged as his starched shirtfront. "Flora! Your husband . . ."

"Yes, where is he?" Flora said with a touch of asperity. "He was here and then he vanished!"

"Those shots . . ." Nicolas struggled with his emotions. "There was an assassination attempt on the minister with Monsieur de Broceliand. The minister is safe. But . . ." He knelt down and took her hand comfortingly. "You must be very brave, Flora. Blaise has been shot."

Claudine gave a little shriek. At least, it looked as if she did. Her mouth opened wide but no sound came out that Flora could hear. Even the noise of the crowd, the wheels of the passing carriages were silent. She seemed to have been struck deaf. Her mouth was so dry she could hardly speak. "I . . . I beg your pardon?"

Gradually the silence was replaced by a strange buzzing in her head, which resolved into Nicolas's voice. He now had Claudine's hand clasped in his other. "My dears, it looks very serious. I fear he . . . he may be dead."

"Dead? No!"

"He cannot be!" Flora caught at Nicolas's sleeve. "Where is he? Take me to him, at once!"

They crossed the street hurriedly. Claudine's legs refused to hold her, and her husband supported her on his arm. Flora walked a little apart, as if tragedy had sealed her inside a clear glass sphere. Her entire body was numb.

Order had been restored. The crowd, so loud and agitated a moment ago, had fallen grave and quiet. They stood like mourners at a funeral, looking down at the pavement outside the opera house. "Make way," Nicolas ordered. The ranks parted quickly. Illumination from the street lamp formed an arc on the wall behind, making the scene look like something from a play.

Blaise lay pale and crumpled, his coat open, a dark and ominous stain spreading across his shirt and over the cold stone. Flora felt as if her blood had been drained from her body as well. *"Ah, no!"* Terrifying, impossible, that a man of such vital energy could be so still and unmoving!

She forced herself to go to him, moving with the stiff, jerky motions of a marionette. She dropped to her knees beside him, as the crowd edged back. Odd, irrelevant thoughts flitted through her head. How very young, how very vulnerable he looked. How long and thick his black eyelashes were, casting soft shadows on his cheekbones. Strange that she had never noticed before.

Voices murmured behind her. "The widow," a man's voice said quietly.

The words stabbed through her. *The widow?* she thought. *How can that be, when I have never even been his wife?*

She took his hand in hers. Still warm. "Blaise! Blaise, it is Flora!"

His head shifted slightly and he gave a low moan. She looked up, hope shining in her eyes. "He is still alive! Fetch a doctor! Oh, quickly!" She realized she had spoken in English, but she had been understood.

A man moved purposefully through the crowd. "I am a physician." He knelt and placed his hand on the side of Blaise's throat. "His pulse is slow, but strong. How far is your home, madame?"

"In the Place Vendôme."

"Excellent. We will take him there at once. The bleeding has almost stopped." Removing his cravat, he thrust it inside Blaise's waistcoat. "You men! Help me lift him into the carriage. Carefully, now. Good, I will follow you in my own vehicle. And driver, don't spare the horses!"

Nicolas and another man lifted Blaise gently and placed him inside. He was limp and made no sound at all. A lock of his dark hair had fallen across his forehead, damp from the cold sweat upon his brow. His breathing was so quiet she couldn't even see the rise and fall of his chest. Life was ebbing even as she watched, Flora thought in despair.

She was helped up into the carriage, and cradled his head tenderly in her lap. Nicolas and Claudine joined them inside, their faces almost as white as that of the wounded man. Neither spoke. They sat close, clutching each other's hands as the door was slammed and the carriage set off at a spanking pace. The same thought occupied all their minds: alive, true, but for how much longer?

To Flora, the short ride back seemed endless, a nightmare journey where the clomp of the horses' hooves marked the passing seconds, like the sound of a muffled heartbeat. Every time they passed beneath a street lamp his color seemed more gray. By the time they reached the Place Vendôme she feared the worst had already happened.

Nicolas was opening the door before the carriage came to a complete halt. Within a few moments he and the groom lifted Blaise, carrying him up the stairs. The door was flung open as the alarmed servants rushed to help. Flora mounted the stairs with dread. She couldn't help but contrast their

arrival tonight with the first time she'd set foot inside this
door.

"Madame . . . ?" Pierre stood in shock at seeing his master's condition. Flora saw that she would have to take
charge of the situation.

"Take him up to my . . . to our chamber," she directed
briskly, when Nicolas started toward the salon. "Pierre,
have plenty of hot water and clean linen cloths brought up
to us. And brandy. At once."

The household snapped to attention. They recognized the
voice of one used to wielding authority. Monsieur was injured and there were things that must be done. Servants
scurried in all directions to obey.

Flora started up the staircase. "Claudine, go to Johanna,
and stay with her, if you please. I will join you as soon as
I may."

"I am here, Flora."

Johanna stepped out of the library, in her robe, a volume
of poetry in her hand. The book thudded to the floor when
she saw her uncle, unconscious and bloody, as he was carried up the staircase. She blanched and looked as if she
might faint. "Dear God, what has happened?"

Claudine hurried to the girl's side. "Come, *pauvre petite*.
Let us go upstairs. I will explain all."

But Johanna tried to follow. "Go with Claudine," Flora
ordered. "The doctor must attend to him first. I promise I
will send word to you the moment you may see him."

Flora mounted to her bedchamber with the doctor at her
heels.

Nicolas had placed Blaise upon the bed, and his valet
was already stripping away his master's clothes. "Cut the
shirt off," the doctor ordered. "We must disturb the wound
as little as possible or he will begin to bleed anew."

Another servant lit all the lamps, while one of the chambermaids added wood to the fire before being dismissed.
Flora stood at the foot of the bed and watched the tableau
unfold. Blaise soon lay naked to the waist, the dark hair of
his chest streaked and matted with blood. He had the physique of an athlete, all lean, defined muscle and sinew.

"A well-made man in his prime," the doctor said.

Oh, yes, indeed! Flora thought. Exceptionally well made. This closer view put any doubts to rest; but his very stillness heightened the effect seeing it had upon her. She noticed the great strength in him, remembered the way he had lifted her in and out of the carriage so lightly, wondered breathlessly, against will and all reason, what it would have been like to be clamped close against that broad, masculine chest in the heat of passion, held tightly by those powerfully formed arms.

The physician turned to her. "Perhaps it would be best if you leave us now, madame."

She lifted her chin. "I will stay with my husband."

The doctor shrugged. She was English, after all, and the English were known to be eccentric in their ways. "Very well. But it will not be a pretty sight, I can guarantee."

"I understand."

The next twenty minutes were ghastly. There was much ripping of linen and sizzle of metal in the fire. Nicolas broke out in a sweat and the valet looked distinctly ill. The physician probed, grunted, probed some more and removed a small, flattened piece of metal. "Here is the culprit."

"So small, to do so much damage!" Flora exclaimed.

But the doctor was frowning and he looked about the wound further. "The rib is cracked but not splintered. I see no other signs of damage. Unless another bullet went in the same place, I cannot account for his continued lack of consciousness."

"There were only three shots fired," Nicolas murmured. "One creased De Broceliand's sleeve, the other embedded itself in the door of the opera house. He took the third, as you see."

"Well, then."

Flora spoke up. "There is a large knot on the back of his head. I noticed it in the carriage. He must have struck his head when he fell."

"Ah, that would explain it, then."

The doctor cauterized the wound, then put a folded dressing in place and bound it tightly. He palpated the lump at the back of Blaise's head, and gave Flora a look that was much more cheerful. "Nothing broken, as far as I can tell. His pupils are equal, his breathing regular, and his pulse steady. And if he should come around in the next few hours, madame, I believe the outlook will be good.''

''And if not?'' she said sharply.

''The wound did not bleed as freely as I should have liked at the outset. I excised as much as I safely could, to prevent the flesh from mortifying. But infection is only to be expected.''

Flora's stomach tightened. Blaise was a healthy man in his prime, but infection could strike him down within hours. ''What are his chances, monsieur? You must speak frankly, without trying to spare my feelings.''

The surgeon cocked his head and eyed her appraisingly. A woman of sense, without an excess of sensibility. ''The longer it takes for him to rouse, the worse the prognosis. Fortunately we live in enlightened times. Modern medicine has done what it can, madame. The rest we must leave in the hands of *le Bon Dieu*.''

Then he smiled. ''And of course, your own, madame. A tender and beautiful wife at the bedside is the best medicine a husband can have.'' He sketched her a bow, his dark eyes alight with a distinctly Gallic twinkle. ''I understand you are newly wed. No doubt, with so lovely a nurse to whisper encouragement in his ear, Monsieur Cheney will soon be restored to his former health.''

Flora thanked him distractedly and went to Blaise's side, taking his hand in hers. It was no longer cold. She looked down at him for several moments, her head filled with nothing but a blank emptiness except for one thought: he must live. He *must*!

Nicolas coughed discreetly. Flora looked up again, dazed. She cleared her throat. ''If it is safe to leave him for the moment, I will go reassure Claudine and Johanna.''

She fled the room with what dignity she could, but checked her pace. Out in the corridor the staff was lined up near the servants' stairs. ''You may seek your beds. The doctor says that all is well. Monsieur Cheney will survive the wound.''

A murmur of thanks went through the assembled servants, followed by mumbled prayers and a few soft sobs. ''God bless you, madame,'' one of the maids said aloud. ''You will see Monsieur safely through this!''

Once again Flora felt the weight of her deceit descend upon her. She hurried to Johanna's bedchamber. They looked up like startled deer as she opened the door and went in.

Lamps had been lit to keep the night at bay. Claudine perched on a small gilt chair beside the rose-draped bed, her niece's hand clasped in her own for mutual comfort. Johanna lay back against the pillows, her eyes smudged with exhaustion.

"I have given her a mild sleeping draught," Claudine said in low tones, "but it has not had time to take effect."

Johanna moistened her lips. "He is dead. I know it!"

"Nonsense," Flora said in her brisk, schoolteacher's voice. "The bullet has been removed, and the wound dressed."

"And he is awake, then?" Claudine asked hopefully.

"No. Not as yet. It is to be expected," she added, seeing their distress, "for he has suffered a blow to the head as well."

"Like little Jean-Maire from Pont du Mor," a voice said from the corner. "He has Cheney blood, they say."

Flora turned and saw Malin sitting there in the shadows, her hands folded in her lap. "He fell upon the rocks near the château years ago, and was carried home on a litter. He lived, but from that day to this, he has neither spoken nor moved again. Another victim of the Mermaid's Curse—and now it strikes again!"

A chill silence filled the room, then Johanna gave a small cry and began to sob. "No, no! It must not happen again."

Claudine shot Malin a frightened look. "Stupid girl, see what you have done?" She embraced the weeping Johanna. "Hush, hush, *petite*. It is only a story. Blaise will be well."

But Malin leaned forward defiantly, her eyes sly and knowing. "It is true. Some say that the real Jean-Maire was stolen away by the *fée,* and a changeling put in his place. Perhaps they will take Monsieur as well."

Flora turned on the maid. "I have warned you before that such foolishness will not be permitted, Malin. Leave us now! I shall ring for you if you are needed."

The maid rose. As she passed by, she spoke in low tones that only Flora could hear. "You do not believe me. But it is not foolishness. You shall see for yourself, madame, when you go to the château. *I* have warned *you*.''

Malin opened the door and slipped out. The damage she left behind lingered. It took time and a dose of medicinal brandy to calm Johanna's emotions. Flora was still up in arms.

''Curses and changelings, indeed! I shall speak to Malin again later. I will not have her frightening everyone with her ignorant superstitions. Perhaps she should be sent back to Brittany.''

The Frenchwoman started to say something, then changed her mind as Johanna fought to keep her eyes open. ''We will talk later, you and I. Meanwhile, I will soothe this poor child.''

Claudine sang songs in a soft, pretty voice with her arm around the girl until her eyes closed. Within minutes she fell into a deep, dreamless sleep. Once she saw Johanna was settled, Claudine rose and went to Flora.

''You are a sensible and educated Englishwoman, and I do truly understand your reaction to Malin's story.''

Flora raised her eyebrows. ''However . . . ?''

Claudine colored. ''As you say. *However.* I do not know how to explain what I am about to say. I, too, am an educated woman. I do not believe in witches and fairy godmothers and blocks of wood left in a baby's cradle when the child is snatched away to live among the *fées.* Here, in Paris, I can laugh at the old ways.''

She gave a moue of amused distress. ''But only quietly, you see. Like Malin . . . like Johanna and Blaise, I am Breton. And when you do go to the Château Morgaine, you will see why I look over my shoulder when I say this. There is strange magic in the air there. At times I feel almost as if reality might shift like a bank of fog, giving glimpses of strange worlds we neither know nor understand.''

Before Flora could laugh, an image rose up in her mind: her wanderings through the black heart of Swarthern Woods to Saint Piska's Well on the eve of the winter solstice, and the sense of something not quite real—or of something perhaps *too* real, in the midnight air. She shivered and drew her shawl around her shoulders more closely.

The chamber door opened and both women jumped a little. Johanna slept on. "Yes?" Flora rose to her feet as a maid entered.

"The doctor wishes to speak with you, madame."

Flora rushed out without another word and hurried past the turn in the corridor, her nerves jangling with every step. She thought she heard someone whispering, but there was no one in sight. The carved mermaids held their alabaster lamps aloft beside the staircase, spilling pools of pearly light to guide her way. Even so, she almost stumbled as she went past.

Catching at the ornate rail for balance, Flora found herself eye to eye with one of the mermaids. The creature's carved tresses seemed to literally float up and away, as if stirred by invisible sea currents. Why, Flora even imagined she could smell the salty tang of the ocean, and hear the sigh of distant surf.

Light from the lamps flickered softly, making the polished features come alive with movement. Flora gave a gasp of surprise. The mermaid bore a startling resemblance to Johanna. *How very peculiar!* And how odd that she had never noticed the likeness. Nor the necklace that hung around the mermaid's slender throat. Surely it had not been there before!

Flora stared at the precious bauble lying between the mermaid's small, thrusting breasts. Shaped like an egg, it glimmered with swirling layers in all the colors of the sea: silvery streaks and bubbles lit depths of azure and sapphire and deep emerald-green. She felt compelled to touch it, yet conquered the urge. She had no time for mysteries now.

Gathering her skirts, she hurried along the hall to Blaise's room. The door was slightly ajar. She stopped on the threshold in dismay. The lamps had been dimmed and a screen placed between Blaise and the light source, creating a funereal atmosphere. All color was leached from his skin, and deep shadows painted hollows beneath his eyes and cheekbones. She felt her heart turn over slowly in her chest.

"Is he . . . ?" She could not go on.

"Merely sedated." The physician came to meet her. "I believe he rests comfortably, Madame Cheney, although he has not yet regained his senses."

Flora advanced to the side of the bed and touched Blaise's hand. Hot. Too hot. "He has the fever already!"

"It will continue to rise until it reaches crisis, I fear. I advise you to let his valet sit up with him tonight, and rest yourself a while. I shall look in upon him in the morning. Meanwhile, should he take a worse turn, you must send a servant to fetch me. I will come at once."

Flora thanked him but ignored his advice. After the doctor took his leave, she dismissed the valet. "There is no need for you to keep from your bed, Georges," she said. "I shall stay the night and keep vigil."

Nicolas touched her shoulder. "Is that wise, Flora?"

"Perhaps not. But I would be unable to sleep in any case."

Reluctantly, the others left her, but only after she agreed that Georges might stay nearby, and that she would call him if there were any change. The moment the door closed behind them, Flora let out a sigh. She smoothed back the hair from Blaise's forehead, almost expecting him to wake in surprise at her audacity. He slept on.

So many feelings whirled through her as she sat there, staring at his face. While the clock ticked away, spinning the seconds into minutes, she had time to examine them. They were chaotic and raw. She couldn't imagine what would happen to her if he died. Like Ruth in Moab, she was a stranger in a strange land, and had no hope of returning to her own country. But this wasn't foremost on her mind. No, what robbed her of breath was the realization that on a profound and personal level, she cared very much what happened to this enigmatic man.

She couldn't say she held Blaise in deep affection. That would be a lie. She hardly knew him. But in the short weeks of their marriage, in the very few hours they had spent in one another's company, he had cast a strange spell over her. Attraction was too tepid a word for it.

Flora bit her lip. What was it then? Definitely not love: neither the idealized, yearnings of the poets, nor the comfortable affection of shared views and experiences. Nor yet that dizzying head-over-heels *coup de foudre*, the thunderclap and lightning that occurs when two gazes meet and hold across a crowded room, and the world falls away. No, this was far wilder and more frightening.

He groaned softly, and she touched his hand. "I am here, Blaise." Instantly his hand closed over hers.

How beautiful his hands were, she thought, so masculine and strong. Unbidden, her mind conjured an image of his hand upon her breast. Her skin tingled and her stomach tightened. She found herself blushing as if he were awake, appalled to admit the truth: he had stirred to life passions she had thought long dead and buried. It was the calling of like to like. Passion to passion and flesh to flesh. A hot and primal hunger in the blood.

She tried to withdraw her hand, but his fingers curled over hers in a painful grip. She sat there, scarcely breathing, until his breathing evened out and his grasp gradually relaxed. The clock struck four and she was amazed to find the hour so late. Little wonder that her hand had gone numb holding his.

The fire was dying down. Rising, she put another small log on, and looked for something with which to wipe her hands. The valet had removed the linens, but Blaise's shirt and coat lay on the bench near the fireplace, ruined beyond repair. She rubbed her hands across the clean sleeve. The movement released the fragrance trapped within the fabric. *His* fragrance. She felt a pull deep in the pit of her stomach.

Her fingers brushed the fabric where the bullet had entered. It was stiff with dried blood. But beneath it was something thin and flat. Sliding her fingers inside the hidden breast pocket, Flora withdrew a rectangular metal case about the size of her palm. The heavily chased surface was covered with row upon row of masterful scrollwork, like the waves of an endless sea. A fresh diagonal crease marred the gold. So this was what had deflected the bullet and saved his life. She turned it over. A small blue-green stone, cut *en cabochon* and engraved with the initial *E*, was affixed to the center.

Flora opened it slowly. The woman in the miniature smiled back at her, an older, more sophisticated version of Johanna Cheney, with hair dressed high and a rather shocking display of décolletage. Turning it toward the lamp, she scrutinized the lovely, painted features. So this was Johanna's mother, Eve Cheney.

She looked young and ethereal but, to Flora's jaundiced eye, rather insipid. Yet the artist had captured a face and figure fit to inspire a man's dreams. And a man's passions. A jolt of something she refused to acknowledge as jealousy shot through her. She snapped the case shut. The brittle click of the hasp sounded loud in the stillness.

Holding the oblong of metal in her hands, she stared into the fire, and saw patterns take shape amid the leaping flames. So much was made clear now: Flora knew, beyond any doubt, that Blaise had been in love with his brother's wife. That he was still in love with a woman who had been dead for ten years.

It was plain to see that he had provided materially for Eve's daughter, yet had been unwilling to face her in the flesh, because she was a constant, painful reminder of his lost love.

And, Flora admitted wryly, something else was also made very clear: she was not only becoming obsessed with the man who was her husband merely in name, but she had been—yes, admit it!—on the verge of imagining a vastly different relationship between them. *Fool, fool, fool!*

It was a struggle, but she resisted the urge to fling the case violently against the wall. If not for finding it, she might have let her romantic imagination and passionate temperament overturn her common sense. Strange, the tricks that loneliness could play upon the human heart. Her grandfather had been right in saying she had a susceptible nature. In future she must be on her guard.

Why, by morning she might have convinced herself that she was falling in love with Blaise.

Sliding her nail beneath the catch, she opened the portrait case again. *Thank you, Eve. You have saved me from making a fool of myself yet again.* The portrait smiled up at her placidly. This time Flora felt compassion for its object. *Poor thing, not knowing what tragedy the future held for you!*

Something caught Flora's eye. She looked at the miniature more closely. Almost hidden in the ruffles adorning the painted bosom lay a small blue-green jewel suspended from a jeweled chain. A chill ran up the back of Flora's arms. The pendant appeared identical to the one she'd seen earlier on the mermaid carving at the head of the staircase.

She glanced at the bed where Blaise lay unmoving, then went softly to the door and opened it. Light from the alabaster globe still illuminated the carved mermaid at the end of the hall. There was no necklace. The polished throat was bare. Flora went out and along the corridor. Had the necklace fallen?

When she reached the mermaid her heart skipped a beat. She had been wrong. The mythical beauty still wore an egg-shaped pendant on an intricate chain—but this one was part of the carving. She touched the smooth wood of the raised relief. Had it been compounded of shadows and tiredness, or was it merely a figment of an overactive imagination? *One more mystery in this house of secrets.*

She brushed a strand of hair from her forehead and went back to the room. Shutting the door again, she went to the bedside and slid the portrait case gently beneath Blaise's pillow. Shadows danced around the room. She stood a moment staring down at his face, sternly handsome beneath its pallor. So pale that the scar that slashed across his cheek almost blended in. Flora steeled her heart against a sudden pang of pity.

I will not let my passions lead me astray again, she said silently. *I will not permit the weight of my own loneliness to delude me into making such a fatal mistake. This I vow.*

She was startled to hear a soft sound behind her, like muffled laughter; but it was only the popping of the wood in the fireplace. There was no one in the room but the two of them, and the ghosts of the past.

Chapter Six

Flora entered Blaise's room purposefully, and waited for her eyes to adjust to the dimness. Outside a brilliant morning sun gilded the stone façades of the Place Vendôme; but here, with the draperies drawn, it was like a shadowy cavern.

For three days Blaise had hovered in private purgatory, suspended in a restless state halfway between coma and consciousness. He was unaware of his surroundings, enmeshed in nightmares that made him cry out hoarsely from time to time. The fear in his voice was so real it made the hair rise on Flora's nape.

Despite the doctor's reassurances she had the distinct feeling—no!—the certain knowledge that Blaise's life hung in the balance. That he had traveled so far and fast into those terrifying realms that the very next breath might be his last.

The room was hot and close. Resolution filled her. The stuffy air could not be healthy. Despite the French fear of drafts, it was time to apply a little English common sense.

"Enough of this gloom!" She went to the nearest window and threw open the curtains. Rich golden light poured through the sparkling panes.

"But madame . . ." the doctor protested. "So much brightness! The shock to his system . . ."

"Nonsense!" She went to the next window and drew the draperies open, then turned the handle and opened it to the small balcony beyond. A light breeze danced into the room, bringing the scent of warming earth and the promise of early spring. "The fresh air will cool his fever," she announced briskly, overruling his continued protests.

Approaching her husband's bed, she drew back the heavy coverlets to his waist. His fine linen nightshirt, damp with sweat, clung to his muscled torso. He was burning up with heat. Flora loosed the ties at the neck, exposing Blaise's strong throat and upper chest. He murmured something unintelligible and turned his head away. An erratic pulse beat beneath his jaw and his skin glistened.

"Georges, fetch me a basin of cool water and some fresh linen cloths. At once, if you please!"

The valet hesitated only a fraction, then went to do her bidding. The affronted doctor clucked his tongue and looked grave. "Should he suffer a relapse, Madame Cheney, it will be upon your head, not mine."

Flora's mouth tightened at the corners. "I am willing to take that responsibility."

She opened Blaise's nightshirt and felt the heat radiating from him. His skin was like the top of an iron stove. Wringing out the sponge in cool water, she bathed him in an attempt to bring down the fever. She bathed Blaise's brow, as she had done for her students when they had fallen ill. As she had done for her own mother in her last days.

Her thoughts winged back in time. That was what had led to Flora's final breach with her stern and unforgiving grandfather. Blaise moaned, and Flora pushed the ugly memories away. Soon she was too involved in trying to soothe him to worry over her disastrous past or the uncertain future.

In the next half hour she began to fear she'd taken on more than she should have. As Blaise's fever dropped, he tossed instead on a sea of restless dreams, uttering incoherent cries. Or so Flora thought at first. Then she realized that he was speaking phrases in the Breton tongue of his childhood.

She jumped as the door opened and Johanna paused on the threshold. She was more pale than usual, and looked like a wraith blinking against the bright light streaming in the windows. She was, Flora knew, terrified that her uncle might die. Her heart went out to the girl, facing yet another terrible tragedy in her short and lonely life.

Johanna's gaze skittered about the room, never once falling on the occupant of the bed. Guilt tormented her night and day. *Everything has gone wrong since we left England,* she thought, *and it is all my fault. If not for me, Uncle Blaise would be safe and well, half a world away.*

She swallowed around the knot of anxiety in her throat and tried to act composed. Flora was under terrible strain, and she must be brave and not do anything to add to it. "Claudine has come to take me for an airing in her carriage. She asks if you will come with us?"

"I can't leave while he is so restless. Perhaps tomorrow, if his fever breaks."

Reluctantly Johanna stepped into Blaise's bedchamber. How quiet it was, how large and empty the house seemed without the force of her uncle's presence in every room! While Flora continued at her task, Johanna restlessly roamed about. Her eyes were huge and dark, focused on her thoughts. She was agitated and nervous, as if the slightest noise would send her leaping like a startled cat. Finally she approached the window.

"Flora . . . what will you do if he . . . if he *dies*?" she blurted out.

"He will not die," she answered, more sharply than she'd intended.

"But if he does," his niece persisted, "will you return to England?"

"Johanna . . ."

"I am not a child! I know the fact that he is no better is an ominous sign." She choked back a sob and fought for control. "And I have a right to know what is happening to him. And what will happen to *me*."

"Indeed, it is too soon to know the course his fever will take."

Reaching out, Flora took the girl's hand in hers. The slender fingers seemed as translucent and sharp as pieces of broken china, and trembled beneath her touch. She had become close to Blaise in the past few weeks, and her terror of losing him was great.

Flora chose her words delicately. "Naturally you are concerned for your own future. I am certain that he has provided well for you, and . . ." She forced herself to continue around the constriction in her own throat. "And should the worst occur, Claudine and Nicolas would surely offer you a home with them here in Paris."

"I do not *wish* to stay in Paris." Tears filled Johanna's eyes. She glanced over to the bed where her uncle lay. "I could not bear it!

"If . . . if he should . . ." Impossible to put the awful thought into words again. "if anything *happens* . . . I shall go to the château at once."

She glanced over at her uncle, then away, frightened and unsure. "I cannot remember much at all of my mother and father. Everything before . . . the accident . . . is like a vague dream. But I remember bits and pieces about the château. I think . . . Oh, Flora, I *know* that I was happy there! I will go there, to Brittany."

"Don't borrow trouble, Johanna. He is strong and he will fight with all his might," Flora began, but was immediately interrupted.

The girl looked at her imploringly. Her blue eyes were enormous in her thin face. "Flora, you are fond of me a little, are you not?"

"Of course, silly goose." She put her arms around Johanna. "You know that I am *exceedingly* fond of you."

Johanna's whole body went slack with relief. "You look so very different from the days you were at Hawthorne—like Cinderella before the ball, then—that I could pass you on the street now without knowing you. I was afraid that you had changed inside as well: but you are still my own, dear, dear Miss O'Donnell beneath that elegant gown!"

"Yes. And I will always be."

"Oh, you are such a comfort to me! More than you know." Johanna lifted her face, with tear tracks glistening on her cheeks. "If anything happens you won't abandon me? You'll go with me to the château, Flora, at least for a while?"

"I give you my word! But you are letting your imagination turn morbid," Flora exclaimed, forgetting that only a few minutes earlier her own thoughts had followed the same painful path. "I fully expect your uncle to recover. Then we shall all go to Brittany for Easter, as planned. And now you must hurry, for Claudine is here and you must not keep the horses waiting.''

Johanna searched Flora's face and appeared satisfied. The talk of Brittany and her former schoolmistress's brisk speech reassured her. This was familiar territory. She gave a tremulous smile. ''I should have known you would not forsake me. You are so good to me, Flora. Far better than I deserve.''

''Silly chit! Is this why you've been so quiet and withdrawn?'' Flora smoothed the girl's hair back from her temple. ''I won't desert you, Johanna. I promise you.''

''Thank you.'' A warm smile and faint flush added color to Johanna's wan features. She looked almost like her old self again. ''I must not keep Claudine waiting,'' she said, squeezing Flora's hand. She turned and slipped out of the room again.

It was only a minute or two before Flora heard the sound of a vehicle pulling away. She went to the window and caught a glimpse of Johanna's bonnet at the carriage window. *Poor child,* Flora thought. *Whenever I feel sorry for myself, I have only to think of the life she has led, and everything is put into perspective. At least I can remember a time in the distant past, when my parents were happy together and I was dearly loved.*

But that had been before her father's suicide. Before her mother had begun her desperate descent from the widow of a charming ne'er-do-well to the mistress of a decadent peer, until she'd gone through a succession of lovers, and she'd landed in the squalor of the streets.

And when her mother had come to Grandfather's house, disheveled and dying, in hopes of seeing her daughter one last time, he had turned her away and tried to shut the door in her face. Would have succeeded, if Flora had not overheard the entire episode from over the upstairs banister.

Remembering, Flora's hands fisted at her sides. That day was etched in acid in her heart. She had been told that her mother had died years before, and could hardly reconcile the wretched creature on the doorstep with her beautiful and fastidious mother. She had begged Grandfather to take her mother in, but he had refused. It had ended with Flora packing her few belongings in a valise and leaving to nurse her mother in her final days. They had left the house with Grandfather purple with thwarted rage, his threats and curses ringing in the air.

"Go to perdition with her, then! I disown you completely! You are nothing to me, either of you. From this day you are both dead to me."

And that had been that. Her mother had died three days later, raving with fever in a hired room above a chandler's shop, with Flora at her side. She had never regretted her decision to be there in those final, desperate hours.

She was jolted from her reverie when Blaise gave out a strangled cry. Wheeling about, Flora found him thrashing wildly, trying to raise himself off the pillow. Despite his illness he was too strong for her, and she had to call his valet to help.

"A dose of laudanum is what he needs," Georges said when they'd calmed Blaise down. It was duly fetched, but had little effect. Flora was pitched headlong into a worrisome hour, as Blaise tossed and turned with increasing agitation.

Suddenly he opened his eyes. They were wild and unfocused, darker than coal. He didn't seem to recognize her.

She took his hot hand in hers. "Do you not know me? It is I, Flora. I am here with you."

His lids lowered abruptly, as if he were too fatigued to hold them open. "Don't go," he said in slurred French. "Don't leave me! Promise that you won't leave me!"

Her heart gave a little leap of unexpected pleasure. She stroked the damp hair back from his brow. "I shall stay until you sleep. I give you my word."

His fingers wrapped so tightly around her wrist that Flora's hand went numb. She tried to withdraw it.

"No!" He cried. "Do not go!"

"You are hurting my hand," she protested, and tried to prise his fingers loose.

Still he clung to her fiercely. "I let you go once before. I was a fool! But now that I have found you, I will not let you go. Never again, Eve. Never again."

Flora's breath came out in a little sigh. It was her hand he held, but it was Eve he saw through his fever.

She wasn't prepared for her own reactions: disappointment, a feeling of profound foolishness, swiftly followed by helpless anger. But she couldn't say if she were angry with Blaise and his persistent longing for a dead woman, or herself for that tiny spurt of joy she'd felt when she'd thought he was speaking to her.

How pathetic I am. And how desperate to be needed. Wanted. Indeed, that had been her undoing before.

His eyes closed and he lapsed from French to Breton once more. He released her hand. Flora rubbed her wrist, trying to restore the circulation. There would surely be a bruise there.

Georges looked across the bed at Flora with great sympathy in his brown eyes. "Is it not strange how one can return to the past while in the grip of fever? My mother did the same when she had an inflammation of the lungs."

Flora smiled at him. "You are a born diplomat. I expect that you might have done well in the foreign office, Georges, had you not turned your skills to other matters."

The valet pursed his lips but seemed pleased with her answer. He turned back to his master, who was now breathing quietly. "I believe the crisis has passed, madame."

She sighed in relief and leaned back in her chair and closed her own eyes, suddenly exhausted. What must it be like to love someone so strongly that that love transcended death? And what must it be like for a woman to be so loved? And by such a man? She couldn't begin to imagine it.

Flora could only wonder at the reasons Eve had preferred Blaise's younger brother to himself. From the small portrait of him she'd seen, Hilliard Cheney had certainly not been any more handsome; and if the artist had rendered true, he had none of Blaise's magnetism.

The next hour passed without much change. Once Blaise mumbled something. She leaned closer to hear. Blaise's eyelids flickered up. She was disappointed to see his eyes were as clouded as before.

"The *mari morgan* calls to you, Eve. Can you hear her?

Do not heed her song. I will save you this time. I swear it!''

"Hush, hush. I will not heed her." He seemed to believe that Eve had said those words, and nodded. A few minutes later he dropped into a more restful slumber.

The *mari morgan*. Flora remembered the story of the mermaids that Malin had used to frighten Johanna with on their journey. How strange that Blaise, a modern and educated man, reverted to the terrors of his childhood in his delirium! How sad that he still called out for Eve, who had been dead these ten years and more.

And how foolish she had been, Flora mused ruefully, to have thought he'd been speaking to her. To have ever wondered, even remotely, if someday there might be something more than a marriage of convenience between them. It was the curse of the feminine heart, she decided.

Once again her loneliness, her romantic nature and longing to belong somewhere, had set her imagination to building castles in the sky—faster than her independence and common sense could knock them down!

Well, she would guard herself against making the mistake again. In two years she would have honored her contract with Blaise. Johanna would be happily settled with some enterprising young man. Flora lifted her chin. She would be free of the Cheneys and they of her. At least this time, when she started anew, she would have the funds necessary to live in comfort.

And safety. She mustn't forget that.

The clock chimed the hour, and she was amazed to see how much time had passed. Blaise was resting quietly now, but the strain had taken its toll on Flora. She could hardly hold her head up for weariness. Surely the danger point had been passed. She rose. "I am going to rest for an hour. Send someone to me if there is any change."

Flora went to the guest room she had taken over as hers temporarily, longing to close her eyes and sleep until morning. As she bathed her face with cool, scented water from the basin, she examined her reflection. Johanna was right. There was little resemblance to prim Miss O'Donnell, with her sleek bun and drab garments, who had taught French and history to girls who were far more interested in learning to waltz, and exchanging flirtatious looks with red-haired William Black.

Clothed in fine silks, with her hair dressed in the latest mode and expensive jewels at her throat and ears, she looked every inch the pampered French society matron. A great weight came off her spirits. She was perfectly safe in her new identity.

Malin rapped on the door and entered. "There is a visitor requesting to see you, madame."

"You must deny me."

"I did, madame, but the Englishman, he insists. Pierre has put him in the drawing room."

Flora's heart thudded in her chest. An Englishman seeking her? All sorts of horrid possibilities went through her mind. It couldn't be Robin, she told herself sternly. Her break with the past had been complete. The visitor must be one of Blaise's acquaintances, come to inquire after him. She could carry it off.

"Very well, I will see him briefly."

She went down to the drawing room, hoping to dispose of the unwanted caller swiftly. Flora picked up the visitor's card from the silver tray and stopped in amazement in the doorway. The man was no stranger to her: the Englishman was none other than the Reverend Mr. Tompkins, vicar to the denizens of Hawthorne Village.

He had wandered to the far side of the room, and was gazing up at an oil painting of *The Rape of Europa*. From the way he peered up at it, she realized that he was extremely shortsighted. Odd that she had never noticed before. Perhaps that accounted for some of his detachment from the rest of the world.

He turned his vague blue glance from the half-unrobed woman, artfully draped across a muscular bull's back, and eyed Flora in mild puzzlement. Then he gave a little cough and cleared his throat twice, exactly as he always did before delivering a sermon.

"While I have no fault to find with the artist's skill, one cannot give credence to such a spectacle. It must be physically impossible for a bull to breed with a human woman," he said, as if they were in the midst of a discussion.

"One would certainly hope so," Flora replied acerbically. He had spoken in French, and she'd answered unconsciously in the same tongue. "I was unaware that you intended a visit to France."

He looked at her more intently. "Have we met before, Madame Cheney?"

She realized that his nearsightedness and her altered appearance had confused him. She took advantage of it, staying in the shadows cast by a piece of statuary.

"My niece Johanna has spoken of you," she said, praying he would not recognize her voice.

"I am on my way to Venice this afternoon. I wished to pay my respects to Miss Cheney, and deliver a letter to her from my sister before I left France. I had meant to come earlier in the week, but the cathedrals, the museums . . ."

He waved a hand as if this explained everything. "I trust that Miss Cheney is well, and enjoying Paris?"

"Exceedingly. Johanna will be sorry to have missed you. She has gone out for the day."

Dear God, I must get him out of the house before he recognizes me! With anyone else she would have had to observe the formalities and offer refreshments, but Flora doubted that he paid any attention to society's rules. If he did, he wouldn't have insisted upon seeing her when the servant announced that she was not "at home" to visitors.

"You must forgive me, Mr. Tompkins, but I am needed abovestairs. You will have heard that my husband is still recuperating from the injuries he sustained in the assassination attempt at the opera house." The newspapers were full of little else.

"I know nothing of that," he said dismissively. "I have no interest in the politics of government, and all the petty bickering that accompanies it."

Flora was stunned. He was the kind of man, she realized, who was capable of totally ignoring anything that didn't capture his intellectual interest. But when something *did*, he focused on it completely. Civilizations might rise and fall unnoticed, while Mr. Tompkins pondered the revelations of Saint John.

Or, Flora smiled to herself, while he mused on the inherent difficulties of a human woman mating with a god, in the guise of a bull.

Indeed, Mr. Tompkins's dazzling blue gaze wandered back to the painting as if drawn by a magnet. He seemed to have forgotten her presence completely. Flora began to wonder if it was the mythological subject that interested him so much, or the life-sized depiction of the unclothed woman. She sincerely doubted that he had ever seen one in the flesh.

Now, if she could only speed him on his way! "You said you have a letter for Johanna?"

"Letter . . . ?" He frowned, then reached into his pocket and pulled out an envelope, much wadded and considerably the worse for wear. It appeared to have been dropped in the mud and stepped on. By its thickness, it was no wonder Miss Tompkins had asked him to bring it in person: receiving it by mail would have cost Blaise a very pretty penny.

He looked down at a calling card he'd accidentally pulled from his pocket. "There is an English scholar, an acquaintance of mine, looking for a temporary position in Paris. Most gentlemanly and well read. I recommend him most highly. I don't suppose that Monsieur Cheney would be in need of someone to catalogue his library or do similar work?"

"Not," Flora said rather sharply, "under the present circumstances."

"Well, then, I must be off. Good day, Madame Cheney. Venice awaits me!" At the doorway he turned back, glanced once more at the painting soulfully, then took himself off.

Flora heaved a sigh of relief when the door closed behind him. He had scarcely even glanced her way during the entire conversation. *What a very eccentric man: the mind of a genius, the face of an angel, and the social awareness of a lamppost—and thank God for that!*

She looked down and realized the sheets of the letter had fallen out of the envelope. Why, the back was torn quite in two. As she picked up the fallen pages, she noticed her own name on one. Her heart skipped a beat. Holding her breath, she scanned the sheet quickly.

. . . and Miss Pemberly, unable to shake off the sustained bout of pleurisy, has resigned on her doctor's advice and gone abroad for her health. Her position is taken over by a Scotswoman of good heart and equally good sense.

Miss O'Donnell is greatly missed by the students at the academy. She would be glad to know that her friend Miss Melbourne unexpectedly inherited a cattle ranch from a distant relation in a place called Lonesome, Texas. She has gone off in great haste to bring civilization and culture to the wild American West.

There have been two weddings since your departure. Miss Evans, who kept the dry-goods store, has made a splendid match of it with a well-to-do merchant, and gone off to care for his motherless young brood. That handsome scallywag, William Black, has broken the hearts of all the local girls by marrying Sara Hemple, a prosperous widow who owns a large farm and is not only six years his senior, but outweighs him by a good two stone . . ."

Flora smiled at the indignant comment, shook her head at young Will's opportunism, and hoped that Johanna wouldn't be upset to hear of it. She suspected that her former pupil had once had a *tendre* for the good-looking red-headed lad.

As she put the letter away without reading further, she smiled at the image of Miss Melbourne serving tea, crumpets, and recitations of poetry to bewildered, sunburned cowboys wearing chaps and gun belts. Flora felt great happiness for her former colleague, and enormous relief for herself: with Miss Pemberly gone and Miss Melbourne safely off to America, two more links to her past were broken.

Pierre coughed discreetly behind her. "Monsieur de Broceliand," he announced formally.

Flora sighed. There was no escape. De Broceliand had sent hothouse flowers for Flora, and baskets of fruit for the invalid, and had twice called before. This was the first time she had been able to receive him.

He entered the drawing room, pausing briefly in the doorway with his head slightly turned. She wondered if he did it to show off his profile. It was certainly a handsome one. He looked her way, smiled warmly, and bowed.

"Madame Cheney! I have come to inquire after your husband."

Stepping closer, he took the hand she offered and proceeded to clasp it between his. "Forgive me for intruding, but I am going away to the country for a time. Word reached me that your husband's condition has worsened. I couldn't leave until I expressed to you personally both my sorrow at the situation, and my gratitude for his brave act."

He looked down into her eyes earnestly, retaining her hand. "Madame, I am desolate that our paths have crossed over such a tragic event."

Flora withdrew her hand firmly, but gently. "While I appreciate your gratitude toward my husband, your fears are premature, monsieur. I believe the crisis to have passed."

His expression was a study in contrast. Relief and rue chased one another over his handsome features. "Excellent news! I felicitate you, madame."

Why didn't she quite believe in his sincereness? Murmuring her thanks, Flora accepted his congratulations.

"I must be away, then," he said, bowing low over her hand. His lips brushed her skin, a violation of etiquette that she found most unsettling. "Be sure that I will pay you a visit upon my return to Paris, and hope to find your husband well enough to receive me."

Flora's cheeks were flushed. Why did he insist on paying her these unwanted gallantries? She suspected he was the kind of man who pursued any fashionable female who crossed his path, as a matter of course. Her glance fell on the card that Mr. Tompkins had left with her. A chance for a little revenge, if the visiting scholar were anything like his friend, she thought mischievously.

"I understand that you are looking for a learned man to research the history of your family. This gentlemen is not known to me, but he comes highly recommended by an old acquaintance."

"Excellent." He took the card and slipped it into his pocket. "I hope to hear good news of your husband upon my return to the city."

When he was gone she closed her eyes and stood there a moment, wondering when she had last enjoyed a good night's sleep. Upon entering her strange marriage, she had seen herself playing a very small role in an established and well-ordered household. Instead she found herself running it.

And all the while her thoughts were acutely tuned to the man lying upstairs, naked and vulnerable, in his bed. Unlike Johanna, she did not feel the rooms were empty. Even ill and floating in delirium, Flora was aware that Blaise's strong, masculine presence still dominated the house.

Feeling too restless to nap, she went to the library, intending to select a volume to read at his bedside later. The room smelled of polished wood, leather bindings, and Blaise's distinctive cologne. Rich colors gleamed behind the glass-fronted doors and along the rows of high shelves. A table beneath one of the tall windows was spread with the papers and stacks of books that Blaise had been engrossed in at the time of his injury.

Idly, Flora scanned the spines of three volumes: *The Fairy Folk in Celtic Oral Tradition* lay atop *Folktales of the Welsh and Cornish Countryside* and a well-thumbed copy of Malory's *Morte d'Arthur.* Nearby were similar tomes in French, all dealing with myths and vanished cultures.

She glanced at the papers filled with lines of spiky black ink in Blaise's hand. One stack apparently held his research notes. The other, thicker one appeared to be a manuscript. So this is what he had been working on!

Her curiosity was greatly aroused. She picked up the thick papers and examined them. There were several sheets of neatly drawn illustrations, all of them featuring rows of standing stones. In addition, there were at least fifty pages of sentences in closely written French, some with notations or corrections that Blaise had made in the margins. She rifled through and found the title page:

The Survival of Celtic Myth and Religion in Brittany, Volume II
Blaise L. Cheney

INTRODUCTION

Beneath Brittany's devout Christian traditions, there lurks a Celtic heritage as dramatic and enduring as the peninsula's jagged coastline, as fierce and wild as the waves that batter its shores.

The independent Breton traits are nowhere more evident than in the area of myth and magic. Despite the benefits of modern education, and the strong efforts of the Catholic church to stamp out such beliefs, the ancient Celtic superstitions thrive. There persists a widespread and deeply seated belief in mermaids, magic wells, dancing dwarves, and fairy spells. The countryside is rife with tales that the giant standing stones uproot themselves on starlit nights and roll down to the sea to drink.

While the rational mind rejects such stories as utter nonsense, there is something in the very air of Brittany which, on misty mornings or shadowy twilight evenings, makes it seem that anything is indeed possible.

Flora was amazed. She had imagined Blaise's "research" to be connected with his business dealings. Certainly she would never have expected a man so seemingly pragmatic to be interested in anything so fanciful. It revealed a side of him she hadn't known existed

She would have to tell him about St. Piska's Well when he recovered. *If he recovered,* a small, internal voice whispered. She stifled it quickly. He would regain his health. She mustn't allow herself to think otherwise.

Setting the manuscript down, her eye was caught by a thin volume of blue leather, intricately stamped with gold leaf with the design of a mermaid. Intrigued, Flora opened and found a title: *Tales of the French Countryside.* She skimmed down the list of chapters, past "Lost Lyonnesse," and "The Counts of Lusignan and the Legend of Melusine,'' and ''The Standing Stones of Carnac,'' but stopped abruptly when she saw the heading: ''Château Morgaine, or the Jeweled Mermaid's Egg.''

Flora was familiar with the Melusine legend and the story of the fabled city beneath the sea. She had never heard of a mermaid's egg, jeweled or otherwise. She flicked through the pages to the fourth chapter.

THE JEWELED MERMAID'S EGG
or
THE CURSE OF CHÂTEAU MORGAINE

One of the most intriguing legends of the French countryside is that of the Mermaid's Egg. It features many of the classic elements, from magic, love and betrayal, to a beautiful ghost and a most formidable curse. This tale comes to us from Brittany, that haunted and beautiful peninsula where some say the adventures of Arthur and Merlin actually took place, and where the last of the faeries are said to have taken refuge from our mundane civilization.

What rational man, the author might add, having tramped the dark Breton woods or strolled its sea-lashed cliffs and felt the magic in the air, would dare to disbelieve?

THE LEGEND

Centuries ago, a young man named Yvon Cheney returned to his mother's homeland in Brittany. Although handsome and clever, he was an unsuccessful fisherman, eking a meager living from the sea. One day, after a violent storm, he found a beautiful woman sunning herself on the shore.

Because her shimmering fair hair was long, like a golden cloak, he didn't realize at first that she was quite naked beneath it. Her only adornment was a lovely gemstone the size and shape of a robin's egg, suspended around her slender neck by a golden chain.

This precious jewel was unique, its transparent blue-green body glowing with streaks and swirls in all the colors of the sea: aqua, azure, emerald, and sapphire.

Yvon did not notice the jewel at first, however, for his eyes were all for the beautiful creature. He fell in love with her on the spot. Falling upon his knees, he offered her his heart, hand, and eternal devotion. The charming maiden returned his regard, and agreed to marry him.

It was only after the vows were exchanged that he learned her secret. His wife was a mermaid (*morgan*), in fact a daughter of the Sea Queen herself. The egg was a magical talisman, carved by the Sea Queen from a solid gemstone. This talisman held the mermaid's soul when she walked upon the land, enabling her to breathe the air as a mortal woman and survive out of her natural element. She had only to throw it into the sea to release the spell and become a mermaid again; but love for her human husband and their subsequent children kept her on land.

The mantel clock chimed and Flora closed the book. It was a charming story—blue-green jewels, naked mermaids, and yet-to-be-learned-of curses were intriguing indeed, but she had no time to read of them now. She slipped the slim volume into her pocket and went upstairs.

She found herself pausing to examine the carved mermaids at every turning. Their sinuous grace and remote, inhuman beauty struck a chill in her heart.

The guest rooms which she'd taken over as her own suite were off a branching side corridor, and Flora decided to retrieve her silk shawl in case the afternoon turned cooler. As she turned the handle she heard the crash of glass and a smothered oath. She threw open the door.

Malin stood frozen at the dressing table, her eyes round with apprehension as she saw the mistress of the house reflected from behind her. Now that Flora had her own maid, there was no reason for Johanna's nursemaid to be in here.

Flora stepped inside. The air reeked of expensive scent,

and light winked from the shattered remnants of a once-exquisite perfume bottle. She was very upset. The perfume and crystal container had been a gift from Claudine.

"What are you doing in here, Malin?"

"I . . . I was looking for . . . for Mademoiselle's pearl necklet."

"And expected to find it among my personal things?"

As she advanced into the room Flora realized that one of her drawers was ajar and her small jewel cask was open on the dressing table beside Malin. It had come with her from England and held nothing of value, except for the diary she had begun to keep. It was obvious that Malin had been leafing through it, and the invasion of her privacy infuriated Flora.

"How *dare* you!"

"I meant no harm, madame. I was only—"

"Only snooping where you have no business. None at all!" Flora interrupted. "I will not tolerate such behavior. You will leave now and you will not enter this chamber again without my express permission. Do you understand?"

The girl's face went from frightened to sullen. "I have taken nothing. I meant no harm."

"Let me make myself clear, since you willfully misunderstand me. If you have the temerity to come here without my sending for you, or if you ever—*ever*—go through my personal possessions again, I will have you dismissed!"

A sly smile spread over Malin's features. She drew herself up defiantly. "I think not, madame. It is only Monsieur Cheney who can dismiss me. And he will never do so."

"We shall see about that!"

"Yes. And you will see that I do not lie when I say this."

Flora rang the bellpull so hard it almost came down. Her own maid appeared in the doorway. "Jeannette there has been an accident. Please be so kind as to clean it up. And if you discover Malin in my chambers again, you will report it to me directly."

Jeanette curtsied, glancing from one to another with great curiosity. "As Madame wishes."

Holding the door open, Flora waited until Malin exited

the room, then followed her out into the hallway. "I mean what I said. I will not tolerate your snooping. If there is a next time, you will be sent packing."

The maid shrugged her shoulders. "Threaten me all you wish, madame, but you will see: he will never send me away."

A cry from the main corridor startled them both. Flora whipped around. One of the chambermaids stood where the hallways branched. "Madame! You must come at once!"

Forgetting Malin entirely, Flora followed the servant to Blaise's chamber. Her heart was pounding and her hands shaking as she entered. The thick draperies were drawn tight and the room was silent except for the ticking of the clock. A chill of fear swept up the backs of her arms. When she'd gone downstairs he'd appeared to be on the mend. How could everthing have changed so drastically in so short a time?

Her husband's valet and another servant stood unmoving at the foot of the bed. They looked up gravely, then stepped aside at her approach without speaking. Flora's heart thudded painfully in her chest. She was afraid to look.

The bed lay in the deepest shadows. Her feet made no sound on the thick carpet as she moved closer. Blaise lay like an effigy against the embroidered linens. The sheet had been pulled up to his chin and neatly folded back. She felt the blood drain from her face. Dear God, she wasn't prepared for this!

Flora stared down at him. He looked so much younger, with the lines of care smoothed from his face. He looked at peace. Tears stung her eyes. Perhaps he had found his Eve, after all.

She raised her eyes and saw that Georges was weeping silently. Her own tears overflowed. She was thunderstruck. Impossible to think that someone of Blaise's vitality could be snuffed out like a candle flame! She couldn't believe that he was gone. It was like a sword through her chest, robbing her of breath. Through the devastation came the dreary knowledge that she would have to tell Johanna.

Georges dabbed at his eyes with a handkerchief, then blew his nose with a Gallic honk. In the quiet room it sounded like Gabriel's trumpet announcing Judgement Day.

Flora wiped her tears with her lace-edged handkerchief, one of the things he'd provided for her trousseau. Somehow that made everything more poignant.

"I wish to be alone with him," she said simply.

The others nodded and left. Georges turned back on the threshold to the dressing room with an odd little shrug. Flora waited until they were gone. When the hallway door was closed she knelt down by the bed and took Blaise's hand. So cool now, when it had been hot as a metal brand.

"I wish that things had not ended this way," she whispered. "I think . . ." *I think, under different circumstances, that I could have loved you.*

But she couldn't say it aloud. Instead she touched her lips to his hand. "Farewell, Blaise. God grant you peace."

His fingers curled tightly around her hand, frightening her half to death. "No," he said clearly, although his eyes were still closed.

Flora gasped and struggled to find her voice. "He lives!" she cried out. *"He lives!"*

Georges popped back into the room, still wiping his reddened eyes. "But of course, madame! Did you think . . . ?"

But Flora wasn't listening. Her emotions had plummeted so low, then risen so high that she was giddy. And Blaise was trying to speak. He held her hand firmly, but gently. "Don't go. Don't leave me."

She caught her breath on a sob. He was very much alive—and mistaking her for Eve again.

But Blaise opened his eyes and fixed his intense dark gaze on her face. "Don't leave me, Flora!"

She drew a shuddering breath. "I won't," she soothed, wondering even as she spoke, just how much she was promising. "Sleep now."

Her reward was his smile just before he dropped into a deep, untroubled slumber.

She took her meals on a tray, and stayed beside his bed until nightfall, searching his worn face while he slept, as if all the answers to her life were written there.

It was only later, when she was finally alone in her own room, that Flora let her façade crumble. The emotional pendulum of the past few days had exhausted her, yet she was too restless to sleep. Blaise had survived the purgatory of his illness. Now she must survive the hell of her present situation. That it was of her own making was ironic.

Originally, she had accepted his outrageous proposal because she was a hunted woman in her own country, and the Bow Street runners were hot on her trail. At the time it seemed she was escaping into a fresh new world.

Before she had been imprisoned by poverty, circumstance, and fear. Now she realized the sensation of freedom on leaving England was just an illusion. She was still in a prison of sorts, albeit an elegant one. But despite the lovely surroundings, a houseful of servants, beautiful gowns and jewelry, it was all a mockery. She was the wife of a man who had drawn up a legal partnership, nothing more. A man in love with a dead woman.

And a man to whom, against all her better judgment, she was strongly attracted, like a moth to a candle flame. She must take care, lest she singe her wings and fall into the fire.

Chapter Seven

$\mathcal{F}$lora looked out the window of the commodious traveling carriage expectantly. Flowers grew thick along the roadside, nodding as they passed. They were far from the sophisticated diversions of Parisian society. After leaving the green, forested interior of the Breton peninsula, the land had turned rocky and wild. Now the breeze carried the rich scent of the sea.

Blaise leaned forward. "Caesar's legions once camped here. Do you see that granite outcrop?" he asked, indicating a tumble of boulders some yards from the road. "I unearthed several old coins and pieces of Roman armor there, when I was a boy. Some claim that the wizard Merlin sleeps nearby in his secret cave."

"I can almost believe it," Flora replied. "The very air sparkles with magic."

Sea birds sailed in curving arcs overhead, their wings like silver. This peninsula was the legendary Armorica, settled in the mists of time by cultures ancient even when the Celts arrived, six centuries before the birth of Christ. They had passed through Argoat, the land of the forest; now they were in Armor, the land of the sea.

Before they reached a narrow stone bridge, Blaise ordered the coachman to stop. "You will have your first sight of the château from here."

They pulled to the side of the road. The second vehicle that carried the luggage had been sent ahead earlier, along with Pierre, Blaise's valet and Flora's maid. She had chosen Jeanette from a field of three highly qualified applicants for two reasons: her pleasant and quiet manner soothed Flora's frayed nerves; and secondly, Jeanette and Malin had taken one another in acute dislike. There would be no exchanges of gossip about the habits of their master and mistress between the two.

Johanna reclined against a pile of cushions, with Malin in attendance. She was a poor traveler whether by water or land, and had been a fine shade of green since leaving Paris. Flora touched her gently on the arm.

"Come with us. The fresh air will clear your head."

The girl didn't even bother to open her eyes. "All I want is to reach the château and put this journey behind me," she groaned. "If I had my way, I would never travel more than ten miles in any direction from home again!"

Blaise opened the door and jumped lightly down. The doctor had deemed him recovered enough to travel, but Flora thought he was still far too pale. She was sure he was in pain, although he denied it. She shuddered, remembering the last time she had seen the scar from the gunshot and the surgery to extract it. The impulse to soothe that red, ragged seam of flesh with her cool touch had been almost overwhelming. She'd had to clasp her hands tightly to restrain herself.

Now, as Blaise extended his hand to help her alight, she was incredibly aware of his touch: the strength, the texture, the warmth of his strong fingers as they closed over hers. It made her skin tingle and her pulse race. From the smile on his face, she was certain that he had felt her hand quiver in his.

It would not do to let him know the effect he had upon her. He was playing a cat-and-mouse game for his own amusement, and she refused to play along. Her position was too vulnerable, emotionally and legally: as her husband, he had every right to make demands upon her. Here in his own country—and even more so on his own estate lands— he had the power to invoke those rights, promises notwithstanding. Without saying a word, he seemed to be going out of his way to remind her of it.

Their eyes met and locked. Blaise heard her swift intake of breath. Silently, he dared her to look away. She was skittish as a woodland creature, he thought, and more than a little afraid: but whether of him or of her reaction to him, he couldn't tell. Perhaps he was moving too fast, forcing matters too quickly. He let his gaze linger on her face. Lovely, tempting, Flora.

Flora smiled coolly, as one would to an acquaintance with whom one did not wish to become too intimate, and turned her head. When he held out his arm to her, she pretended not to notice.

"Why do you refuse my arm?" he said softly. "Have I done something to offend you, Flora?" His voice sounded serious, but when she glanced up at him his dark eyes were mocking.

"You are still recuperating from your injury, and I am perfectly capable of walking a short distance over the plateau," she said, and promptly tripped over a rock hidden among the wildflowers.

He caught her against him with his good arm and managed to keep them both upright. He took her chin in his other hand and lifted her face up. "You are a very poor liar, *chèrie*."

He was wrong there, she thought guiltily: necessity had made her quite an accomplished liar, but Flora certainly didn't want to disabuse him of his notion.

When he released her abruptly, she almost stumbled again. But this time it was the effect of his nearness, and not the rocky ground. Every day Flora thanked heaven that they no longer had to make a pretense of sleeping together. In Paris, his injury and recuperation had been her excuse to remain in the guest room.

Matters would be less awkward at the château, where there were separate bedchambers for the master and mistress, and she would have her private boudoir. At his level of society it was not unusual for a husband and wife to have separate bedchambers, and after a while everyone would forget that they'd ever shared a room. Except, of course, Blaise and herself.

While they were talking Malin decided to scramble down after all. She stretched and arched her back for the benefit of the watching groom, who smiled appreciatively. Encouraged, she strolled over to him. "You are new to Brittany,'' she said, casting a flirtatious glance from beneath her lashes.

''That I am, mademoiselle; but I am rapidly falling under the spell of her beauties.''

Malin laughed at the scarcely veiled compliment. She liked the look of the fellow, with his thick brown hair and admiring gray eyes. ''I hope you will stay long enough to see more of them.''

He blushed at her boldness. ''You're a tempting little morsel with a teasing way, but I hear that Breton girls are very religious, spending all their time in prayer.''

''Ah, but who knows for what we are praying?''

She laughed at his eager look. It wouldn't do to lead him on too far. She had no intentions of giving away anything until she had a ring on her finger and the marriage vows exchanged. A man did not value what came too easily.

She changed the subject. ''Have you been in service to Monsieur Cheney long?''

''Only since his return to France. But I understand your family has served his for generations.''

''Indeed.''

''What do you think of your new mistress?'' he asked idly. ''Is she harsh or foolish? Or kind and wise?''

Malin's eyes followed Flora as she walked arm in arm with her husband through the meadow. ''I do not gossip about the family,'' she chided, to show him she was a superior house servant, while he was from the stables.

The groom lowered his head. ''I meant no offense.''

''Well, you will know better than to ask in the future.'' The sly look that Flora so disliked came over her features like a mask. ''But I will tell you this: she is very learned, so I am told. But for all her book knowledge, she does not know half as much as she thinks she does.''

With a flounce of her skirts, Malin went back toward the carriage. Meanwhile Blaise and Flora had stopped on the side of the ridge.

He seemed startled by the view. ''Pont du Mor was a simple fishing village on my last visit. It has grown considerably.'' Flora followed his gaze through a leafy gap in the trees and spied a jumble of roofs and chimneys silhouetted against a sliver of sky and dark blue sea.

"Where is the château?"

"There. It is called Kastel Morgan in Breton, and Château Morgaine when we speak of it in French."

She scanned the distant landscape and spied a small castle, straight from a fairy tale, perched on the lip of the vale below. It was complete with a bridged moat, conical roofs on the towers, and graceful stone traceries over the arched windows.

"Impossible!" Flora declared. "I refuse to believe that you were born there."

Blaise frowned. "Why do you say that?"

"Why, it looks like a marchpane confection. All airy turrets and delicate lines. It is impossible that something so dainty and whimsical could be the ancestral home of the brooding Cheneys!"

"No," he said, touching her cheek to turn her head a few degrees to the right. "That is one of De Broceliand's properties. He and his family will come down for the *grand pardon.*"

Claudine had told Flora about the *pardons,* Breton religious festivals to honor the local patron saints. The pageantry sounded fascinating, and she was looking forward to seeing one. Flora was not so sure that she wanted to see De Broceliand again at such close quarters. He had come by to visit her with alarming frequency while Blaise was laid up with his injury. The man's insinuating manner and dissipated air made her acutely uncomfortable. In the country they would necessarily be thrown into one another's company even more.

But Flora's thoughts strayed from De Broceliand. Blaise's nearness distracted her. The soft edge of his sleeve brushed her throat like a caress. "Over there. On the far side of the valley. Look straight through the line of menhirs. Standing stones, as you say in England."

His hands were warm and strong on her shoulders. Almost possessive. She knew he was waiting for her reaction, and wouldn't give him the satisfaction of trying to pull away. But oh! how his nearness affected her.

She made out the menhirs in the cool distance: a group of large, irregularly shaped standing stones were strung out along the high ridge that bounded the valley. Roughly man-shaped, they formed a line, like sentinels all in a row. There appeared to be six of them, and the road ran spear-straight between the center two. As her eyes adjusted, she could discern a high stone wall, and dark slate roofs of the sprawling château.

She shaded her eyes. Four towers were visible against the blue sky, as gray and ancient-looking as the standing stones that guarded the approach. There were peaked roofs in abundance, jutting angles, and intriguing windows in odd places. On the whole, a dark and forbidding place. She sensed Blaise was waiting for her reaction.

"Ah, now that is much more in keeping with the way I had imagined it. A Gothic fantasy come to life. I trust there is a donjon beneath the keep, and an oubliette full of moldering skeletons?"

A smile flickered around the corners of his mobile mouth. "No donjon, and I am afraid that the oubliette is not much in use these days," Blaise said, steering her back toward the carriage. "Although I might consider it as a method to tame the tongues of saucy wives."

She had to laugh. "I am not saucy, sir, only disillusioned."

He helped her step inside, his hands lingering at her waist. He closed her in the vehicle, then climbed up on the seat and took the reins from the groom for the short journey across the vale.

Malin had overheard the end of their conversation. "There are ghosts, madame, so I hope your disappointment will not be severe."

"You are joking of course."

"That you must discover for yourself. One is said to appear only to the women of the family. You may hear her singing of a night."

"Mermaids, and now ghosts," Flora said, shaking her head. "I do not listen to servant's tales."

Malin gave up and leaned back against the squabs. Flora was relieved to have a few moments to compose herself before they reached the château. She was even happier that Blaise had not joined her in the carriage. She needed distance from him, for even a short while.

Blaise Cheney was most dangerous to her peace of mind when he was good-humored and charming, as he had been just now. On the whole, she preferred him in his distant, sardonic mode. It was much safer, for it put her on her guard.

Their relationship had changed during his rapid recuperation. He seemed determined to charm her; yet there were times when she caught him watching her with an odd, calculating gleam in his eye.

She turned her attention toward the high walls surrounding the *kastel*. Flora was an educated woman, but the stern appearance of the château was enough to set her imagination roaming. It wouldn't take long to reach it.

First they had to pass along the avenue that ran between the standing stones. The great gray rocks were over fifteen feet tall, and beyond the initial row of six there were dozens more, all carefully aligned.

As the carriage rolled between the menhirs a tingle ran down Flora's spine. Johanna seemed to feel it as well. She bolted upright and looked out the window. "The Druid Stones!" she exclaimed, suddenly wide awake. "I remember them!"

"Why druids?" Flora asked.

The girl's cheeks were suffused with excited color. "After the Romans conquered Britain, the druids fled back to their old home in Brittany. At the summer solstice, they held a great procession. But when the bells of the first Christian church in the parish were rung, the druids were turned to stone, every last one of them."

Flora eyed the stones warily. There was something uncanny about their stolid, gray forms up close. They resembled cloaked and hooded figures, turned from flesh to stone. "I can see how the legend began."

"Every ten years," Malin said, "at the time of the summer solstice, the Druid Stones uproot themselves and roll down to the sea to bathe in the waters, where they become men again for the space of an hour. Then the air is filled with the sounds of the harp and voices raised in chant. While they are gone, those brave enough may dig the soil where the stones were planted and remove the golden treasures hidden there."

She made a hasty sign of the cross and leaned forward. "But if the treasure seekers are not swift enough in removing the gold, the stones will roll back in place and crush them to death. It happened in my father's lifetime," she said, "to a man of the village."

"Nonsense." Flora tried to discourage the girl's tales. "More likely the poor treasure seeker tried to dig at the base of a stone, and undermined the rock so that it toppled over upon him."

Malin shrugged. "Believe what you wish, madame. The man was still crushed by the stone, so it is really the same."

Flora gave up—for the time being. Malin's superstitions were deeply rooted.

They were almost at the château now. The high wall surrounding it was of the same dark granite as the Druid Stones, and pierced by two wrought-iron gates. As the carriage drew near, the road swung abruptly to the right. Flora gave a little gasp of dismay. The land fell away without warning, a sheer drop of at least a hundred feet, to the frothing waves below. There was nothing between her side of the carriage and disaster, but empty, shimmering air.

Fighting off giddiness, she caught another glimpse of Pont du Mor, all dark slate roofs and wide stone chimneys from this vantage; but her main impression was of sparkling spume and crashing waves. Then the sea was gone, hidden from view, blocked by a tangle of flowering shrubs bent landward by the prevailing winds.

Just ahead the château gates opened as if by magic. Flora was almost disappointed when they passed through them, and she spied the two gnarled men who had pulled them wide. A wave of a magic wand or a command of "open sesame" would have been more appropriate, she thought, smiling inwardly at her strange fancies. Next she would be expecting the Druid Stones to roll down to the sea, as Malin believed.

Once they were inside the gate, the gloomy atmosphere was completely dispelled. Greenery and colorful blossoms contrasted with the weathered stone of the wall. The drive wound through a grassy park overhung with massive trees. Yellow, orange, and white flowers sprung between their roots, and pink and red blossoms swarmed up the mossy walls to her right.

"Yes," Johanna murmured beneath her breath. "I *do* remember. It looks exactly as it does in my dreams."

"A pleasant welcome from Mother Nature," Flora said, craning her head for a better look at the château itself. "Why, in Paris the first flowers are just coming up."

"Spring comes early to Brittany," Johanna answered. "It is because of the warm currents that flow just offshore, Uncle Blaise says."

Malin had a third version. "It is part of the pact that Yvon Cheney made with the Sea Queen," she said mysteriously.

As she spoke they passed beneath an arch in another thick stone wall, and entered an immense courtyard. In the center, the cobbled drive split to pass around an oval pond some sixty feet across, built of the same weathered stone as the rest of the kastel. A lone swan rippled the mirrored surface with its wake, creating a gentle disturbance among a mass of floating lily pads. And on the far side of the expanse, Flora had her first real look at the Château Morgaine.

It was quite old. Despite its newer wings, it was more castle than traditional château. Three rambling stories of carefully fitted stone, topped by slate-roofed gables, rose into the blue sky. Unlike the De Broceliands' airy storybook place, this was heavy and masculine, and seemed to have sprung from the Breton bedrock.

The round towers glimpsed earlier, with their pointy witches'-hat roofs, were more massive than she had realized from a distance; but the somber effect was softened by splotched patterns of moss and climbing vines, and the edges of the stone blocks were worn smooth from centuries of wind and spray. Casements on the second floor were thrown open, leaded panes reflecting their sage-green shutters, and the massed flowers in the matching window boxes beneath. The bright pinks and purples, scarlet and white of the petals were almost shocking against the sober gray walls.

A figure in a black dress, with a headdress of stiff white lace, came out of one of the buildings against the far wall.

She made a striking picture against the blue hydrangea and bright yellow blossoms, as she dropped a curtsy. Flora had only a glimpse of plump cheeks and sloeberry eyes nested in wrinkles. The woman bore a distinct resemblance to Malin, and smiled widely as they passed by.

"So," Malin murmured beneath her breath, "the old witch still lives."

Flora was startled. Then she saw that Malin was looking elsewhere. Craning her own neck, she caught sight of another face at an open window. Long, thin, aristocratic, and female. Her features were obscured by light dancing off the panes, but Flora was sure of one thing: this woman was much less pleased to see her than the other had been.

Johanna had seen her, too. "That must be Gaelle," she said quietly. "I do not remember her at all."

Flora knew little of Madame Morceau, who resided at the château, acting as its chatelaine. She and Blaise's late mother had been cousins. Because of that, Flora had pictured her as quite elderly. While it was difficult to tell from such a fleeting glimpse, she had the impression that her assumption was wrong.

The carriage slowed and stopped before an ancient set of doors in the main tower. Johanna's stiff posture suddenly relaxed. She had been afraid of what she might feel on seeing the château again, of the terrible memories that might come flooding down upon her. Instead she felt a sense of peace. Her breath came out in a sigh of relief. She was home.

Blaise dismounted, opened the vehicle and handed Flora down. He leaned close to her ear. So close that anyone watching would have thought he'd kissed her cheek. "Welcome to your new home, *chèrie*," he said aloud. "Welcome to Château Morgaine."

The château was even more imposing at close hand. Flora examined the granite façade. A mermaid was carved into the lintel above the main door, the only fanciful element visible. Everything about the château suggested unadorned masculine strength. If the one down in the vale had reminded her of Sleeping Beauty or Cinderella, this had more the air of Bluebeard's castle. But once again, the flowers of Brittany rioted over the gray stone, tempering the effect with their soft, wild beauty.

The household servants were lined up to greet them like soldiers at a military inspection. The men were dressed in black breeches and short jackets over red waistcoats, both richly embellished. The women wore white blouses and skirts of black or green, with brilliantly embroidered aprons, and the beautiful lace headdresses of Brittany.

On their journey Flora had seen these traditional coifs in every form, from small caplike coverings to towering cylinders of starched lace a foot and a half in height. Those worn by the women at the château resembled Spanish mantillas, rising from low combs, but folded behind so they looked like dainty moth wings when viewed from the back. Their workmanship was exquisite. The women curtsied and looked, Flora thought, like a field of Queen Anne's lace bowing to the breeze. She was utterly charmed.

The housekeeper, Madame Kerjean, was greeted by Blaise with respect and affection. A brisk woman with kindly eyes, she looked like an older version of her daughter, Malin, with none of the latter's slyness.

"Welcome home, monsieur." She dipped a curtsy to Flora. "Welcome, madame."

Flora thanked the woman and Blaise led his bride inside to meet his cousin. After the sunshine of the courtyard it took her eyes a moment to adjust to the lower light. The door opened inward on oiled hinges, to reveal a great hall with a stone-flagged floor, two fireplaces that were each large enough to roast an ox whole, and several dark chests, chairs, and cupboards ranged along the walls.

There the resemblance to a medieval fortress ended. The interior was sensual and sumptuous. While most of the older furniture was heavy and right-angled in shape, every square inch of every surface seemed to be ornately carved, and polished to a fare-thee-well.

Here and there a more feminine, sinuous piece of the cabinetmaker's art announced its Paris origins. The silky Persian carpets, the lustrous oriental porcelain, the intricate tapestries, the crystal chandeliers and gilded twelve-foot-high candelabra might have come from a palace. Certainly they had come from the four corners of the earth.

She had no time for closer observation. Gaelle Morceau stood stiffly, like one more shadow in the vaulted room. She wore a severe gown of dark gray silk with a wide collar and cuffs. Her thick, silver-streaked dark hair was skinned back and coiled tightly at her nape.

The austerity of her garb was relieved only by the large, ruby-studded crucifix which adorned her flat bosom. Except for the bloodred gemstones and a hint of rouge at her cheeks, Flora would have taken her for a nun.

The woman looked coldly through Flora, as if she were invisible. Her gaze flickered over Johanna, paused briefly, and went on. As it lighted upon Blaise she was transformed.

"You cannot know how I have waited for this moment! Welcome back, Blaise. Welcome home!"

"Gaelle!" Blaise strode forward and put his hands on her shoulders. "You have not changed a bit." He leaned down and kissed his cousin's cheek. "You are as beautiful now as you were then."

Her entire demeanor changed when she looked at him. When she smiled she almost lived up to his compliments. Flora watched, acutely uncomfortable. Although she was two decades older than Blaise, his cousin had the glow of a woman greeting a lover after a long absence.

Then she remembered Claudine saying that Blaise had been raised by Gaelle Morceau after his own mother's death. Her heart went out to this woman, who had waited so long to see the man she thought of as her son.

Madame Morceau linked her arm through Blaise's. "While I appreciate your letters and gifts from abroad, this is the best one yet. You have been away far too long, *mon coeur,*" she said.

"I shall rectify it by staying until you wish me gone again," he answered, leaning down to kiss her cheek.

"Than you shall never leave."

He didn't answer and the woman lowered her eyes. When she lifted them again, it was to regard Flora steadily. "So this is your bride."

The flat voice and stiff face were at odds with the alert hazel eyes. Flora straightened her shoulders. "I am pleased to make your acquaintance at last, Madame Morceau."

The woman nodded dismissively and examined Johanna, hovering in the background. "How very like Eve you are," she said.

Her overbright gaze moved on and finally came to rest upon Blaise once more. "I will take you up to your rooms."

"I must have a word with my steward," he said. "If you would be so good as to escort Flora and Johanna to their rooms, I will join you shortly. Have you put us in the West Tower?"

"But, no! I have moved my own things there," she said. "Naturally you will want to have the Yellow Suite for yourself."

Blaise protested. "But that has been yours as long as I can remember. I don't wish to put you out of them. My old rooms in the West Tower will suit us well enough."

Gaelle shot a look in Flora's direction. "I am sure your wife feels otherwise. As mistress of the château she must take precedence over me." As she spoke, she touched the heavy silver chain that hung around her waist with its ornate chatelaine and its dozen keys. "I will turn these over to the new Madame Cheney, also."

Flora was taken aback. *Manage this large household?* she thought in alarm. She smiled and tried to hide her nervousness. "Madame Morceau, you have been mistress here for many years, while I have no experience at all in such things. I would not presume to usurp your place."

If she expected thanks for her speech, Flora was sadly mistaken. Her admission that she was unfit to manage the household earned her a look of total disbelief, followed almost immediately by one of disdain. *"Blaise has married beneath his station,"* it plainly said, *"for any well-born lady would have been educated to fill my shoes."*

Aloud she was only slightly more diplomatic. "Then you must learn, for you are the mistress here now."

"There is time enough for that later," Blaise interjected. "Do not forget that Flora and I are still on our honeymoon." He touched her bare arm and she flinched involuntarily.

"Oh! You startled me," she said quickly to cover up her gaffe.

Gaelle Morceau's eyes narrowed. She looked from one to the other and a tight little smile twisted the corners of her mouth. Flora's heart sank, but she squared her shoulders and pretended not to notice. She had not counted on having an enemy at the château. Perhaps she could win Madame Morceau to easier terms in time: otherwise the next two years would be unbearable.

Blaise felt the tension thickening between the two women. He should have prepared the way better. A mistake on his part, which he would have to rectify soon. Meanwhile, he had every confidence that Flora could play her part well.

"Go with Gaelle," he said, smiling down at her. But his eyes gave a warning meant only for her. "She will see you settled, and I will join you shortly, *ma belle.*"

His cousin watched this interchange, her face unreadable. "Come. After you have freshened up we shall partake of a light meal. Malin, take Mademoiselle Johanna up to her room. I will personally escort Madame Cheney to hers."

Gaelle went along the hall in a whisper of silk, and Flora had no choice but to follow her. They went up a wide, branching stairway built against one wall. There was no rail, and it gave her a sensation of vertigo to look down. She saw that Johanna was hugging the wall just as tightly. At the top was a windowed gallery, hung with portraits of Cheneys long gone. Flora saw Blaise's firm jaw and aquiline nose reflected in portraits stretching back generations.

The men looked strong and firm of purpose, the women gentle and meek. No doubt, she mused, it would take a more yielding character than hers to live in peace with one of the Cheney males.

In the center was a larger-than-life canvas of a lovely woman with two young boys. Her pose was artless perfection, her hair and gown exquisite, her smile serene; but Flora thought the artist had captured a shadow in the woman's eyes and the way the corners of her mouth turned slightly down. The thought came to her with utmost certainty: *She was unhappy here.*

Her gaze shifted to the boys. It was easy to pick out the elder of the two as Blaise. The fierce intensity in his eyes, the sense, of passion and temper strictly controlled, were already there.

"Uncle Blaise and my father," Johanna said, stopping short. "I remember this portrait. But the last time I saw it, I was even younger than they were when it was painted. And that, of course, is *Grandmère*. I never knew her. She died before I was born."

Gaelle glanced up at the portrait with a strange expression, as if she had not really looked at it in a long time. "Poor Anne. How young she was. How young we all were then!"

She gave herself a little shake. "Come, there is time enough to look at the portraits later."

As they walked away, Flora turned for one last look. The painted eyes in Anne Cheney's face seemed to be watching her sorrowfully. *A trick of the light,* she thought, with a tiny shiver. *Only a trick of the light.*

At the end of the gallery they parted ways, the two younger women proceeding to the left, Flora and her guide turning off to the right. They passed door after door standing open along the way on either side, each chamber filled with the finest examples of the cabinetmakers' skills, with fabrics and treasures from around the globe. The tall, arched windows gave views of courtyards and gardens and the distant fields. Never once even a glimpse of sea.

The Yellow Suite, traditionally that of the master and mistress, was at the far end of the corridor. The splendors of the house in the Place Vendôme paled in comparison. A small anteroom, painted all around to resemble a misty landscape, led through high double doors into a wide sitting room, larger than the drawing room in Paris. The walls were hung with yellow silk jacquard, and wainscoted with glazed pearwood in pale amber. Elegant sofas and tables were arranged in comfortable groupings, interspersed with more of the intricately ornamented but straight-edged Breton furniture.

Double doors on either end stood open to tantalize with glimpses of a masculine bedroom on one side, all done in shades of gold and bronze, and a more feminine boudoir on the other. Gaelle led her through to it. "Your bedchamber."

Flora felt as if she had stepped into a sunlit, undersea grotto. Her first impression was of a magnificent, lavishly ornate bed recessed in a deep alcove. Satin draperies in pale seafoam green fell from a central medallion shaped like a gilded scallop shell. At the moment they were swagged back, but they could be freed to close off the alcove from the rest of the room.

It would not have looked out of place in a sultan's harem, she thought in amazement. Remembering her nunlike cell at Hawthorne Academy, Flora almost laughed aloud. The bed alone was larger than her tiny chamber had been.

The rest of the furniture was every bit as unique. It was sensual and feminine and beautifully bizarre, like nothing she had ever seen before: silver-gilt tables mounted on leaping dolphin bases; chairs with slender, sinuously curving fish for legs, their backs carved to look like scallop shells; a matching dressing table and console, their mirrors and every inch of decorative banding edging the furniture encrusted with more carved and gilded shells. Flora looked around in wonder. They would certainly take some getting used to!

"I hope you are pleased with the chamber," Gaelle said without expression. "The furnishings are in the Venetian Grotto style, purchased there by Blaise's father, during his travels."

"They are unusual, but quite beautiful," Flora replied carefully.

Gaelle arched her thin brows in scorn. "Myself, I find them grotesque. I have always preferred to sleep in the other bedroom, and kept this one closed up."

So, Flora thought, *this is war. Well, I will not be drawn into this little skirmish. Not yet, at any rate . . .*

She went to the open casement windows, hoping for a view of the sea. One framed a pleasant courtyard scene, another looked out over the château's tumbled slate gables toward a picturesque wooded ravine.

"I've lost my bearings," she said. "In which direction is the sea?"

Gaelle folded her hands. "There is no place within the château from which to view the sea."

"How very strange! Is it because of the cold winter winds blowing in off the bay?"

The older woman shook her head. "Do you know the story of Yvon Cheney and the mermaid?"

"I have read something of it."

"Then you will understand. The blood of the *mari morgans* runs through our veins. Should the Sea Queen call to us, we might be tempted to return to her watery kingdom."

Flora swung round. "Surely you don't believe that, however romantic it may be?"

Gaelle's eyebrows drew together in a frown that was not feigned. "Many have heard her call. Some are able to resist it, while Blaise's mother could not. She leapt to her death when he was just a boy." She regarded Flora steadily with her changeable hazel eyes. "What will you do, when you hear the mermaid's song? Perhaps you, too, will be unable to resist."

"I am made of stronger stuff than that, Madame Morceau," Flora said coolly. "You will discover that it takes more than a legend to frighten me."

Gaelle Morceau's lips drew back in a parody of a smile. "Ah. That is exactly what Anne used to say. Let us hope that history does not repeat itself."

She turned on her heel and left Flora standing there alone.

Johanna, gowned in rose and white silk sprigged with embroidery, almost danced into Flora's dressing room. Twisting her hair up in a neat chignon, Flora smiled at the girl's reflection in the mirror. The sea air had put color in her cheeks and a sparkle in her eyes.

The girl traced one of the carved and gilded shells with her fingertip. "I remember my mother sitting at this very dressing table. She looked exactly like a fairy princess. Oh, so much is coming back to me now! I feel close to her at the château, Flora, as if she were watching over me."

Flora had the same sensation of being watched; but in her case, she suspected that Gaelle Morceau had set the servants to spying on their new mistress. It wouldn't surprise her one bit.

The change in Johanna since their arrival a few hours earlier did, however. She seemed almost the same spirited schoolgirl that Flora had known at Hawthorne Academy; but the strain of the past weeks, since Blaise's near-fatal accident, had altered her features. There was a new maturity in her face and bearing.

Johanna realized that Flora was still wearing her wrapper. "What, not ready? It is almost time for dinner."

"I am almost finished. My maid cut her hand on a broken perfume bottle. Madame Kerjean is tending to her."

"Shall I send Malin to aid you?"

"No. I have only to put on my stockings and gown. Go down to the drawing room, and I promise I will join you shortly."

"Very well." But Johanna lingered at the door. "I hope you will come to love the château as I do Flora," she said softly. "For the first time I feel I am home."

"I am so very glad."

Johanna returned her smile and left in a far happier frame of mind from when she had arrived. It was true, what she had said to Flora. For the first time that she could recall, she was not a stranger. An outsider. Everywhere she wandered through the château, she found things that jogged her sleeping memories: a large blue and white porcelain vase in the drawing room, decorated with a motif of drooping willows, quaint little boats, and arching bridges; the smiling silver Madonna in a wall niche in her room; a glimpse of leafy arbor and an alley of trees, seen from a window.

And earlier, when Malin had brought bread and chocolate, and tucked her in for a brief nap, she had drifted off imagining that someone was singing softly to her, that a gentle hand had stroked her hair and soft, cool lips had kissed her brow. Only a dream, she knew, but a most comforting one. It gave her the feeling that she was safe, that everything would finally turn out well.

Meanwhile, Flora found her situation far from satisfactory. She had been eager to leave Paris, thinking only of putting as much distance between herself and the chance of being recognized, as possible. Now she found herself beneath the same roof with a woman who resented her presence bitterly, and who would no doubt go out of her way to make it apparent.

Too late now. Sighing, she swung her legs over the side of the ottoman and reached for her silk stockings. They were fine as cobweb and it was a delicate task to don them without snagging a thread on her nails.

She had just smoothed the first one over her thigh and slipped on the satin garter, when she heard a soft footfall behind her. Johanna had not closed the door on the way out. Blaise materialized at her side.

''Allow me,'' he said, bending down on one knee, before she could cover her legs. His face was almost level with hers, dark eyes alight, as he took her bare foot firmly in his strong hand. It had a shocking effect on her. Heat rose in a slow wave and she felt tongue-tied and giddy. She couldn't withdraw her foot without losing both her dignity and her balance.

Blaise lifted the other stocking, already rolled up neatly, and slid it over her foot, then slowly stroked the clinging fabric up her slim ankle. He felt the tremor that went through her, heard her soft gasp at the deliberate sensuality of his touch. His own breathing was strangely affected. It had been too long since he'd dressed—or undressed—a beautiful woman. A desirable woman. There. He had admitted it to himself. The attraction. And the danger.

Perhaps he had proposed to the wrong woman after all. Things would have been far less complicated if he'd taken to wife that shy little mouse of a creature who had gone to fetch Flora on his second visit to Johanna's school: Miss Melbourne would have been a far safer choice. A conformable wife, who would have put up with much to escape the life of drudgery.

He remembered what Flora had said that fateful night at the opera: *"To be deceived by one's husband would be unforgivable . . . If there is not trust . . . and truth . . . then there is nothing."* He hadn't anticipated such a romantic attitude from a woman who had seemed the soul of practicality.

Only time would tell if he had made a mistake. And meanwhile, here was Flora, half naked beneath her silk dressing gown, with flushed face and sparkling eyes, and her mouth as soft and open as a rose. Perhaps, he thought, it was the danger that heightened the attraction. It was stronger now than it had ever been.

Flora was trembling, but finally found her voice. "Please unhand me. I am perfectly capable of dressing myself."

His fingers smoothed the fabric upward and he smiled. "I am sure, lovely Flora, that you are capable of almost anything."

"Then release me, if you please. At once!"

He smiled into her eyes, but refused. "You must accustom yourself to my touch, *ma petite fleur.* Unless you wish to advertise that all is not as it seems. Gaelle saw how you pulled back from me like a scalded cat, earlier."

His hands moved up her calf, sliding the silk along her leg. All the while his gaze was locked with hers. Flora couldn't look away. Yet she dared not let him know how he affected her, how the warmth of his touch ignited a pool of flame in her blood. She was melting inside with the heat of it.

"Do you see, it is not so bad," he murmured, sliding her wrapper open even higher. Her scent surrounded him. A surge of sudden hot desire caught him off guard. His hand tightened involuntarily. *Gently, gently,* he reminded himself. He must keep his head. He must not frighten her. He must not let himself be caught in this web of his own dark spinning.

"What lovely limbs you have, Flora. They are just as I imagined them . . . soft and smooth and shapely, like the rest of your figure." A flush of color stained his cheekbones.

She felt an answering flood of fresh color in her face. "Don't . . ."

Was that her own voice, so husky and low? Her breasts felt full, the nipples taut and hard. She realized that her wrap had pulled open at the bodice when his rough cheek grazed her bare skin above her lace corset. He gave a sharp intake of breath. They both froze. For a moment there was nothing but the sound of their breathing. As he slid the silk stocking onto her slender thigh he realized his hands were shaking. God, but he wanted her!

But first she must be ready. Blaise fought for control. He must be completely sure of her. He must use her passionate nature as the snare, and make her a willing partner in her own seduction. Blood pounded at his temples.

In his time he had played the role of seducer with women of the world who had enjoyed playing the sensual game of cat and mouse between the sexes. He had always known when to touch, when to retreat. How to fan the flames until they both surrendered in the fire of mutual need.

With Flora it must be different. He saw her catch her bottom lip between her small white teeth, and knew her breasts ached with desire. Knew, just as surely, that if he reached out to her now he would ruin everything. *Patience,* he counseled himself. *Patience, and everything you want will be yours.*

Letting his fingertips glide along the satin skin, he watched her marvelous eyes dilate with fear and pleasure. Her female scent was all around him like perfume. Oh, she was hot-blooded, this cool-seeming Englishwoman.

He leaned forward and touched his mouth lightly to hers. She didn't protest, but her tiny moan of despair shattered the spell. Blaise tipped her chin up and searched her face. "You have nothing to fear from me, *chèrie.* I shall not force my attentions on you. When I seek the pleasures of a woman's boudoir, it is with the expectation of caressing a willing partner in my arms."

Flora was afraid to answer. Her body was awash with heat. When he first touched her the only thing she wanted was for him to stop. Now that he had, it was all that she could do to keep from flinging herself at him. She wanted . . . oh, how she *wanted!*

She found her voice at last. "If it's a willing partner you seek, then you will have to look elsewhere."

Blaise only smiled. "Do you believe that, *chèrie?*" He laughed low in his throat. "Do you believe that *I* do?"

As he rose his hand brushed her breast. It happened so fast she didn't know if it had been by accident, or design. All she knew was that her skin was on fire with it. He stood looking down at her, his face dark and flushed with the same heat that rose in hers.

"You are a passionate woman, Flora. And I, I am a passionate man. All it would take would be one spark to ignite us. And there would be no going back."

She shivered at his words, at the danger and the truth in them. If he touched her now she could not be responsible for her actions. If he touched her now, she would be consumed.

His gaze held hers. She could not look away. "Remember this, Flora: *If I want you, I will have you.* And you will come to me full willing!"

He left her boudoir without looking back. Flora sat there, unable to move, gasping air as if she were suffocating. Her legs were shaky when she got up and turned the key in its lock. She leaned against the door and dragged in a ragged breath. She caught her reflection in the shell-rimmed mirror above the mantel. Her image shimmered in the firelight, like one of the mermaids in the Place Vendôme come to life. Her breasts were ripe and full, her waist slender.

Once before a man had stirred her passions in the same way, and it had ended in disaster. Robin Harding had fed her spoonfuls of honeyed lies, and she had swallowed every one.

At least Blaise did not pretend anything more than animal attraction. Flora stood in the growing shadows of the chamber, examining her body. Her hands cupped her aching breasts. That long moment when he gazed on them had almost been her undoing. She had fought the urge to let him caress her with hand and lips and tongue. And he had known it. The thought was humiliating.

His voice echoed in her head. *"If I want you, I will have you. And you will come to me full willing."* A shuddering sigh wracked her. Oh, yes. She would.

And hated herself for it.

The only thing to do was to avoid ever being alone with him again. Hastily she threw off her silk wrap and slipped into her garnet evening dress. The cool silk settled over her heated body like mist. Her every sense seemed heightened.

How could she face him at the dinner table and pretend nothing had passed between them? But of course, he had stated that as his very intention. He wanted to take her awareness of his masculinity to another level, one so obvious that the others could not help but notice her response to him.

That was even more humiliating.

With trembling fingers she did up the tiny buttons that went up the bodice from waist to low-cut neckline. She wished she had chosen something less revealing. She knew he wanted her. Did Blaise find her truly desirable, she wondered, or was it only the need to conquer and possess?

And if he had reached inside her open wrapper and placed his strong, bare hand against her flesh—would she have cared about the reason?

Dinner was a formal affair in a chamber outfitted with a long table and several chandeliers the size of carriage wheels. The corners of the long room, with its coffered ceiling, were hidden by shadows. The Cheney crest, with its sinuous mermaid, was carved into the stone chimney breasts at either end of the room. High-backed chairs, upholstered in ancient tapestry, lined the table. More tapestries hung on the walls, this time hunt scenes with fine ladies and gentlemen of the court, chasing noble stags.

She wondered if Gaelle always dined in such splendor, even when she dined alone. It was, Flora thought, like being sent back in time. All it needed was a dais for the nobility at the head of the room, and a few trestles for the lesser folk below. Little wonder that tales of ghosts were spun about the place.

Gaelle made a great show of giving up her place to the new bride: "It is only right," she said with an icy attempt to feign good will. The servants who stood near the sideboard, waiting to serve the family's pleasure, watched the interplay without seeming to do so.

Flora hesitated briefly. It seemed she had two choices: either to accept the role of mistress that was thrust upon her, or spend the next two years beneath Gaelle's thumb. There was no doubt in her mind that the older woman would then do everything she could to make her life miserable, as long as she was seen to hold the reins: Flora had lived with domestic tyrants before. She inclined her head.

"You are very gracious, Madame Morceau. Thank you for making me so welcome in my new home."

A spasm of emotion twitched Gaelle's features before they settled into a smooth mask. She had chosen her first battle ill. Blaisc's wife had risen to the challenge, and now was formally acknowledged as the female head of the household. Her dark eyes burned with resentment as Flora took the large chair at the foot of the table, opposite her husband.

Flora picked up the little bell at her place setting and rang it to signify the meal was to begin. The servants hid their surprise and began the service, and she had her introduction to hearty Breton cuisine: *cotriade,* the stewlike fish soup traditional to the region, colorful with red potatoes, green leeks, onions, shrimp, and white fish, seasoned with bay and thyme. Next came a bounty of winter carrots and early vegetables roasted with *pré-salé,* the flavorful salt-meadow lamb; and *homard à l'Armoricaine,* chunks of lobster in a fabulous sauce of tomatoes, garlic, and cognac.

Since glasses of apple brandy were drunk between courses, Flora began to feel very mellow indeed. She was particularly glad to see that Johanna's normal schoolgirl appetite had come back. She not only partook of every dish offered, she sampled all of the desserts and encouraged Flora to do the same. "And you must try the *gâteau breton.* It is superb. Madame Kerjean let me assist her in baking it."

Flora eyed the buttery confection, but declined. "Another time, perhaps. If I continue to indulge myself like this on a nightly basis, I will have to let out all the seams in my new gowns."

Gaelle looked up sharply and frowned. All through the meal her eyes had kept coming back to Flora, as if against her will. As if she could not believe that this foreign usurper was sitting in the place that had been hers for so many years.

Flora was also uncomfortably aware of Blaise, sitting opposite her. It seemed that all he had to do now was look at her in a certain way, and the blood thrummed through her veins. She glanced across the table to where Blaise sat, handsome and commanding in the warm candlelight. It highlighted his strong features, his chiseled cheekbones and firm mouth. Her husband.

An intriguing and powerful man. She had a share in his wealth, his name, his status. Perhaps she even had his admiration. But not, of course, his heart. Their marriage was hollow, but it had provided her with an escape from the bleak past, and the very real possibility of a bright future.

She might even have more, if she had dared to risk it. The scene in her dressing room was proof of that. There were women who, even knowing the truth of her position, would envy her. Who would welcome him to their beds for the duration of their arrangement, and no hard feelings or emotional entanglements when it ended. Flora almost wished that she were one of that sisterhood. Blaise was an experienced man of the world. She had no doubt that he would be a skilled and passionate lover.

Blaise glanced down the table at her at that exact moment. Their gazes locked. After a few long seconds he smiled, as if he had read her mind. Flora looked hastily away.

Only Johanna seemed oblivious to the charge in the air. She was eager to visit a site she remembered from her childhood.

"There was a ruin near the château . . . a cottage perhaps? The roof had fallen in and the walls were crumbling, but the garden was magical, all wild and overgrown. Is it still there?"

Blaise tossed back another glass of apple brandy, in the accepted Breton style. "I do not recall such a cottage."

Flora knew that he was lying. Intuitions stirred. Had it been a trysting place?

Johanna was remembering more. "And there was a place near a church. It used to frighten me . . . a dark building without windows, and many curious statues nearby. I did not like to go there."

"The parish close in Pont du Mor," Blaise said. "It is quite famous. The statues are part of the *Calvaire*. You will be fascinated by it, Flora, I am sure. Carvings of stories from the Bible, used to teach the villagers in the days when few, even among the gentry, could read. Some are lovely, others quite strange and primitive, as if the stonemasons had imbibed a little too much local brandy."

"You must not be disrespectful, Blaise," Gaelle said sharply. "The windowless building is the ossuary, Johanna, where the bones of the dead are kept. There is nothing to be afraid of there." She turned to Blaise again. "Loic Kersaudy is preparing a book about our parish close. I told him you would not be pleased."

"What, do you think he is poaching on my territory?" Blaise laughed. "I take care of my own," he said, with a glance at Flora. "As for Loic's village stories, he may write of them all he chooses. My work is in another field."

"Loic and Ysuelt!" Johanna exclaimed. "Yes, I have never forgotten them. Their grandfather was a *chevalier*. They lived in a cottage down by the strand, just outside the village, I think. I used to play at dolls with Ysuelt. Of course Loic was much older—ten years at least—and far too superior to spend time with two little girls. Although he did bring me pretty shells from time to time. Do you think . . ." She blushed prettily. "Might we pay a call on them tomorrow, as well?"

"We shall see."

Flora wondered if Blaise's niece had once had a childish *tendre* for the young man in question. That might explain the eager animation in her face—and the reserve in Blaise's voice. Her mind went leaping ahead: "Is Loic Kersaudy married?"

He frowned. "Why do you ask?"

She shrugged. "I was just making conversation."

But actually, her agile imagination was developing possibilities. Johanna seemed disposed to like the young man. If this Loic's grandfather had been a knight in the old regime, his bloodlines must surely be acceptable. Now, if only he had a fortune equally as acceptable, her task of seeing Johanna married off might be over sooner than she had anticipated.

And, after the breathless, pulse-pounding incident with Blaise in her dressing room, earlier, she thought that sooner would be a very good thing.

After dinner the household retired early. Flora didn't want another confrontation with Blaise just yet. She parted ways with Johanna, and entered her own bedchamber through its private door from the corridor, instead of going in through the sitting room.

Without bothering to ring for her maid, she undressed and put on her nightshift. The effects of the day's travel, the excitement and nervousness of her arrival at the château, and the meeting with Gaelle Morceau should have all combined to create fatigue. Instead Flora found herself too wakeful for sleep.

It was Blaise, she thought, and the knowledge that they were only separated by two doors and an empty room. There was no one else in this entire wing. What would she do if he decided to claim his legal rights?

Nonsense! her intellect said firmly. Hadn't he told her that he had no wish for an unwilling partner?

Ah, that other, traitorous voice whispered, *but are you really so unwilling? If he came to you now, could you resist?*

Unbidden, her mind conjured up a picture of him in his dressing room. She imagined those same strong, brown hands that had touched her so evocatively earlier, now stripping off his shirt to reveal his magnificent physique. Flora's breathing quickened.

Her grandfather's parting words echoed in her head: *"You are just like your mother! You suffer from the same fatal character flaws that brought her to grief. I know where your headstrong ways will lead you. If you bring shame upon yourself, do not come to me . . . for I shall turn you away!"*

There had never been any love lost between them. Long before her mother had come begging at the door, Flora had resented his harshness, his conviction that she came of bad stock, and was doomed to fall. Flora rubbed her temples. Perhaps, she thought, his understanding of human nature was greater than her own knowledge of herself. Certainly everything he had predicted had come to pass.

And now, despite the terrible lessons of past experience, her passionate nature was in danger of leading her onto the shoals. She must remain firm. Blaise would soon tire of his little game, and by the autumn they would be back in Paris. Claudine had promised to sponsor Johanna, even to giving her ball at the Le Vecs' fabulous mansion, while Flora could remain in the background as much as possible.

And, if fate smiled upon her, Johanna would not even have to go to the bother of making a successful debut. Perhaps she and Loic Kersaudy would make a match of it. By this time next year, Flora told herself happily, Johanna might even be happily married. As for herself, she would be a free woman of independent means, able to travel or take up her abode anywhere she chose. Blaise Cheney and the Château Morgaine would seem like a fading dream.

For the present she had nothing to do but guard herself against his charms, and enjoy the luxury with which she was surrounded. And he would be closeted with his research a good deal of the time.

That cheered her immensely. Yes, she would concentrate on the positive aspects of her new role—one of which was lying in a comfortable bed with a good book for as long as she pleased before sleep.

There were three biographies, some poetry, a novel or two and several volumes of foreign travel in the packet Claudine had sent with her as they were leaving. Flora picked out a slim book on the Mediterranean islands. Perhaps she would visit them when her arrangement with Blaise ended.

Taking the volume back with her, she slipped between the velvet-soft linen sheets. The fire in the hearth cast a warm golden glow over the walls. Flora sighed with pleasure. At least for tonight she would set aside her current problems and relax. The pillows were finest down, her nighshift exquisitely embroidered, her lamp bright with the best burning oil.

Flora leaned back against the luxurious pillows, prepared to enjoy the author's travels on the island of Crete. But when she opened the pages, she realized she had taken up the wrong volume. This was the book she'd gotten from Blaise's library the day the Reverend Tompkins had come to call. Very well, she was too cozy to get up and rummage about for the other one.

Turning to the legend of Château Morgaine and the jeweled Mermaid's Egg, she began to read at the place where she had left off in Paris:

The Sea Queen was enraged that Yvon Cheney had won her daughter's heart and hand, and tried to lure her home; but, although she sang to her daughter by day and by night, the beautiful mermaid was so besotted with her human lover, that she turned a deaf ear to her mother's grief. In time she began to forget her past, and to believe that she was a human woman.

Yvon was accosted by the Sea Queen herself, riding in her seashell chariot drawn by twin crabs. She offered him the treasures of her kingdom, pearls, coral, and chests of gold from sunken ships, if he would release her daughter from human form by throwing the gemstone into the sea.

Blinded by visions of great wealth, he agreed. Of course, he never intended to honor his promise to the Queen of the Mari Morgans. That night, while the mermaid lay sleeping beside him, Yvon slipped the gold chain and the jeweled egg that held her soul from her throat. Stealing from the house, he hid it beneath a stone in the churchyard, on hallowed ground, where his wife dared not go.

Years passed. Investing the treasure wisely in land and goods, Yvon Cheney amassed great wealth. But while he tended to his business empire, his lovely wife grew restless, as mermaids always do. One day, when the wind blew in from the sea and waves crashed upon the shore, the mermaid heard her mother's singing and remembered everything. She wept and begged to visit her mother in her kingdom beneath the sea. Yvon refused to give her the jeweled egg, knowing that her mother would never allow her to return.

The mermaid slowly pined away and died, without ever seeing her mother or her home beneath the waves again. Her ghost is said to haunt the château, trailing ropes of wet seaweed along the stone corridors. Keening and weeping, searching, endlessly searching for the little jeweled egg that contains her poor, lost soul.

Flora sighed. She'd hoped for happier bedtime reading. It was the familiar story of a woman foolishly giving up everything she valued for love, only to learn she'd made a bad bargain. Her own mother had followed that tragic pattern, and so had she.

She almost set the book down, but decided to finish the chapter.

And now to the curse of Château Morgaine, which is said to remain to this day: Yvon Cheney's broken promise and the lonely mermaid's death brought retribution down upon him and his future descendants. Although the Sea Queen could not take Yvon's wealth back, as long as he kept possession of the mermaid's egg, she would still extract her vengeance: each decade, so the legend goes, one member of the family will be claimed by the sea, a hostage for the return of the mermaid's soul.

The curse came true in his own lifetime. Yvon Cheney's second wife and infant son were lost in the treacherous waters off the Ile d'Ouissant. Still the stubborn man, afraid of losing his wealth, refused to throw the mermaid's egg into the sea. He retrieved the gem from the churchyard and took it back to his château, where it remains to this day.

While the family has indeed prospered since Yvon's time, it is equally true that his descendants seem cursed. The most recent victims were Hilliard Cheney and his English wife, Eve. The couple were lost when their small yacht, the Mari Morgan, sailed forth on a sunny day, and went down to the bottom of the sea when a squall of supernatural fury arose off the Isle d'Ouessant.

The villagers of Pont du Mor attribute the terrible event to the Sea Queen's wrath. Only when the egg containing the mermaid's soul is returned to the ocean once more, they say, will the curse be lifted and the surviving Cheneys left in peace.

Flora shivered and closed the book. Isle d'Ouessant. The Isle of Terror.

For a moment she could almost feel Eve's fear and suffocating panic, as the cold waves closed over her head. And both Johanna and Blaise had been there. She could only imagine the memories that haunted them. And she wondered who had dared to tempt fate by naming the ship after the mermaids of legend.

Not, of course, that she believed in such things. But all the same she touched the small gold cross at her throat as if the reassuring feel of it could ward off disaster. Perhaps, Flora thought, she should keep it on always, as an amulet to ward off Blaise's charm.

Her ears pricked up. She heard the sound of a door opening nearby. She had neglected to lock the door leading to their sitting room. Tiptoeing to the door of her bedchamber, she leaned her head against the carved wood and listened. Was Blaise moving about on the other side? It was difficult to hear anything over the pounding of her heart. She waited a while longer. Nothing. After a long moment Flora turned the key. As it rasped inside the keyhole she couldn't help wondering if she were locking him out—or herself in.

It was in the still hours of the night that a strange sound awakened Flora. She had been in a deep, dreamless sleep, and was disoriented by her surroundings. The room was dark as a tomb. Then she remembered she was at the château, and that she had closed the shutters against the night air.

There it was again. She sat up and listened. At first she thought it might be Blaise, in the grip of a nightmare, like those that had plagued him after his injury. But no, these came from the other direction.

Rising, she went softly toward the door leading directly out to the corridor. Her bare feet made no sound on the stone flags. Yes, the sounds came from the other side of the paneled door. As if someone stood only inches away. She stopped and listened. Muffled sobs. A low moan of despair. Both so lonely, so terrible in their hopelessness that it made the hairs at her nape stand up.

Flora wanted to run back to her bed and clap her hands over her ears to drown out the sounds. The weeper in the night might not welcome a witness to her woe. But her instincts would not let her ignore such suffering in another human being. She turned the key and opened the door cautiously.

A cool wind blew down the corridor, filled with the salt and iodine tang of the sea. It set the flame in the wall niche's oil lamp dancing. A flare of light sent giant shadows racing up to the ceiling, before it guttered and went out. A full moon shone through the great window at the head of the staircase, and there was still enough light to see. The wide hallway was deserted.

Now the moans seemed to come from behind her. Spinning about, she found the corridor just as empty in the opposite direction. It might be the sound of the sea carrying on the night breeze, Flora mused, stepping back inside her chamber. Or the wind in a chimney. Yes, that would explain it.

Laughing at her foolish fantasies, she turned the key in the lock once more and walked back toward her bed.

"Are you the one?"

The low voice was so near at hand that Flora jumped. So soft that she wondered if she had really heard it at all. "Who is there?"

"Are you the one? I have waited so long. So very long . . ."

Something touched her cheek. Cool, silky, like a brush of ghostly fingers. A sudden draft swirled through the room, and the voice faded to a sigh.

"I am dreaming," Flora said aloud. But the sound of her own voice, hoarse with fear, was real enough. And the stones of the floor were so cold beneath her bare feet that she felt as if she were standing on a block of melting ice.

Flora looked down. This, at least, was neither dream nor illusion. Even in the dimness she could make out a liquid sheen. She stepped toward the bed, reaching for the flint box on her night table, then gasped and recoiled. Something sleek and wet had brushed against her foot. Something alive.

Her hands were shaking with more than cold as she struck the spark and lit her candle. She lifted the taper. The window was tightly closed, the door to the parlor still bolted. She turned back to the center of the room, afraid of what she might see. Candlelight shone like hoar frost on a puddle of water and the thing that lay glistening in its center.

What she had mistaken for the tentacles of a living creature was a six-foot length of thick, green, gelatinous seaweed: an ominous memento—or perhaps a warning—fresh from the cold depths of the Sea Queen's realm.

Chapter Eight

$\mathcal{F}$lora lit the branch of candles on the mantelpiece with shaking hands, but it was bright anger, not fear that made them tremble. *A silly prank to frighten me! Well, I shall not give them the satisfaction of screaming the house down in the middle of the night.*

Had one of the servants done it, as a test of their new mistress? Or was it something more sinister, orchestrated by Gaelle and carried out by one of her pawns? Well, except for that first horror, it hadn't worked.

Flora smiled grimly. There was hardly a schoolmistress alive who hadn't found a frog or a cricket put in her desk by mischievous students. Attempts to intimidate her only put her back up. Of course, they didn't know her here yet.

They will learn, she vowed, *that I am made of sterner stuff!*

But how had the perpetrator entered the room? Both the corridor door and the one to the sitting room had been locked. The keys were still in the keyholes. Flora went to the window and threw the casement open wide. A gust of cool sea air swirled through the room, making her shiver in her thin nightgown. She leaned her head out. Moonlight turned the ancient stones of the sheer wall to pewter and silver. No human could have made the climb. In the morning she would take a better look at the doors and their locks. Perhaps they were defective.

Fetching the poker from the fireplace, Flora tried to lift up the sodden seaweed. Limp frills, each as thick around as her wrist, trailed from supple stems. They writhed and

slithered off the blackened metal as if alive. The gelid
clump spattered on the floor and broke into several pieces.

She was forced to pick the seaweed up in her bare hands.
It was heavier than it looked—cold and wet, with a horrid
texture, like slimy fur. Steeling herself, she carried the first
piece to the open window and cast it out. By the time she
had disposed of them all and mopped the floor with a towel
from the washstand, she was thoroughly wet and shaking
with cold.

She thought of ringing for hot water, but decided against
it. The hour was late, the household abed—except, possibly, for the person who was waiting for the sound of her
bell, before rolling over for a chuckle and a good night's
sleep. Flora wouldn't give the prankster the satisfaction.
Stripping off her damp gown, she changed hastily before
the banked fire and climbed back into bed. Many long
minutes passed before she stopped shivering and fell into
a deep and troubled sleep.

*She was walking along the edge of the sea at sunrise, filling
her pockets with smooth, white shells. Waiting for someone.
The sand was tinted pink and gold with the rising sun, and
the water was frosted green glass. Waves rippled over her
bare feet and legs, warm and soothing.*

*Her dream-self looked around. She had wandered too
far. She really should turn back toward home and safety.
But she couldn't remember where she had come from, or
to where she was going. Just ahead, past that tumble of
fallen granite, someone was singing. A woman's voice,
crooning softly in some forgotten, ancient tongue. Flora
followed it, knowing she had been summoned.*

*Suddenly something wound around her ankles and jerked
her off her feet. It coiled about her body tightly, pulling
her out toward the deeper emerald waters. She fought to
break free of the clinging tendrils of seaweed but could not.*

*The dream changed, as dreams always do. It was not
seaweed holding her, down on the damp sand, but Blaise.
Her heart pounded like the surf. His mouth was ardent and
demanding on hers. Then his lips skimmed her temple,
down the line of her jaw and the soft curve of her throat,
the perfumed cleft between her breasts. Her body warmed*

against the hard planes of his, pliant and yielding. She felt the heat of his skin against hers, and knew that she was naked in his arms.

And she was no longer struggling to be free . . .

Flora was heavy-eyed when she joined her husband and Johanna in a walled garden where breakfast was served in fine weather. As she dressed she had wondered how to conduct herself when their paths crossed again. The best she came up with was to act as if the incident in her dressing room had never happened.

Easier said than done, when the sight of his dark head bent over his cup was enough to remind her of her dream, and set her pulses racing one more. She was glad his niece was there to act as a buffer.

"You must try some of this *krampouezh,*" Johanna said, cutting off a piece of a square buckwheat crêpe, filled with ham, onion, and cheese. "It is splendid."

"I don't have much appetite this morning. Only coffee, if you please."

The servants exchanged glances. Flora supposed they were shaking their heads at the strange habits of the British, mauling their insides with morning coffee rather than chocolate, and drinking tea at all hours.

"You did not sleep well?" Blaise asked, noting with satisfaction the shadows beneath her eyes.

"I never sleep well the first night beneath a new roof," she said, glancing away.

He had spent a wakeful night as well, tossing and turning. He remembered rousing, too soon, from a dream where he had been making love to Flora on the seashore. Even now he could recall the way the flush of rosy light and desire had warmed her fair skin, the way she had felt in his arms. He found himself staring and turned away.

So she, too, had tossed and turned during the night; but he doubted the reasons were the same. The episode last evening had gotten out of hand. He was a man who prided himself on his control, but he had let it slip badly. What he'd intended as a little flirtation, a casual kiss on the cheek to accustom Flora to his touch, had flared into something far more dangerous. It had been a foolish mistake for a man of his experience to make. If he was not careful he would ruin everything.

"Isn't this comfortable?" Johanna said brightly. "Everything has worked out so well. Here we sit, like a happy family, as if we had always gone on this way!"

Flora looked anywhere but at Blaise. The garden was beautiful, and rendered even more pleasant, at least in her view, by Gaelle's absence. Blaise's cousin was an early riser, who spent the morning in prayer, fasting in the château's small chapel. Flora only wished that Blaise were absent as well.

She could not look directly at him. It was like staring into the sun. He dazzled her eyes and blinded her.

Instead she took in her surroundings. The garden was a lovely setting for a meal or an afternoon's diversion, with cushioned benches and settees. Great pots of flowers spilled their rainbow bounty all along the stone balustrade that overlooked a wooded ravine. The air was warm, the breeze soft, and the sun screened by trellised vines just leafing out. Wrought-iron gates stood open on the far side, giving views of a winding walkway. Soft coos came from the nearby dovecote, and somewhere a stream splashed merrily in its hidden, headlong rush to the sea.

And that brought her thoughts circling back to her erotic dream of Blaise. It was his fault, for staging that little scene in her dressing room. Last evening her wrath had been directed at him. Today she was more angry with herself for letting him affect her so, than for the way he'd acted. There would be no repetitions if she had any say in the matter.

She would keep her door locked and avoid any opportunities of being alone with him. Let Gaelle and Johanna act the roles of unwitting chaperons. Surely, in a place so large and rambling, and with so much to see outside the château, she could keep the danger of being private with Blaise to a minimum.

Johanna set down her fork. "Gaelle says we shall all make a pilgrimage to Mont-St. Michel when Claudine and Nicolas come to visit us. Not Nicolas and Uncle Blaise, of course. Will you like that?"

Flora's mouth quirked up at one corner. "Yes, indeed."

She had heard of the famous site, an island at high tide, a pinnacled mount rising like an apparition when the sea rolled back for miles at low tide. If she had to tour the whole of Brittany to keep from having another exchange with Blaise like yesterday's, she told herself, she would cheerfully do so, even in Gaelle's dour company. The older woman evidently lived like a nun, spending hours on her knees in the château's chapel, telling her rosary beads and offering novenas. She rarely left the château at all, so Malin had told them, except to visit various shrines.

Meanwhile, Blaise tried to concentrate on finishing his breakfast. It was difficult when he could smell Flora's light perfume, mingling with the scent of the massed flowers and the windborne tang of the sea, undermining his resolve. She had turned to talk with Johanna, and he surveyed her, unnoticed. The sun struck fiery highlights from her hair and caressed her ivory skin. He remembered exactly how soft it had felt, how sweet her full mouth had tasted. How that spark had blazed in her eyes so suddenly, that he had wondered for a moment if she meant to strike him or return his kiss with equal ardor.

Beyond a doubt—beyond his will—she intrigued him. He couldn't guess completely how she might react to any given situation. Certainly her handling of Gaelle last night had been masterful. It had surprised him as much as it had his cousin. At the time he had felt a pang of pity for her. Gaelle had given her life to raising Hilliard and himself, when she would have been far happier in some cloister, no doubt.

He would have a talk with Gaelle soon, and smooth the way. Once that was out of the way, he would consider how best to approach the problem of Flora.

But Johanna was addressing him. He had lost the thread of their conversation completely. "Is there truly nowhere within the château from which to view the sea?" she was asking. "I do not recall noticing that, as a child. It seems very strange."

"There were once several windows overlooking the bay, but they were bricked over in my grandfather's time. Now there is only the Mermaid's Tower."

Both Flora and Blaise's niece were agog. Both looked up at the roofs and turrets rising into the soft azure sky.

"Which one is that?" they asked simultaneously.

"You can barely see it from here. It is in the oldest section of the château. Part of the original keep that once stood here, according to tradition. It is where my ancestor Yvon, who married a mermaid, so they say, kept his wife locked up so she would not return to the sea."

"How cruel!" Johanna exclaimed. "Was it because he loved her so much?"

"No. Out of greed," Flora said. "According to the legend, he thought his wealth would vanish if she left him."

Blaise shrugged. "That is one version. Perhaps he loved her. Or perhaps he did not want to lose what was his." He fixed Flora with a long look. "There is a family motto engraved over the mantelpiece in the old section: *What is mine, I keep.*"

Johanna craned her neck for a better view of the jumbled walls and slate roofs. "Can we go up into it? Will you take us?"

Blaise seemed disinclined to humor their curiosity. "I do not recommend it. No one has been there in years. It is sure to be the home of bats and spiders."

Flora added her entreaties. "I should very much like to see this Mermaid's Tower."

He hesitated, then gave in and pushed back his chair. "Come along, then." They followed with alacrity as he led them back inside and through a maze of rooms and passages. Flora tried not to stare at everything in amazement.

The château was far larger than it looked from the entrance courtyard. Formal reception rooms gave way to more intimate parlors, most with the furniture in holland covers. One unwieldy object was surely a harp tucked into a corner. She wondered what grandiose plans the builders had had in mind: surely there were not enough people in the village to fill the place!

Blaise again seemed to read her mind. "In other times, the château was filled with large parties of friends and acquaintances for weeks on end. There were balls and feasts and hunts through the interior. I was younger than Johanna when the last house party was held here. They came for a month in the spring to celebrate Easter and to attend the *grand pardon* which was held that year. Forty guests, each with their attendant maids, valets, coachmen, and grooms.''

It seemed hard to imagine now, walking through the empty, echoing corridors. Short staircases went up at odd angles here and there. The passages grew dark and narrow, and the massive walls and beams were black with time and the smoke of centuries. Their route ended abruptly in a small room with unglazed windows.

The shutters were opened wide and wind moaned through the stone arches. Moss grew in the chinks between the massive stones. Blaise stopped beside a low door banded with iron hinges. He took a lamp from a wall niche, and lit it, then held the door open. Circular stairs were barely visible inside the shadowed maw of the tower's base. A breath of clammy air blew past them like a sigh.

Blaise went in but the other two hung back a little. He laughed at them. ''Come, the legend is only a story, made to frighten the servants away. This was no prison for wives, like Bluebeard's castle. It is where the strongbox and arms were kept in days of old. Old Yvon Cheney was said to have kept his treasure in the tower. I will show you how it got its name when we reach the top.''

They followed him inside and up the winding stairs. There was a definite atmosphere of strangeness to the place. An indefinable air of melancholy clung to the dank stones like dust-clotted webs. Flora's skin prickled. She was almost ready to turn back when they suddenly came out into the top of the tower.

They all blinked at the sudden brightness. Blaise blew out the lamp. The room was twenty feet across and rudely furnished with a small table and bench of ancient vintage. Scraps of leaves and a few bird droppings stained the floor, but there was no dust to speak of. Flora had expected the place to be thick with it. As they stood in the center a gull flew in one of the two tall, unglazed windows in a flutter of wings. It took one look at them and sailed off from the sill, scolding and squawking that strangers had invaded its private kingdom.

Flora noticed the pink granite stone sunk into the wall between the windows. A primitive design of a mermaid was carved into its surface. She realized they had passed a similar stone at the tower's base. "So this is how the tower got its name?"

"No, that came later. No one knows the story behind that stone and its twin. It is lost in the mists of time."

Flora drifted to the window. The walls were more than two feet thick. A row of scallop shells was lined up along the sill. She wondered who had placed them there, and when. Perhaps it had been Blaise himself.

Or Eve.

No. She was being foolish. In that case they would have been rimed with salt from the sea air. These were as clean and polished as if they had been placed there only moments before. She turned one over and recoiled. A bit of seaweed, fresh and green, lay coiled against the pink interior. Flora turned her attention to the view.

The window looked out over the château's steeply pitched roofs and the village of Pont du Mor. The granite walls, rising from the dark shingle of the strand, made it seem as if the village had sprouted out of the very bedrock of the land. She could see a church steeple and deep buttresses, a large walled churchyard, and a group of curious ornate stone columns rising in its grassy green center. Although she shaded her eyes, she could not make out any clearer details.

"The parish close and calvary," Blaise explained, from just behind her. "They are structures unique to Brittany, as you will see."

Johanna stood at the other window. "I feel like Rapunzel," she announced, to no one in particular.

Flora joined her, as much to get away from Blaise, whose nearness made her heart pound so erratically, as to see the view. It was breathtaking. The tower was built into bedrock and seemed to rise directly from the sea. To the left, the land curved out sharply into a narrow-necked peninsula. Flora caught a vague glimpse of a slate roof and chimneys beyond a stand of twisted trees. Straight ahead the water stretched out like crumpled blue-green silk, seemingly to infinity. The beauty of it was so keen, she thought, it was almost a physical ache.

Blaise touched her shoulder lightly, sending a jolt of sensation all the way to her toes. She loved the way he smelled, of exotic woods and leafy forests and his own erotic manscent. It took all her effort to appear unaffected.

"There, Flora." His breath stirred the hair at her temple. "If you look to the right, past the strand, you shall see the mermaid that gave the tower its name."

She strained her eyes. "I don't see anything . . ." she began, then caught her breath in surprise.

Out in the bay, just past the line of frothing surf, she spotted a form. A sweep of dark, sinuous tail, long tendrils of hair floating on the waves, and white limbs flashing like pearl just beneath the surface. As she stared in astonishment, it seemed the creature lifted one slender arm and beckoned to her.

"What is it?" she asked huskily.

"No, this way. You are looking in the wrong direction," he told her, turning her head so her gaze was directed right, toward the strand. "There. Do you see that tumble of rocks in the bay beyond the village? How the one is vaguely shaped like a woman, with the tail of a fish?"

"Yes," Johanna cried. "It does look very much like a mermaid! Do you not think so, Flora?"

It was true. The striated granite did have the rough shape of a human form, ending with a curve where the legs would be. But it was nothing compared to the figure Flora had spied out beyond the surf. She blinked against the shimmering light off the water and looked from Blaise to Johanna and back again.

"Did either of you see anything . . . *odd* out in the bay just now?"

They shook their heads, puzzled. "What do you mean?"

She searched again, afraid of what she might see. There was nothing but an endless procession of waves, looking now like ripples in a piece of blue stained glass from their great height. The sea was as empty of golden-haired mermaids as the clear, azure sky was of clouds.

"I thought there was a woman swimming out there, where the water changes from blue to green."

Blaise laughed. "No woman would swim in that sea. There is a fierce riptide there. What you saw was a seal, most likely."

A seal with a woman's white arms and long golden hair floating out behind her? Feeling foolish, Flora didn't say that aloud. It had been nothing but a trick of the eye, caused by sunlight slanting off the waves. An illusion conjured by those twin deceivers, imagination and expectation.

And, of course, the lingering effect of the childish prank someone had played upon her the previous evening. Try as she might, Flora had still not figured out how the seaweed had been put into her bedroom, with both doors locked.

She was glad when Blaise suggested they go, relieved to leave the tower and its melancholy secrets behind. They were all silent as they retraced their steps to the great hall.

"I have business in Pont du Mor this morning," Blaise announced. "Have you any errands to commission?"

Johanna paused as they went through the old door and back into the newer section of the château. "Are we not to accompany you? I want to see the village. You could drop us off at the *enclos paroissial*. You would like that, Flora, would you not?"

The idea of getting away from the château held great appeal for Flora. "I should like very much to see this famous parish close, if it would not be out of your way."

Blaise was reluctant. "It is to the church that I am going, as a matter of fact. I promised Abbé Gastel that I would stop in to discuss the arrangements for the *pardon* and the feast afterward. However, I may be some time with him, and you are both fatigued from yesterday's journey. We can attend Sunday Mass together. It is expected of us."

"I would prefer to go today, not when there is a crowd of churchgoers." Johanna twisted her hands together. "I wish—very much—to visit my mother's grave."

A shadow crossed his face. "Are you sure that is wise?"

Her reply was low. "I cannot rest until I have seen it."

Blaise's features were very still, as if carved from the Breton granite; but Flora saw flickers of raw emotion in his eyes. "Very well," he said abruptly. "I will order the carriage."

"We'll fetch our bonnets and gloves."

"Before we visit the parish close," he said, "it would perhaps be wise to stop by the lace shop where the ladies of Pont du Mor display their handicrafts. It would be a gesture of good will if you were to wear one of the local head coverings when you enter the church, as is our custom here."

"I should like that very much," Johanna said warmly. "I can vaguely remember *maman* in her *coiffe* at Sunday Mass."

Blaise hesitated. Once again Flora was aware of thoughts and emotions flickering like will-o'-the-wisps in his eyes. "I will meet you here in five minutes' time."

When they returned with their bonnets and gloves, Blaise was waiting for them. He produced a small parcel done up in silver tissue. Handing it to his niece, he bowed gravely. "I think this belongs to you, now."

Johanna took it and held it a moment before unwrapping the contents. Inside was a high comb of polished wood and a double curve of delicate lace. The traditional *coiffe* of Pont du Mor. Her fingers tightened on it, crumpling the fragile fabric. She had such a strange look upon her face she seemed to be scowling in anger. Then Flora realized the girl was smiling through her tears.

"Thank you," she breathed, holding it to her cheek. "I could not prize any gift more highly than this small piece of lace."

A muscle worked at the corner of his jaw as Blaise fought to master his emotions. Eve had been wearing it when he'd come back from India, after more than a year's absence. He'd arrived unannounced one warm summer afternoon, while everyone was away at a festival. Everyone but Eve. He'd found her alone in the garden of the ruined cottage nearby. He had courted her there when they were younger.

She had been incredibly beautiful in her gauzy summer dress, with blue ribbons threaded through its bands of scalloped lace, and the delicate coif pinned to her golden hair. It had been his gift to her on her fifteenth birthday.

"I knew you'd come today," she'd said simply. *"I dreamed it."*

And he had swept her up in a passionate kiss without uttering a word. Eve had returned it, wantonly. *"Take me, Blaise. Take me here. Now!"*

Blaise recalled lowering her to the mossy ground, still wrapped in his embrace. That was when the coif had fallen from her hair, snagged by a climbing rose. He remembered nothing else until the sound of the church bells, ringing the Angelus, had recalled them both to their senses. And that was when his world had begun to crumble.

Her ripe mouth still bruised from his kisses, her hands still clinging to his naked shoulders, raked bloody by her nails in the heat of their passion, Eve had ripped his living heart from his breast: she had told him that their urgent lovemaking was her parting gift to him. She had tired of waiting for him and was pledged to marry his brother. The wedding was less than a week away.

Even now he could remember the expression on her face, as the blood drained from his head. He'd rolled off her and covered his eyes with the back of his hand. His heart had seemed to stop in his chest, and he'd been unable to think or move or breathe: *So this is how it feels to die.*

During those few moments of stunned immobility, she had slipped on her moss-stained dress and gone away, leaving him among the ruins of his life. Afterward, when he'd come to his senses, he'd found the lace of her *coiffe* hanging from a thorn. He had folded it and tucked it inside his pocket, like a bandage to staunch the flow of blood from the gaping wound where his heart had been.

Blaise shook off the memories. He watched Johanna hold the coif against her cheek. Parting with it had never entered his head until a few moments ago. This was the right thing to do. He had meant to have it put into his coffin one day and be buried with it; but Eve, Eve had been dead these ten long years. Now it belonged to her daughter.

Flora looked at Blaise in surprise and admiration. She had guessed at something of his struggle. This souvenir of his lost love was more dear to him than gold. To part with it must be wrenching. She was touched that he would give it to his niece. A glint of tears shimmered before her eyes before she could blink them away.

His eyes met hers in sudden awareness. A flush rose up over his cheeks. He felt naked, as if he'd exposed his soul. But he didn't look away. Something flowed between them in that moment. Something as real and as genuine as a touch.

Johanna was unaware of the emotions swirling about her. She held the lace out to Flora. "Will you help me put it on?"

"Of course."

There was a lump in Flora's throat that made talking difficult. The lace smelled of both cedar wood and the light scent she recognized as Blaise's custom-made cologne and shaving soap. She smoothed it almost reverently. Untouched by the shadows of their tragedy, she was nevertheless usurping Eve's place, with her daughter and the man who had loved her to death and beyond. It humbled Flora.

Her fingers were awkward as she entwined the comb at Johanna's crown and arranged the lace to fall gracefully from it. Two pins from her own chignon helped keep it in place. Johanna turned to her uncle and lifted her head with shy grace. Her blue eyes shone with emotion and her cheeks bloomed the same delicate shade as the pink hydrangeas behind her.

"Shall I pass muster? What do you think?"

"I think you look like a lovely Breton maid, about to go for an outing on a fine spring day." The harsh lines of his face softened. "And I think that your parents would have been very proud to see you."

To Flora's surprise, the compliment unnerved Johanna. Her rosy flush deepened to a bright crimson, quite spoiling the effect. At times she forgot how very young Johanna was.

Blaise offered them each an arm and escorted them out to the waiting carriage. The farther they went from the château and its sad memories, the higher Flora's spirits rose. It occurred to her suddenly that she was living the life of which she had always secretly dreamed: travel abroad to intriguing new places. But in her wildest fantasies she had never expected to do so in such luxury. Or, for that matter, under such odd circumstances.

*   *   *

The village of Pont du Mor was small, but enchanting. Blaise pointed out the arching of wave-carved rock near the headland. "The 'Bridge of the Sea,' which gives the place its name. In French we say the feminine *mer* for sea, but in Breton it is called *mor,* a masculine form. The fishermen believe that the sea is an old male monster, far more ancient than the land. And that someday we will anger it enough that it will wash over the land and sweep it all away."

"A pleasant thought," Flora said dryly. "Are all your legends so somber?"

"Not all. There are the *korrigans,* dwarves who will invite you to join their circle dance, and when the dance is ended you will discover a hundred years have passed, while you have not aged a day yourself."

"I shall look for them when I am considerably older, thank you."

Johanna laughed and Flora turned her attention to the scenery. The water sparkled in every shade of blue to their left, and the village fanned out around the small harbor. It was separated from the water by a stone seawall and a wide expanse of sand and shingle.

Most of the houses were of the same gray granite as the château, although a few had been painted or washed with white. An occasional house was trimmed in green or a striking red-orange, like ground paprika spice; but the majority had shutters and doors painted a glossy, intense and brilliant blue that made Flora think of Bristol glass, or polished lapis lazuli. Even the boats in the harbor had hulls or stripes of the same vibrant Breton hue.

"For good luck, and to ward off evil," Blaise told her, when she commented upon it. "Even the lobster pots and fishing nets are blue in this area."

Here and there, an older half-timbered structure with a thatched roof peeked out from between taller buildings. Every one of them faced south, keeping their solid back walls to the cold north winds. The only windows, she noted, were in the front of the houses. The freestanding ones had wide chimneys on either end, while others butted up cheek by jowl against their neighbors. The backs of the houses were completely blind. The north wind must blow cold off the sea, she thought with a shiver.

They drove along the cobbled street, the subject of much interest. No one stared at them directly, but it was apparent that they were under intense scrutiny. Whether it was the return of the Cheneys to the château, or an inspection of herself as the new mistress, Flora could not tell. At least she sensed no hostility.

It did not take them long to reach their destination. The strip of shops along the harbor was small: a confectionary, a cafe, the lacemaker's, and a dry-goods store flanked the village hall on one side; a doctor's surgery, a post office and stationer's, a greengrocer's, a butcher shop, and a fishmonger on the other. Each building was augmented by its own wooden sign, from a plain rectangle with the physician's name, to a green and pink pig complete with curly tail, and by flowers spilling out of wooden tubs, window boxes or hanging planters suspended from the walls.

At the far end of the strand the ground rose up sharply, and the dark walls of the parish church loomed against the soft blue sky. The day was warm and sunny, but from time to time the breeze came in fitful bursts. As the ladies descended from the carriage it almost snatched Johanna's coif away. Flora gathered her skirts to keep them from blowing.

"So much wind for such a fine day," she exclaimed, holding on to her bonnet as well.

Blaise turned to scan the horizon, frowning at the sharp-edged clouds that were piling up in heavy layers. "Not as fair as it seems. Look at the boats pulled up along the strand. The fishermen know when a storm is brewing. They did not even wait to fill their nets."

She hadn't noticed before, but he was right. A few more boats were pulling in, their blue nets only half-filled with silver fish. "How can they tell when the sky is so clear?"

"It is something born in the blood. There is an old saying that seawater flows around a Breton's heart. The sailors know the face of the sea in all its moods, more intimately than they know their own in the mirror."

They went into the lace shop, where Flora purchased not only a coif in the local style, but two collars and a shawl of great beauty. The latter was so expensive, because of its size and workmanship, that she hadn't really considered it;

but Blaise had no sooner seen her interest than he told the shopkeeper to wrap it up.

"I have three shawls already," Flora protested.

"But none like this." He leaned down so that only she could hear. "Consider it in the way of an apology," he said.

"Or a bribe?"

The corners of his mouth turned up. "Perhaps. Time will tell, *chèrie.*" He moved away, leaving her flustered and off stride.

Just as he had planned.

Blaise signaled the coachman to let them down at the church. "St. Mary of the Sea," he said with pride. "Anne of Brittany founded the original chapel. The remains of it are enclosed by the church wall, and the parish close is the finest in all of Finistère."

Johanna stood in silence, fitting her memories of the scene with the actuality. It looked both strange and familiar, and despite enclosing a large area, was much smaller than she'd expected. *Why,* she recalled, staring down at a fat little cherub near the door, *the last time I was here I had to look up at it!*

The parish close was certainly like nothing Flora had ever seen before. Her first impression was of overwhelming grays in every possible shading. A monumental gateway, ornately carved of the gray native stone, led into a walled compound. Straight ahead, behind the secretive walls, was the *cimetière,* the edges of the mossy headstones rounded by weather and time.

On opposite sides, separated from the rest by barriers of wrought iron, were two mausoleums, severe and blackened with age. There was nothing about them to offer comfort to the grieving: she hoped that Johanna's parents were not interred there.

The ossuary stood a little apart with the rectory opposite, so that the area was laid out like a cross. The church stood in the center, relatively small for the grandeur of its surroundings, like a rocky island in a cobbled sea. Its geometric lines were almost obscured by elaborate carvings in the Gothic style, over every door and gable and window.

The stained glass in the narrow, peaked windows looked dark and dull from the outside. Flora didn't relish the thought of going in.

"The *calvaire*," Blaise said, indicating the archway they had just entered. "In the days when few could read, this is how the priests taught the Gospel and stories of the Bible to the parishioners."

Flora tilted her head back and looked up. And up. On the roof of the enormous stone gate and all down the sides were more than a hundred statues carved out of the solid stones. A huge column with a central, many-armed crucifix crowned it. Each of the branching arms was lined with statues of saints and apostles, like a row of crows along a tree limb.

Before they had time to examine them more closely, the door of the rectory opened, and a middle-aged woman came out. Her hair was as white as the towering *coiffe* upon it, quite distinctive from the one worn by the local women.

"That is Madame Rohun, the abbé's widowed sister," Blaise said.

Johanna looked at the woman in awe. "Malin says she not only keeps house for the abbé, but warns him whenever a parishioner is fated to die, whether by illness or accident."

"Quite a convenient talent," Flora said crisply. "And how, exactly, does she accomplish this marvelous feat of prediction?"

"She is one of those who 'sees' the ghost funeral processions. She has only to look at the corpse upon the bier passing by, to know who is going to die. Within three days that person is dead."

Madame Rohun saw them and smiled. Johanna pretended not to notice and moved away, ostensibly to look at one of the scenes carved into the gate. Flora suspected it was to keep out of Madame Rohun's view. She was exasperated.

"I have spoken to Malin several times, about not frightening Johanna with her silly tales, to no avail. Perhaps she would heed it better coming from you."

Blaise was silent a moment. "Madame Rohun's warnings come true," he said simply. "It is a fact."

Flora couldn't hide her astonishment. "You must think me extremely gullible."

He frowned down at her. "I am not making sport of you. It is a common thing in these parts, to have such sightings."

"I cannot believe an educated man such as yourself would give credence to superstition!"

"Superstition is a belief without proof," he said sternly. "Madame Rohun's warnings have proved true time and again. We are an old race, we Bretons. The people are close to God and to their roots. We do not always understand these things, we only know that they exist."

"I do not! I believe in the existence of things I can see and touch and hear."

Blaise cupped her chin in his hand and tilted her face up to his. "If I believed that, I should be very sorry for you. Tell me, Flora, do you do not believe in hope? Or love?" His dark eyes searched hers. "What has happened in your life to make you so cynical, *chèrie*?"

He watched a rosy flush rise to her cheeks, saw the confusion and, yes!—the spark of sensual attraction that flared in the depths of her wonderful blue-green eyes. The temptation to lean down and kiss her was almost overwhelming. If not for the time and the place, his fine resolve would have vanished like morning fog. She clouded his senses, this fiery little English rose.

He rubbed his thumb along her jawline, over her creamy skin. "Tell me, Flora, have you never once known or dreamed that something was going to occur, only to have it come true? Have you never once heard a voice, and turned, only to find yourself alone? Have you never once walked through a place and felt a certain atmosphere, as if there were unseen things swirling all around you?"

She wanted to deny it. Yet she thought of Swarthern Wood on the night of the winter solstice, and St. Piska's Well. Of a time during her childhood when she had stood alone upon a wild moor in the rising wind, and had the sudden sensation that she was surrounded by a host of men in steel and leather armor, battling for their lives. Of last night, when something—or someone—had spoken to her and touched her cheek in the darkness. And only this morning, when she had imagined she'd seen a mermaid swimming through the sapphire waters of the bay.

Blaise was smiling down mockingly, still waiting for her answer. "You see, you *do* believe."

"The abbé will see you now, monsieur," a voice said, breaking the spell. Madame Rohun had joined them.

Blaise made the introductions, and Flora was nonplussed by the way the woman looked her over sharply. For the smallest fraction of an instant she had the feeling that Madame Rohun knew everything there was to know about her, every flaw and fault and sin. Then reason asserted itself. It was only the curiosity of meeting Blaise's wife that made the woman look at her so strangely.

Madame Rohun offered her good wishes on their marriage, and her hopes that Flora would find Pont du Mor to her liking. "I came here as a stranger myself, ten years ago," she said. "Now it is my home. The people are honest and devout. To me, there is no more beautiful place in all of Brittany."

Her French had a foreign sound to it, and Flora realized that Celtic-rooted Breton was the woman's first language. She made appropriate thanks. "I must not keep my husband from his appointment," she added.

"I will meet you back at the carriage," Blaise said.

As he went off with Madame Rohun, Flora heard them speaking together in their native tongue, which reminded her of Welsh songs she had heard.

Johanna joined Flora. "Malin says that Madame Rohun is kind, but that some of the village women can ill-wish a person, and cause them bad luck."

"Malin and I must have a little talk," Flora said between clenched teeth. "She seems to delight in spinning dark tales to frighten both of us."

Johanna laughed. "I cannot imagine you frightened of anything, Flora. Oh, look! There is Noah!" She wandered to the side of the enormous gate. She clapped her hands in delight. "Come and see!"

A relief of the ark was carved into the stone, with the head and torsos of Noah, his family, and many pairs of animals exuberantly rendered above it. Although each figure was done in stylized fashion, the happily grinning faces appeared to be those of different individuals, and Flora wondered if she was looking upon the faces of villagers, dead three hundred years. The animals were more whimsical. It was apparent that the artisans who'd crafted them had never seen giraffes or elephants, but the effect was charming.

She walked with Johanna, discovering more: the miracle of the loaves and fishes; the raising of Lazarus; a full Nativity scene complete with shepherds, wise men, and a host of chubby, goggle-eyed angels. Another showed Abraham preparing to sacrifice Isaac, and beside it David slaying lumpish-looking Goliath. A stone Salome danced for Herod in the panel above, while Adam and Eve, naked as the day God had made them, cowered from an angel with a fiery sword. Near their feet the gloating serpent coiled its lithe body around a huge stone apple, with a large bite missing.

"Which is your favorite?" Johanna asked.

"Noah and his happy little group. And this is certainly my least," Flora added tartly, pointing to the last panel. A grinning skeleton in a king's crown and peasant's sabots leered down at them. He carried a banner with the legend: *High or low, I shall claim you all.* Flora shuddered with distaste. "Not a pleasant reminder of one's mortality."

While she contemplated it, Johanna drifted away once more. Flora stayed back as the girl roamed up and down the rows of slanted tombstones, ending up at one of the mausoleums.

Shall I go to her, or will I be intruding? she wondered. She waited for some sign, while Johanna scanned the inscriptions. Her face looked more puzzled than sad. Finally she looked up. "She is not here. Or, at least, her name is not."

"Look to the monument with the *morgan* on it," a masculine voice said from behind them.

Flora turned. A compact, athletic man of about her own age came strolling through the close. He doffed his hat to reveal thick, curling brown hair and smiling eyes that were neither gray nor brown. He bowed to her, but addressed his remarks to her companion.

"Forgive me, Mademoiselle Cheney, if I presume upon old acquaintance. You will not remember me, but I used to feed you barley-sugar candy, and bring you scallop shells when you were last at the château.''

Johanna's eyes widened. "Loïc?" she asked uncertainly. "Is it you?"

"At your service. And yours, Madame Cheney, as well." He swept them a bow. "I recognized the carriage as I left the rectory, and guessed at your identity; however, I should have recognized Mademoiselle anywhere, even after all these years."

The girl's cheeks were pink with surprise and pleasure. "Because I resemble my mother?"

"No. Because you resemble a little girl for whom I had a certain fondness." He tilted his head. "But you do have the look of your mother. I remember her well."

"She is not here," Johanna said. "My father's body was not recovered, but I always understood that *maman* was buried in the churchyard of the parish close."

"Those claimed by the sea are there," he said gently. He indicated the small area on the far side of the mausoleum, railed off by iron pickets. "A Cheney tradition."

Flora examined it. It was not a conventional monument like the others, but a small standing stone, like one of the menhirs that Johanna had called the Druid Stones. The dark granite was liberally streaked with white and rose in a curious, swirling pattern.

Johanna eyed it somberly. "Why are they not with the others?"

"A family custom. It is said that the first Yvon buried his mermaid wife here when she died, and had her likeness put upon it. It is called the Morgan Stone."

Flora stepped closer to examine it. A chill ran up her back. A small picture had been incised into the stone. A woman's head and shoulders rose gracefully above a line of curling wave. She had seen that beautiful, remote face before, on the mermaid lamps at Blaise's town house. Yes, there was that same necklace carved in low relief, an egg-shaped talisman hanging from a cleverly wrought chain.

She wondered why he'd had the design copied for his home in Paris. Was it Blaise's way of thumbing his nose at fate? Or perhaps, given his superstitious background, bowing to the inevitable?

Brass plaques were fixed to the lower portion of the rock, and her eyes scanned the names below. So many of them! Far too many to be buried here beneath this small memorial. Flora wondered how many had vanished beneath the crashing blue waves, never to be seen again.

"There," Johanna said softly.

Her fingers reached out to trace her mother's name. Her face looked serious and mature. As if she were reaching across time to caress her mother's cheek.

"You may rest now, *maman*," she murmured so that only Flora could hear. "I am home."

A wind blew through the *cimetière*, light and warm and filled with the scent of the sea. Flora drew her shawl around herself more tightly.

After a moment Johanna turned back to them, her eyes overbright with unshed tears; but her voice was steady when she spoke. "Flora is not familiar with the parish close, and I do not recall much of the church. Perhaps you would be so good as to be our guide, Loic? That is, if you do not have other errands?"

"I am at your disposal." His smile was equally warm as it beamed over each of them in turn. "In fact, you may find it difficult to be rid of me."

A dimple appeared at the corner of his mouth, making him even more attractive. "I am writing up my research on the *enclos paroissiaux* and the *grands pardons* of Brittany; but while the details I've learned excite me, I tend to get carried away. I will surely bore you to tears, in which case you may feel free to send me packing."

Despite his modesty, he proved an entertaining guide, full of local lore and gentle humor. He showed them the lovely fountain that sparkled in the grassy center of the close. "It comes from a well that is said to have curative powers against leprosy and plague. This *enclos paroissial* was built by the devout of Pont du Mor, in hopes of escaping a terrible epidemic of bubonic fever that devastated the countryside. You may wish to throw a coin into that opening beside the fountain."

"To prevent the plague?" Johanna laughed.

"No. To make a wish. The ancient Celts believed that all the wells in the world were connected beneath the earth,

by subterranean rivers. A wish made here would flow
through the underground chambers to every magic well in
existence, multiplying its power.''

Flora looked down the deep cistern beside the fountain,
and saw nothing but black water and sunlight dancing off
it in the shape of a golden bow. It reminded her of the
students' escapade at St. Piska's Well on Midwinter's Eve,
and how she'd lost her gold pin in Swarthern Wood.

It struck her suddenly that she had made her own wish
that night, not at the well, but when she was safely back
in her own cold bed at the academy. Oddly enough, it had
still come true, in a manner of speaking, although not at all
in the way she'd intended.

Johanna took a coin from her reticule and tossed it in.
She closed her eyes and lifted her face up to the sky for a
few seconds. "I hope it works," she said after a moment.

"Do not tell your wish," Loic cautioned her, "or it will
not come true.''

He led them out the triumphal gate, and in through the
main doors of the church. The interior of Notre Dame du
Mor was astonishing, all carved and gilded wood, winking
candles in polished brass holders, and brilliant stained glass.
The only gray to be seen was in the stones that paved the
floor; but they were transmuted into opaque jewels by the
sunshine pouring through the colorful panes.

Flora had not been in a church like this since her father's
funeral, of which she had only vague memories. It fascinated her. Since she had been baptized in her father's faith,
she supposed it had been in a similar church. She had not
set foot in one since she'd gone to live with her grandfather.
The difference in religion had been one of his strongest
objections to her parents' marriage. The faint trace of in-
cense in the air, the sense of peace, of . . . *presence* was the
only word that came to mind—were somehow familiar. It
was the same thing she had felt in Westminster and St.
Paul's. And in the oak grove in Hawthorne Village, where
druids were said to have worshiped.

Johanna knelt at a *prie-dieu* before the altar to offer up
a prayer, while Flora and Loic continued their tour of the
interior. He led her to a small grotto built into a side altar.
Light from the tall windows and the glowing candles spar-

kled back from mica chips in the pink granite boulders forming the artificial cave. The mortar between the stones was crusted with tiny seashells of every description.

"Here," Loic said, "is the symbolic center of Pont du Mor's famous *pardon*."

Flora followed his gesture and saw a marble niche, designed to look like a giant opened cockle shell, which was set into the wall halfway up. From there, the molded features of the village's patron saint gazed calmly down at her. It was an exquisite work of art, almost three feet tall.

The statue was not that of a saintly matron draped in flowing robes, such as Flora had seen in paintings. It was like an exquisite doll, depicting a young and beautiful woman, fabulously dressed in the style of a medieval queen. The white silk gown was richly encrusted with pearls and a web of gold beadwork, and the blue velvet cloak studded with the same winking jewels that adorned the ornate necklace and golden diadem. From beneath the coronet fell a replica of the lace butterfly *coiffe*, distinctive to the women of Pont du Mor.

"How exquisite! And surely worth a king's ransom."

"Yes. For three hundred years she has stood thus, and even during the worst of the uprisings over time, not so much as one thread of her gown has sustained any harm."

"She is glorious," Flora said in wonder.

"I love this church above any I have ever seen," Loic added, almost to himself. "The contrast of the colors, the intricate carvings and the statues against the dull stone, are like a promise of heaven in a cold, dark world."

Caught up in the same enchantment, Flora spoke without thinking. "I quite horrified my grandfather once, by stating that I felt the Reformation had thrown out a little too much of the early church's pageantry. I was forced to spend the next week in my room, writing out tedious sermons in my best copperplate."

Loic eyed her with surprise. "Surely a heavy punishment for so insignificant a comment; but I take it that your grandfather is minister in the Protestant faith?"

A jolt of anxiety shot through Flora. The peace of the church had affected her, but still! How *could* she have been so indiscreet as to bring up her past? "Only a man with little tolerance for any ideas that differ from his.''

She moved deeper into the grotto, as much to see the statue of the church's namesake, as to remove herself from a dangerous conversation. St. Mary of the Sea stood in a gilded chariot decorated with seashells, drawn by a pair of carved crabs so real looking that Flora almost expected them to wave their huge claws in the air. She remembered a similar one in the painted medallion on the ceiling in Blaise's bedroom.

"I have never seen the Virgin Mary in a chariot before. It is unusual, is it not?''

Loic laughed. ''Highly! Perhaps that is one of the reasons your grandfather objected so strongly to your comment. In ancient times, the monks and priests found it easier to convert the local gods and goddesses into Christian saints, than to convert the Bretons directly. They would decide which saint in the church calendar bore the greatest resemblance to the local deity, and effect a name change.''

"Like Lugh and Saint Michael, or Saint Brigit and the Bridey wells.''

"Exactly.'' He smiled down at her. ''I had heard you were an educated woman. How my sister will enjoy your company, Madame Cheney. She is eager to meet you,'' he added before going on.

"Our patron saint is an interesting mixture of Christianity and our own local beliefs. According to Breton legend, that is the chariot of the Sea Queen, who lives in caverns of pearl in the ocean off Brittany's coast. A combination of Mary, mother of Jesus, as Queen of the Sea, with the queen of the *mari morgans*.''

"And she is the focus of Pont du Mor's *grand pardon*?''

"Yes. On the second day of the *grand pardon*,'' he explained, ''she will be paraded through the village and then carried all the way up to the *kastel*. By tradition the master of the *kastel* will make a donation in the saint's name for repair and upkeep of the church, and another to the fund to provide for the orphans and widows of our fishermen who are lost at sea. I believe the custom actually began as a way to invoke the saint's protection for the Château Morgaine and its inhabitants—to guard them from the Sea Queen's wrath.''

"Is that in your book, Loic?"

They both turned at Johanna's voice. Neither had noticed her enter the grotto with Blaise at her side. Her husband did not look pleased that Flora had gone off alone with the other man, and he and Loic exchanged curt greetings.

Loic answered Johanna's question, looking uncomfortable. "It is not exactly a book in the sense you mean. Only for my own edification. A history of the *pardons*."

"Perhaps you will let us read it one day," Flora said.

"Yes," Johanna echoed. "I should like that very much."

Loic blushed and stammered a reply. "It is a small effort only. Nothing to compare with your own respected publications, Monsieur Cheney."

"The carriage is here," Blaise interrupted. "We must get back to the château. Good day, Kersaudy. My respects to your sister, and we hope to call upon her soon."

With an abrupt nod for the other man, Blaise took Flora and his niece by their elbows and guided them out of the grotto. Loic followed a few feet behind. Outside he stopped to speak with Johanna, while the other two went ahead.

Flora waited until they were out of earshot to express her displeasure. "That was rude of you in the extreme."

Blaise's dark brows came together. "I do not appreciate the impertinence of handsome young men who take my wife off for quiet tête-à-têtes in secluded corners. He will not make the same mistake twice."

"Now you are being ridiculous!"

Blaise glowered down at her. He had not been prepared for the spike of jealousy that had stabbed him at seeing Flora so rapt with Loic Kersaudy's conversation. The urge to throttle the other man had been sudden, violent, and out of all proportion to the circumstances. He knew that. But it had come over him like a red rage. An emotion so primitive and raw it had shocked even him.

Blaise found it hard to believe that this woman, a total stranger a few months earlier, had assumed such ascendancy in his thoughts. What had begun as a necessary evil had turned into an intriguing situation—and was rapidly becoming an obsession.

He tried to rationalize it away. Really, it was simple. He was a man who guarded his possessions. Flora was his. She belonged to him.

He made the mistake of saying as much.

"For a period of two years, until our contract is fulfilled," she hissed beneath her breath. "And only in a limited capacity. I am surprised I should have to remind you of this again so close upon the heels of yesterday's . . . *conversation*."

He waited to hand her up into the carriage. His mouth was grim, his eyes hot. "I remember everything you said to me quite clearly, madame. I only hope that you remember *my* words as well!"

How could she forget them? They had echoed in her dreams all night. Erotic, sensual. So tantalizing that she had awakened toward morning with her body shuddering beneath waves of pleasure. Even now she blushed to think of it.

She slanted a sideways look at him from under her lashes. "I do recall you making a threat of sorts."

His grip tightened on her wrist as he lifted her hand. He touched his mouth to the soft skin exposed between her sleeve and glove. "It was not a threat, *ma fleur,* but a promise."

The gesture had not been one of a lover, but of a seducer. A conqueror. White with anger, Flora still could not quench the wave of heat, the dark flare of desire that swept over her. She tried to snatch her hand back. "You flatter yourself. It will not come to pass. I am immune to your practiced charms."

Laughing, he released her. He had seen that telltale flush rise up from the top of her low bodice to mantle her throat and face. "You cannot fool me, Flora. As I said before: you are a woman of passion, and those passions will not be denied."

He toyed with a lock of her hair that had escaped her bonnet, winding it around his strong, brown finger. "Perhaps we should not fight it. Ah, Flora, I could give you pleasures such as you have never imagined."

He heard her small gasp, saw the quick rise and fall of her breasts, and went on: "But I shall not go back upon my word. It will be difficult. Because, you see, I do want you, Flora. But I will not press you. I will wait until *you* are ready to admit your needs. Until it is *you* who comes to me.''

"Hell will freeze over first!"

"Do you know, I have always thought of the underworld as a place of cold and ice, rather than heat and flame. So it has already come to pass, *ma fleur*.'' His smile widened and dark lights burned in the depths of his eyes. "Accept the inevitable!''

Since Johanna joined them at that moment, they had to drop the subject. While Flora fumed, Blaise helped his niece into the carriage, climbed up after them, and signaled the driver to move on.

Johanna waved to Loïc Kersaudy as they drove off. Her cheeks were rosy and her eyes sparkling. The fresh sea air must be doing her good already, Flora thought. But the girl's first words were about Kersaudy.

"How kind and funny he is," she said wonderingly. "I remember him as being terribly studious and quiet, and thought he was so much older than myself. Why, he must be very near in age to you, Flora!''

"Yes, I believe not a year separates us.''

Blaise folded his arms across his broad chest. "You must have had quite an extensive talk, to have exchanged so much information.''

Flora ignored him, at least outwardly. Inside, she was still shaken by her response to his words. The deep timbre of his voice as he spoke them. His careless kiss upon her wrist. If such minor incidents could set her pulse hammering and throw her thoughts into total confusion, what could a more determined seduction do to her?

She could not help glancing at his mouth, remembering how those firm lips had felt against her own when he had kissed her yesterday. Remembering how her blood had heated as he held her crushed against his chest. The urge she had to throw her arms around his neck and lose herself in wild, sensual surrender to their mutual need. Even now, the recollection flustered her.

From the corner of her eye she caught a flash of his teeth in a sardonic smile. Did he have the power to read her very thoughts? Turning her head, she looked out the open window and hoped the breeze would cool her flushed cheeks. *If he thinks he has bought my services as a wife in more than name only, he will have to be made to see his great error!*

Meanwhile, she would have to fight her growing attraction to him, ward off the loneliness and sense of isolation that made her vulnerable. If only she had the willpower to see it through! But, God help her, she was lonely. And her body ached for him to make love to her.

It was going to be a long two years.

Gaelle was standing at the window in the sitting room when Flora went up to her chamber. She turned around. "I am told that you went up in the Mermaid's Tower today." Her voice was agitated. "That was most unwise. You must not do so again."

Flora's eyebrows shot up. "Did you think me trespassing? I was with my husband."

"He would not have gone up without your insisting upon it."

"I fail to see why this has so upset you."

The older woman sent her a piercing glance. "You are tempting fate. Blaise's mother fell to her death from one of the windows, into the sea below."

The blood drained from Flora's face. "Dear God! Had I known, I would never have asked him to take us there. It must have been painful for him."

"He does not know. We told him she fell from the headland. It was better that way."

"Do you mean . . ." Flora stuttered to a stop. The windows in the tower were too high, their sills too deep to fall out of easily. One would have to lean far, far over the edge.

Or jump.

"You are saying her death was not an accident?"

Gaelle twined her hands as if in prayer. "Call it what you will. The *mari morgans* called to her, and she could not resist their song. What will you do, I wonder, when you hear it?"

Anger flashed in Flora's eyes. "I do not frighten so easily, madame, if that is your intention."

"Ah, no." A gleam that might be malice was hidden by the older woman's hooded lids. "Make no mistake, I mean only to warn you. For you are a Cheney, too, now."

"First Malin, and now you, madame. Let me remind you both that I am a Cheney only by marriage."

"The curse follows the name, not merely the blood." She slanted an oblique look Flora's way. "And the child you bear in your womb will inherit both."

Flora was aghast. "You seem to be suffering under a misapprehension. I am not with child."

The hazel eyes narrowed and regarded her steadily. This time the malice was definite. "No? Then I cannot think why Blaise would marry you. I expected him to look high for a wife. He is a wealthy man, master of this fine château. And who are you? A mere nobody. I could not have been more astounded had he brought home a . . . *salope* from the Paris gutters!"

The attack was vicious and unexpected. The blood left Flora's face, then came flooding back in a rush of heat. The masks were off now, and she knew her enemy. Her initial astonishment turned to fierce anger. *Jealous old witch!* Her reply came swift and sharp as an arrow, with the same intention to wound.

"The answer must be obvious: perhaps, Madame Morceau, it is because he loves me."

She was astonished at how easily the lie came to her lips. At how convincingly she had uttered it. The effect was the same as if she'd struck the other woman. Gaëlle Morceau's face went deathly pale, and she stumbled back a step. Gasping for breath, she turned and made her way to the door.

But she gathered her wits and paused for a parting shot from the threshold. "There is only one woman whom Blaise has ever loved—and she is dead!"

The door swung to behind her.

"Horrid, odious woman!" Flora muttered beneath her breath.

"Only frightened, I think," Blaise said from somewhere behind her.

She jumped. He stood in the doorway to the master's chamber. "I did not hear you come in," she said quickly, wondering how much he had overheard.

"My aunt is set in her ways and afraid of losing her position as mistress of the château," he said soothingly. "She will come about." He gave her one of his intimate smiles, the kind that melted her bones. "You handled the situation well."

Flora backed up. His smile grew. "I . . . I didn't really know what to say. It was difficult to lie to her."

"Really?" He leaned against the jamb, his lips curved cynically. "You almost had me quite convinced, myself. You lie remarkably well. A quality a man does not usually praise in his wife."

"Are you saying you have never bent the truth? You lied to me at Hawthorne, when you said there was no one to look after Johanna. I cannot understand why you did not bring her to Madame Morceau to raise in the first place."

He took a turn about the room, touching articles restlessly as he passed.

"My aunt divides her time between her duties to the château and her religious affairs. She is quite devout, and does not go much into company. Certainly she could not properly oversee Johanna's debut and accompany her to balls and parties in Paris."

"No. But Claudine could."

He stopped his wandering and set down the ivory snuffbox he'd been examining. "Claudine and Nicolas might be living in the West Indies by the end of the year."

This was news to Flora. She felt a pang of dismay. "Claudine has said nothing to me of this."

Blaise looked up then, frowning. "She does not know. It is only a possibility, you understand. You will not speak of it with her, if you please."

"But . . . !" She was still flabbergasted. "The West Indies? Surely that is something Nicolas should discuss with her!"

Blaise made an impatient gesture. "Why upset her over what might not come to pass? Frankly, I do not think it will happen. They spent six of the last ten years in Algiers, and the hot weather does not agree with either of them. Claudine had a miscarriage shortly after their arrival, and Nicolas was quite ill at one time with a tropical fever. But it was said to me in confidence. I spoke out of turn, and you must forget that I have mentioned it.''

Flora was still incensed. "This puts me in a terrible position. It isn't right. Men! If I ruled the world, it would be illegal for a husband to keep such secrets from his wife.''

He laughed aloud. "Then, *chèrie,* the prisons would be as full as they could hold. All husbands have secrets from their wives.'' He eyed her shrewdly. "Just as I would suppose all wives have secrets of their own.''

Flora felt herself blushing. "You have a suspicious nature, sir. I prefer to think more highly of my fellow creatures.''

"Do you?'' Again that strange look from Blaise, as if he saw through her like crystal.

Her blush deepened. The lies came so easily out of her mouth now, like honey dripping from the comb.

She sighed. "I am in over my head. I thought it would be less difficult to keep up a pretense here than in Paris, but it seems that it will prove the opposite.''

"Just follow my lead.'' Too late, she realized that he was at her side. Blaise tilted her chin up with his finger. Before she could pull away, his lips came down upon hers. They were warm, ardent, and robbed her of thought. He lifted his head. "Was that so very bad, *chèrie*?''

"N-no. Yes!''

But it was too late. He was kissing her again. This time his arms came around her, pressing her against his chest. She was aware of her heart racing, the steady beat of his own, the metal edge of his coat button pressing against her breast. Then she was aware of nothing but him.

His embrace was a flame around her, enveloping her senses. She thought she heard him breathe her name against her mouth, before claiming her lips again. This kiss was altogether different from the first, hungry and demanding.

Blaise was wild with desire for her. It surged through him like wildfire, sweeping away everything else. All his fine resolve vanished when their lips met in that second kiss. He couldn't wait a moment longer. His mouth conquered hers and he took the kiss deeper. Her lips parted in a small sigh that sent his blood flaming through his veins. He burned for her.

She felt an answering need, a pull of passion deep inside her body, rising through her like a fiery tide. And with it came panic. His thumb traced an arc of flame down her throat from ear to collarbone. His warm breath tingled against her ear. Flora mustered all her will to push him away. "Stop it!"

"Why, Flora?" he asked huskily. "Because you do not like it when I touch you? Or because you do?"

Her breasts rose and fell with her suddenly ragged breathing. Again he reached out to run the back of his fingers down the side of her jaw, along the soft curve of her neck and down to the front of her throat. His face was mere inches away, his mouth hovering close to hers. He trailed his index finger down her bodice to the tip of her breast, where her nipple stood erect beneath the silk. His nail circled it erotically. She was riveted to the floor. Waves of heat and cold alternated through her body as she was shaken by the winds of spiraling desire.

His hands cupped her breasts, weighing their supple heaviness against his palms. She could neither move nor breathe as he lowered his mouth to hers in a bruising kiss. While her brain was still reeling with sensation, he pulled abruptly away and looked down at her face. She had never seen him look more intense, more brutally handsome.

His hands slid down to her waist, then around to her back, pulling her tight against his broad chest. Twining his fingers in her hair, he tipped her head back. Desire burned in his eyes and lit an answering flame within her. "Let us end this mockery, Flora. Here and now!"

Then his lips were on hers again, heated and commanding. She could not resist him. She was lost. With a tiny moan of frenzied surrender, she melted against him. Her mouth opened to him and his tongue darted in. She had never been kissed deeply, intimately before. Her blood sang in her veins like a chorus of a thousand tiny silver bells.

But the ringing came from behind Blaise. They both became aware of it at the same moment. As he released her and stepped back she looked past his shoulder. Gaelle Morceau stood just inside the room, her face as white as her starched collar. She held the dangling silver chatelaine in her outstretched hand. It was the tumble of the chain and its myriad keys that had made the tinkly chimes.

"Pardon me," she said hoarsely. "I did not know you were here, Blaise, or I should not have intruded." She placed the keys on one of the side tables for the new mistress, and marched back out. The door closed with a slight click.

Blaise cursed softly beneath his breath. The moment was gone. Flora had taken the opportunity to change her mind. She'd put the distance of the room between them. Her body, so soft and pliant in his arms, was rigid with tension.

She held both hands to her burning cheeks. Passion had been replaced by anger and shame. What had she been thinking, to let him addle her so? Fool, fool, *fool*! She would not be used to slake his passions, and then cast aside.

Lifting her chin, she stared at him defiantly. "There are some women who let men take liberties with them in return for payment—perhaps you are in the habit of frequenting them: they are called whores. I am not one of them."

His face darkened, his voice flayed like a whip. "You were not so unwilling to receive my advances only minutes ago. And, may I remind you, in case you forget, that you are my wife before the law."

"And may I remind *you* that what we pledged was not a true marriage. I am as much your servant as Malin, or the man who grooms your horses." She lifted her head defiantly. "We have a bargain, you and I, sir. And this is not a part of it. If you try again to break it, I shall consider it null and void, and leave this place immediately!"

"A bargain I heartily regret, *ma fleur*! One day, Flora—I swear by all the gods—I shall make you regret it, too. Till then, I give you my word as a Cheney that I will not touch you until you give me your leave."

Flora bit her lower lip. She had never seen him so intense, so wildly out of control.

Blaise faced her, jaw squared and eyes dark with the same hunger that thrummed in her veins. All his cool sophistication had dissolved in the heat of his emotions, leaving his breathing ragged and his pulse throbbing at his temple. "You need not lock your door to me. I will not force myself upon you. And one day, sooner than you think, you will come willingly to me . . . and then, we shall finish this!''

He strode out, leaving her alone in the room. Flora stood in the center of the floor, burning with anger, and shaking with need.

Chapter Nine

The evening breeze ruffled Blaise's hair as he paced the west terrace. Inside Flora was seated at the pianoforte, playing something bright and restless that echoed his internal chaos.

He stopped at the far end and leaned on the low wall. Below it the ground sloped down to a deep, wooded ravine, lost in blackness. Earlier, high winds and lashing rain had scoured the sky clean. A splash of stars burned clear and white in the fresh-washed heavens, illuminating the sharp angles and contours of the château.

He ground his teeth. His shoulder ached abominably from the weather, the scar was pulling, and he was furious with himself. He had acted like a fool. He, who took such pride in his self-control. Blundering like a schoolboy trying to snatch a kiss from a chambermaid on the back stairs. But, given the same circumstances, he could not guarantee he would not react in just the same manner again.

The kiss yesterday had been a mistake; the episode earlier today had been a disaster. If he wasn't careful he would ruin everything, and his fine plans would collapse about them like a house of cards.

He slammed his fist against his palm. The jolt to his still-healing shoulder sent a ragged blade of pain lancing down his arm. Why the devil had he acted so rashly? And why hadn't he chosen some plain little dormouse of a woman to act the role of wife? Far better if he had approached someone all meek and earnest and biddable, so nunlike in appearance as to make herself practically invisible. Not a passionate woman like Flora, with her lovely face, her flashing eyes and tempting lips . . .

"Have you and Flora quarreled?"

He spun around and saw Johanna standing at the terrace doors. She came across the flagged terrace to his side.

"Go back inside. It's damp," he said. "You'll catch a chill."

"I don't care." She lifted her face anxiously in the starlight. "Have you quarreled? Neither you nor Flora spoke directly to one another at dinner tonight. Gaelle remarked upon it. I thought perhaps . . ."

He touched her cheek. "This has nothing to do with you, child. Do not be overly concerned. Now go inside before the damp settles in your lungs."

Johanna twisted her hands together. "I had so hoped everything would work out between you. I was sure it would, once you got to know one another. And we would come to the château, and everything would be as right as rain."

"And so it shall. Do not be overly concerned. Flora and I are both strong-willed. It is inevitable that we clash from time to time. But it will all work out in the end."

She rose up on tiptoe and kissed him on the cheek. "You are the best of all possible uncles." Then, as if surprised by her own daring, she fled back to the drawing room.

Blaise smiled after her. She was charming. He wondered what Hilliard . . . what *Eve* . . . would think if they could see her now. It was a difficult time for Johanna: one day a girl, the next a woman. He hoped life would be kinder to her in the future than he had been in the past. A few months ago he was scarcely aware of her existence. He had cheated them both of the relationship that should have been theirs, and he was sorry for it now.

But there were times—and this was one of them—that he wished he'd never left Egypt. He was in a damnable coil. There were three choices left to him regarding Flora. He could cut his losses, admit that he had failed, and rid himself of his reluctant bride. No doubt that would be her preference at the moment. But he wouldn't . . . *couldn't* take that route. So his choices were really narrowed down to two: he could bide his time a while longer and hope to smooth matters out before it was too late—or he could force them along entirely.

All he had to do was decide which of them was the least dangerous.

After a moment he pushed himself away from the balustrade. He had made his decision.

Flora shut the piano and went to pour out evening tea. She and Johanna had brought the English custom with them to the château, and for once Gaelle had no objections. In fact, she had gone out of her way to be pleasant, after their scene earlier in the day.

Gaelle set aside her embroidery. "Will Blaise be joining us?"

"I don't know. He is still out on the terrace, brooding."

His cousin lowered her voice so that Johanna, reading on the other side of the room, would not hear. "This is a painful day for him. For both of us. It is the anniversary of his mother's death."

Flora frowned. "You said she leapt to her death. Intentionally, if I understood correctly. She must have been frightfully unhappy to take such a desperate measure."

"How could she be?" Gaelle said with a sting of bitterness. "She had everything any woman could want! A handsome, virile husband, two fine sons, great wealth and position in society."

"A woman does not dash herself upon the rocks for no reason."

"Some women carry the seeds of their own unhappiness with them. They are never content with what they have. They always want more."

Her fingers toyed with the jeweled cross upon her breast. "Anne was a restless, selfish creature, caring more for herself than for those she purported to love! Everything she wanted fell into her hand like a ripe plum, but still she was not satisfied. Our family, too, claims descent from Yvon Cheney several generations back. There is a dark streak that runs in the Cheney blood, and leads to destruction. Perhaps that is the true curse upon us all."

Flora glanced out the open windows. Blaise was silhouetted against the starry sky. He must have been very young
at the time. Gaelle followed her gaze.

"He is the last of his line. The last Cheney male. After
him, the name dies out." She turned back to Flora. "I pray
for your husband unceasingly, that he may make his peace
with God and find happiness. I had the raising of him after
Anne's death. He is . . . is like a son to me," she said halt-
ingly as she struggled with her emotions.

"I want only what is best for him. That is why I was so
upset to learn of your marriage. At first I was sure some
fortune hunter had sunk her claws into him, and that only
grief could come to him. I see now that I was too hasty."

Flora was surprised. She didn't think Gaelle liked her
any better than she had initially. But something *had* altered.
"May I ask why?"

The older woman took the cup of tea Flora poured for
her, but did not meet her eyes. "A woman can sometimes
change a man. I see that in Blaise. His moods are not so
black as they were the last time he came to the château.
Perhaps you will save him from meeting the same fate as
his mother."

The cup rattled against the saucer in Flora's hand. "I
cannot believe he would do such a thing!"

"Ah," Gaelle murmured, regarding her with an unfath-
omable look. "But you see, I thought the same of Anne."

*Flora was dreaming. She knew it, but she couldn't wake
herself. Once again she was back in that cold marble corridor. Once again the black door loomed at the other end.
She longed to know what was beyond it. Almost as much
as she feared to know. Almost, but not quite.*

*Reaching down for the ring of keys she wore, she real-
ized there was only one. Silvery metal, with a handle
shaped like a mermaid. She reached the door and put the
key inside the lock. It turned! The door swung inward.
It was dark. Someone was singing. A woman. Her voice
was so beautiful Flora could have wept. It lured her on,
into the darkness. She stepped over the threshold onto the
black marble of the floor beyond. It crumbled away be-*

neath her feet. She was falling. Falling onto the jagged rocks below . . .

Flora awakened before dawn in a cold sweat. The dream again! But as she tried to get out of bed, she realized it was more than the dream affecting her. The room spun dizzily as she tried to sit up. Her empty stomach rebelled.

She barely managed to ring for Jeanette before falling back against the pillow. She could feel her heart racing, but so weakly it was just a flutter of bird wings in her chest. Chills wracked her body.

The maid came hurrying in and gasped to find her mistress white-lipped and filmed with sweat. "La! Not you also, madame! The mademoiselle, she was taken ill this morning, just before dawn."

"Johanna?" Flora struggled to sit up. "How . . . is she?"

"Not so ill as you, madame." Bringing her a cold cloth for her head and a basin in case she became ill, Jeanette went for aid.

Blaise came, took one look at Flora's pallid face and glittering eyes, and sent for the doctor. "Tell him to come immediately."

Flora was too sick to argue. Every time she opened her eyes the room spun like a carousel. Her fingers clutched the quilt as if it would keep her from spinning off into space.

"Is she increasing?" Gaelle asked Blaise in an undertone. "I thought . . . She swore she was not with child."

Blaise frowned her to silence as Jeanette came back into the room. "It is early days yet."

I am not with child, Flora tried to say, but her mouth and throat were so dry her tongue seemed to cleave to them. As she opened her eyes the room seemed to give another sickening lurch. She closed them at once, and quickly lost interest in everything but holding on to the quilt for dear life.

The next time she opened them Gaelle was at her bedside, accompanied by a swarthy man with liquid black eyes and a gentle manner. The dizziness was gone, leaving her weak and wan.

"I do not believe it to be infectious," the man said after checking her pulse and pupils and looking down her throat. "Tainted food is the most likely culprit. Can you recall anything that you and the young mademoiselle ate that might be responsible?"

Gaelle pursed her lips. "There was a clear soup and *fruits de mer* for a first course, followed by *poulet au cidre,* but we all partook of it. No one else in the household was taken ill, Monsieur Mathau."

Flora tried to remember. Her tongue was as thick as the fog in her brain. "We had refreshments at the inn in Pont du Mor yesterday afternoon: *moules marinières,* a platter of *andouilles* and *boudins noirs,* served with cheese and cold asparagus."

He cocked his head like a curious blackbird. "A typical luncheon, then. Nothing else? With mushrooms, perhaps?"

"No, monsieur."

"Well, then. I myself ate the same mussels in white wine sauce there yesterday, with no ill effects. Perhaps the sausages had gone bad. I shall inquire of the innkeeper if any of his guests were also stricken."

He dosed Flora with a foul-tasting elixir, ordered a diet of plain food and bed rest, and promised to visit again the following morning. The medicine sent Flora back to sleep. *At least I don't have to talk to Blaise,* she thought, as she went sinking down into a deep and welcome warmth. But she had forgotten about Johanna. Struggling against the medicine, she heard Blaise questioning the doctor about their condition.

"They have taken no harm. A day or two and they will both be fine," Monsieur Mathau said, from some rapidly receding reality.

That question answered, Flora gratefully surrendered to sleep.

She was in a boat beneath a sky as dark as lapis lazuli. The wind-lashed waves towered over her and the boat bobbed wildly in their deep troughs. She clung to the sides in desperation, soaked through by the icy spray. Something flashed beside her in the water, sleek and sinuous. Light glinted off shimmering scales.

The wind moaned in her ears, an eerie sound mingling with the thunder of the waves. She could almost imagine she heard voices in it. Soft voices calling out to her . . .
"Are you the one?"

"You make me feel old, Johanna. Your stomach must be made of the same iron as those enormous kettles I saw in the kitchens."

Flora had spent three miserable days in bed, although Johanna was back on her feet almost immediately. Although the girl remained pale, she was free of the weakness and pains that had continued to plague Flora for the best part of a week since.

Today was the first day she felt like herself. But watching Johanna stuff down a luncheon repast of mussels *à la Saint-Malo,* in their rich cream sauce, made Flora shudder. "I cannot believe that eating tainted food would leave me so washed out."

"You need fresh air," Gaelle advised briskly. "I will order the carriage. A sedate drive will do you good. Perhaps by Sunday you will be well enough to attend Mass with us in Pont du Mor. In the *ancien régime* the château had its own priest," she added wistfully. "Mass was celebrated in our own chapel, with the family and upper servants. They attended only on special occasions."

Flora listening while toying with the bowl of broth and dumplings Gaelle had made for her with her own hand. The older woman's attitude had changed even more since the episode of food poisoning. Although there was no warmth in her manner—perhaps, Flora thought, the woman was constitutionally incapable of any—she had been quite solicitous. "I suppose a change of scene would do us all good."

"We could pay a call upon Yseult Kersaudy," Johanna suggested. "She has been visiting with an aunt in Dinard, but should be back by now."

"I do not wish you to encourage that friendship," Gaelle said sharply. "The Kersaudys put on airs because Loïc went away to study, and because they have a distant connection with the Cheney line. But they are not our equals!"

Oh-ho! Flora thought. *So Gaelle sees which way the wind is blowing. I wonder if Blaise does yet?* Loic had come every day to inquire after their health. He brought by a book of poems one time, a bouquet of flowers another. Although he divided his attention among them, Flora was sure her continued indisposition was just an excuse: it was Johanna who was the attraction.

"I suggest a ride along the strand," Gaelle told them. "The air is very invigorating." Not to mention it being in the opposite direction from the village. "The two of you must go; as for myself, there are household matters to which I must attend. There will be many mouths to feed after the *grand pardon*, and there is the baking and cooking to organize."

"Enough *kouign-amann* and *far* and *gateaux bretons* to feed the entire village," Johanna announced, "and all washed down with cold cider. And here is a dessert for us to sample now. Oh, my favorite!"

A serving maid came out with a heavy dish holding a *far*, a flan of apricots and brandy-soaked raisins baked with sugar, eggs, and cream. Flora's mouth watered and she realized her appetite had come back after all. The dense cakes and fruit flans and crumbly cookies of the region were so rich and buttery they seemed to melt on the tongue. The household here, she surmised, used more butter and eggs in a month than were used to feed the entire Hawthorne Academy for a year. "By the time the *pardon* is over I shall have to let out all my seams!"

"That is as it should be." Gaelle cocked her head. "You are far too thin and hollow-eyed since you fell ill. We must build your strength up again. I shall make you my special broth."

All this unwanted attention was weighing Flora down. Then she caught her reflection in the mirror across the room. Her eyes did have dark circles beneath them, but they were not from the tainted food. It was lying awake at night, knowing that Blaise was only a few feet away, on the far side of the closed sitting room doors. Wondering if he were as aware of it as she was.

But perhaps not. There had been no repeat of his brash behavior. In fact, he had kept his word, and his distance.

He was unfailingly polite, unquestionably charming. Indisputably remote. Had he been a different sort of man, she might have imagined that he'd found a more willing woman in the village to accommodate him. Certainly it would not be unusual in a man of his wealth and station. No matter how much he loved Eve and grieved for her, she doubted someone with his strong passions had lived the life of a monk all these years.

But it was strange all the same. Almost as if he'd forgotten everything he'd said—and done—the day they'd visited the parish close. Flora was not so lucky. She had tried and failed a hundred times and more. She was haunted by the memory of how his arms felt around her, the hardness of his lean body against the soft curves of hers.

Just thinking of it set a fire raging in her blood. The emotions and longings his kisses had stirred to life would not go back to sleep again. They prowled like restless lions through her mind, slinking in and out of conscious thought. And if he could do so much to her with a few kisses and caresses, what more could he do to ruin her peace of mind? Flora shivered. If she were prudent, she would make sure that she never found out.

"Where is Blaise?" Gaelle cut a piece of the tantalizing *far* with her fork. "Perhaps he should accompany you on your airing."

"He has gone off to do his research," Johanna announced, "and won't be back until the evening meal."

Flora was glad of it. The less she saw of her husband, the better. Fortunately, he'd been quite busy with this book research, whatever that might entail. In addition to it his time was taken up by details of the feast planned to follow the *pardon,* and the business affairs of the château, which were extensive.

And there were also Johanna's business interests. It seemed that she was quite an heiress, although she would not come into her fortune until the age of twenty-five. Little wonder that Blaise planned to have his niece make a big splash in Paris society, followed by a brilliant marriage.

The carriage was duly ordered, and Flora set off with Johanna at her side and Malin in the seat opposite them. It was warm but overcast and the rough waters of the bay had turned a pale, translucent blue. It was difficult to find the horizon separating sky from sea. The light had an odd quality, bouncing off the waves to color their troughs in sapphire, emerald, and turquoise, and highlighting their flashing crests with moving streaks of light.

It reminded Flora of something . . . ah, yes. That strange illusion she'd had on the staircase at the Paris town house, when she'd thought the wooden mermaid had worn a necklace with an egg-shaped jewel. The same kind of necklace she'd seen in Eve's portrait. It gave her an uneasy feeling.

"Shall we go along the harbor front?" Johanna asked. That route would lead them past the Kersaudys' home.

Malin, primed by Gaelle, had another suggestion. "Perhaps Madame would care to see the château from the strand. It is most imposing."

"Yes, I should like that." Anything to keep away her thoughts away from Blaise. His words taunted her: *"I could teach you pleasures such as you have never imagined."* She didn't doubt it.

And she heard her grandfather's voice, as well, an echo from the past: *"You are a whore, like your mother before you! And like her, you will die alone in some foul gutter, cast off by an indifferent lover . . ."*

Flora hugged her carriage cloak about her more tightly. She had already been used and discarded by a man once before. Robin Harding had wooed her and won her, and betrayed everything she held most dear. She must not give in to her attraction to Blaise.

It would destroy her.

The carriage went along the strand until Pont du Mor was just a huddle of stone beside the sea. The ground rose up sharply opposite the water and became towering granite cliffs. A few trees, stunted by salt air and bitter winter gales, clung to them, but soon there was nothing but massive rock and sky and sea. There was magic in its wild loneliness. Except for the carriage and its occupants, it seemed a place where humankind had never gone before.

It created the strange sensation in Flora that they were approaching an invisible boundary line between reality and myth. Finistère, this section of Brittany was called in

French, and Pen ar Bed in Breton: World's End. The name was certainly fitting.

"The Mermaid's Rock and the view of the château are just ahead," Johanna said, a little too loudly, as if she had also felt the strangeness in the air.

The carriage bumped along and around a rounded hump of rock. "The way is blocked, madame," the coachman said, reining in.

It was indeed, not only by a rockfall that littered the sand with enormous boulders, but by a festive group. A gig and an open carriage were drawn up at the edge of the sand, and six people, attended by liveried servants, were finishing an al fresco meal.

"Ah, it is Madame Cheney!" a too-familiar voice rang out. "And the young demoiselle."

Flora was startled. "Monsieur de Broceliand?"

He came up beside them, as suave and handsome in the informal setting as he had been in Paris. His smile for Flora was particularly warm.

"Well met, ladies! Come and take a glass of wine with us. I will introduce you to Madame de Broceliand and the rest of my party, and we shall toast your health."

Giving in to his persuasions, Flora and Johanna joined his party. He led Flora forward by the hand. "May I present to you my wife, Odile?"

A stunning woman with spun-gold hair came forward to greet them. She was exquisitely dressed in the very height of fashion. Her eyes were a hazel-green with clear, golden centers, her skin as flawless as the pear-shaped pearls that hung from her perfect earlobes. Claudine had called her the most beautiful woman in France. Flora realized that she had not exaggerated.

"Madame Cheney! How I have looked forward to making your acquaintance," Odile de Broceliand said, with every evidence of sincerity. But Flora detected a sparkle of ironic amusement in her eyes.

"I must introduce you to my friends. You have already met Monsieur Kersaudy, who is preparing a history of my husband's family, but not, I think his sister?"

Yseult Kersaudy was only a year or two older than Johanna, but more mature in figure and in bearing. Pale and fragile-looking, she had her brother's gray-brown eyes, and a very pretty face framed by wings of waving black hair. She dipped a polite curtsy to Flora.

"I have so longed to meet you, madame. And I am delighted to become reacquainted with my old friend Mademoiselle Cheney. It is many years since we have met. I do not know if you remember me?"

"But I do! We played at dolls together, and looked for shells and crabs along the strand, while my parents strolled along the breakwall. And when Loic would tell me I was a pest and threaten to send me back to my mother's side, you would take my part." Yseult laughed, pleased to be remembered.

The other couple strolled over and were introduced as the Pattersons, Americans who were houseguests of the de Broceliands. "It was Blaise Cheney who saved my husband's life at the opera house with his quick thinking," Odile de Broceliand told the others. "I look forward to thanking him personally."

"Odile was just going to show us the Mermaid's Rock," Mrs. Patterson remarked.

"Yes." Odile smiled her charming smile. "Do come with us."

Johanna hung back. "Are you coming, Loic?"

"No, I have seen the rock a thousand times." His smile took the sting from his refusal, but Johanna's face fell. She turned too quickly for him to see, but Flora noticed.

Falling in step with Odile and Mrs. Patterson, she linked arms with Johanna. Her earlier daydreams of an attachment between the young Breton and Blaise's niece had been banished when she learned of Johanna's large fortune. It would be an unequal match, one bound to end in resentment and unhappiness on either side. In any event, Loic now appeared to regard Johanna as very much the same little girl who had tried to tag along on his adventures. It seemed she would have to find her Prince Charming in Paris, after all.

Yseult Kersaudy walked a little apart from them. She continued to survey Flora from time to time with an unnerving intensity. Johanna noticed it, too. "Perhaps she has had a vision of you," she whispered. "She is one of those who sees things, Malin says."

"What kind of things?" Flora asked, torn between annoyance and apprehension.

"The future, some say. Perhaps the past. I do not know. She warned the apothecary not to go along the cliffs with his young son. The man left the boy home because of it. His son slipped out of the cottage and fell on the rocks. They found him lying at the foot of the cliffs. He recovered, but is not right in his head." Johanna made a sign of the cross. "Malin says the *fées* stole him and put a changeling in his place."

"Malin says a lot of ignorant things," Flora snapped. "And what good does it do for a person to see the future, if they cannot change it?"

"I don't know. There are many things in this world that we are not given to understand."

"Yes," Flora replied. *Like strange voices and seaweed in my locked room. Or magical lights in Swarthern Woods at the winter solstice.* "But there is some logical explanation, if only we know where to look for it."

"I don't believe that is always so. Miracles happen. It is God's doing. We are merely too human to understand."

Flora had no intention of getting into a philosophical debate. "Perhaps you are right."

The women went on together for a goodly distance. The way was strewn with cockles and oyster shells and drying bits of seaweed, especially near the base of the cliffs, but nowhere did Flora see anything like the strange tangle of seaweed she'd found in her bedchamber. When she looked back the carriages were out of sight. To get to the viewing spot it was necessary to cross an area of rough shingle and turn past a long tongue of rock, before they came out to a broad sandy area, backed by the high cliffs. Three crosses had been deeply cut into the granite rock face, all with recent dates carved below.

"Memorials to those who have drowned here," Yseult said. Johanna looked apprehensive.

"Are you sure it is safe for us?" Flora eyed the crosses with misgiving.

"Perfectly safe." Odile pointed back the way they'd come. "Do you see that little post with the red stripe upon it? As long as one stays on this side of the post, the tide cannot reach you."

Shading her eyes, Flora found the striped post near where Malin was standing in conversation with one of the servants. Guy de Broceliand leaned against the cliff face and lifted his hand to wave.

It wasn't far to the Mermaid Rock, and Mrs. Patterson exclaimed over the likeness of the shape to its namesake. Johanna was disappointed. "It is even more apparent from the château's tower is it not, Flora?"

"Ah," Odile exclaimed, "then you have been up there, also? It is true," she told the American woman. "From the château, the resemblance is uncanny." She tilted her head upward. "We are almost directly beneath it; however, one must go along a bit farther to actually see Château Morgaine from the strand."

But Mrs. Patterson's shoes were wet from the damp sand and she wanted to go back. Johanna volunteered to accompany her. "I shall return also," Odile said, but she waited until the others were gone. Putting her hand on Flora's arm, she favored her with a blinding smile.

"We arrived early this week. I have been so impatient to meet you! Only word that you were not well enough to receive company has prevented me from calling upon you."

"I am fully recovered. I should be very happy to receive a visit from you, Madame de Broceliand." Flora meant it. In the past few days she realized how dreadfully she missed Claudine. It would be wonderful to have a friend in Brittany. One who would not be so interested in scrutinizing her relationship with Blaise.

"You must call me Odile, and I shall call you Flora, *hein*? I am sure that you and I will become fast friends: we have so very much in common."

Flora could not hide her surprise. "Because the château is so close to your estate?"

"That also," Odile replied with a dismissive wave of her hand. "I am referring to things of a more personal nature."

Now Flora was totally at sea. "I am afraid I do not understand."

"No? Now, that is very bad of Blaise!" The laughter was back in Odile's green-gold eyes. "Well, I suppose I that must be the one to tell you then—for it is widely known and will surely come to your ears: before my marriage to Guy, I was your husband's mistress."

Mrs. Patterson had turned around and was calling to her hostess. Odile winked at Flora. "We shall not let old history stand in the way of our friendship, I think. But now I must go and attend to my guests. If you wish to view the château, you must continue on a little farther. *Adieu.* I shall call upon you tomorrow."

She left Flora standing alone, dumbfounded.

There was no use in following her. *Blaise's mistress.* Flora laughed wryly. And all this time she'd imagined that he'd been pining for Eve, his lost love. She was even more of a fool than she'd thought! Shaking her head, she wandered beneath the base of the granite cliffs.

From time to time she glanced up, hoping to see the château. Perhaps it was hidden by the trees? Looking back to make sure she was still on the right side of the striped post, Flora continued on, paying more attention to Odile's words than her surroundings. Her mind was filled with questions: what was the protocol for receiving one's husband's former mistress as a guest? It boggled the mind. *Perhaps I should ask Gaelle for guidance.*

She stopped short. No. There was no use playing games in her head. The Frenchwoman might take the situation lightly, but Flora could not. Hearing that Blaise and the beautiful Odile had been lovers had given her a severe shock. Emotions had rocketed through her like a shower of fireworks: disbelief followed by mortification, swiftly succeeded by a surge of unreasoning anger.

No, Flora admitted. *Not anger.* It had been jealousy, pure and simple. How long had they been lovers? Which of them had broken it off? And what were the chances of them ending up in each other's arms again?

And why did she even care? Blaise was nothing to her. Not on that level. He was her employer, and whether or not he still carried a *tendre* for Odile de Broceliand, or she for him, was none of her business. Especially after she had rebuffed him herself.

Flora took a deep breath and tried to turn around. She couldn't lift her feet. They felt as if they'd turned to lead. Looking down, she realized that her boots were sunk into the sand past the ankles. It was like being caught in a steel-jawed trap. How could she not have felt it?

Then she saw that the sand, which had looked damp but solid, was the consistency of thick gruel. It appeared to ooze up her boots even higher. Horrified, Flora realized she was actually sinking further. The more she struggled the deeper she went.

She tried to wrench herself out by twisting around, but lost her balance and fell. Her elbow and hand pushed into the cold sand as if it were yesterday's porridge. Water seeped up to her wrist. She couldn't free her numbed fingers. She tried to wriggle them free, and they plowed deeper into the sand.

Flora fought for calm. With a mighty effort she gathered her strength and almost pulled her hand free. The recoil set her further off balance, and now both her hands were trapped. She could feel the quicksand flowing like a sluggish river, tugging at her ankles and arms as if it were alive and intent on swallowing her whole. When she tried to call out for help, only a frightened croak came from her panic-constricted throat.

This was ridiculous. She couldn't be sinking in quicksand, mute and panic-stricken, with people a mere two hundred yards away. As she looked to see if anyone had noticed her plight, her stomach knotted in fear: the De Broceliands' carriage was driving away toward the village, and the huge granite boulders effectively hid her view of the others.

She took a deep breath to call out for help, but only uttered a sharp cry, like the sound of the seabirds overhead. The fluid sand beneath her right arm had given way, throwing her backward with a sudden jerk. She was leaning back in a half-sitting posture, facing the sea, her legs buried to the calf, her elbows and forearms rapidly disappearing beneath the quicksand. Flora had visions of being sucked completely under, sand clogging her mouth and filling her nostrils, smothering her to death.

Her breath came out in a ragged sob. Whatever her sins, she did not deserve this. She would not die this way! She would not!

"Help me, someone, for the love of God!"

"*Mon Dieu!* It is Madame Cheney, caught in the sands!"

She recognized Loic's voice, and heard him sprinting toward her across the shingle nearer the cliff face. "Do not struggle, it will only make things worse."

From the sounds, she could tell he was slithering toward her. "Get more help. You'll be trapped as well," she exclaimed.

"Help is on its way. Now you must trust me." She felt him touch her shoulders. "Lie back against the sand."

"Are you mad?"

"It is the only way. The situation is urgent, madame. Listen to me. Do not fight it. You must float atop the quicksand by spreading your weight across the surface. You shall be all right, I promise you."

Gently but firmly, he applied pressure to her shoulders. She found herself almost lying flat in a most awkward position. His strong hands brushed the sides of her breasts, then caught her under her arms, pulling so hard she thought her shoulders would dislocate.

"Forgive me," he said near her ear. "You will be bruised, Flora, but you will be safe."

Another tug and she felt the suction loosen against her elbows. They pulled free. She would be saved. Tears of relief and gratitude stung her eyes.

"*Sacrebleu!*"

"Cheney!"

"Unhand my wife, Kersaudy!"

Loic's hands let go of her and Flora flopped back like a beached flounder. A pair of boots straddled her, and other, stronger hands leaned her forward, then caught her in a bruising bear hug beneath her ribs. She was pulled up and back with such abrupt violence that it squeezed the breath from her lungs. Another jerk and the sand released her with a liquid, sucking sound. She was free.

Flora could hardly stand to thank her rescuers. Both were liberally streaked with sand and water. Loic offered her his handkerchief to wipe the muddy sand from her arms. Blaise merely glared at her, arms akimbo.

"Where on earth did you materialize from?" she asked.

"I was up on the cliff path by the château, and saw you from there. Why in the name of *le Bon Dieu* didn't you stay behind the marker pole? This area is dangerous for those who do not know it well!"

"But I did!" She whirled and looked for the striped post. She was surprised to find herself quite a distance forward of it now. Surely it had been in line with the edge of the rocks earlier? "I thought . . ."

"Not *enough*, evidently. If the tide had been coming in you might have been in real trouble."

Shucking off his jacket, he wrapped it around her. She was shivering violently with reaction. "Come. You are soaked through. I will take you back to the château."

"My house is closer," Loïc interrupted. "Flora is chilled to the bone. A warm fire and a glass of brandy—"

Blaise's temper flared. "I am perfectly able to look after my wife."

Loïc's eyes locked with his. "Are you, monsieur?"

Blaise's mouth was rimmed in white. "You need not make it your concern, Kersaudy."

"No?" Loïc gave Flora a penetrating look, released her hand and walked away.

"Insolent young jackanapes!"

Flora was indignant. "He saved my life."

"Nonsense. The quicksand is strong from the water currents running beneath it, but it is not very deep along this coast. Unless it was high tide, you were in no real danger."

"Monsieur Kersaudy's opinion is quite the opposite!"

"Well, that is his error," Blaise said coldly, assisting her back toward the carriage. "The sand would not have come up as far as your hips. He is a man of Pont du Mor. He should know this area like he knows his own face."

"Perhaps he had forgotten."

"Or perhaps he wanted to play the hero, so you would shower him with gratitude." He slanted a darkling glance at her. "And when did you give him leave to call you by your given name?"

"You are insufferable." Flora tried to pull away, but Blaise had her firmly by the shoulders.

"And you are my wife," he said through gritted teeth. "If you have any plans for a romantic dalliance with Kersaudy, you may forget them."

She stopped short and glared at him. "If I am not mistaken, when you proposed this marriage to me, you gave me carte blanche to seek out lovers on the side, as long as I did not cause a scandal."

Blaise's face went white with suppressed fury. "Did I? Well, it will cause quite a scandal if he is found strangled to death some dark night! I saw how he touched you before attempting to pull you out of the sand. My hands itched to go around his throat!"

She schooled her features. Loic was nowhere in sight, but Johanna and Malin stood less than ten yards away. "You are causing a scene. I refuse to speak with you when you are in such foul temper."

As she tried to flounce away he suddenly swept her up in his arms. She was light and soft in his embrace and he tightened his grip, pressing her head against his shoulder. She gave a faint gasp and her body quivered not from cold, but from the sudden sexual fire that leapt between them. Their mutual anger had only heightened it.

Her hair had come loose in the struggle to free her, and the fresh breeze whipped it against his cheek. Blaise cupped her chin in his hand. "Do you know what I wish, Flora? That the ground would open up like a giant mouth, and swallow the others whole, leaving us alone."

His voice was like a razor, cutting away all pretense. Slashing to the heart of the moment. "Now, when your passions are stirred. Now, while our blood runs hot!"

She was every bit his match in ardor. He knew it. Their coming together would be wild and fierce. His breath caught in his chest at the thought of it.

Flora trembled in his strong arms. She fought the urge to twine her arms around his neck. If they were anywhere but here, the outcome of this moment would be inevitable. Thank God they were in full view of half the citizens of Pont du Mor. Johanna came running up to them and Flora pushed away.

"What has happened? Did you twist your ankle and fall, Flora? Your clothes are all wet and dirty."

"I . . . I stepped into one of the treacherous places, and was caught in the sand. Monsieur Kersaudy kindly came to my aid."

"Did he?" Johanna's face lit up.

"Oh, yes," Blaise said sarcastically. "He is quite the hero."

Sweeping Flora off her feet, he carried her back to the carriage. Neither Flora nor Blaise said another word all the way back to the château.

During her long, hot bath, Flora had time to think over the afternoon's events. Someone had moved that post. She was sure of it. It was only a painted stick, after all, stuck into a jumble of rocks. Easy enough for someone to pick it up and move it a few feet without anyone noticing.

Someone like Odile de Broceliand, perhaps?

It was a malicious trick but if, as Blaise contended, the only danger had been to her dignity, there was no harm done. Still, it had been frightening at the time.

After toweling off and changing before the fire Jeanette had roaring in the hearth, Flora dressed early for dinner and went down to the Green Salon, which the family used as an informal sitting room. Johanna usually joined her there, but Blaise was always locked away in his library and Gaelle on her knees in the small chapel, praying for her sister's soul.

Checking the console table where the Paris papers and mail were placed, Flora was disappointed to find it empty. She had written to Claudine just before falling ill with the food poisoning, and had expected an answer by now.

Voices drifted in from the adjoining room, where the door was left ajar. As she was about to leave in search of Johanna, her ears pricked up. She had heard her own name.

"You have not spoken with Flora yet?" Gaelle's voice carried from the open window of the Green Salon.

"You know I have not." Blaise's voice was sharp.

"And you know that you must. You cannot put it off indefinitely."

"In my own good time, Gaelle! And the time is not yet right."

Flora went to the door and opened it. "Perhaps I should be the judge of that, if it affects me!"

Blaise uttered an oath and Gaelle looked nonplussed— but for only a moment. "Had I known you make it a habit of eavesdropping," she said coolly, "I should have closed the door before embarking on a private conversation."

"I merely came down to see if Claudine had written as to when they are coming to join us here. And, since this 'private' conversation evidently concerns me, I see no reason why you should not disclose the matter to me now."

Blaise lounged against the mantelpiece and reached inside his jacket. "There is a letter for you here in my pocket. Claudine and Nicolas will arrive late next week, the day before the *grand pardon*."

She took the envelope he removed and held out to her. "Thank you. And this is the dire news that you were keeping from me? I hardly consider the arrival of invited guests to be on the same level as a state secret!"

Gaelle gave him a significant look. "I will leave you two."

After she was gone, closing the door behind her, Blaise took a turn about the room, frowning. "I neglected to mention that we will have other houseguests on the last day of the *pardon*, for the *fest noz*. It is a tradition, since the celebration lasts into the small hours. A small party only: Claudine and Nicolas, of course; Monsieur Lampoul, the mayor, and his wife, Margot; Loic and Yseult Kersaudy; and Guy and Odile de Broceliand," he said offhandedly. "I hope it will not discommode you to have them at such short notice."

"I see." Flora's eyes darkened. She folded her hands primly and spoke with quiet emphasis. Any of her former students would have realized what that meant. Blaise watched her warily.

"It is very considerate of you to be so concerned for my convenience. However, since Gaelle continues to oversee the household and the servants do all the chores, I do not understand why you think this would put me out. Unless," she said straightly, "you feel it might be awkward to have your wife and your former mistress under the same roof?''

He let out the breath he'd been holding. ''So,'' he said slowly. ''You know.'' Flora never ceased to amaze him. He caught the throb of anger in her voice. He might yet turn this to his advantage.

''Oh, yes. Madame de Broceliand, in our one, short private conversation this afternoon, managed to inform me of the fact. A refreshing frankness on her part.''

A little smile played over his lips. ''I see. I realized that someone would tell you, and wanted to do it myself, to spare your feelings.'' Blaise tilted his head and eyed her appraisingly. ''If I did not know better, I should think you jealous.''

''I will not dignify that with a reply!''

''Excellent.''

He leaned against the mantelpiece, his smile widening. She was magnificent when she was angry, with her eyes sparkling and fresh color in her cheeks. ''There was no graceful way for me to decline. De Broceliand as good as invited himself. It is quite a coup for you, Flora, to receive such notice from so important a man. Your credit will rise in all the best circles.''

She tucked the letter from Claudine in her pocket and moved to the door. ''If the De Broceliands are examples of the best circles, I am not much impressed. I do not know which of them I dislike more!''

He laughed at that. ''As to myself,'' he said smoothly, ''I infinitely prefer Odile.''

Flora went out, shutting the door with more violence than she intended. His laughter echoed in her ears.

The news that the De Broceliands were going to be houseguests weighed on Flora's mind. How many people knew of Odile's past relationship with Blaise? she wondered. She wasn't certain about Claudine, but Nicolas would surely have known. Did Guy de Broceliand? She was not naïve enough to think that such situations never arose among the upper classes. What was the etiquette in receiving one's husband's former mistress as an overnight guest?

Flora looked forward to an extremely uncomfortable week during the *grand pardon*.

Inventing a headache that gave every evidence of becoming real, she took a tray in her room that evening instead of coming down to dinner, and retired early. Jeanette brought her a small vial as she prepared for bed. "Valerian and herbs, madame. My own concoction. You will sleep well and awaken refreshed. There is nothing in it that will harm you."

Flora thanked her and took a few drops of the remedy in water, not really expecting it to work. Her mind was too active. She lay with her eyes closed, pretending the valerian was working, and Jeanette tiptoed out. The next thing she knew, it was morning, and she was trying to hold on to a rapidly fading dream.

Something about a woman, Flora thought vaguely. A woman weeping her heart out in the shadows of a stone tower.

She heard a small sigh and was instantly more alert. Someone was moving about in her room. "Jeanette?"

"Are you the one?"

It was more like a breath than a question. The words hung in the still air, softer than her own heartbeat drumming in her ears. Fright made her angry.

"The one for *what*?" Flora said, sitting up quickly. "Who are you? And *where* are you?"

"I think you are the one . . ."

Rubbing her eyes, she looked around. There was no sign of her maid. She was alone in her chamber and the door to the dressing room remained closed. A gust of wind rattled the casement and the room felt still and empty again.

Just the remnants of a dream, Flora told herself bracingly.

Turning back the covers, she sat up and swung her legs over the edge. As she stood up her foot slipped on something hard and sharp. "Oh!"

She barely saved herself from a nasty tumble by grabbing the edge of her nightstand. Her foot hurt abominably. She looked down to see what she'd stepped upon. It was a scallop shell, the size of her palm. The top was a rich cream with bands of yellow and orange, and the satiny inside looked like a fiery sunset. She had never seen such a large scallop, nor one so glossy and gaily colored. Surely nothing so exotic and tropical-looking grew this far north in the Atlantic!

She remembered, uneasily, that one of her students had brought a similar shell back, as a souvenir of her sojourn in the Leeward Islands.

And there were more. She looked about gingerly. Her bed was encircled by them, three deep. It reminded her of a fairy circle, the ring of mushrooms that sometimes formed in grassy areas where spirits and gnomes were said to dance in ages past. Flora ran her fingers over the edges of the banded scallop. Who had put them here?

Why hadn't she wakened?

But, most of all, what did they mean?

There was nothing menacing about them. Excepting, of course, the fact that someone had been in her bedchamber, undetected, while she lay fast asleep. Perhaps that was the point.

Flora sat on the edge of the bed for a while, thinking. First the seaweed, then the quicksand—the more she thought of it, the more she was sure that the striped pole had been moved—and now this. Someone was playing tricks, trying to frighten her. Perhaps to plant the idea that she would become the next victim of the so-called family curse.

More likely, merely to irritate her already frayed nerves. If so, their plan was succeeding admirably.

Chapter Ten

*F*lora pondered what to do. Like the incident with the seaweed, she would not give the prankster the satisfaction of rousing the household. She swept up the shells and hid them in the fireplace basket, beneath the kindling, until she could dispose of them. Originally she had imagined that Gaelle was behind the tricks. Knowing the older woman better now, she doubted that. The only person who would do such a thing was Malin. But why?

After Jeanette brought her morning chocolate, Flora dressed and started downstairs. Light from an open casement brought in fresh morning air and a bright shaft of sunlight. It slanted across the gallery to illuminate the portrait of Blaise, with his mother and brother. She paused to look up at Anne Cheney and her two sons.

What made you so unhappy that you took your own life? she silently asked the painted woman. *How could you leave your children behind to suffer so? Was your love for them too weak, or was your pain too strong?*

But the sad eyes merely gazed back at her from the gently smiling face.

Flora examined the two boys. Hilliard, slightly younger, appeared outgoing and energetic, as if he barely had patience to sit still for the artist. Blaise looked grave and intense even then, his eyes . . . His eyes were troubled. It bothered Flora. Had he somehow sensed the tragedy that lay ahead? Or was Gaelle right in thinking he had inherited his mother's dark streak of melancholy? And Johanna as well? She had never known a more mercurial family, either in alt or in gloom.

Not that she was particularly placid herself, these days.

She examined the woman again. Anne Cheney must have been about the same age as Flora was now, when she sat for the portrait. As she searched the lovely face in the artist's rendering, she had a better view of the necklace the woman wore. She'd noticed the gold chain before, of course, but in the clear morning light from the windows she could make out a jewel nestled in the pale blue ruffles at the woman's breast. It gave her a jolt: egg-shaped, the stone was swirled with blues and greens and bands of shimmering white. All the colors of the sea.

"Are you the one?"

Flora jumped and looked around. The whisper had sounded as if the speaker stood at her shoulder.

She was alone.

Hurrying down the staircase, she almost ran into Malin at the bottom. "Did you speak to me just now?" she asked sharply.

"No, madame." Malin's gaze swept up to the gallery. "I saw you looking at the portrait. Do you see the chain with the jewel hanging from it? It is the Mermaid's Egg, of the legend. By rights, it is given to every mistress of the château, to protect them from the curse." Her dark eyes shifted slyly. "That one, she took the necklace off. To have the clasp repaired, she said. The next day she was dead."

Flora was furious, but managed to keep her features schooled and her voice icily calm. "Are you trying to frighten me again? It will not work, I assure you."

Malin shook her head. Her dark eyes were solemn. "No, madame. I am trying to save you." She dipped a curtsy and vanished through the servants' door near the foot of the stairs.

It was early and the others were not down yet. Instead of seeking her breakfast, Flora wandered about, trying to find a sense of Anne Cheney in the various rooms. Trying to imagine what it was like for two motherless boys, left alone in this sprawling pile of stone.

Somehow she ended up in the oldest section of the château, at the foot of the Mermaid's Tower. Something compelled her to open the door and go up. A gust of wind blew steadily past her, like the breath of the sea.

The view was particularly splendid this morning, the sapphire bay shot with glints, the sky like a crystal dome. At the horizon line they blended together in a muted, opalescent blue. If she leaned out just a bit, she could make out a triangle of sand and shingle. She spied a noticeably smoother surface, one unlittered by shells and pieces of fallen rock. That was the place where she'd been caught in the shifting sands. How easy it was to view things more clearly at a distance, she thought. Time had the same effect. Little, separate matters became part of a readily discernible pattern.

And there was the cliff path, from which Blaise said he'd seen her. How had he scrambled down to her aid so quickly? The suspicion formed that he'd arranged for Malin to move the post, so that he could "rescue" her and earn her gratitude. That might be why he was so out-of-reason angry with Loic Kersaudy, for helping her before he himself could reach her side.

No, she couldn't believe he would be so petty and devious. And he had no way of knowing that she would be on that section of the strand.

A movement startled her and she whipped around, half expecting to hear the strange whisper that had roused her from her bed. It was only another seagull. It cocked its head and looked at her, as if expecting food. "Shoo! I have nothing for you." The bird flew off with a shrill cry.

Flora left the room and started down the narrow, winding steps. There was a melancholy air to the place, but she doubted there was ever a Cheney wife held prisoner here. It made sense that this was the keep of the ancient structure, where the family would retreat in times of attack. Legends had grown from smaller things than this.

But as she left the Mermaid's Tower, Flora noted a very strange thing: the door of a keep should have some way to keep would-be assailants out, but there was no heavy bar to secure it from the inside.

It was on the outside, as if to keep someone locked in.

Flora turned away quickly, and something plucked at her sleeve. She started and gave a gasp of alarm. She was still alone. A thread from her lace cuff had snagged on the pink granite stone with the mermaid etched into its surface.

"Poor creature," she said, touching the engraved lines of the woman's face. "I do not believe in mermaids and *fées,* but I do believe there must be a kernel of truth somewhere behind your legend. We share a kinship, you know. We are both exiles from our homes."

For a moment Flora was struck with a longing for England, its tidy villages and hedgerows, its familiar customs and language. For a moment she felt almost ill with it.

The loneliness threatened to overwhelm her and spill out in hot tears. She sighed and traced the outlines of the mermaid's billowing hair. The first, according to legend, in a long line of unhappy Cheney wives. "Did you love him, too?" she whispered hoarsely.

Flora gasped at her own words as if she had been slapped. She hadn't meant it. She didn't love Blaise. She couldn't. She *wouldn't.*

No, it had been a mere slip of the tongue. Something brought on by the atmosphere of the château and her sleepless nights.

"If it is your restless spirit that haunts my dreams, I wish that I could help to set you free."

A sudden gust of wind blew through the stone corridor, and a thin voice cried out: *"Help me . . . help me . . ."*

Flora's heart turned over in her chest. Then she heard a flap of wings and laughed in relief. It had only been the forlorn cry of a seabird, echoing down the stairwell. Even though it was explained, her pulse still drummed in double time.

The Breton atmosphere was soaking into her. "I must get a grip on myself," she said sternly. "If I am not careful, I shall imagine I am seeing *fées* dancing in the moonlight, and standing stones rolling down to the sea!"

Fleeing the ancient tower, she made her way out through the main section of the house. After stopping to fetch her sunbonnet and shawl, she went out into the sunny garden. Shimmers and glints of golden fire darted in and out among the colorful blooms.

Dragonflies, so early in the year? But this was Brittany, after all, where the warm sea currents advanced the season considerably. Her grandfather had called them darners, and told her they would sew her mouth up; but Flora's mother had always claimed that dragonflies were magical creatures, the graceful steeds of the fairy folk.

Her thoughts flew back in time. How beautiful her mother had been in those early days, and how happy! But for so short a time. Hannah O'Donnell had married above her station, a runaway match with a handsome and feckless gentleman who had never worked a day in his life nor had any desire to do so. Her parents had refused their permission, and Franklin McCall's family had been even more appalled by the mésalliance.

When his family cast him off without a farthing to his name, Flora's father had refused such genteel occupations as tutoring, and tried to make his fortune at the gaming tables. Instead he had ruined himself. An accident while out shooting, her mother had claimed, but everyone—except little Flora—had known that he had taken his own life rather than face bankruptcy.

At the time she only knew that her father was gone, and all their happiness and ease had gone with him.

A flash of light caught Flora's eye again as she drew closer. Bright gleams of gold flickered near the nodding stalks of the early lilies, like darting wings of fire. She was glad to have been given the gift of this happy memory to assuage her loneliness. Surely their appearance was a good omen, that there were better days ahead.

Stepping softly toward the lilies, she stopped short in dismay. Her imagination had led her astray once more. There were no graceful dragonflies hovering over the heady blooms. The fiery glints between the stalks were the silken snares of an orb weaver's web, stirring in the breeze. The spider, fat and patient, sat in the center of its glittering circle, waiting for its unsuspecting prey.

Shivers danced frantically up Flora's spine, like the brush of frail wings. If this were indeed an omen, it was not at all the kind she fancied. Turning abruptly, she went back inside.

Blaise was alone at the breakfast table, when she found her way there. He glanced up at her enigmatically, through his thick lashes. He looked incredibly handsome in his close-fitting riding jacket, with his hair ruffled from the wind of his morning ride.

"You are up early," he said, regarding her closely. "I trust you slept well?"

"Very well," she said, for the ears of Malin, or anyone who might have taken part in the trick played upon her earlier.

A strained silence fell as she broke her fast. She had the strange feeling that he was waiting for something. Biding his time, like the orb weaver in the garden.

In reality he was through with waiting. Blaise set down his cup. His original plans had been knocked to flinders for some time now: he could do no worse by opting for action.

"Johanna is joining me in an expedition this morning, to the Druid's Isle. I am researching its history. I wonder if you would care to accompany us?"

"The Druid's Isle?" Flora took a cup of coffee from the sideboard, a new addition made to the usual breakfast, to accommodate her habits. "An intriguing name. Is it very far?"

"It is actually a narrow peninsula at the foot of the cliffs, quite near the château. At low tide it is an easy walk. High tide floods over it at the neck, separating it from the mainland."

"What does your expedition entail?"

"Nothing more strenuous than a picnic. Madame Kerjean has already sent Malin down with the hamper of food. I think you will find the isle a fascinating place. The druids are said to have buried their dead beneath the standing stones, and I intend to take some measurements."

Flora was intrigued. With Johanna along, there would be no danger of being private with him. It seemed innocent enough. "I should like that."

"Excellent. Johanna has gone up to fetch her bonnet. She will join us on the cliff path."

"Very well."

They went back toward the Mermaid's Tower and past the stone with the figure carved into it. "Why is the bar on the door placed on the outside, rather than inside?" she asked him.

"To keep the wind from blowing it open, I imagine."
A light sparked in his dark eyes. "What, are you disappointed?"

"A very little. It is a more logical, but less romantic reason than I expected. I thought perhaps it was where the Cheneys stored their recalcitrant wives."

He laughed at that. "We Cheneys have far better methods of persuasion. As you will learn, in time."

She couldn't think of any way to answer that. Blaise led her through a low wooden door in the stone wall, and down a pathway that descended gradually into a wooded area behind the château. Now and then Flora caught a glimpse of the bay through the wind-blasted trees.

The way was paved with stones, and wound gently, but ever downward until it came out into the open. They stood on a wide and rocky ledge, and from there the landscape grew wild and steep, but the path continued on at an easy grade, guarded by a metal rail. The view was breathtaking. She wanted to pause and take it all in.

"Let us stop and catch our breath," Blaise said, in that disconcerting way he had of seeming to read her mind. "Magnificent, isn't it?"

"Fabulous." She shaded her eyes and looked out to sea. Flora couldn't remember ever seeing it so calm and placid. Now it shone like a great silver mirror beneath a hazy blue sky. Not a whitecap to be seen.

"There it is," he told her. "That great pile of rock."

A long crescent rose from the steely waters not too far out from shore.

"But you said it wasn't an island!"

"At low tide, if you recall. However, it is quicker and safer to go around by water most of the time," Blaise told her. "With a boat we can always be sure of getting back if the seas run high. Otherwise we could be cut off from the land."

They continued on to the bottom where a small sailboat was moored in a little cove. It was painted the same lapis blue that Flora had seen throughout Brittany. He helped her into the sailboat and took a seat at the tiller. The picnic hamper was already tucked beneath the bow.

"I hope Johanna will enjoy our sail to the island more than she did our trip across the Channel," Flora said doubtfully.

"She is most anxious to see it. The Druid's Isle is where our family began. The first of the Cheney line lived there," Blaise told her, "eking a living from the ocean's bounty. Not much has been changed in generations. It's a wonder the old house hasn't fallen to ruin. You can see it from here."

Flora shaded her eyes against the glare off the water. By a great leap of imagination she could almost make out a steeply pitched roof behind a huddle of twisted trees.

A woman's voice called from above them on the cliff path. Flora looked up and saw Malin waving to them from halfway down. "Madame, monsieur!" She cupped her hands to her mouth. "Mademoiselle sends regrets. She forgot that she is promised to Ysuelt Kersaudy and Madame Rohun this morning. They are to decorate the grotto chapel at St. Mari du Mor."

Blaise waved to indicate they had heard and Malin turned and ran lightly up the path. Flora was disappointed. She wanted very much to see the Druid's Isle.

"Perhaps we can go another time," she began—and realized, too late, that Blaise had already cast off the line. The sail filled with wind and the little boat was already leaving the cove.

"There is no sense in aborting our plans because of Johanna's absentmindedness," he said smoothly.

The cove was retreating fast as they headed out into the water. Flora was upset. She did not want to be alone with Blaise. "I suppose that a request to return to shore would be ignored?"

"Why should we turn back? The morning is beautiful and I am anxious to finish this phase of my research." A smile played at the corners of his mouth. "If you are afraid I shall force my attentions on you again, let me put your mind at ease. I gave you the word of a Cheney."

She flushed. Yes, he had. She remembered exactly what he had said: *"I give you my word that I will not touch you again until you give me your leave. And you will! One day you will come willingly to me . . . and we shall finish this!"*

Flora turned her head and looked out to sea. It seemed to change constantly, depending on the light. With the sun higher now, the waves had turned a milky, opaque blue almost the same hue as the sky. Beyond the bay they gleamed like polished steel.

It was less than half an hour by water to the tip of the peninsula, and she enjoyed the sail. Blaise was as at home on the sea as he was in a drawing room. Despite the family legends, he seemed to have no fear. He guided the little boat around a spill of giant boulders edging the side of the isle, and into a sheltered spot.

The rocky base of the Druid's Isle rose fifteen feet above them. It seemed to Flora that there would be little protection from high waves and winter gales. It canted steeply on the other side. What kind of man was Yvon Cheney, who had founded his family in this savagely beautiful and lonely place?

Blaise watched her. Could she see the same ravaged splendor that he did? Did its wild essence call to something equally untamed in her soul? She smiled and gave a sigh of contentment, without realizing it. His tension eased. Yes, he had not been wrong about her.

They moored at a curving inlet where wavelets lapped and sighed like fairy voices. An ancient iron ring was mounted in the living rock, staining the granite with its rusted blood. Blaise slipped on a knapsack, lifted the heavy picnic hamper as if it were a feather, and stepped out upon the shore. His hand was warm and strong as he helped her out of the sailboat and along the overgrown path. Neither of them spoke. There was no need. For the first time they were in perfect amity, content to merely *be*.

Although it had been cool upon the water the air warmed once they clambered up the rock-cut steps to dry land. The sharp tilt of the land protected them from the wind, and hid all views of the coastline. It seemed to Flora as if they had journeyed back in time. It could be any year from any era since the dawn of creation.

At first there was no sign of any house. Blaise led her around a granite outcrop and there it was, tucked against the island's rocky spine, as if it were part of the bedrock. Beyond there was nothing but a hammered silver sea. He stopped in the middle of the path. For a moment he seemed to have forgotten Flora's presence, although he still held her hand in his.

Of all the lovely views he had seen in his travels, nothing owned him as this did. He belonged to it completely. He could never set foot upon the Druid's Isle without feeling that he had returned home. For him, it was a place of comfort and renewal. Of fresh beginnings.

He hoped it would be so for Flora as well.

Blaise released her hand and swept her a bow. "Welcome, Madame Cheney, to my ancestral home."

They set off toward it. Flora was enchanted. Like all the houses she had seen on the Breton coast, it faced south, with huge chimneys taking up the end walls. Flowers gone to the wild still tumbled around the foundation. Double windows flanked either side of the bright blue door, and the open shutters were covered with the same paint. She thought that she would never remember Brittany in years to come, without picturing that strong hue burning like blue flame against the sturdy granite blocks. It gave her a little pang.

He placed the hamper of food on one of the wide windowsills. "There is our destination."

An undercurrent of tension ran through his voice and she saw the excitement in his face. It communicated itself to her. She spied the standing stones at the very tip of the peninsula, three great oblongs facing westward out to sea, where each sunset would bathe them with the light of the dying day. "They look like sentinels," she said.

He lifted one eyebrow. "That is what they are called: the Sentinels. They are waiting for someone. Some say the return of King Arthur, others claim it is the return of the men—or the gods—who raised the stones before Christ was born. All that is remembered now is their name."

They picked their way over the stony ground toward the menhirs. Blaise was eager and strode ahead so quickly that Flora was forced to scramble to keep up with him. The going was not easy. The perspective against the backdrop of the wide sea gave the illusion of smaller stones near at hand. When they finally reached them, Flora found that the tall center stone was well over thirty feet high. Their seaward sides were blasted almost smooth by centuries of wind and rain, but their backs still bore intricate traceries of circles.

Flora touched her finger to one and felt a strange current run up her arm, like a strong tingle of static electricity. "Oh!" It startled her. Gingerly, she reached out her hand again. Nothing. The stone was inert.

Blaise laughed. "I thank you for confirming part of my research. There is a belief that a form of energy is stored inside the stones, and can be released by a human touch. I do not know the truth of it, but I have felt the same shock that you apparently did. And on more than one occasion."

"It was quite peculiar! I felt almost dizzy for a moment."

"I hope you are recovered now." He handed her one end of a measuring tape. "I am a hard taskmaster, and you will earn your picnic luncheon."

Any fears she had at spending time alone in such an isolated place with Blaise were soon put to rest. They spent well over an hour taking exacting measurements of the stones and their placement in relation to one another.

Afterward, Blaise made quick preliminary sketches and diagrams in his notebook, and set Flora to work taking rubbings of the concentric circles etched into the menhirs' backs. Details were revealed in the rubbings that did not show up well on the dark stone surface, and she became completely engrossed in her task. Enjoying herself, she was oblivious to the passage of time, until the wind freshened and the first drops of rain spattered on the granite.

Looking up, she was astounded to discover the blue sky had vanished. Thick gray clouds had amassed overhead, turning the sea as dull as lead. Now that she wasn't preoccupied she could hear the crash of the waves, and realized that she had been dimly aware of it for some time. The spatters came down harder and thicker now, and the breeze tugged hard at her bonnet and whisked her skirts around her legs.

Blaise raised his head from his sheet of drawing paper, snapped his notebook shut, and grabbed up his measuring tools. "Hurry! We'll take shelter before the rain comes down in earnest."

They scrambled back toward the house. Halfway there the skies opened and the rain bucketed down. By the time they reached the door they were both soaked to the skin. The door pushed open easily. Flora hadn't known quite what to expect: cobwebs and mold, perhaps. Her first impression was of gloom and the smell of woodsmoke and beeswax polish, and the faint odor of centuries of damp and salt sea air absorbed into the structure. She shivered in the chill air.

She almost tripped over a low stool, but Blaise made his way across the room toward one end of the house as if he could see in the dark. She heard him open a metal box, then the strike of a match. Light bloomed on the mantelpiece as he lit the lamps on either side of the chimneybreast.

"There will be wood for the fire somewhere," he said. "I'll get it started. Meanwhile, there should be blankets in the chest in front of the bed."

Flora looked around. This was her first time inside a typical Breton house. The floor was as solid as slate, but she saw it was *terre battue*, the hard-beaten earth that Blaise had told her housed the village floors. The furniture was heavy and solid and as intricately worked as the Breton pieces at the château. A table was built in a nook beneath one window, with settles of dark wood on either side.

A stone sink with a pipe leading to a rainwater cistern on the roof, and a low dresser with a hutch, were on the front wall at right angles to where Blaise was building the fire. Plates and bowls and platters in colorful faïence ware still lined its shelves. It looked as if the family had stepped out for Sunday Mass one morning and never returned.

"Has someone been living here?" she asked, trying to keep her teeth from chattering.

"No. But in the past I have sometimes spent a few days alone, working on my manuscripts." He shrugged out of his wet jacket. His fine linen shirt clung to his sculpted body. Flora looked away quickly.

The opposite wall held a long bench in front of a row of floor-to-ceiling cupboards, whose chestnut wood and metal fittings gleamed faintly in the dim light. Although it was much larger than the houses of Pont du Mor, the house was not as deep as she'd thought, and all one room. She didn't see any bed. That was a relief.

The kindling had caught well, putting forth a golden light. Blaise glanced over his shoulder. "The *lit clos*," he said. "It is behind those center doors."

She crossed the floor to the row of cupboards and found that they slid to either side rather than opening outward. At first she thought she was looking into another room. Then Blaise came to her side, carrying the lantern. She saw it was a box bed, enclosed on all four sides. There were curtains that could be drawn for privacy when the doors were open.

"Why, it's large enough for an entire family," she exclaimed.

Blaise smiled. "Yes, it was the custom. When the cold north wind blows they were cozy with the shared warmth of their bodies."

Two recesses were built into the paneled walls of the *lit clos* and held melted stubs of candles, while the third was a *niche de dévotion,* with a few dead wildflowers lying at the foot of a small wooden statue. He showed her the hook near the top where a baby's cradle could be hung, as well.

"There is another, smaller bed built into the back of the settle by the table. I used to play in it as a boy. The settle itself can be turned into a sleeping surface by tilting the top back, and laying a featherbed atop it for guests."

He saw that she was shivering from the cold rain. Opening one of the wall compartments, he drew out an enormous feather bed and spread it out inside the *lit clos*. A quilt and pillow followed. "Climb inside and take off your outer garments. I will spread them by the fire to dry along with my jacket and shirt."

"They will dry well enough with me inside them!"

His eyes lit with laughter. "Do you still not trust me, Flora? I have given you the word of a gentleman. And do not forget we must make the trip back across the water when the rain stops. I will refuse to take you if your clothes are not dry. The wind is too cold on the open water. If you are wet and chilled during the crossing, you would surely develop an inflammation of the lungs."

He was right. "Very well," Flora said, trying not to let her teeth chatter too badly. "They should be dry by the time the rain stops."

She sat on the bench and removed her muddy shoes and stockings. Slipping inside the *lit clos,* she unbuttoned her wet day dress and peeled it off. She was careful to tuck herself up in the quilt before handing her garment out of the box bed to Blaise. By now her teeth were clicking together as shivers racked her.

"Your corset cover and petticoats, too," he said indifferently. "We must warm you from the skin out."

She hesitated only briefly. Really, she was being absurd. After a brief struggle, she worked the damp garments off and handed them through the curtain as well. Within minutes she knew she'd made the right decision. The chill that had taken hold of her was abating.

Snuggling back against the featherbed, Flora resigned herself to a pleasant hour or two, trying to imagine herself a simple Breton housewife of centuries ago. The quilt was warm, with none of the dampness she would have expected of it so close to the water. The house was indeed snug against the elements.

She heard Blaise moving around in the room for several minutes. He came back, bringing her a lighted taper to stick in the wall niche. He had removed his shirt and hung it to dry on a chair back. His face was in shadow, but firelight shone on the muscles of his chest and arms, bringing red lights in the crisp, dark hairs there. Flora's stomach felt suddenly hollow and fluttery. The setting was too intimate for the sudden state of her nerves.

He moved out of her view, then returned and held out a wine glass of golden liquid. *"Choucher,"* he said. "Mead, made from honey. It will chase the chill from your bones."

She took the glass and sipped the drink. It was very sweet and heady. The Celts drank it before going into battle, Flora knew, to stimulate their courage. Perhaps she had better have more of it. It would take a lot of mead to steel herself to look away from Blaise, to turn her back on the sensual pleasure the mere sight of his naked torso gave her.

He looked down at her and smiled. Her courage wavered even more.

"Shall we still have our picnic, Flora? The food will be no less tasty for our being *en déshabille*. You need not even come out of your hidey-hole to dine."

If that was a hint to invite him into the *lit clos,* she was not having any of it. "I will come to the table."

She stepped out clumsily, holding the quilt around her with one arm and balancing the wine glass in her other hand. He caught her arm to steady her balance and it was the same as when she'd touched the standing stone: a jolt of stabbing electricity ran up her arm and set her heart pounding. She moved away as quickly as possible.

If he noticed he pretended not to. Escorting her to the settle, he put out the contents of the picnic hamper while she sipped the mead. There was a crusty loaf of bread, thickly sliced smoked ham, a stone bottle of the inevitable *cidre bouché,* sliced boiled eggs, a wedge of cheese, a crock of butter. Next he removed a packet of *gallettes,* the flat scones which were Johanna's particular favorites, and rolled *krampouez,* stuffed with stewed apricots and jam and dusted with sugar.

"We certainly shan't starve while we wait the rain out," she said, taking the plate of bread and ham he offered.

He didn't answer, absorbed in his own thoughts for several minutes. An air of melancholy had settled over him. Something was weighing on his mind. For a long while the only sounds were the patter of rain on the slate roof, the crackle of the fire in the hearth, and the sighing of the wind.

"The happiest days of my life were spent in this house," he said finally. "I used to say that one day, when I grew up, I would leave the château and live here, earning my living from the sea."

"Did you come here with your parents?"

"With my mother and brother."

He went back to his brooding thoughts, and Flora was sorry she'd brought the matter up. It was cozy sitting with him in the half-light, sharing a simple meal. She tried to imagine what it would have been like for a woman living in this sturdy house, with nothing to disturb her peace but wind and wild weather. Sleeping in the *lit clos* with her husband by her side, a baby asleep in the hanging cradle. Listening to the soft sounds of their breathing. Cuddling into his side for warmth on cold winter nights. Feeling Blaise reach out for her and . . .

Flora gave a little start. The potent mead, the intimate mood, the warmth of the fire had almost put her to sleep. She wanted to crawl back into the *lit clos* and snuggle beneath the quilts and doze to the lullaby of the wind and rain.

Blaise rose abruptly. "The rain has blown over. Our clothes should be dry. We must get back to the château quickly."

"Why such a hurry?" she said, feeling a little cross at the shattered mood. "If the rain is gone we have plenty of time."

"The weather can be treacherous." He handed Flora her gown, dry and warm from the fire. "Get dressed."

She did as he asked, still out of sorts. It was so pleasant here, and she did not want to return to the château. To Gaelle's thinly veiled dislike and Malin's dire predictions. To her luxurious bedchamber, where voices asked whispered questions and seashells and seaweed materialized, seemingly out of thin air.

Blaise gave her no choice. When she got down from the box bed he was dressed and waiting at the door. He opened it and they stepped out. The rain had stopped but the ground was muddy. A brisk wind plucked at the strings of Flora's bonnet and tugged at her skirts, but she had seen the village fishermen out at sea in the same stiff breeze. They squelched through the mud.

As they rounded the huge upthrust of granite that sheltered the house, the wind struck them like a fist. Flora gasped and staggered. If Blaise had not caught her by the arm she would have fallen. From their vantage point she could see that the seas were running high. The water rose in great gray walls all the way to the horizon.

They fought their way to the sheltered spot where the boat was moored. She half expected to find it smashed to kindling, but there it was, bobbing crazily with the ebb and swell of the waves. It made her ill to watch it.

"Can we make it back safely?"

"If the sailboat holds up. I am a man of Brittany," he said. "I know these waters like I know my own face in the mirror."

She remembered him saying the same thing of Loic Kersaudy. "Then you should have been prepared for the change in weather."

He frowned and pointed to the low line of black clouds scudding swiftly toward them. "I became preoccupied by my work; one forgets. If we don't go back now, we'll be stranded here."

She eyed the sky doubtfully. "I can stand your company until it passes, if you can put up with mine. It seems the lesser of two evils."

Blaise looked out to sea. "I don't like those clouds. This might be worse than a few hours of inconvenience. When one of these wild storms blows up out of the northwest, it can last for two or three days."

A tree branch snapped with a mighty crack not ten feet away. The torn limb went spiraling off the low cliff. Flora's hand fluttered to her throat. "What shall we do?"

He didn't answer at once. When he did, his voice was harsh.

"The choice is yours, Flora. If I were alone, I would be willing to make a run for it. Now, before the high tide comes in and complicates matters. But it may already be too late. I leave it for you to decide if we should stay. Shall we risk it, you and I, and accept the consequences? What is your decision?"

Her heart sped up a little. It seemed as if there was more than one meaning to his words. The craft rose and fell, rose and fell, until Flora was dizzy from looking at it. The wind tore her hair loose from its chignon, sending it out like streamers behind her. The hull scraped against the rocks with a sound like a moan of pain. A wave crashed with a deafening roar, filling the bottom of the sailboat with foaming gray water.

A vision flashed through Flora's mind: Blaise's battered body washed up upon the strand, her own trapped below the waves by constricting tentacles of seaweed. "If we attempt it, the boat will surely capsize!" she exclaimed. "I

would much rather wait out the storm here in safety, than
be dashed to pieces on the rocks.''

"So be it," he said. There was relief in his tone, and
something she couldn't identify.

Flora glanced across the waves toward the cliff. "They
will be concerned when we do not return in this weather."

"Someone will see lights from the house, and guess that
we are there. It will not be the first time I've waited out a
storm in the cottage."

He sheltered her against his side as they turned back
toward the house, blocking the growing gusts of cold air
with his body. By the time they reached the safety of Yvon
Cheney's cottage, the wind was howling like a beast. Blaise
caught the door and pushed her inside, barely managing to
shut it against the violent wind. Perhaps it was only a grim-
ace of effort that flickered across his face, but Flora could
almost have sworn that he was smiling.

Hard rain beat a midnight tattoo against the roof. The
wooden storm shutters Blaise had closed earlier rattled beneath the onslaught, until Flora thought the glazing in the
windows would shatter. The wind shrieked like souls in
torment. Flora covered her ears against the din; but it was
not the storm outside that kept her from sleep. Curled up
on the feather bed in the *lit clos,* she was warm enough,
although she'd given Blaise the only quilt. He'd gotten
soaked to the skin battening the shutters. She'd made him
finish the rest of the mead to ward off the chill.

"There should be several quilts, along with a supply of
candles and matches," he'd complained. They'd searched
high and low for more linens, but the cupboards were bare
of them.

He was supposed to be sleeping before the hearth fire.
Instead she heard him pacing up and down, restless as a
caged tiger. The same restlessness stirred in Flora's blood.

She felt hollow inside, but not with hunger. They'd eaten
the eggs and some of the ham, and stored the rest in a stone
box on the floor. He'd found two jars of preserved pears
in the larder earlier. If they were careful, there was plenty
of food to last out a three-day storm, and a goodly quantity
of firewood. They were safe from the outer elements. It

was the heavy atmosphere in the cottage that threatened them.

Flora snuggled into the feather bed. She was sorry that he was going to have to sleep on the floor, though, and she felt a little guilty that she had the warmth and comfort of a bed so large it could hold four adults with ease. . . . but she was *not* going to invite him to share it with her.

She jumped as something slammed against the house with a mighty clatter. One of the exterior shutters had torn loose and slammed against the stone wall. The wind wrenched it away, and in the flare of lightning that followed, she could see Blaise silhouetted in front of the dazzling glare illuminating the window.

He braced his arms on the sill and looked out at the storm while rain lashed the glass panes. As she watched he turned abruptly away, sat on the low bench and buried his head in his hands. There was such woe, such despair in his posture that it frightened her.

She rose from the feather bed and climbed down from the *lit clos*. The hard-beaten floor was cool beneath her feet and smooth as stone. ''What is it, Blaise? What is wrong?''

He lowered his hands but turned his head away. Between the golden-red firelight and the icy-white lightning he seemed sculpted of fire and ice. A muscle worked at his jaw. ''Go back to bed, Flora. Leave me be.''

Tentatively she touched his arm. ''Won't you tell me what is wrong?''

He flinched, then went still. ''I am not fit company for you,'' he said hoarsely. ''For the love of God, go back to bed and stay there until morning.''

Instead she knelt on the floor beside him. ''You are frightening me. Are we in danger?''

He turned then, and took her face between his hard palms. His eyes glimmered in the strange half-light. ''Not from the storm, Flora. The danger is here in this very room. Can't you sense it? Can't you feel it, flowing between us like a swift current?''

His thumb traced a line of heat along her cheek. His eyes were dark with either passion or anger, but which she could not tell. Nor could she speak. Her heart pounded so hard inside her rib cage that she felt the next beat might shatter it like glass.

His breathing was harsh and rapid, as if he had run all night through the storm. "Flora, Flora . . . *Sacrebleu!* I am a man in hell, and only you can release me."

Blaise's self-control returned, and he let her go so suddenly she almost lost her balance. He rose and strode over to the fireplace, leaning his naked arm against the mantelpiece. "When I proposed our little arrangement to you, I had only one thing in mind: to see Johanna safely settled and out of my hair, so that my life could go on as it always had, with nothing to interfere with my work or my pleasures. I saw no reason for either of us to waste our energies in trying to make a real marriage of what was an inconvenient necessity. And so we agreed, you and I, that ours was to be a marriage in name only."

Turning, he met her gaze full on. The impact of his look almost sent Flora reeling. Everything she had secretly hoped—and feared—was there in his eyes.

"I cannot pretend that I have not changed my mind," he said fiercely. "Almost from that first day, I realized how grievously I had erred. Knowing you were mine in name, knowing you were just a few feet away from me in the long, lonely hours of the night, has driven me to the brink of madness. I lost my head, not once but twice. In the process I frightened you badly."

He prowled the firelit room with lithe, masculine grace. "I gave you my word, and I will keep it. But, God in heaven, how I want you, Flora!"

She sat there listening. Barely breathing.

He stopped before her, his face in shadow now.

"I have cursed myself for a fool a thousand times. I lie awake at night, torturing myself with the knowledge that you are lying in your own bed on the other side of our sitting room. Knowing that it was my arrogance in offering you a marriage of convenience only that has brought us to this impasse."

He held his hands out toward her, then let them drop to his side. His agitation was only betrayed by the rough timbre of his voice: "I did not expect to care for you, you see."

Flora's breath caught in her chest. She had never expected to hear those words from him. It sent her into confusion. What was in her own heart? She didn't know. She was desperately attracted to him. There. She had admitted it. But did she love him, or was it just desire calling to desire, need to need?

Did it matter?

Her heart pounded in her throat. "What is it that you want of me, Blaise?"

"Don't you *know*? Haven't I confessed my feelings to you?"

She was shaking so badly her teeth almost chattered. "Say it in words. Tell me what you want . . ."

"I want *you*! In my arms and in my bed. Sharing my life. My wife in all ways, not just in name." He touched her cheek. "Flora, my beautiful love."

Another tremor ran through her. If this were love she felt, it was not at all what she had expected—this pain and doubt and longing, this fire in the blood that urged her to yield herself up, body and soul. There was only one way to resolve it and end this exquisite torture. The decision, the choice was hers to make.

She had no words to give voice to her tumultuous emotions. Instead she lifted her hands and let her silk chemise slip from her ivory shoulders. It whispered to her feet. The light in Blaise's eyes, his ragged intake of breath, made her knees go weak.

When he strode forward and pulled her into his arms, she was dizzy with fear and longing. With wild, hot desire.

They were locked breast to breast, their bodies melding together like molten metal. His mouth found hers, and his kiss was filled with passion and possession. Flora responded, leaning into him as she surrendered her conscious will to deeper, more primitive instincts. His fingers dug into her flesh. He would not be a gentle lover. He would be fierce, insistent, demanding. And she was glad of it.

He gave in to the desire that flamed between them. All the agonizing hours of knowing she was a touch away, and yet not truly his to touch, burned away in the heat of it. He buried his face in her hair and swept kisses down her temple to the angle between her jaw and throat. Her body moved against his, fitting her soft curves against the hard masculine planes of his, as if it had done so a hundred times before.

His blood roared like a blast furnace. They would come out of this refined and tempered by their fire. In Flora he had found an equal partner in passion. He knew that she could no more rein in her desires than he. Hadn't he somehow sensed it from the start?

Her skin was soft against his lips, and he found the delicately fluttering pulse with the tip of his tongue. She shuddered in his arms, and he felt his need for her grow until it was almost overwhelming. But he must make the most of this first, blazing encounter. He must seal her to him with the act.

He drew her toward the bed, and her footsteps matched his eagerly. Swooping her up in his arms, he lifted her into the *lit clos,* and pressed her down into the feather mattress with the weight of his body. For a few seconds he held her without moving, reveling in the sensations of their embrace, exulting in his victory. It had been easier than he'd expected, but it was every bit as sweet and heady as he'd imagined.

His long fingers cupped her breasts. They were white and full against his rough palm, their tips lush and ripe. He had dreamed of this, yet tried to deny it far too long. His mouth roved from the tender notch at the base of her slender throat and down to the vee of her breasts. *Mon Dieu!* but she was beautiful.

Flora thought she was dreaming, lost in some erotic paradise of the mind: any moment she would wake up and find herself alone in her room. But the skim of his fingers gliding over her breasts, the fire of his warm breath upon her skin, her swelling nipples, was so real, so intense she could hardly bear the pleasure. Her hands smoothed over his strong arms and shoulders, touched his chest with tentative, questing fingers. She rejoiced when he threw his head back and gasped at her touch.

"Do you love me, Flora? Let me hear you say it. Say it and make a vow that you will never leave me, *mon coeur.* Swear it!"

"I will never leave you, Blaise. I do swear it. My husband, my *love*!"

And she knew then, beyond a doubt, that she did love him. Had loved him almost from the start. Denying her feelings had only driven them deeper. She could not believe her sudden giddy happiness.

There was no need for further words between them. He shifted away and stripped off his trousers. She stifled a laugh when a button, torn loose by his hurry, pinged against the wall of the *lit clos* and landed on the pillow beside her head. He was as helpless to fight their desperate need to come together as she.

Then his naked body touched hers. Fire met fire. She arched against him and her arms wound around his neck. It seemed that she could not get close enough to him.

His fingers trailed across her stomach and along one thigh. When he touched her intimately, she stiffened briefly. He cupped her with his hand, not moving, and kissed her mouth until she was accustomed to his touch. Gradually she relaxed.

"Don't be afraid," he whispered. "I will give you such pleasure, I promise you!"

He was experienced in the art of seduction, and she soon learned how little she knew, how little she had tasted of love. As he skillfully stroked and probed and tantalized, she was greedy for more. Even in her most fervid longings, she had never imagined anything like this. When the feelings he evoked became too exquisite to sustain, she twisted away from his seeking hands.

"Easy," he murmured. "Let me pleasure you, Flora. Let me make love to you as I have longed to do."

Her breath was jagged as a knife, but she let him gentle her with his low murmurs, his sensual talents. She wondered, fleetingly, where he had learned to give such intense delight, and how many women he had bedded and pleasured. Then the thought was lost in the swirl of sensation, as his tongue caught her nipple and his hand moved between her thighs. She was rising on a hot, red tide that swept her along before it. Helpless to stop it, she let it carry her away.

As it crested she was suddenly catapulted into space. She uttered a cry that was half fright, half amazed joy, and gave herself up to it willingly. Her body shuddered with desire as he held her, urged her on. She clung to him, shaken and desperate for their union. Instantly he was there, filling her emptiness with his body, raising her hips to meet his and plunging deep.

A fierce joy coursed through her blood as she gave herself up to the wild storm of release. He drove into her again and again, each thrust an intense lightning bolt of exquisite pleasure. Then she shuddered and groaned and arched back on a final thrust that sent her up and over the edge again. After they lay entwined, slick with sweat and replete with satisfaction.

He whispered against her hair, murmuring indistinguishable words. As he held her in his embrace, Flora would have been content to spend the rest of her life like that. The moment was too perfect.

And he had barely started. He slid his torso down her body inch by inch, the crisp hair of his chest making her skin tingle delightfully. Caressing and kissing her throat, her breasts, her belly. The softness of her inner thighs. The secret places between. Tasting her delicately, teasing her with lips and tongue, teaching her things she hadn't guessed her own body was capable of feeling and doing. With relentless skill and exquisite timing, he brought her to the brink a dozen times, retreating at just the right moment to leave her writhing with desire.

"Shall I go on, Flora?" he breathed against her sensitive skin. "If you do, you must say it."

"Oh, yes. Oh, God! Now!"

Lifting her hips, he lowered his head and pressed his mouth against her, kissing her intimately. Urgent need swept through her. She was shaking with want, aching with desire. And then she was tumbling off the earth once more, hopelessly lost. He held her while her body bucked and shuddered again and again until she was breathless and gasping for air.

And still he wasn't finished with her. She moaned as his mouth found her breasts, as he took her nipple into it and rolled it with his teeth. Her blood was on fire. His hands moved lower, stroking gently as she opened to him. But this time she wasn't just satisfied with his touch. She wanted more.

"Tell me, Flora," he groaned against her flesh. "Tell me you want me. Let me hear you say it."

"I want you, Blaise. I want you now!"

He speared into her and she cried out with pleasure. "More?" he asked softly. "Harder? Deeper?"

"Yes . . . oh, yes. . . ." Her voice trailed off into a series of gasps as he took her with practiced strokes. Deeper with every thrust until they were both moaning with the sheer physical joy of their consummation. He plunged into her again and again until she arced up against him and he shuddered and spent his seed in her.

"You are mine, Flora! You are *mine!*"

They lay sprawled together, listening to the small mantel clock strike three. He kissed her until her mouth was swollen and tender. She was sleepy and content and more than a little sore, but thoroughly satisfied. Flora wanted to lie awake, enjoying this perfect peace between them; instead she drifted into dreams almost immediately, locked in Blaise's arms.

He pushed himself up upon his elbow, and looked down at her face. How different she looked like this, with her lips swollen with his kisses and her cheeks flushed with the glow of passion. Her damp hair was spread over the pillowcase in wild tendrils and he wound a curl around his finger. So ardent! So beautiful! He had chosen well.

Now that he had her safely in his arms, he was too relieved, too wide awake, to sleep. He blessed the good fortune that had led him to enroll Johanna in the English academy. He thanked the gods for his foresight in choosing Flora. Things could not have turned out any better.

But he must not let his arrogance trip him up. It was early days yet, and she had a mind of her own, this little wife of his! First he must bind her to him, use her own passionate nature to ensnare her further, until a look, a touch from him could set her on fire—as she did him. His loins tingled thinking of it.

He went over every moment of their lovemaking again in his mind while she slept beside him. After a while Blaise reached for Flora again and drew her to him, cupping her breast against his palm as he lowered his mouth to hers. She murmured sleepily.

His lips closed over her nipple and tugged lightly, until she came fully awake. His teeth nipped and teased until she moaned in anticipation of yet more pleasure, and wound her bare arms around his throat. Her body moved beneath his, inviting him. Enticing him to further heights of passion.

A light touch told him she was ready, the shiver of her body and the shifting of her limbs told him she was eager. *Not yet,* he told himself, *not yet,* although his loins were hot and aching for release inside her.

There was still so much to show her, new heights that he would take her to, new sensations that would delight her and send her shuddering over the edge to ecstasy again. He stroked and caressed and let his mouth rove lower, skimming her breasts, the feminine curve of her rib cage, the rounded swell of her belly. His thumbs slid between her legs, gently parting her satin folds like the petals of a flower. She was honey and nectar on his tongue, sweeter and more heady than mead. This time he was bolder yet.

Flora could not believe what he was doing, and that she was letting him do it. He was touching her in places she had never dreamed of being touched, and the rasp of his cheek against her inner thigh, the flicker of his tongue, the sharp ecstasy as he found the most sensitive spot, were so intense she thought she would die from them. He urged her, stroking and probing and sucking until her body was racked with sensation. Nothing had ever prepared her for this giving of self, this taking of pure, physical pleasure, this blending of heat and breath and soul.

Her body was a fragile craft, tossed on the wild seas of passion, and she gave herself up to the greater force. Rough waves of sensation overwhelmed her, sweeping her away. "Now," she said hoarsely. *"Now!"*

He rose above her, naked and splendid as a young god. She arched up as he plunged inside her and lost herself in the storm. He clasped her hips and drove deep inside her, claiming her with every thrust. Deeper and deeper, as she cried out his name. Their lovemaking was urgent and savage, consuming and renewing itself while the winds howled in the eaves and the raging rain drove against the windows. Its left them both shaken, and forever altered.

Flora lay with Blaise's naked limbs entangled with hers. His breathing was deep and regular and she knew he was asleep. Their man and woman scents mingled with the smell of peachwood in the fireplace. He had invaded all the secret places of her body, and she reveled in the victory of her surrender. This then was love.

In the space of a few hours her universe had expanded and collapsed. Nothing remained of it but this curtained bed and the two of them, throbbing in the aftermath of passion. She was satiated and replete beyond the power of thought. And she was *loved*! Hugging that thought to herself, she drifted back into dreams.

It was the silence that awakened Blaise an hour after dawn. Through the window with the missing shutter, he could see a sky of pink and gold, promising a glorious new day. *An omen*, he told himself.

He lifted himself up on one elbow. Flora lay naked beside him, rosy with sleep. Her hair spread out on the feather bed like a fan of dark silk. She was his. Finally, his.

He kissed her face, her throat, her smooth, thrusting breasts. He laved the swollen nipple with his tongue and took it into his mouth again, feeling it tingle and go hard. He was half insane with the need for her. He could not get his fill of her. And he wanted her to feel the same, fierce desire.

Her lids fluttered open and she smiled up at him radiantly. It made his heart turn over in his chest. Blaise felt the weight of the days ahead settle on his shoulders. What had happened here was only the beginning.

He must make Flora his completely. Instill so deep a craving in her that it was like a fever in her blood. An insanity. An obsession so great, so overwhelming that— even when she finally learned the truth—she would forgive him anything.

Chapter Eleven

Flora awakened at first light, curled up against Blaise. Listening to his breathing, feeling the heat of his body permeate hers, she could still almost believe it to be a dream. Any moment, she thought, she would awaken and find herself back at Hawthorne Academy in the cold gray light of a winter's morning.

But it was the warm dawn of a Breton spring shining in through the cottage window, and her husband—her *husband*!—sleeping beside her. She hugged her joy to herself. That their paths had crossed at all was incredible. The fact that Blaise loved her, an unexpected miracle.

He *had* said that he loved her, hadn't he? Or had that been something she'd dreamed? Reality and dreams had merged in her waking hours, and she could no longer tell one from another. All she knew was that she was the most fortunate of women. Four months ago she had been a lonely and hunted creature, desperately hiding behind a new identity. That seemed like another lifetime. She refused to let Robin Harding shadow her happiness and pushed the ugly memories away. Now she was Madame Cheney, starting life completely anew with the man she loved to distraction.

There! She had admitted it: her heart, so bruised and wary, had been given to Blaise long before last night. It had only been fear of being hurt again that had made her refuse to acknowledge it sooner. She had seen many sides of him, from sardonic and sophisticated, to haunted and vulnerable, wracked with the pain of physical suffering and his deep emotional scars.

She snuggled closer to his side, breathing in his scent. The sun rose higher, and she felt him stir. "I wish it were still raining," she said softly. "I wish we didn't have to go back."

He buried his face in the cloud of her hair, his hands skimming possessively over her skin. "The sun is barely up *ma fleur*. We don't have to go back . . . yet."

Flora turned her face for his kiss, and lost herself once more in his arms.

It was still well before noon when their little sailboat put in to the cove beneath the Mermaid's Tower. One of the men was loading a rowboat with cartons. "Bonjour, madame, monsieur." He touched his cap. "Malin said you wanted blankets and supplies out on the island. I was going to bring them earlier but . . ."

"That is quite all right," Blaise said curtly, and hustled Flora over to the cliff path.

She stifled her laughter with difficulty. "A good thing he did not set out earlier!"

Blaise leaned down and nibbled her ear. "An even better thing that Johanna chose not to accompany us yesterday."

They made their way up the steep path hand in hand. The strength of his, the warmth with which it enfolded her own, made Flora feel protected and cherished. As they entered the old part of the château they went by the door to the Mermaid's Tower.

The pink stone with the engraving struck Flora as poignant in the extreme. She touched it lightly in passing, and felt a chill ripple through her. Today she had discovered great happiness at Château Morgaine, while the legendary sea creature had found only unhappiness and death—or so the story went. But it was only a story, after all.

The days passed in a delirium of contentment. Flora hadn't dreamed she could ever be so happy. The two weeks following their night on the Druid's Isle were perfect. The weather was glorious, and even Gaelle seemed to have fallen under the enchantment that filled the château. The preparations for the *grand pardon* were well under way, and the halls bustled with a sense of excitement. Not even the pending arrival of Guy and Odile de Broceliand could dampen Flora's spirits.

One afternoon, as she and Blaise were up in the Mermaid's Tower, indulging in a brief romantic interlude, they heard the sounds of carriages rolling over the cobblestones.

"Who on earth can that be?" Flora said, reluctantly tugging at her open bodice. "The guests are not due to arrive for three more days."

He sighed and kissed her. "The mayor is coming to see me this morning." He grinned and kissed her again. "I had quite forgotten, so taken as I was with other matters. You will have to put in an appearance, as well, if he has brought Madame Lampoul with him."

"Wretch, for not telling me!" Flora hastily did up her buttons and smoothed her hair. "If we hurry I can make it up to my chamber and freshen myself before they are inside."

They retraced their steps and hurried to the main hall, where there was great activity. They were met by the housekeeper.

"The first of the guests have arrived for the *pardon* madame."

Flora was aware of her rumpled appearance. "Oh, dear. You must make my excuses for me. I will hurry upstairs and change before greeting them."

Blaise looked out through the open door and recognized the maid and valet standing beside a mound of monogrammed luggage. "No need. It is only Claudine and Nicolas. Those two are so wrapped up in each other, they wouldn't notice if we met them in our night clothes."

Laughing they stepped into the sunny courtyard. The baggage coach was already gone and a light traveling vehicle pulled up at the front door. The swans stopped their imperious gliding on the ornamental pond, to eye the new arrivals. Nicolas jumped lightly out and put down the steps for his wife. The sun shone on his fair hair like a cap of gold. Flora thought what a lovely couple he and Claudine made, both so elegant and so devoted. If only their marriage had been blessed with the children they so desperately wanted!

"Blaise! Flora!" Claudine descended from her traveling carriage.

Her eyes took in Flora's glowing face and Blaise's air of deep content. "There is no need to ask how you are doing! The country air . . ."—she cocked her head to one side, as if considering—"or perhaps marriage itself, has done you both a deal of good."

Nicolas clapped Blaise on the shoulder. "Indeed you look well. I am glad of it. You gave us quite a fright, *mon ami*. There was a time when I feared you would not live."

Blaise gripped his friend's arm. "I should have been dead at the opera house, without your quick thinking. I can never repay my debt to you."

"Let us not speak of past debts," Nicolas responded, flushing. "Let us think instead of the future."

"We did not expect you for three more days," Flora said, as she strolled inside with Blaise's cousin, ahead of the men. "How fortunate that you could come to us sooner."

Claudine blushed and lowered her voice so that only Flora could hear, as they entered the cool great hall. "You know that after the *pardon* I intend to make a pilgrimage to Mont-Saint-Michel? Perhaps Blaise would bring you and Johanna, and we could tour together. Ooh, la! To see the tide roll in for miles and turn the Mont into an island is something you will never forget! And there is this quaint little goldsmith's shop that has—"

She stopped herself before she could go off on one of her enthusiastic tangents. "Enough of that for now! But meanwhile, there *is* another place I wish to visit while we are in Brittany. A shrine to Saint Yvonne near Plouzané. Nicolas and I thought we might go tomorrow and perhaps spend two or three days there, then return to you so we might have a little time together, as planned, before the festivities begin."

"Tell me about the shrine," Flora said, leading her to the stairs.

Claudine's dark eyes sparkled with new hope. "We chanced to hear of it at a soirée. It is said that if a barren woman offers up a prayer and drinks from the well there, just before the full moon, she will conceive. I do not know if this is true, but oh! how I hope it might be so!"

"Claudine! Nicolas!" Johanna came flying down the corridor from the small sitting room where she had been sorting out Gaelle's silk floss. She threw her arms around Claudine. "You have come at last, you and Nicolas!"

Claudine kissed her and then held her at arm's length. "This sea air agrees with you also, *petite*. You look young and carefree, as a girl your age should." She pinched Johanna's cheek lightly. "It is good to see you with color in your face and a sparkle in your eyes. Exactly as a debutante must look if she hopes to snare herself a rich husband, eh?"

Johanna stiffened. "I do not wish for a husband, rich or otherwise. I should be perfectly happy staying here at the château forever!"

"Oh, la! How vehement you are." Claudine sent Flora a look tinged with laughter. "I recall thinking the same at a certain stage in my life; but like all women, you shall change your mind completely, when the right man comes along!"

The girl did not look at all convinced. Blaise took Nicolas off for a glass of brandy and Johanna offered to fetch Gaelle. "She will be in the chapel, no doubt. She repairs there every day before noon, to say her rosary beads, and again each evening. I have never known anyone so devout."

She said this so respectfully that Claudine turned to Flora the moment Johanna was gone. "I hope she does not intend to follow in Gaelle's footsteps—or worse yet, decide to take the veil!"

Flora laughed. "No, she is only suffering from a disappointment. She had a letter while we were still in Paris, saying that the handsomest lad in Hawthorne village had married a wealthy widow many years his senior. Although her heart is not broken, I am sure it was quite a disillusionment. And Loic Kersaudy, who used to be very attentive, is immersed in his writing. Come, let us go upstairs and you can change out of your traveling clothes and tell me all the news. I feel quite cut off from the world here."

That was all the encouragement Claudine needed. All the way up the stairs she bubbled over with news, comments about their journey and the weather, and all the latest gossip of the *haut monde*.

She waited until Flora had escorted her up to the best guest chamber to freshen up before she delivered the most delicious of her tidbits.

"No doubt you have heard that the De Broceliands retired earlier to Brittany this year than is their habit?"

"Yes," Flora answered, with a wry lift of her eyebrow. "In fact, I met them on the strand. In an effort to spare my feelings from learning of it from another source, Madame de Broceliand kindly informed me that she had been Blaise's mistress for many years."

"No! But she is too much, that one!" Claudine was torn between indignation and scandalized amusement. "To be the mistress of an unmarried man, that is one thing: to announce it to a man's bride is the outside of enough! Has she no shame?"

Flora laughed. "Very little, I imagine. She seemed quite proud of her frankness, and extended an offer of friendship to me. I was in no particular hurry to take her up on it; however, it appears it will be thrust upon me. Blaise says they will be our overnight guests during the *grand pardon*."

"*Oh, là!*" Claudine stopped in the act of removing her bonnet before the mirror and stared at Flora's reflection, openmouthed. "Well," she said when she recovered her voice, "you need have no worries on that score. Blaise is a gentleman. If she were still his mistress, he would draw the line at inviting her to sleep under the same roof as his own wife."

"As would I!" Flora exclaimed. Claudine's more worldly view of extramarital liaisons did not exactly shock her: Frenchwomen were much less hypocritical about such matters than the English upper classes, although she was sure the incidence of infidelity was much the same in either country. But it gave Flora pause.

"Is every husband expected to take a mistress, then?"

Claudine threw her arms around her friend. "Do not be concerned about Blaise. He is as loyal as Nicolas, to death and beyond."

She put her hand to her mouth, realizing she had made a terrible faux pas. Now was not the time to remind Flora of poor Eve. "You have worked a miracle. Why, I can see that he is head over heels in love with you. He has never looked happier."

She pressed her lightly powdered cheek against Flora's. "And you are blooming! I am overjoyed for you!"

She stepped back and slipped off her pelisse. "Do you like my new brooch and eardrops? A gift from Nicolas for our anniversary."

Flora admired the extravagant pin and earrings of scintillating opals surrounded by clusters of garnets and diamonds. "How fabulous! And they suit your coloring extremely well. But I understood your marriage took place in the autumn?"

"Oh, it did." Claudine laughed. "But Nicolas is so sentimental. We met in the spring, you see. Every year, on the anniversary of that day, he sends me gifts—jewels, flowers, candy. Which reminds me, I must have my maid unpack the things we have brought for you and the others from Paris."

She smiled and posed in the mirror, watching the light strike fire from the opal and garnet earrings in their diamond frames, then recollected herself.

"But I forgot my story I was relating to you: the reason the De Brocelliands came so early is that Guy fought a duel." Claudine sniffed. "Over Odile's *honor*. He came home unexpectedly and found her *en flagrante* with a handsome young naval officer." The dimple peeked impishly at the corner of her mouth. "On the table in the dining room, amidst the remains of brandy and strawberry-rhubarb tarts."

Flora burst out laughing. "You are making that up!"

"Ah, no. It is all quite true. It was hushed up, of course, but it was deemed best that Guy and Odile retire to the country until the scandal blows over. There is a new dessert being served at Paris dinners: *Pêche Odile*—poached peach halves in brandy, served with strawberry and rhubarb sauce. It is *fort amusant*, is it not? But you must pretend you have not heard!"

Flora gasped for breath and tried to control her laughter. "You should not have told me, Claudine. I do not know how I shall be able to look them both in the eye, without giving myself away."

"Yes," the Parisienne said with a twinkle in her eyes. "That is what makes it so much fun, *hein*? Myself, I look forward to meeting them with great eagerness."

Half an hour later they went downstairs, arm in arm, in high good humor. Flora was delighted to have Claudine and Nicolas with them. She missed having another woman to talk to, one who shared some of the same interests as she. For all her fashionably frothy appearance, Claudine had a solid understanding. She was very well read, and interested in history and the politics of the day.

As they passed the large portrait in the gallery, Claudine stopped. She glanced from the painted likeness of Blaise's mother to Flora. Her face, so pink with laughter a moment earlier, went white with alarm.

"But you do not have on the necklace! You must wear it always, when you are at the château. The Mermaid's Egg will protect you from the curse."

Flora was torn between curiosity and dismay at Claudine's superstitious belief. "Do you mean to tell me that it really exists?"

"Of course it exists. It has been handed down to every Cheney bride for generations. Whatever can Blaise be thinking? I will speak with him. He must give you the Mermaid's Egg at once."

Flora started down the stairs again. "I am in no danger. Blaise and I rode out a storm on the Druid's Isle, and the worst I suffered for it was a night spent in my shift." Not that she'd had in on very long. She blushed at the memories.

"Now I know that he is mad for love of you," Claudine exclaimed. "Blaise is too good a sailor to go out when foul weather threatens. I tell you what it is: you have addled his brains, Flora."

"No, no. The day was fair and sunny when we set out. But I was glad we were stranded. It was the first time we've truly been alone together." She'd thought that she knew what occurred between a man and woman. Her initiation into the sensual arts, by Blaise, had been a revelation.

"Well, then, I am glad of it also." She scrutinized Flora's face and her own softened. "In Paris, I admit I was worried when you and Blaise seemed so distant to one another at times. Nicolas is very wise. He said you needed time to be better acquainted. And now, *chèrie,* you have the look of a woman well loved. I am so happy for you!"

"Yes. I am the most fortunate of women. Claudine, you spoke earlier of making a pilgrimage to Mont-Saint-Michel, after the *pardon.* If that is your intention, I should like to accompany you. I wish to give thanks for all that I have been given."

Claudine sighed without realizing it. "Yes, I intend to make the visit, and also to make a pilgrimage to Saint Anne of Auray. Perhaps the saints will intervene with *le Bon Dieu,* and he will bless my efforts to conceive." She sent a sly look at Flora. "Perhaps you will have to wish for other things, eh?"

From below they could hear Gaelle's voice, calling to Blaise rather imperiously. Claudine saw the look on her friend's face. She put her hand on Flora's sleeve. "You must not mind Gaelle's possessiveness toward Blaise. She has no one else, you see. I used to think that she was almost relieved when Eve died, hoping it would end his misery. Almost, I say, for she did most sincerely grieve for her."

Flora felt chilled. Such jealousy was unnatural. "She must have been a handsome woman in her youth. I wonder that she never married."

"She was betrothed to man of Normandy, who jilted her on the eve of their wedding. Her suffering and humiliation were great. She suffered a decline, and came here to live with the family and recover her health. Her devotion to God and to Blaise kept her here after Anne's death. Otherwise, I think she would have taken the veil and entered a convent. That one, she was born to be a nun!"

Their tête-à-tête was interrupted by Blaise and Nicolas coming up the staircase. Claudine gave her cousin a scold. "You have not given Flora the Mermaid's Egg."

He gazed up at the portrait as if he had not really looked at it in years. "How young we all were then!" He stared at it a moment, then turned away. "I had almost forgotten about it. The clasp was never repaired. I will see if I can fix it myself, Flora, so that you may wear the necklace for the *pardon.*"

He touched her cheek with the back of his fingers. "I should not want anything to happen to you, *chère.* Especially now."

The two men continued on up the stairs while Flora and Claudine went down to the drawing room in search of Johanna and Gaelle. Remembering that first evening at the château, Flora could not help contrasting it with today. She was indeed the most fortunate of women.

At the foot of the stairs she paused and looked back. Anne Cheney stared down from her portrait, forever beautiful and young. Forever sad.

The afternoon was a busy one, for the privilege of dressing the statue of Saint Mari du Mor fell to the ladies of the chateau. Flora had been looking forward to seeing the new garments Gaelle had fashioned, placed on the statue in the church's grotto.

By the time they finished a light repast, there was scarcely time to look at the gifts Claudine and Nicolas had brought them from Paris: a gold locket with her initial for Johanna, fine chocolates and a new cologne in a crystal bottle for Flora, a rosary of carved coral from Jerusalem for Gaelle, and several bottles of a marvelous burgundy for Blaise's appreciative palate.

The men decided to sample the wine, "in case it has gone off from the journey," Nicolas said with a grin.

"Or in case it has not, which would be even better," Blaise said, laughing.

Flora and Claudine climbed into the closed carriage beside Johanna. Gaelle had taken the seat opposite so her precious cargo would not be jostled by the others.

She sat as rigid as a poker, looking incongruous in her plain black gown with the splendid garments she'd sewn for the statue spread out on her lap. She would not entrust the delicate fabrics to be wrapped, afraid that the ornaments might snag the fine golden threads on which she'd spent so many laborious hours.

Although the *pardon* would not begin for several days, the streets of Pont du Mor were bustling with relatives and friends of the villagers, as well as visitors from all over the country. The inns for miles around were already as full as they could hold. Most visitors were dressed in the colorful costumes of Brittany, and Flora had never guessed at such a variety of *coiffes*. The men were also wearing their best, the short black jackets and trousers, and the flat black boater hats with streamers of ribbons hanging down the back.

At least a third, however, were fashionably dressed, some obviously straight from Paris and the House of Worth. A few appeared to be English. There was no mistaking her fellow countrymen abroad, both by their clothes and their ingrained British attitude of superiority, which they carried with them to the earth's four corners. The French and *bretonnes*, feeling much the same about themselves, were seriously annoyed.

Flora wondered if anyone could guess that she was born and bred in England, attired as she was in an elegant bronze day dress from Callicot Soeurs, with the Pont du Mor *coiffe* pinned to her hair. Tonight, and for the duration of the celebration, they would all don the traditional garb. Gaelle had presented her that morning with an apron she had personally embroidered. The work, in colored floss in every possible hue, was magnificent.

"I began this long ago, in the hopes that someday Blaise would marry and settle at the château," she had said. "I have added this English rose and the Irish shamrock in the center medallion for you."

The gift had marked a watershed in the relationship between the two women. Flora knew her own feelings had softened after learning of the woman's tragic history. As for Gaelle, the change in her attitude since their first meeting was startling, if a little unnerving. She seemed determined to take Flora under her wing and mold her in her own image.

As their vehicle approached the parish close Johanna was pensive, torn between anticipation of the coming festivities, and vague memories of the past. "There is so much I do not remember," she said. They came to a stop before the triumphal arch. "But I think I can recall my mother in the drawing room on a winter's evening, embroidering garments with gold thread."

"Yes." Gaelle nodded. "Eve was a notable needlewoman. She helped me prepare the finery that adorns the statue now. And for the next *grand pardon* it will be Flora, as mistress of the château, who has the honor of making the garments."

She spoke as if she were bestowing a great boon. Flora was horrified. Needlework was not her strong point. "Then I must rely on you to teach me, so that I can carry on the tradition in a befitting style," she said diplomatically.

Ten years was plenty of time for Gaelle to discover and help correct her inadequacies as a seamstress. But, in the midst of her almost comic dismay, Flora felt a glow of unexpected pleasure. For the first time in her life, she saw the years stretching out in an unbroken chain of acceptance. She belonged to Pont du Mor now, just as the rest of them did. Her children—God willing—would be born and raised here. A sheen of tears misted her eyes.

After a life of wandering, she had found her home.

They dismounted the carriage and went directly into the church, instead of going through the arch into the parish close. The mayor's wife was waiting for them in the nave. "Ah, Madame Lampoul," Gaelle greeted her. "I am told this will be the best *pardon* yet, thanks to the good work of you and your husband."

The woman, a stout gray-haired matron with eyes as bright as a bird's, beamed with gratification. "The bishop says that not even Guimiliau's will eclipse ours this year."

She startled Flora by dropping a curtsy as they were introduced. A young girl stepped forward at Madame Lampoul's signal and bestowed a bouquet of flowers upon the new Madame Cheney. Flora thanked her charmingly, and received nods of approval from the older women. Inside she was filled with amazement. She had never, in her wildest daydreams, imagined herself as the lady of the manor, yet here she was being offered every civility.

Despite France's love affair with democracy and egalitarianism, she thought, *the old social distinctions die hard.*

Yseult Kersaudy was already in the grotto and the wooden statue stood on a low stand, ready for the changing of the garments. She was taking the gilt crown off the statue's carved head, and looked up as they entered. She paused in mid-movement. Gaelle came forward, tsk-tsking, and took the crown from her. "You must be more careful," she chided.

Yseult blinked, as if waking from a dream, and looked at Flora strangely. Claudine frowned. "What is it? What is wrong?"

"Nothing. A dream I recalled." She had their complete attention, all except Flora's.

"You must tell us," Claudine demanded. She turned to Flora. "Yseult dreams true."

Madame Rohun nodded and gave Yseult a warm and knowing smile. "Mademoiselle Kersaudy has the gift of dreams—even though at times it seems to her more like a curse. The things that she sees in her dreams will come to pass."

Flora's heart gave a lurch. "And you dreamed of me?" she said slowly. "Was it . . . was it anything bad?"

"No, Madame Cheney. I do not recall all of it, which is why I was staring so, trying to remember. I do not know exactly. A document with a seal upon it." She wrinkled her brow. "I am afraid that is all."

"Ah, a document with a seal. The marriage license, no doubt." Claudine sounded quite relieved. "Let us proceed with robing the statue."

Flora wanted to ask more, but decided not to pursue it. It was, after all, just a dream. She would not let superstition take hold of her imagination any more than it already had.

The abbé's sister tenderly removed the old garments from the statue, wrapped them in tissue, and placed them in a box. This she presented to Johanna. "We thought you would like to have these, mademoiselle, since they were embroidered by your mother. Perhaps you will use them in your own chapel, one day."

Johanna took the box with trembling hands, but there were stars in her eyes. "Thank you, madame. I shall treasure them always."

Gaelle's handiwork was duly admired and then placed upon the statue. First the undergown of cloth of gold, next the lace overdress, and finally the magnificent blue outer robe with its embroidery of amber, gold beads, and tiny pearls. She started to reach for the crown, then stepped back and motioned imperiously to Flora. "Come. It is for you to do now."

Flora lifted the tiny crown. She held the diadem out to Johanna. "Perhaps you should . . ."

"No." Johanna stepped back, hiding her hands behind her. "It is for you to do. It is the tradition."

Carefully, Flora placed the crown upon the statue's graceful head. She felt as if she were sharing the moment with all the other women, past and present, who had undertaken the task. It was both humbling and exhilarating.

"Now," Johanna said solemnly, "you are part of the history of this place."

"Yes," said Madame Rohun. "Now you are truly a woman of Pont du Mor."

Flora, who had never belonged anyplace in her entire life, fought the urge to bury her face in her hands and weep with happiness. She swallowed past the constriction in her throat and bowed her head in a simple prayer.

When she turned to the others her face was radiant with the same joy that illuminated her heart. But later, as they stood back to admire the figure of the saint in her new robes, Flora was aware of Yseult looking at her in that strange way again. She managed to get her alone as the women went out a side door and into the grassy close. "I think perhaps that you remember something more of your dream?"

Yseult nodded. "I did not want to speak before the others, in case they misunderstood. This document, it is not your marriage lines." Her face became grave. "It is something from out of your past. What, I do not know, Madame Cheney—but it will change your life entirely."

She stepped out into the sunny enclosure, leaving Flora stunned among the shadows of the church.

"Here is your necklace," Blaise said that night, when they were finally alone in their chambers. Much as Flora adored

Claudine and Nicholas, and reveled in their company, she had been waiting all night to be alone with her husband.

Blaise placed a lacquered box on the table beside her. "I had planned to give it to you tomorrow, but I must leave for Saint-Renan in the morning."

"Saint-Renan! For how long?"

"A day or two. Perhaps three. I will be back in time for the *grand pardon,* never fear." He saw the disappointment in her face and kissed it away.

"I wish I could go with you," she whispered against his mouth. "If only our guests hadn't arrived so early. Think of it, Blaise. Just the two of us, alone . . ."

He groaned, and kissed her again, deeply. Heat leapt between them like lightning. "Do not think I haven't thought of it, *ma fleur.* But it cannot be this time. There is business to conduct, and you will only be a distraction—albeit a beautiful one. Come, let me show you the necklace."

Handing her the box, he waited expectantly while she opened it. The interior was lined with rich velvet, and the necklace lay coiled gracefully in the center of its jeweled chain.

"The Mermaid's Egg!" Flora breathed. "It is far more beautiful than I imagined!"

She lifted it out carefully. Flora saw that it was attached by a clever piece wrought in gold in the shape of a seahorse. The intricate gold chain sparkled in the warm glow of the candles, and the stone set into the links glittered like rainbow spume from the waves along the strand. But it was the extraordinary jewel hanging from it that caught and collected the light.

The egg-shaped gem was as cool as seawater against her palm, and reflected the blues and greens of the ocean in every tint and hue. Its beauty was strangely hypnotic. Staring at the glorious jewel, she felt as if she were looking into the sea itself, as if she could look and look and look into bottomless depths forever.

"I have never seen any stone such as this before. Is it Venetian glass or some exotic gemstone?"

"No one knows." Blaise shrugged and smiled. "I took it to a man who specializes in rare stones in Paris once, and do you know what he told me? He said: 'I have never seen its like, monsieur. Perhaps it truly *is* a mermaid's egg."

She laughed with him. "Shall I put it on?"

"Only when you are properly dressed."

"Oh?" Flora looked up at him. "What should I wear with it?"

Blaise took the necklace from her and set it aside. "Why, what a mermaid wears, of course." His hands were already undoing the buttons of her gown with disconcerting ease. "Which is to say, nothing at all."

She reached to help but he stopped her. "No. Let me."

Only when he had her stripped bare did he take the necklace and place it around her throat. The lovely egg hung in the cleft of her breasts, feeling both warm and cool at the same time. Or perhaps that was because of the way Blaise was touching her, Flora realized. He let his hot mouth rove along her shoulder, down one breast to its very tip, then slowly worked his way down to her feet, kissing her from head to toe.

He worked his way up more slowly, tantalizing her with expectations, fulfilling them until she was trembling with need and anticipation. "You are so beautiful, my love!"

While she stood there, bathed in golden candlelight, he taught her new intimacies and delights, took her to levels of rocketing sensation that left her swaying against him breathless and weak-limbed. Then he picked her up in his arms and carried her into his bed and began anew.

He stripped off his evening clothes, revealing the taut muscles of his body to her questing mouth and hands. Although he wanted to prolong the moment, she was burning with longing and ready for him. Her fingernails dug into his back. "Now, Blaise! Now!"

He thrust into her and she welcomed him, urging him on in a frenzy of desire. They lost themselves in it together, isolated for a brief span from the dark pain of the past and the gray uncertainty of the future. Nothing else existed but the spiraling fury of their union, as they rode it to its heights. His body arched over hers in wild possession. At the height of his passion, as he thrust into her, he gave out a hoarse cry.

She realized that it was her name he called out. *He loves me. Not Eve. Me!*

On that joyous note she went over the edge of rapture, falling through time and space, knowing she was safe because she was in his arms.

It was not quite light when Flora heard someone call to her. She tried to rouse Blaise, but he was in a deep sleep.

"Are you the one?"

Rising quickly, Flora tried to stand and instead fell heavily to the floor. She could not get up. Where her legs should have been, was a mermaid's shimmering tail. "Blaise! Help me!"

"You are the one!" *the voice said, more loudly. The tones were no longer soft and sad, but menacing.*

Flora scrambled up, trying to claw her way back on the bed. "Blaise! Help me!"

He turned and held out a hand; but it was not Blaise's hand. It was cold and blanched, and blood dripped thickly down between the plump fingers. As she shrieked in alarm, the dark head raised off the pillow. Not Blaise's black hair, but a woman's bloody head. "You are the one! You brought him to my home. You unlocked the door for my murderer!"

"*Miss Hansen! Oh, God! Oh, God. I am so sorry. I never meant for him to hurt you! I trusted him. I thought he loved me. I didn't know him for what he was!*"

A hand clapped down on her shoulder. Flora tried to run, but her mermaid's tail was useless. She turned toward the unseen person. He leaned into the light. A handsome face, and innocent-looking. Until one saw the darkness that lurked in his eyes.

"Robin! *How did you find me?*"

"*You asked me to come,*" *he said, laughing as he ripped away her nightgown.* "*You begged for me. I heard you call my name.*"

Candlelight bloomed somewhere in the room. It was not Robin who held her, but Blaise. His face was smeared with blood.

"No!"

*   *   *

. . . Flora opened her eyes to terrible silence. This time she was really awake, and the room was still pitched in darkness. Blaise slept beside her, his body warm and still, his breathing deep and regular. It had all been a dream. Dear God, it had seemed so real!

The knowledge didn't help much. Her heart was pounding like a kettledrum and she was shaking so hard she feared she'd awaken Blaise. *Only a dream,* she said, over and over, trying to soothe her nerves. *It was only a dream.* Dreams weren't real. They couldn't come true.

Except, perhaps, in Brittany.

In the morning Flora saw her husband off, heavy-eyed. Not because they had resumed their lovemaking in the dawn hours, but because of her nightmares. She had lain awake until first light, comforting herself with his presence. Afraid to close her eyes because the horrible dreams that had plagued her for so long had come back to haunt her. *Dear God, will I never know peace again?*

But she put on a brave smile for Blaise. "Hurry back to me, my love."

He kissed her long and deep. "If I had my way, *chérie,* I would not leave your side. *Au revoir.*"

He drove out of the courtyard, waving as he reached the gates. Flora wondered if she would sleep at all until he returned. The thought of going up to her room held no appeal. She wished that Claudine and Nicolas were not intending to start for Plouzané, after an early breakfast.

Instead of going back inside, Flora decided to take a turn in the walled garden, where no one else went of a morning. The flowers were in high bloom. It amazed her that they grew so lushly all along this rocky coast, as if in defiance of nature's furies. The Bretons had a great love of flowers, and she hadn't seen one house in the village without its tubs or boxes of blossoms.

She heard the sound of wheels, and then voices from the courtyard. Nicolas must have ordered his carriage brought round early, so the luggage could be put aboard. Flora wandered down a mossy path beneath arching trees, toward the little pond. Water flowed from the spout of a bronze water lily, and the gurgling drowned out the sound of footsteps behind her. She didn't realize she was no longer alone until a hand clapped down on her shoulder.

"So, I finally ran you to earth."

Flora froze. It was just like her dream.

"You *are* Madame Cheney, aren't you?" a voice asked in English. "Used to go by the name of Miss Flora O'Donnell?"

She turned slowly. She recognized him, of course. Not Robin Harding from her dream, but still someone out of her worst nightmares: the Bow Street runner who had followed her through the streets of Tunbridge Wells.

Chapter Twelve

The man reached into his coat and removed an envelope secured with an official-looking stamp and an unbroken wax seal. "Here. This is for you."

An arrest warrant. Flora kept her hands at her sides, trying to quell the panic that rose inside her like a cold frost. "I do not believe that it is enforceable here in France."

"Well, you're wrong there. It's good in England, and that's what matters."

Could she be extradited? Flora wasn't sure. Bluffing was her only course. "Leave now, sir, or I shall call the servants and have you forcibly thrown off the château grounds."

"After the merry dance you've led me? No, ma'am. I'm here to do my job, and do it I shall! No one stops Barnaby Jerome from doing his duty."

"Flora?" Nicolas came through the garden entrance, eyeing the stranger keenly. He'd heard their voices. One quick look at her white face, and at the man—obviously no gentleman—told him that something was wrong. "You, fellow!" he called out in English. "What is your business?"

"Now, now. Don't get all testy with me. The name is Jerome, and I've been trying to track this young lady down since the turn of the year. I've been charged to deliver some papers to the lady, from her grandfather's solicitor."

Flora almost fainted with relief.

"Here," Nicolas said, helping her to a stone bench and chafing her hands. "Sit down in the shade. Shall I send for your maid?"

"N-no. A . . . a sudden indisposition. I shall be all right in a moment."

Mr. Jerome stood by, flushing ruddily and shifting his weight from one leg to the other. "I'm sorry, Mrs . . . er, . . . Madame Cheney. I thought you knew the old man had cocked up his toes, or I would've broken it to you more gently."

Nicolas showed his surprise. "I understood you were alone in the world."

Flora looked away. "I was, to all intents and purposes. We were estranged." She took a deep breath. "These documents, Mr. Jerome, do you know what they are?"

"A copy of his will, so I was told, and a letter from the solicitors. Petersham and Petersham, the firm that hired me to find you."

"And how *did* you locate me?"

"Lord, ma'am, I've spent twenty years and more hunting up missing people for as many reasons as there are hairs on your head. I don't give out my secrets."

"Then it is not always easy to do?"

"Not unless you're Barnaby Jerome. I'm the best there is, which is why Mr. Petersham hired me for the job. Not but what it isn't coming out of your inheritance, I'm sure."

"Well, you have successfully completed your mission. Thank you. And now, you must be hot and thirsty after your travels. Nicolas, if you will be so good as to see that Mr. Jerome is given some refreshments, I would like to be alone for a few minutes."

"No need to put yourself out on my part," the man said. "I've taken a room just a few miles from here. If you'll just sign a receipt for the letter, I'll be on my way. Don't say I wouldn't mind a pint of ale, to wet my whistle first, if you've any in the house."

After assuring himself that she was all right, Nicolas led the man away. "I'll send Claudine out to you after you've had the opportunity to read the documents."

Flora waited a moment before breaking the seal. So her grandfather was dead. The last link with her own kin broken. Hateful as he was, her grandfather had provided an anchor of sorts to her parents, and now he was gone. She felt nothing at all.

Yet, if not for Blaise, for Johanna, Claudine, and Nicolas—and yes, even Gaelle—everything would be quite different. It would have disturbed her terribly to know she was totally alone, without any bonds of either blood or affection in an uncaring world. A chilling thought. Thank God for them!

She opened the envelope. Inside was a letter from one Donald Petersham, informing her that she was the sole inheritrix of her grandfather's considerable estate. Although he had lived humbly, Mr. Petersham wrote, Calvin Fraser had invested wisely in Funds. These, along with the monies from the sale of his house, were left to Flora entirely, providing that she claim them within a year of his death. The monies could be reinvested, or the solicitor would forward a draft to a Paris bank, if she so desired.

She stared at the sum, and the date of her grandfather's passing. He had already been buried six weeks before Blaise Cheney had first come to visit his niece at Hawthorne Academy. It was so ironic: if she hadn't fled from Mr. Jerome, thinking he was a Bow Street runner, she would have learned of her inheritance long before Blaise and Johanna returned from London. She would not have been at Hawthorne to receive his strange proposal of marriage.

In fact, even if she had, she would have surely refused his unorthodox offer. There would have been no need of it. How strange fate was: her current state of happiness was based on a fear-induced leap to the wrong conclusion. Because of it, she was sitting now in the gardens of a fine château, happily married to a man she loved beyond distraction, while her grandfather lay cold and unloved in his grave.

What miracle had led to this change of heart on that bitter old man's part? There were more questions, to which she would never know the answers: had illness turned him sentimental? Had he repented his harshness toward her mother and herself, or had he merely hoped to redeem his shriveled soul by bargaining with God as the fatal hour approached?

She looked again at the copy of the will. It had been made years ago, when she had first come to live with him, and he had never changed it. Perhaps he'd thought he would live forever. Well, now. What should she do with his money, which she neither needed nor desired?

A whisper of silks, and Claudine came out into the garden, her face puckered with concern. "Nicolas said you have received ill tidings. I am so very sorry!"

Flora folded the letter and slipped it back inside the envelope. "It is all right. But I've received a bequest—a rather substantial one, it seems." Her troubled eyes sought Claudine's. "My grandfather was a cold and cruel man. He had nothing to do with me the last several years while he was alive, and I want nothing to do with his money now that he is dead. I don't know what to do. Is it possible to refuse the legacy?"

Claudine's practical French soul was horrified. "Refuse it? *Mon Dieu,* Flora, have you taken leave of your senses? If you do not want it for yourself, then place it in trust for your children. They will thank you for it one day. Especially if you have a daughter. It is always good for a woman to have an income independent of her husband!"

The idea struck Flora as a wise one. She held out her hand to the other woman. "You are so wise! Thank you, dear friend. I shall take your advice."

It wasn't long before Nicolas and Claudine left for Plouzané, and Flora went back inside the cool walls of the château. It was quiet with Blaise gone, as well. She touched the mermaid's jewel hanging on its lovely chain, and wondered how she would occupy her time till her husband returned.

She picked up a book she had left in the drawing room, but it failed to keep her interest. She opened the box of chocolates she'd left on the mantelpiece, and saw that someone had already eaten most of her favorites, took one and replaced the lid. There was always needlework, for which she had no talent, or a nap, for which she had no inclination. The situation was novel: for the first time in her life, time weighed heavily on her hands—and she was bored.

She perched on the edge of a tapestry-covered chair and searched her brain for something to while away the hours. It was a shame she had no watercolors. She should have asked Blaise to bring her some from Saint Renan; but for now, what to do? Gaelle was in the small chapel, saying her endless rosaries, but Flora felt no urge to join her. Johanna had not come down yet. Perhaps she would ask if Johanna would like to drive out in the carriage. They might go down to the village.

Or, if they were particularly bored, they might even go to pay a morning call on Odile de Broceliand. Flora laughed aloud at the thought of it.

"I do not care whether Blaise had a hundred mistresses in the past, each more beautiful than the next! It is me he loves now." She hugged her arms around herself. "Only me!"

Flora started for the chapel to ask if Gaelle would like to go for the drive also, but ended up in the room Blaise used for his study, and found herself absorbed again in his books of legends and folktales. This was not boring at all.

Moving toward the long library table he'd set near the window, she saw that he'd gotten quite a bit accomplished. Blaise's angular writing filled many sheets of paper, most neatly stacked in piles. One lay where he had left it on the blotter to dry. Flora scanned it and saw the château mentioned.

> Like most legends, the tale of the captive mermaid at Château Morgaine is surely rooted in fact, no matter how the truth may have been twisted and altered by time. There is a strong streak of jealousy in the Cheney line. Is it possible that the Yvon of legend was so possessive of his wife that he locked her away in a tower, where she subsequently died? Or, as the local people assert, was there indeed a mermaid ancestress who pined away because she could not return to her home in the pearly caves beneath the sea?
>
> There is certain to be a strong basis for the legend to have taken hold so firmly. One must remember, of course, that in Brittany the old beliefs are strong: ask any villager and you will be told, with a hasty glance over the shoulder and a quick sign of the cross, that the fées still grant boons or play tricks upon mere mortals, and standing stones rip loose from the earth to dance in the light of the moon.

As to the magical talisman, the jeweled egg that is supposed to contain the mermaid's soul, clues are few. The jewel does exist, a remarkable stone of great beauty and unknown source. The workmanship of the chain and fittings is exquisite [fig. 3–1.], and not like anything previously known. The closest, perhaps, would be the goldwork of the ancient Scythians.

The blue-green mineral forming the so-called Mermaid's Egg has never been identified, although many experts have examined it. Naturally, chemical tests such as that done with sulfuric acid are out of the question, since they might destroy the stone.

One thing is certain: its beauty is so unique that it is no surprise that mystical origins and qualities have been assigned to it. There is widespread belief that the Cheney fortunes are linked to possession of the necklace and that they would be lost if the stone were ever returned to the sea.

To learn more of the stone, the foundation of the legend must be uncovered. Only by sifting through the various versions of the legend and comparing them with the Cheney family history can fact be separated from fancy, and the truth be winnowed from the myth.

Flora was enchanted. She had never given much thought to the origins of folktales. To her they had always been fairy stories and legends woven whole cloth from vivid imaginations, or the need to explain things that ancient people, in their ignorance, could not explain by other means. Hunting for clues among myths and fairy tales appealed to her greatly.

Perhaps he would let her help more with his research. Both in the library and out in the field, as well. She had enjoyed herself immensely measuring the menhirs with Blaise on the Druid's Isle. She could continue to be a great help to him. They might travel around the world, once Johanna was safely settled.

Unless, of course, other things interfered. Like a child, for instance. Smiling, she placed her hands over the curve of her belly. Had a little soul already found a home inside her?

She lost herself in pleasant fantasies: a perfect child, a boy, who looked exactly like Blaise. Or, no, a girl with Blaise's black hair and her own blue eyes. Or perhaps one with chestnut hair and his dark ones. If it were a girl, she would ask to name it after her mother and Anne Cheney, if Blaise did not object. A son, however . . .

Flora realized one of the upstairs chambermaids was hovering nervously in the doorway. "Yes, Youna?"

"Madame, you are to come with me at once, if you please. It is most urgent."

The girl turned and started off before Flora had time to ask a single question. She rose and hurried up the stairs after the maid and along two branching corridors to Gaelle's chamber, imagining all manner of disasters: nothing could have prepared her for what she found.

She threw the door open and stopped short. Splashes of blood splotched the pastel carpet like wet, red roses. There were more soaking the tumbled bedclothes at the foot of the bed. Malin stood by the washstand, wringing her hands. Madame Kerjean, the housekeeper, was hunched over the mattress, blocking her view.

A low moan of pain, terrible to hear, greeted her entrance. Flora rushed toward the bed. "Gaelle . . . !"

As the housekeeper stepped aside, Flora froze and stood rooted to the floor. It was Johanna who lay still amid the twisted, bloody sheets. Her face was gray and beaded with moisture.

Flora went to her side. "Dear God, what is happening here? What is wrong with her?"

Madame Kerjean choked back a sob. "Foolish, wicked girl! She is too far along to try and rid herself of the child. *Mon Dieu!* Now there is danger that they will both be lost."

It took a moment for the true meaning of her words to sink into Flora's brain. When they did, they burned like brands. *Johanna with child? Impossible.*

"Hush!" she exclaimed. "You must not say such things, for they are untrue!"

"Alas, madame, they are not." The housekeeper wiped her eyes with the corner of her apron. "Have I not borne seven children myself? Have I not aided the midwife with every birth beneath this roof since first I came here?''

''You are mistaken!''

The old woman shook her head. She was weary with all the pain her eyes had seen in her lifetime. At the moment it overshadowed all the joys and triumphs. ''Me, I know of what I speak. This poor child is carrying one of her own. But not for much longer . . .''

The housekeeper's certainty convinced Flora against her will. Emotions and questions shuddered through her mind. *But who . . . ? And when?* The girl was never alone with any man. Unless on one of her visits to Yseult, Loic had been there instead? And yet she couldn't believe he would have taken advantage of an innocent like Johanna.

''How far along?''

''Since before she left *l'Angleterre*,'' Malin said softly.

Flora was stunned speechless. Johanna had gotten pregnant in England? She did some rapid revising. Despite her sorrow—and, yes, anger—her sympathies were stirred. Poor, poor Johanna, carrying this secret in her heart, all alone. ''You should have come to me,'' she said, smoothing the matted, sweat-soaked hair from the girl's brow.

There was no response. Fear stabbed its cold knives through her. It was terrifying to see Johanna, so young and full of life, looking like a broken porcelain doll. Perhaps dying . . .

But she must put aside all such thoughts for the moment. They must take action. Flora took the girl's hand in hers. So frail, so cold. Her mouth was dry with fear. ''Where is Madame Morceau? Does she know of this?''

''She set out on foot to visit an old servant on the estate lands who has fallen ill. I have sent someone to bring her back.''

''Good. And the doctor, has he been sent for?''

''No, madame.''

''Malin! Send someone to fetch him here at once!''

''But madame . . . think! The scandal . . . !''

''Scandal be damned! Her life is at stake. I will not let her bleed to death for propriety's sake!''

Malin, frightened half out of her wits, hurried away to do her bidding. Flora faced Madame Kerjean. "Tell me what to do. There must be something!"

The housekeeper indicated a glass of dark liquid on the night table. "Try to get a spoonful of the fluid down her from time to time. And madame—pray!"

Flora did. Her religious background was tangled between her father's Catholicism and her mother's Calvinistic leanings, but her basic personal beliefs held firm. There was a God, and surely, if there were any justice in heaven, He would listen.

All the discarded and forgotten words she had learned in childhood came back. While Madame Kerjean worked to staunch the flow, Flora prayed and fought back tears and slipped drops of the medicine between Johanna's bloodless lips. An hour passed. Suddenly she was heartened to see those gold-tipped lashes flutter and open partway.

"Flora. . . . ?" The girl's voice was thin and ragged, like a tarnished silver thread. "Ah, do not leave me . . . I am so afraid . . ."

Leaning down, Flora spoke in soothing tones, despite her inner trembling.

"Yes, darling. I am here, and Gaelle soon will be. The doctor is on his way. Everything will be all right . . ."

The lie stuck in her throat like a sharp bone. A tiny smile flickered over Johanna's features. Her eyes glazed over with pain and she moaned again. A drop of water fell onto Johanna's cheek; Flora was astonished to realize it was one of her own tears.

"Look you, the hemorrhage is slowing." Madame Kerjean stood up.

Flora swallowed. "Surely that is a good sign."

The old woman shrugged. "It may be, madame," she said in low tones. "Or it may be that her heart is failing, and has no strength to pump it out."

"How can I ever face Blaise?" Flora said to herself, not even realizing that she spoke aloud. "Oh, how can I ever tell him?"

Johanna's eyes opened wide. *"Blaise?"* she breathed. "Blaise? But he knows. He has known all along . . ."

Her eyelids closed as she grimaced in pain, and slipped into blessed unconsciousness.

Flora wished that she could do the same.

The bleeding had stopped, and Flora sat beside the sleeping girl's bed in a state of utter exhaustion. Numbness had set in after the shock. Beneath it was a layer of rage and pain so sharp, so deep, that if it surfaced she thought it would kill her.

Gaelle tiptoed into the room with a bowl of broth for Flora. "You must take some sustenance."

"I cannot eat. The very thought of it makes me ill."

"I shall feed it to her then, when she awakens."

"*If* she awakens. You should have let me send for the doctor. You should not have countered my orders!"

The older woman's face showed her churning emotions. "I have been mistress here for many years. The servants' loyalties are still to me. But you are overreacting. Johanna did not loose as much blood as at first appeared. That fool Malin splashed so much bloody water everywhere in her first panic, that it made it look much worse that it was."

"She is still in danger. The physician should be called. If she loses the child now, she may lose her life as well."

"She will not die, I tell you! And this was not for you to decide. It was Blaise who made the plan, with Johanna's cooperation. He did it to save her from ruin. If word of this got out—and it would have, once the doctor came into it, make no mistake—she had been better off dead!"

Flora's nerves snapped. "You may get your wish!"

"Now you are being foolish. Think! Where can a woman go when she has been abandoned and betrayed by her lover?"

Flora rubbed her temples. Where, indeed?

And how could she fault Johanna, so young and so long neglected, for her folly, when she had done the same thing herself—twice. Willingly let the wool be pulled over her eyes, making herself blind to the reality of Robin Harding, and then Blaise.

Blaise!

She could hardly bear to hear his name, to even think of it. What dreams and fantasies she had woven around him.

And it had all been lies. Nothing but a tangled web of lies.

Her fingers were still as she held Johanna's hand in hers. Inwardly she was trembling, no, shaking from the whirlwind of the past hour's revelations. "So he thought to pass the child off as mine. How unfortunate that he neglected to tell me his plans!"

Gaelle gripped her ruby cross so tightly her fingers blanched. "I cannot speak for Blaise; but he meant to tell you after the *pardon*, when the moment was right. Hear him out when he returns. I beg of you, Flora! He needs you . . . we all need you, to see us through this."

"Blaise!" She ripped his name with scorn. "I do not wish to ever see or speak with him again! I will be packed and ready to leave at the earliest opportunity. The very minute that Johanna is out of danger, I will leave this place forever."

"How can you be so hard-hearted? I thought you loved them."

Flora sat there with silent tears streaming down her face. "And I thought that he loved me."

Flora paced her room. The setting sun washed the casements with streaks of gold and rose. It had been a long and terrible day. Johanna was resting as comfortably as possible, dosed with poppy juice. She hadn't lost the baby. At least, not yet.

Some tale had been passed off to the household to explain her indisposition. Flora was sure it would be a good one: these Cheneys lied all too well.

As soon as possible she would see the last of them. For now, there was nothing to do but wait. She took a deep breath and a pain pierced Flora's chest. Her heart, broken and shattered by this unthinkable betrayal, had rearranged itself in jagged, bloody pieces.

Rage, sorrow, pain, disgust chased themselves through her mind in an endless circle. Her fury and disappointment were directed as much at herself as they were at the Cheneys, who had lured her into their dark plot. So much made sense to her now: Johanna's malaise in Paris; later, the way she had begged Flora to accompany her to the château if Blaise died; Blaise's rash proposal.

No, she corrected herself, not rash. He had planned it carefully, calculating just what it would take to make her accept his offer. And the sail to the Druid's Isle. She understood now why he had cut off the servant who had talked of blankets and supplies on their return—the man had carried out his errand a day too late. The whole episode, the sensual seduction in the privacy of the *lit clos,* had all been carefully planned.

But why? To ensure her cooperation? To bind her to him with ties of sensuality? Or merely for the sake of conquest? Because she "belonged" to him, like that bureau, or that chair, and therefore must be used?

The door opened without warning, and she whirled around. Blaise stood on the threshold, his eyes dark and dangerous. The light gilded his high cheekbones, the strong lines of his nose and jaw. He shut the door solidly behind him. "We must talk."

"I have nothing to say to you. And you have nothing to which I wish to listen!"

She turned her back, afraid to let him see the pain in her eyes. He had used her to further his own lying ends. By God, she at least had her pride!

Blaise came up behind her and put his hands on her shoulders. Flora snatched herself away and turned on him. "Don't touch me. Don't ever touch me again! It makes me sick!"

His head snapped back as if she had slapped him. A white line rimmed his firm mouth. "Flora . . . for the love of God!"

"Love? How *dare* you speak of it to me."

Tension shuddered in the room between them and the air shimmered with roiled emotions. He ran his fingers through his hair. "You are angry, and rightfully so. But hear me out—"

"No! Leave me. I cannot bear the sight of you."

He recoiled again. His entire body stiffened and she thought he would turn on his heel. Instead he grabbed her by the arms and shook her till her teeth rattled. He would not let her go so easily.

"I will leave, Flora, but only when I am finished!"

She looked up into his face, the face she had loved, and saw something beyond his sudden fury. A bleakness that still, surprisingly, had the power to wrench her heart. Her pulse drummed in her ears. She could not think clearly so close to him, with the heat of his hands radiating through her body.

It was difficult, but she made her voice level and cold. "Release me, and I will listen. And then you will go."

Blaise uttered an oath. His fingers tightened and she knew there would be bruises there. She winced.

He saw it and released her abruptly, almost flinging himself away. What a monster she must think him! He damned himself for not taking her into the plot earlier. If he had been the one to tell her of Johanna's pregnancy, it would have turned out differently. He was sure of it now; but before he had been afraid to risk it. His fist pounded against her dressing table, shocking in the quiet of the room. His voice was low, rough.

"What good will it do? I am cursed from birth to always make the wrong choices, take the wrong path." He sent her a hard, unyielding glare. "Love the wrong woman."

She stood like a stone, fighting the curl of sympathy she felt winding through her. He deserved none of it.

He swore again, savagely. "So be it. If you will not hear me, it is no use to prolong this agony. I cannot help Johanna now. God save me, I cannot even help myself!" Blaise went to the door, reached out to open it.

"Blaise . . ."

The word was torn from her throat. Flora didn't even realize she'd spoken until his name echoed through the twilight. She struggled with herself mightily. "I will listen. For Johanna's sake. She is practically a child."

A child, bearing a child. She buried her face in her hands a minute, sick at heart. "I never guessed. How could he have taken advantage of her innocence!"

"*Sacrebleu!* I wish I had killed him with my own two hands. I wanted to." She looked up at his violence. His strong fingers curled around an invisible throat. "Only the need to protect Johanna prevented me from doing so at the time."

Flora massaged the skin between her eyes. "I have thought and thought. The girls were watched so closely. I cannot think how she ever came to be alone with young William Black! Unless, perhaps, it was on her way to her Greek lessons at the vicarage."

Blaise's head jerked up. "Then she has not told you?"

"I didn't want to badger her with questions while she lay so ill."

"Let me solve the mystery for you, then." His mouth twisted. "It was not on her way to the vicarage that the seduction took place, but *at* the vicarage."

"But William—"

"You are not a stupid woman, Flora. Think!" His face was dark with repressed fury. "Who was she alone with every week for an hour? Who had the physical beauty to steal a young and inexperienced girl's heart? He had, she told me, the 'face of an angel,' " he said viciously. "That *devil's spawn!*"

"But . . . Mr. Tompkins?" Flora could hardly credit it. "He is so . . . unworldly."

"Not so unworldly as to resist the temptations of lust for a lonely young girl!"

"Or," Flora said slowly, "perhaps to satisfy a remote and intellectual curiosity." Yes, that was even worse, but she could imagine it happening that way.

Afterward, Johanna would have been too frightened and humiliated to tell anyone; and the Reverend Tompkins, having satisfied his curiosity, could have put the matter out of his mind completely. It seemed, from what she knew of him, perfectly possible.

Blaise rose and walked to the fireplace, resting his polished boot against the fender. "It only happened once, she claims." His fists knotted at his sides. "She says the sin is hers. Infatuation for a handsome man, coupled with the charm of the comfortable vicarage—she imagined herself marrying him, living there with him and his sister, of whom she was quite fond."

Yes. Flora could see that: Johanna weaving a picture of the cozy home and the family she wanted so desperately, from the fabric of her loneliness.

"Mon Dieu!" His fist came down on the table so hard a vase smashed to the floor. His hand bled along the edge where he'd scraped it. Blaise didn't appear to notice. "May hē burn in hell for this one day, as I am burning now, with guilt and regret!"

"Did she . . . did she tell you how it happened?"

He calmed himself with difficulty. "She blames herself entirely. Evidently she had wanted for some time to impress him with her budding beauty. Holding her head just so, posing her figure to best advantage, as she had seen the older girls do at the local assemblies. Johanna went to the vicarage that fatal day, filled with romantic fantasies. Determined only to experience her first kiss."

His voice rasped with emotion. Flora wanted to cover her ears, but listened with dreadful fascination. "She wore her most becoming dress and dabbed borrowed perfume at her throat. And she pretended to twist her ankle so he would carry her to the couch, like the heroine in one of the novels from the lending library. With her arms around her neck, it was nothing for a pretty and determined girl to get him to kiss her. And he did. One thing inevitably led to another. The next thing she knew she was on her back with her skirts up, and it was over."

"Dear God in Heaven!"

"After, he made her kneel and pray with him, asking forgiveness for her wantonness, and his weakness in succumbing to her lures. Her lures! And she, a girl not yet sixteen! I should have thrashed him within an inch of his life."

Blaise lowered his head in anguish. "And then, she told me, he arranged his clothes, assigned her several verses of the *Iliad* to translate and memorize, and said he would expect her back for her usual lesson the following week. As if nothing at all had happened!"

Flora was sick at heart. The Reverend Tompkins *was* unworldly. His only passions seemed intellectual. She would have thought nothing of leaving Johanna in his care for an hour or so. Perhaps, she thought, he had been confused by an attraction to Johanna, or even overwhelmed at the moment by a surge of need and desire against which he had no defenses.

No! Her mind made another complete turnabout. She would make no excuses for him. He was a man, a man of God, and Johanna had been a schoolgirl teetering on the edge of womanhood. He, and he alone, was fully responsible for his own actions.

How had he *dared* to visit their house in the Place Vendôme and ask after Johanna, as if nothing untoward had occurred? Had he hoped to resume their relationship? Or come to reassure himself that Johanna was not pregnant?

Or, the thought struck her, that it had never happened at all? She recalled him sitting in the Paris drawing room, examining the unclothed women in the paintings with such interest. If genius was, in some cases, allied to madness, then the Reverend Tompkins had surely passed over the boundary line.

She shook her head, remembering that Johanna had stopped going to her lessons at the vicarage in the beginning of December. At the time, Flora had thought that the lessons were suspended because of the holiday season. Now, too late, she understood.

"Poor child! She said nothing of this to anyone."

"No. Not even to him. From that day to this." Blaise made a gesture of despair.

"As I said, she blamed herself. The sin was hers, she thought, for tempting a man of God. She tried to put it out of her mind, as her seducer had recommended. And when her monthly time did not come, she took it as a sign of her punishment—God did not deem her worthy of being a woman."

He ran his hands through his rumpled hair. When he spoke again, his voice was thick with anger. "It was only a few days before my fortuitous visit to the academy that she overheard the chambermaids gossiping about one of the local girls, and the truth dawned. Until that moment of revelation, she had thought that only married women could get pregnant. She hadn't associated it with what he had done to her."

"And she told you that day you came to see her?"

"No. Not then. When I took her to London, she fell violently ill one morning. I had taken her to a play and late supper, and blamed myself for giving her too many sweets.

But there was some talk of influenza in the city, and I did not want to take any chances. I called in a friend who is a physician."

His laughter was bitter. "Imagine my shock when he rendered his diagnosis."

The room was almost in darkness now. Flora preferred it that way. She knew exactly what his face looked like, dark and haunted with guilt. He had tried, belatedly, to make up to Johanna for his past mistakes. He had done everything in his power to save her reputation. Including this sham of a marriage.

But that, Flora thought, blinking away her tears of confusion, did not erase everything he'd done to *her*. She shook with reaction.

"And so, to save her reputation, you concocted this fantastic scheme, this tissue of lies!"

"What choice did I have? There was no one else I could turn to in the situation. Not if I meant to pass the child off as mine and raise it as my heir. For that I needed a wife."

"You should have told me!"

"Johanna begged me to do so. She trusted you, but how could I? I did not know you at all. I could not confide in you for many good reasons. What if you chose to blackmail me? Or you might have instead reported her condition to your superiors at the academy. How did I know whether or not you would keep our secret, unless you were allied to me in marriage?"

He slanted a look at her in the fading light. "Be truthful, Flora. If I had explained the circumstances to you, would you have agreed to the scheme?"

She searched her heart. What could she say? *Probably not, except I thought a madman and the Bow Street runners were after me, and it was either marriage to you or the hangman's noose.*

"Malin knew all along, I assume." She bit her lip. "What of Gaelle and Claudine?"

"Gaelle only learned of it after we came here. I wanted to tell her face-to-face. Claudine does not know."

Flora was grateful to hear it. At least one member of the family had not betrayed her love. "Tell me one thing— you ignored Johanna for the past ten years, then suddenly you do everything in your power to rectify your neglect. Why? It makes no sense to me at all.''

''I see that you will wring every drop of blood from my soul, Flora. Very well.''

He paced the room, collecting his thoughts. The chamber was large but his restless energy filled it. ''She was beautiful, Johanna's mother, even as a child. I grew up loving her. Her father was English, but his grandmother was Breton, and he had inherited a house in the village, where they would spend the summers. He would tease Eve and say that one day she would wed the master of the château and be its mistress.

''It seemed that it would come to pass. As my father's eldest son, I knew that one day the château would be mine. We would marry and live happily ever after, like the prince and princess in a fairy tale.'' He stopped and touched a small gilt chair that stood before the writing desk. ''I used to imagine her sitting here, in this very room that had been my mother's.''

Flora watched him look around the gathering shadows of the chamber, as if he would find her there. A pang of pity smote her.

''I saw her every summer,'' he continued. ''Our love grew. The year she was to be sixteen, I went to my father and told him that I wanted to marry Eve. I was nineteen. I had not spoken to her of it formally, but she knew. She always knew. My father said we were both too young; but if, when she was eighteen, I was still of the same mind, he would give his consent to the match. I gave Eve a gold locket, and told her that in two years I would take it back, and replace it with a wedding ring, if she would marry me. She agreed to be my wife. That was the happiest day I could recall. A week later my life fell apart.''

Suddenly, as he was telling it, Blaise was propelled back in the past to a certain summer. The day had been warm, almost sultry, and he'd been barefoot on the strand, searching with his brother, Hilliard, for seashells. Not ordinary ones, like the clam and oyster and cockle shells that could be had anywhere along the coast, but special ones that the Atlantic storms sometimes washed up from the deep.

Blaise would have preferred to be out on the bay in his sailboat, but had agreed to accompany Hilliard. Less than one year separated them, but he always looked out for his younger brother, since their mother's death . . .

"Why do you want these shells, Hilliard?"

"To decorate a box I am making. Oh, look! There are several washed into the place where the rocks come together. I can reach them if you grab my pants by the waist and hold on to me."

"You are a pest, but I'll humor you. There. Over you go . . . careful now!"

"A little lower, Blaise. The finest one is just out of my reach."

"Very well. But if you tear your clothes, Gaelle will send you to bed without dessert."

"Just a little farther. I have almost got it."

"What is so special about this box, that you must go to such trouble for it?"

"A birthday gift for Eve. I don't begrudge you the château, brother, for I have a greater treasure in mind. When Eve is seventeen, I shall marry her!"

"And that," he said hoarsely, "is when my hand slipped. My brother fell upon the sharp rocks and was knocked unconscious. I thought he was dead."

"How dreadful! But he recovered?"

"Not completely. And not for a while." Blaise gritted his teeth. "One of the fishermen came to help. He carried my brother up the stairs leading to the Mermaid's Tower. My father saw us from above and came hurrying down, crying out to be told what had happened. 'He fell,' the fisherman said. And my father, thinking Hilliard had fallen from the tower as our mother did, suffered a stroke of apoplexy on the spot. He, too, was carried up to the château, the second victim of my moment of carelessness . . ."

For three days and nights Blaise did not know if either of them would live. It was all his fault. If he had not let himself be startled by Hilliard's response, if he had only held on more tightly, if he had only tried to retrieve the shell himself.

If, if, if.

"It is not good to brood," Gaelle said. "Better to spend the time in prayer, begging le Bon Dieu to spare them. You are still almost a child, and it is said that children have God's ear."

Blaise did not feel like a child at the age of seventeen. He was a man. But he would pray. He had gone to the chapel and bargained with God. "What will it take for you to spare them?" he asked silently. "I will do anything, make any sacrifice that you demand of me."

God had not answered him. Not at first. By the sixth night, Hilliard was no better and their father's condition had worsened. Blaise was sent for in the middle of the night. Walking into the room, he heard the death rattle in his father's throat.

"He is finally awake and lucid," Gaelle said softly, "but I fear he will not last the night."

"Anne? Anne is calling me," his father said, looking into the corner of the room. He coughed weakly but his voice gained strength as he spoke. "I must go to her . . ."

A strange sound made Blaise look up in alarm. It was the first and only time he had ever seen Gaelle weep. It was shattering. The priest finished anointing his father with holy chrism. Blaise stepped closer to the bedside and took his father's hand in his.

"Your son is here," the cleric said to the dying man. "Your father wishes to speak with you, boy. You must be brave, and carry on the Cheney name with pride."

Guy Cheney's eyes opened once more. He stared at his son blankly for a moment.

"It is I, Father. Blaise."

And then his father spoke his dying words to his eldest son. "Blaise. Yes. Your mother chose that name for you. A fitting symbol of the lust and shame in which you were conceived." His voice wavered, and grew strong again: "My father was a proud man. He prevented me from marrying the woman I loved, because her family was obscure and she had no dowry. The last laugh is mine, though—

because now a bastard will inherit everything he treasured most . . ."

Blaise's agony was real, as he relived the events that had scarred his soul. He turned away from Flora. "That was how I learned of my mother's adultery, my own bastardy. From my father's dying lips. My loving memories of my mother died with him. That is the price her sin extracted from me.

"It was only later that I realized the full implications of it: Hilliard was my father's true heir. It was Hilliard who should be master of Château Morgaine. If he lived."

A deep sigh wracked Blaise's body. "I had, without meaning to, robbed my brother of the château and its fine estates. How could I rob him of Eve, the only thing he had left? Hilliard survived his injuries and I—I paid the price that heaven demanded of me in payment for his recovery. I left France. Went away, knowing that Eve and my brother had a real affection for one another. Knowing that, in time, she might turn to him for solace."

Flora was deeply moved. "So it is love for them that caused you to try and save Johanna from ruin."

"And for the child herself, once I came to know her."

"But none of this would have occurred, had you not neglected her in the first place."

His eyes flashed. "Do you think I do not know that? There is more, as long as I am making my confession to you. I came back a few days before their wedding." He couldn't tell Flora the rest. Of how he had lain with Eve in the ruins of the stone cottage on the estate grounds, of how he had made love to her, not knowing that she and Hilliard were to wed, until after. She had not told him of it in her letters to him. No one had.

"Although I had had a hand in it, the knowledge that she and Hilliard were to marry was a terrible thing. I went away for many years, leaving them at the château. It seemed only right that they should have the benefit of what should have belonged to him.

"On my next visit, Hilliard proposed we take my yacht out to the islands. There was a property on the Isle d'Ouessant he wanted to see. Yseult Kersaudy had a dream

that the morgans were going to claim their next victim. I
scoffed. I did not believe her. We left, and the first day all
was well. The next, a fierce squall blew up and the yacht
shipped water and began to sink. We were not far from
land. Hilliard called to me to get Eve and Johanna into the
rowboat. We were going down! I got the child to safety.
When I looked up again, Hilliard was in trouble. He
shouted again for me to rescue Eve. I had to haul her bodily
from the water and into the boat. She was half-conscious
and I knelt over her and tried to clear her lungs.''

He looked up, eyes blind, face ravaged with grief. ''And
while I saved the woman I loved, my own brother vanished
beneath the seas. His body was never recovered. So you
see, I robbed my brother twice: first of his inheritance, and
then of his life.'' And of Eve's virginity and love as well.
He had not touched her again.

The weight of his guilt filled the room, pressing the
breath from Flora's chest. ''You did what you had to do.
It was what he wanted.''

But Blaise was lost in his own private hell. ''Every time
I looked at Johanna, I saw their faces. I could not bear it!
And so I placed Johanna in the English school, as her
mother requested on her deathbed. And I went away
again.''

Flora understood the agony in his voice. He would always wonder if he had tried harder, if he had swum faster
. . . if he had not been still desperately in love with his
brother's wife . . .

She ached for him. It was no wonder he was so haunted.
But that did not change the situation, nor absolve him for
what he had done to her.

She considered her options. Her own sins were great, but
she had been paid back a thousandfold. And she had not
tried to harm either him or Johanna with her own deception.
But Blaise had used her for his own ends, tricked her into
thinking he loved her, and then seduced her for his pleasure.

In return, in complete trust and innocence, she had given
him her heart and soul. That betrayal was something she
could never forgive.

The moon had risen, ripe and full. It sent liquid silver through the open windows, filling the room with surreal light. A perfect night for making love. Instead she proposed a bargain.

"I will make a pact with you, Blaise. For Johanna's sake. And the child's, should she not miscarry. If you agree, we will abide by its terms. But if you break it, I will leave in an instant, without looking back. This will be your only warning."

He turned his hands palms up. "What choice do I have?"

"Very well. These are my terms. I want nothing from you. I will assign my grandfather's legacy to you, in exchange for an equal amount of money to be deposited in my name in Paris. You will see to this immediately. Do you agree?"

"Of course. But why?"

He frowned at her, uneasy at the change in her manner. All the anger had drained out of her voice. This was not the hot-blooded woman he'd made passionate love to, this was a cold stranger. An icy goddess from some distant realm.

"I'll explain soon enough. Suffice it to say that I want nothing from you. Not a single sou!"

Flora collected herself and continued. "We will let it be known that I am with child. Half the village suspects it, in any case. I will stay with you and Johanna, acting the part of your wife in public, until 'complications' of the pregnancy force me to retire to the château for the rest of the confinement. Johanna, of course, will not be seen about the village either, as we will give out that she is in constant attendance upon me. It will be difficult to stay at the château so long, but we will survive the isolation."

"You would do this?" Hope and disbelief warred in his breast.

"Yes." She eyed him stonily. "Until the baby is born and christened. And then I will return your gifts and jewels and expensive Paris gowns and leave this accursed place forever, and you will do nothing to stop me. *Nothing!* Nor will you try to contact me again in any way, ever again."

Blaise swore a violent oath. He turned his face away, jaw knotting with the effort to control himself. It wasn't an easy task.

He strode to the window and stared out blindly. Flora watched him and waited, her back rigid and her insides quivering like blancmange. He turned back and his face was dark with fury.

"I see," he said at last, with great bitterness. "You loathe me so greatly that you intend to leave with nothing but the clothes on your back."

"Those are my conditions. Take them or leave them."

Blaise ran a hand through his thick hair. Flora tried not to stare at it, or remember how strong, how gentle, those hands could be. The intimacy they had shared had meant everything to her and it had been nothing to him. Nothing but lies.

Blaise saw the momentary softening of her face, and the black despair that had settled over him at her ultimatum lifted a little. Yes, it could work. It would still be Hilliard's and Eve's flesh and blood who inherited the château—as it rightfully should be. As to Flora, she would not feel so strongly about his deception, if she were truly indifferent to him. And he knew her weaknesses. He knew her passion.

She would be here with him, essentially confined to the château from the time that Johanna's pregnancy began to show. They would be thrown continuously into one another's company for months. Her very nature was on his side.

Flora, Flora! If I cannot lure you into my arms again, and into my bed, then there is truly no hope! His eyes lit with golden flames in the moonlight, just thinking of it: he would seduce her all over again.

"Very well. Let us seal our bargain." Blaise came forward, reaching out to take her hands.

She stepped back stiffly. "Do not! For that is the last condition, you see. If you touch me—even once—the agreement is severed. I will leave in an instant."

Her vehemence shocked him. His face was like a statue's, sculpted in light and shadow. A muscle ticked at his jaw. He had to handle this carefully. Protestations of love would be useless. She knew him for the liar he was.

He attacked on another front. Swiftly, while her emotions were still vulnerable.

"You ask too much of me, Flora." He advanced on her slowly. "Remember all the hours we have pleasured one another, *chèrie*. Remember that you are still my wife."

He was so close he could almost hear her heart hammering. He knew by the catch in her breath that she still felt the tug of their mutual attraction. One more step and he would gather her up in his arms and kiss her until she came to her senses. Or lost them completely.

"Look at the moonlight, *ma fleur,* and think of how it would be to make love in it. Here. And now." He could sense her resistance dying. Another moment and she would be his. "Come to me, Flora. Let me make love to you."

Fine tremors shook her body. That was exactly what she wanted. Craved, with every fiber of her being. All she had to do was abandon her principles, forgive his duplicity, and surrender her self-respect.

She had hoped once to win his love: instead she could have a true marriage of convenience, with him offering his name, his wealth, the strength and vigor of his virile, masculine body.

Nothing more.

And yet, she wanted him. Merciful God, how she wanted him! Her breasts tingled for his hands, his lips upon them. Her whole body burned with the hot ache of desire.

Blaise heard her gasping breaths and his blood sang with exultation. Yes, this was the way to win her back. Now, before she had time to think.

She swayed a little toward him. Almost, almost. It was exquisite torture, being so close to her. Knowing that victory was almost his. His loins throbbed for her.

But one wrong move would ruin everything. He must not frighten her with his intensity. So then, trying to ease the matter by making it lighter, he pushed it too far instead.

"Let me love you, Flora. What is the harm in it?" His voice and manner were soft. Incredibly seductive. He lifted his hand to her cheek, brushing her breast casually, purposely, with the side of his palm. He could see her trembling in the clear, silver light.

His long fingers touched the contours of her mouth, following the outlines of those beautiful curves. "We will keep our bargain, you and I, if that is what you want. But in the meantime, there is no reason we should not still enjoy all the benefits of marriage."

She jerked back as if scalded, and cursed herself for a fool. She faced him, spine rigid, one hand thrust out before her. "Not another step. Not one! If you touch me our pact is ended, for once and all!"

"Flora, for the love of God—"

"There is no love in you," she cried. "You do not know the meaning of the word. I rue the day I ever set eyes upon you!"

She darted around him and ran to the door, opening it wide. Malin stood in the corridor, all agog.

Blaise scowled at the maid. "Have you nothing better to do than to listen at doors?" he said viciously.

Flora whipped past her and fled down the stairs, her heart aching and shattered beyond repair.

Chapter Thirteen

Johanna lay on a chaise in the walled garden, beneath the shade of an ancient chestnut tree. Her eyes, in a face visibly much thinner, were deeply troubled. "Do you hate me, Flora?"

"Of course not."

"But you are angry."

"We have gone over this ground before. Let us discuss something else."

"Yes. There is something I must say." The girl struggled to sit upright, then collapsed back against the cushions. "I have told Gaelle, and now I swear to you, Flora: I did nothing to rid me of my child. I do not know why Madame Kerjean thinks so."

"Because she is a fool," Flora replied sharply. Instantly she was contrite. "Forgive me. I have not slept well lately. I believe you, Johanna. And I do not place any blame on you for any of this. Not for your situation, nor for keeping it a secret from me."

"You must not blame Blaise. He was only trying to protect me."

Flora didn't answer. Couldn't answer.

The soft breeze fluttered her skirts and ruffled her hair as she strolled along, pretending to admire the colorful blossoms. Seeing nothing but her own inner turmoil. Her emotions shifted constantly, from hot, red anger to cold and black despair, followed by a gray sort of numbness that left her deaf and blind to everything but her own misery.

She plucked a stem of pink hydrangea, hardly knowing that she did so. In her mind, she had gone over the events leading up to this a hundred times in the preceding days. It was not that he hadn't told her of Johanna's pregnancy before their marriage. She could understand his reasoning there. It was his failure to do so afterward, when he knew something more of her character and had seen her real affection for the girl.

He should have known by then that she would not betray or desert them. That she would have seen it through and honored their contract, no matter how upset she might have been at being deceived. If he had told her before that night on the Druid's Isle, she would have been shocked and saddened, but she would have understood. Would have not abandoned them.

Instead he had carried out a coldly calculated seduction of her—for that is exactly what it had been. A carefully plotted campaign to ensnare her with sensual pleasures and the illusion that she was loved. How easy she had made it for him! Flora thought with a pang. She had loved Blaise, in spite of all his flaws. Perhaps because of them. And she had believed that he loved her in return. *That* was what she could not forgive.

The whole thing had been a chess game to him: he had made her feel that she was his queen, but she had been nothing but a pawn. Something to sacrifice and discard in order to achieve his goal.

If he loved her he would have trusted her. If he loved her, she thought with an aching heart, he would have said so. And he had not. She had to give him that. Looking back over what he had said, she realized he had never once told her that he loved her.

Flora closed her eyes against the pain and lifted her face to the warm sun. He had fooled her as completely as Robin Harding had done before. And she had been a willing accomplice in her own seduction. There was one small consolation: at least this episode had not ended in a death.

A shiver ran through her. Flora opened her eyes and realized that pink petals littered her shoes and the ground around her feet. She had shredded the hydrangea.

A shadow fell across the path in front of her. She looked up. Blaise had entered the garden. His masculine presence dwarfed the feminine flowers, the dainty fountain, the mossy pathways weaving through the dappled shade. He was staring at her, his eyes hooded and brooding. She met his dark, smoldering gaze and it was like the punch of a fist to her stomach.

At first it was her physical reaction to him, but it became something more. Without warning her knees went weak and her head whirled giddily. All her blood seemed to be draining out of her body and she knew she was going to faint.

"Flora!" He stepped toward her, arms outstretched to save her from falling.

She grasped the back of a garden seat with clammy hands. "Stop! Do not!" she said through gritted teeth. "Don't . . . touch . . . me!"

Even in her terrible state, she could not let him know how her resolution wavered in his presence, how his nearness undermined her strength.

Blaise went as white as she felt. The lines from the corners of his nose to his mouth deepened. He stopped in midstride, utterly shaken. A few days ago she had lain naked and replete in his arms. Now she could not bear to even be touched by him. She could hardly stand the sight of him. He watched her take great gulps of air in an effort to steady herself. The moment she had recovered her color she edged stiffly away from him and left the garden.

He watched her halting progress toward the house, warring with the urge to sweep her up in his arms and carry her inside. Knowing full well that she had meant what she said—that she would leave at the first opportunity. He had never felt such helpless anger in his life.

Flora managed to get up to her room, where she fell across the bed, so dizzy and sick to her stomach she could hardly reach for her bellpull to call Jeanette. "I am ill," she said, but Jeanette had already seen. She managed to get the basin to her in the nick of time. Flora was violently sick for several minutes. When it was over, she was wringing wet and exhausted.

The maid dosed her with herbal drops in water, undressed her tenderly, and bathed her with tepid water.

"Shall I ask Madame Morceau to come to you?" she asked.

"No! I am . . . it is nothing. I am better. Thank you." Flora closed her eyes.

After pulling the curtains closed, Jeanette tiptoed back into the dressing room with a knowing smile on her face.

The same thought that made Jeanette smile had Flora fighting back shock: God in heaven, could she be with child? Surely it was too soon. She had never heard that pregnancy sickness could come on so quickly! But then, she knew so little about it. Not much more than Johanna, in fact.

She lay there, stunned with the possibility. If so, it would complicate everything. Her first instinct was to flee before any chance of it could be discovered. Blaise would never let her take his child away with her. But could she leave, knowing she carried Blaise's child within her womb? Rob him of his true heir? She didn't think so. Nor could she go and leave her child behind.

And what of Johanna's baby? The more she tried to puzzle out the possibilities, the more tangled and twisted her thoughts became. Was there no way out of this terrible predicament?

Oh! If only she were wrong. Perhaps it was only the food again. Last evening's oysters, or the cream from her morning coffee. Food did not keep well in the warmer months, and it was very likely. That calmed her.

She lay with her eyes closed, trying not to think at all, until the draught Jeanette had given her began to take effect. Flora willingly relinquished consciousness, falling headlong into the well of sleep. Down and down through gauzy layers, into the mermaid dream . . .

. . . *She could hear the mermaid singing. The voice drew her on. A voice so unearthly in its loveliness that it brought tears to her eyes. Filled with the sighs and murmurs of the sea, and the music echoing through the pearly caverns that were home to the* mari morgans. *She sang of love and betrayal, and the loneliness, the longing for what she could never have . . .*

The sorrowful beauty was too much to bear. Flora wanted desperately to wake up, but could not. She had to find the mermaid and set her free.

She looked about and saw that she was wandering the endless marble halls of a vast château. She recognized it now from her dreams in Paris. Then it had been a place of echoing emptiness and locked doors. Then she had feared that she would never be able to open them.

Lately she had been more afraid of what she would find on the other side.

And now she would find out. There was no escaping the knowledge.

It was time. Opening the first door, all rusted iron and shrieking hinges, she discovered Gaelle, weeping at a prie-dieu. She called to her, but Gaelle did not answer. Flora realized that the woman was flanked by two coffins, and shackled to them by ropes of twisted, black rosary beads made up of thorns.

The second door was made of glass. Behind it she saw Johanna, floundering in a lake of blood. Flora tried to open the door but could not turn the crystal handle, because it was slippery with her own tears.

She approached the third door with growing trepidation. The third door opened to the Mermaid's Tower. She knew that Blaise was up there, standing at the window from which his mother had jumped. When she tried to open it she discovered it was locked, this time from inside.

"Ah, no! Blaise!"

There must be a key somewhere. There must be another way inside. It must not end this way.

Blinded by tears, the dream-Flora turned and gasped with shock. She was standing in front of the pink granite stone set into the wall, the one that in waking life had a mermaid design crudely etched into its surface. But the face looking back at her was not incised in stone. It was that of a flesh-and-blood woman, with haunted, hopeless eyes.

"Are you the one?" a soft voice whispered—but it was not the woman speaking. Her lips were sealed with a cross. The dream-Flora turned.

A figure stood behind her, shrouded in shadows. "Yes, you are the one," it said gently. "Come with me. It is time to end this."

And Flora followed the figure down the winding stairs that led to the cliff path, toward the inky glimmer of a midnight sea. A cold wind blew steadily, chilling her to the marrow. Every sense warned her not to follow the mysterious figure, yet she found herself powerless to resist. Down and down and down, into ever deeper shadows.

Even though she knew that the thing that summoned her was Death.

The sun shone brightly over Pont du Mor for the opening of the *grand pardon* and the day was unseasonably warm. The crowds thronged the waterfront and clogged the streets.

Even she was feeling the heat of the noon sun, and the cups of cider they'd been sipping did little to ease her discomfort. Her taste buds had not been the same since her episode of illness, and she set the cider aside.

"This is wickedly foolish," Flora said beneath her breath. The Cheneys' commodious carriage was positioned for the best view of the village, from the parish close to the strand, but her eyes were for Johanna. The girl was as white as eggshell.

"We are here," Gaelle said crisply, "and there is no turning around now in all this milling multitude. We must make the best of the situation."

Flora was less sanguine. "She will suffer a relapse."

"Do not blame Gaelle," Johanna begged. "It was my wish to come. It is expected of me, as a Cheney."

She held her head high. Inside she felt neither the strength nor the confidence she projected, but she would do her best. A new sense of responsibility filled her. She had let so many people down! Now she must face the consequences.

For a time she had pretended that nothing had happened, as if the incident at the vicarage had been no more than a bad dream. Tried to be a child herself again, pretending there was not a tiny life growing within her womb. Putting all the burden of her troubles upon Blaise and Gaelle. And now, Flora.

She had not meant to cause them so much grief. At the time it had seemed so perfect: her beloved Miss O'Donnell would leave her chores at Hawthorne Academy, and come with them to France as Blaise's wife. Johanna sighed. She had convinced herself that everyone would be the happier for it.

She would have a companion whom she loved and trusted, and later would be able to make a new life for herself, free of the shame and social disaster she had brought down upon herself and her family. Her child would be heir to the château, and not a shunned bastard living in the shadows. Oh, yes, she had worked it all out in her mind.

Flora would no longer have to labor as an instructress at the academy and could live a comfortable and fashionable life. Blaise would have not only the heir he wanted, but a wife as beautiful in spirit and heart as she was in appearance. He would fall in love with Flora and she with him, and they would all live happily ever after, quite like a fairy tale.

Which is exactly what had happened. On the surface, at least. But it hadn't worked out that way in the end. The airy dream castle she had created, had been built on a foundation of lies. Now it lay in ruins about her. Her own reputation would be saved, but at what cost?

Flora and Blaise had been so happy since returning from the Druid's Isle. Now they no longer spoke to one another, except when forced to by necessity. Thank God that Nicolas and Claudine were back! Their presence made Blaise and Flora keep up the pretense that everything was well between them. But in a few months, Flora would go out of their lives forever—it did not bear thinking of!

"What is taking so long?" Claudine asked. She sat beside her husband in an open carriage next to theirs, chic beneath a fetching yellow parasol.

Like the other women from the château, she wore her best Paris finery today. On the morrow they would change into their traditional Breton garb for the ceremony at the château, the High Mass in the church, and the *fest noz* in the evening.

"I hear the *couple*," Nicolas said beside her. "The procession has started."

The crowd stilled as the music of traditional instruments of Brittany carried on the warm breeze. Flora shaded her eyes and saw the head of the procession coming out through the triumphal gate of the parish close. It was led by men playing the *bombarde,* an oboelike instrument, and the *biniou,* the small Breton bagpipes. Together the instruments made up a *couple,* so-called because they were invariably played together.

It was like no procession Flora had ever seen in Hawthorne Village. The joyous reverence of the participants was evident in every line of their bodies. Directly behind the musicians came an enormous open litter, carried on the shoulders of six men especially chosen for the honor. It was decorated with garlands of flowers. The statue of St. Mari du Mor, dressed in her new robes, stood in its center in her golden scallop-shell chariot. Gaelle's usually composed face was pink with pride.

Behind them came the members of the church societies, each with their standards and colorful banners, and most of the population of Pont du Mor, in their festive finery. They went from house to house, and at each the family would greet them with more flowers for the litter, and fall in behind. Merchants offered coins in a collection basket for the widows and families of those who were lost at sea.

Flora saw that this was not just a ritual to them, but a community taking care of its own. How close they were to life and death, in this little village clinging to its rocky shore. She was truly saddened to know that she would never be a part of it.

Looking away, she caught Blaise's eye as he stared enigmatically at her. She felt her color rise. How magnificent he was on horseback. It chagrined her that the mere sight of him could still make her heart turn over like a millwheel.

Claudine saw, too, and leaned closer to their carriage. "La! He cannot take his eyes off you, even now," she said, more loudly than she had intended. Several people turned to look at the blushing bride. Even Blaise was discomfited.

The procession passed and the carriages and horsemen fell in behind, with the cavalcade going down to the strand where the fishing boats were pulled up. They had been decorated with banners and floral garlands and the effect was totally charming. Flora, Claudine, and Malin descended their carriages to watch the blessing of the boats but Gaelle and Johanna stayed in the vehicle.

As the abbé went along slowly, sprinkling each vessel with holy water and offering a prayer for safety, Flora became aware of Blaise at her side.

"Walk with me a way," he said brusquely. "We must talk."

She hesitated only a moment. There was no danger in strolling apart with him. There was no danger at all that he would pull her into his arms here in front of the entire village, and kiss away all her resolve, which had grown shakier with time. They walked out of earshot of the others and stood apart from the crowd.

"I have something I must say to you." He looked away from her and out to sea, gathering his words. He must choose them carefully.

Flora looked at his strong profile against the steel-blue waves and felt her heart somersault painfully.

Blaise continued to stare out across the sea. "You say you want to leave as soon as . . . as is possible. I cannot stop you, even though you and I have a signed agreement. But I have given your situation great thought."

He turned back to her and his eyes were flat and black as unpolished stones. "It occurred to me that someday, when this is all behind you, you will meet a man, perhaps fall in love, and wish to marry." The corners of his mouth twisted wryly. "In such a case, a husband in France would surely prove a major inconvenience. I have decided to give you your complete freedom."

Her insides lurched. It was an effort to keep her voice steady. "A divorce, you mean?"

"No. That would prove a bad choice for either of us. I have no desire to marry, but there may come a time when I change my mind and decide to take a wife: the child will need a mother, after all. Gaelle is too old and bitter to have the raising of it, and Johanna must move on and make a new life, have children born within the law."

Every word of his was like a lash to her flesh, flaying her to the bone. Another woman in Blaise's home . . . in his arms . . . in his bed. Flora clenched her hands at her sides so hard her nails threatened to puncture her gloves. It took enormous effort to keep it from showing in her face.

That was the moment when she realized that she still wanted him. Desperately. Still loved him, despite what he was and what he had done. She must not let him see how the thought affected her. "You are determined that this child will be raised well."

His jaw knotted. She hadn't reacted as he'd prayed she might. All hope of reestablishing anything between them was gone. "I will not repeat the same mistakes I made with Johanna, with her child. He or she will be raised here, in the proper atmosphere, surrounded by family. And never suffer the painful knowledge of being born a *bastard.* I have sworn an oath on it!"

How deep his wounds went, she realized, and felt his anguish as keenly as if it were her own. She was too moved with sympathy to speak.

He thought her indifferent. And why should she care, after the gross deception they had played on her?

"What I am proposing is this. Stay on with us, Flora, until Johanna is safely established, as you originally agreed. Two years, only. Help her ease through this painful period. Let the world see you with this child and believe it is mine. In return I will help you in every way I can to see yourself established.

"Divorce would create too much difficulty for you. Our world is cruel to women who live estranged from their husbands. It is worse to those who are divorced. You would not be accepted in higher circles of society. Among those who did receive you, you would be looked upon as easy prey by men, and as a threat by their wives."

He took a deep breath and let it out. "If you do this, I will arrange for a speedy annulment. It can easily be done. Fortunately we were not married in the church. I had intended to have our marriage sanctified by the abbé next month, which would have made it valid in Rome. As it stands now, it will be merely a civil matter."

The sun was still shining, but Flora felt increasingly chilled. A civil matter. Everything that had been between them, reduced to a few sheets of paper. But then, most of it had been a product of her own yearning. To him, she had only been a convenience. A concubine.

Blaise glanced down at her. How remote she seemed. Hard to believe that this was the same woman who had arched and writhed against him with passion. For all her interest in him, he might as well be a stranger.

"The child will still be my legal heir and your reputation will remain intact, Flora. The monies I have agreed to settle on you will be yours, as well as any jewels I have bought for you. When the time is up you will be free to resume your life as a wealthy and highly eligible woman, unencumbered by either a husband or the scandal of divorce. And I swear to God, I will never touch you again as man to woman."

Flora had listened to him in a state of growing conflict. She thought of Johanna and her baby, of what her leaving would mean to them. She had not thought of the other consequences to herself. But perhaps she was only pulling the wool over her own eyes, convincing herself to stay when she knew it would only lead to disaster.

If only you loved me, Blaise, it would be so easy.

Nicolas joined them, unaware that he was intruding on a private conversation. "I've just met an engaging fellow. Monsieur Wolfe, an Irishman, and a scholar of note. He will be helping Loïc Kersaudy assemble and chronicle the records of the De Broceliand family. I thought perhaps you would wish to invite him to dinner at the château tomorrow evening, since he is staying with them."

He glanced back toward the main crowd. "You might be aiding in a budding romance. Mademoiselle Kersaudy seems quite taken with him. I overheard her say that he is quite the most charming man she has ever met."

"Certainly," Blaise said. "In fact, you may be our emissary, if you wish."

"My pleasure." Nicolas took himself off, pausing only to whisper something in his wife's ear. Claudine clapped her hands and smiled up at him.

If only that were us, Flora thought. She was silent a long time, so lost in thought she didn't realize that the blessing of the boats was over, and the crowd was processing back toward the church. Her innate fairness had come into play.

Blaise had lied to her and kept a terrible secret from her and used him for his own ends.

And she had done the same.

She could admit that to herself, now that the first heat of her disappointment had passed. She had pretended, much as Johanna had done, that everything that went before her arrival in France was like a bad dream. But it was real.

"You have not answered me," Blaise said quietly. "Will you stay and see this through? Not just until the child is born, but until he or she is safely established as my own?"

"I must think." Her thoughts were whirling. Her first reaction to his proposal was the fear—no, the certain knowledge—that she would end up in his arms again. It was inevitable. They were too passionate and the sensual bond between them too strong, too vibrant.

But she was a woman and needed love as well as sexual passion, and he was only offering her the one. Day by day, she would lose what self-respect she had left. She would grow to resent him even while she welcomed him to her bed. She would find paradise in his arms, and hell in the lonely hours afterward. In time she would hate them both.

And when the two years were up and he sent her packing, like a paid-off mistress, she would be carrying the pieces of her broken heart away in a basket.

Blaise watched her closely, seeing the emotions that flitted so quickly across her face. It was like watching the reflection of sun and clouds passing over the glittering surface of the bay. He schooled his face, knowing that one wrong blink on his part could destroy all hope.

Flora knotted her hands together and looked up into his face. She could read nothing there to help her. He might as well have been carved from the native granite. Everything he said made sense . . . but then, so had everything he'd told her before. He seemed to know instinctively just how to play upon her emotions and unbalance her judgment until she couldn't tell up from down.

As she looked past his shoulder, she saw Johanna watching them intently, her eyes deeply shadowed in the pale oval of her face. Flora knew what it was like to feel hopeless and abandoned. Without her, Johanna's unhappy fate would be sealed. She would be sent away to the care of strangers again, until her child was born. And she would never set eyes upon it again.

Flora dragged in a shivering breath. "Very well. I have seen it this far, and I will honor our pact. But you must honor your part of it as well. My door will remained locked to you. That part of our life together is over."

A flash of gold lit his eyes. It was gone in an instant. "Then one last boon," he said. "A kiss to seal our bargain. To remember on the cold winter nights."

Before she knew what he was doing he'd swept her into his arms.

Flora braced herself for one of his punishing, demanding kisses. Instead his mouth was gentle and infinitely tender. It lasted just long enough to melt her bones to syrup and send her blood racing through her veins. And then she was out of his warm embrace and standing alone in the cold wind.

Blaise took her gloved hand in his. "*Adieu,* Flora, my love." He bowed formally over it, his lips stopping correctly so that they just brushed empty air. "*Bonjour,* Madame Cheney."

He dropped her hand and turned abruptly. The abbé's sister was standing between them and the road. Madame Rohun's face was grave as she stared up toward the château. Her head moved as if watching an invisible procession, following its progress into the village. Then she blinked, like a sleepwalker awakening, and hastily crossed herself.

The color drained from Blaise's face. "What is it? What did you see, Madame Rohun?"

She started as if she had seen a ghost. Blaise put out a hand to steady the woman, and questioned her in their native tongue. Flora was suddenly frightened. The abbé's sister shook her head vigorously, and strode away, into the crowd.

"Was it one of the invisible funeral processions?" Flora wanted to know. "I was told about them. That she sees the corpse in the vision, and the person she sees will perish within three days."

He frowned at her. "You must not put credence in her powers."

"But you do. I can see it in your face." Flora moved closer to his side, as if he could physically shield her from the dreadful unknown. "Who . . . who was it?"

"I do not know. She claims she could not make out the face, for it was covered with a blue veil."

Flora shivered. The sun had gone behind a cloud, cooling the air and dulling the village. The granite looked cold and gray, the flowers suddenly leached of their bright colors. "The others are quite a way ahead. We shall have to hurry to catch up." They walked back toward the center of the village, together yet separate. As they would remain.

Their absence had not gone unnoticed. "There you are!" Claudine exclaimed. A sly expression came over her. "You were down by the rocks. When next I looked around you were gone." She lowered her amused voice. "I thought the *fées* had carried you off, Flora, but I see it was just your husband. Even in sight of all Pont du Mor, he cannot keep his hands off you!"

Oh yes, he can, Flora thought. *The question is,* will *he?*

Johanna had insisted on getting down from the carriage to join the processional to the parish close. "Ah, look," she announced. "There is Yseult. And . . . and Loic." Two spots of high color formed on her pale cheeks.

Malin looked across the road to the crowd on the other side. "A handsome man, that one," she whispered to Johanna. "Perhaps Monsieur Kersaudy hopes to make a match for his sister, eh?"

A sharp reprimand was issued by Gaelle in Breton. It was not Malin's place to gossip with her mistress or try to ape her betters. "The girl has no sense of what is fitting and proper," she added in an aside to Flora.

But Flora did not hear any of the exchange. Idly glancing over at the festive throng, she had spied Yseult and Odile de Broceliand at the same moment Johanna had. And that must be Loic, half hidden by one of the embroidered satin banners. Then the procession moved on. A man stood in the gap between two carriages, looking at Flora thoughtfully.

She felt as if all the wind had been knocked out of her. Awake and in broad daylight, she found herself staring,

appalled, into a face from her nightmares. A face she had
hoped to never see again.

Robin Harding was still incredibly handsome, she
thought in surprise. It seemed by now that evil side of him
should have wrought some changes. But no, he was still an
Adonis, with fair hair and the face and body of a Greek
statue.

She leaned back into the shadows beside the carriage,
and prayed that he could not see her well enough to recognize her. He continued to scrutinize their carriage for
some time, a slow smile forming on his beautifully modeled
lips. She wasn't quite sure, but she could almost swear that
he winked. Then he tipped his hat and vanished into the
crowd.

Flora was sick with shock and horror. What evil coin-
cidence had brought him here, to the little village of Pont
du Mor? She must think the problem through and not panic.
Not yet.

Everything depended on whether or not Robin Harding
had seen and recognized her. Flora knew she presented a
far different appearance now. When he knew her in London, she had been the hired companion to a kind and elderly spinster. Her clothes had been plain, her hair simply
dressed, her manner quiet and reserved. Even her name had
been different then.

Surely there was nothing to connect that naïve young
woman, drab and practically penniless, with the wife of a
wealthy French landowner, elegantly outfitted in tasteful
jewels and gowned by the House of Worth.

The mass of humanity surged forward, following the music of the *couple* and raising their voices in song. Flora was
carried along, willy-nilly, through the triumphal arch and
into the close. The grassy open spaces and pathways were
thronged as the priest led them three times around the *calvaire*. The central stone column rose high into the sky, sur-
mounted by its crucifixion scene and the figures of saints
and apostles surrounding it.

Flora looked around. Cautiously. She had become sepá-
rated from the others again. There was no sign of Robin
Harding, for which she was grateful. Stepping back, she
managed to put one of the many statues between herself

and the main group, which was still surging forward. If she could just make her way to the safety of the carriage without being seen and recognized she might—

"That second figure beneath the cross," a smooth voice said from behind her shoulder. "Is it the pure Virgin Mary? Or the soiled Mary Magdalene? I have always preferred to disport myself with the former."

Shock froze Flora in place. Even her heart seemed to stop in mid-beat. She turned slowly and looked up into the mocking face of Robin Harding.

There was laughter and something sharper in his voice. His eyes, those restless gold-green eyes that still gave her nightmares, were as clear and dazzling as she remembered.

"But," he went on, "perhaps you are in a hurry to leave, and have no time to talk with an old acquaintance?"

"I beg your pardon," she said haughtily, in her flawless French, "but you have made a mistake, monsieur. I do not know you."

He laughed. "When did you learn to be such a bold little piece? And so deceitful? I think you know me very well indeed."

He cupped her chin in his hand and lifted it. "Did you think I could ever forget that lovely face?" His voice lowered. "That soft and yielding body? A shame you didn't let me explore it more completely. But it is not too late to rectify that, Madame Cheney. That is your name now, is it not? But, of course, I knew you as Katherine McCall. You've done extremely well for yourself, it seems. While I languished in the squalor of a cell."

She tried to pull away. Her head was spinning. "People are beginning to stare!"

"Oh, so you worry about what people will think? Excellent. I think, my little lost love, that you have as much—or more!—to lose from discovery than I. Do not fear. I shan't give you away." His smile widened. "Nor, I am certain, can *you* betray *me*. Let me relieve your mind, my dear. That . . . ah, incident in London was purely an accident."

The yellow eyes bored into hers. "You do believe me, don't you?"

"What are you doing in Pont du Mor?" she asked in an agitated whisper.

"Did you think I had come searching for you? What a romantic imagination you have! No, I assure you, my presence here in the same little village is merely one of those little jokes that fate plays on us."

He dropped his hand from her chin, but closed his fingers over her wrist, cruelly. "And it is all your own doing. You see, I met an acquaintance of yours in Paris and gave him my card. One Reverend Tompkins. At the time I didn't know of the connection." His smile was dazzling. "And then you so kindly presented my card to Monsieur de Broceliand. And now I am staying right here in the village, with Loic Kersaudy and his so-lovely and virginal young sister. So you see, you cannot escape fate. We were destined to be together, you and I!"

He lifted her hand and kissed it. Even through her glove she could feel the hot dampness of his mouth as he pressed his lips against the fabric. "Until we meet again. And, I promise you, we *shall* meet again."

"She was overcome with the heat, that is all. It is unseasonably warm today."

Nicolas helped Flora down from the carriage when they reached the château and got her inside the hall. She was weak and trembly, her legs barely able to support her. "Sit here," he said, taking her to a chair and fanning her with the brim of his hat.

Malin and Johanna hovered anxiously, Gaelle sent for Jeanette, and Claudine knelt beside Flora's chair, chafing her cold hands. Nicolas vanished for several minutes and came back with a glass of brandy, which he gave to Blaise.

"Really, I am quite all right now," Flora protested. "It was only a momentary faintness."

"You look like death," Blaise said, holding the brandy to her lips. "Drink this, *chèrie.*"

His anxious eyes met hers across the rim. *How can I tell him?* she thought in despair. *I cannot.*

Claudine looked to her husband, her own emotions torn between hope for Blaise and his wife, and dismay at her own sudden wash of envy. It must be true, what Gaelle had hinted at, that Flora was with child. Ah, if only she were, too!

Nicolas reached out and caught Claudine's hand to his lips for a quick kiss. "Do not worry, *mon coeur*," he said softly. "Your time will come. Tomorrow night, when you drink the waters of St. Yvonne's Well at Plouzané—"

"Tomorrow?" Gaelle said in surprise. "But that is the *fest noz*!"

"Yes." Claudine looked even more unhappy. "We did not know . . . Nicolas had been misinformed. One must not only drink from the well as the moon increases, but return again on the night of the full moon, which is tomorrow. We had arranged for Nicolas to return in time for the feasting, and I intended to put up at the convent for the night and hear Mass there in the morning. But I will stay here, where I am needed."

"Nonsense." Gaelle looked annoyed. "I am perfectly capable of looking after her. Flora would not wish you to change your plans on her behalf."

"No, indeed!" Flora said, finding her voice. "I will not hear of it." *Especially,* she thought, *if I am halfway to Paris by then.*

"Give her more brandy, Blaise." Nicolas frowned down at her in concern. "Her color is starting to come back."

"I would prefer to go up to my chamber and rest a while, thank you."

"I will accompany you." Claudine rose to her feet. "Blaise, perhaps you should carry her?"

Flora would have none of it. "I am recovered now. I wish only to lie down in the quiet of my room. Jeanette will tend to me."

"You are not well. See how your hands tremble!"

"It was only the heat, and I feel foolish to have spoiled everyone's enjoyment."

Claudine smiled. A woman in Flora's condition should not be upset. "Myself, I was ready to return. It has been a long day. But I will prepare you a *tisane* with my own hands and bring it to you."

Once in her own chamber, Flora undressed with her maid's help and then dismissed her. "I will ring if I need you. I wish to rest undisturbed."

What she really wished to do undisturbed was think. But no sooner had the door closed behind Jeanette, than Flora felt the room spinning around her. Stumbling to the bed, she lay down, fighting painful waves of nausea. It lasted several minutes, leaving her clammy and weak.

When the episode ended she lay there, looking up at the beautifully molded ceiling. The curtains were drawn and sun filtered through like molten bronze. Just when she thought her life was settled, at least for a time, everything had gotten worse. She felt as though she had been sailing high above the earth in a hot air balloon, and the bottom of the basket had just fallen out. Now she was hanging on by her fingernails: any minute she would plummet to the ground.

The thought made her dizzy, and brandy she had taken didn't help. She felt curiously disembodied, floating away on currents of warm, amber light. Flora tried to clear her head. It was imperative that she think clearly. One misstep and she would plunge the Cheneys into scandal and herself into danger.

A rap sounded at the door and Claudine entered with her *tisane* in a porcelain cup. "Drink this, and you will feel much better, I promise."

She perched on the small slipper chair and watched Flora sip the restorative drink. "Blaise is very concerned," she said. "And I think a little jealous. He saw you talking with the Kersaudys' guest, and has been making inquiries about him."

The cup rattled against the saucer in Flora's hand. "I beg your pardon?"

"Monsieur Wolfe. Blaise saw him kiss your hand. I heard him curse beneath his breath. He was quite agitated." She crinkled her eyes in amusement. "La! But it does my heart good to see Blaise head over heels with you, Flora. I never thought to see the day!"

The cup tipped from Flora's suddenly boneless fingers, spilling a few remaining drops of the liquid on the counterpane. "I am tired, Claudine. I would like to rest now."

"Of course, *chère*. I will look in upon you later." Kissing Flora lightly on the cheek, she took the empty cup and went out.

Flora's heart fluttered wildly. She must think the problem through and not panic. Not yet. But she must act quickly. What in the name of God was wrong with her? A madman, a conscienceless seducer and murderer, was loose in the village, staying in the Kersaudy home, and she was worrying about hiding her past! He was probably insinuating himself into Yseult's good graces even now. They had to be warned.

Sick at heart, she knew there was only one solution. She must lay bare her soul to Blaise and throw herself upon his mercy. She would deal with the consequences to herself later. But, oh! she was tired. If only she could just close her eyes and sleep. Wake up and discover this was just one more terrible dream!

Flora rang for her maid. "I must speak with Monsieur. In private. Ask him to come to me here, if you please."

Jeanette dipped a curtsy and hurried out. Flora was on her feet, agitatedly pacing the sitting room, when Blaise arrived. He was pale, his face tense with concern.

"What is wrong? Shall I send for the doctor?"

"What ails me isn't physical," she said. "And it would take more than his skills to repair. I have something to tell you. When I am done you will think me the worst hypocrite in the world." Her gaze slid away from his. "And that is one of the *better* opinions you are likely to hold of me."

She stopped before the fireplace, unaware of the way the light turned her hair to a corolla of dark flame. She looked so beautiful, so vulnerable, that he thought she might tell him anything in the world, and he would forgive her.

He leaned against the mantel with his arms folded across his chest to keep from reaching out to her. What a damnable fool he had been to handle her so poorly. "You need not make so much of it," he said, watching her intently. "I realized that you were not a virgin the first time I made love to you."

In fact, he had rather expected it. There was a certain quality in the way she looked at him, and in the way she moved, that he had recognized. A knowledge, an awareness of her body that belonged to a woman whose passions had been aroused, who had already tasted the forbidden fruit.

In her case, he suspected that it had ended with disappointment. It had added spice to the seduction.

She started and stared at him in dismay. At the moment it was the least of her worries. "I wish that that were all," she said slowly. "What I am about to tell you is something I never thought to tell anyone in the world. When I am finished you may notify the authorities or turn me out of the house. I leave it in your hands. But if you can find it, in your heart to let me go away . . . but perhaps I have come to the end of my race."

Blaise was stunned. "I cannot imagine anything so dire. You may safely place your problem in my hands, and then forget about it."

Tears glistened on her lashes before she blinked them away. "If only it were so easy . . ."

She took a deep, shuddering breath. "I accused you of lying, of harboring secrets, of using me for your own ends." Her blue eyes met his across the short distance. "I have committed every one of those sins, and more. I was escaping my past, and thought that what was over and done did not concern anyone but myself. I was wrong.

"My name," she said, "is not Flora O'Donnell, but Katherine Flora McCall. My mother was born a gentlewoman, who married above her station and was thrown off by her own family, when she ran off with my father. He was a charming and dissolute ne'er-do-well, with a soiled reputation. But she loved him." Flora laughed without humor. "She thought she could redeem him. Women always do."

Her hands twisted together as she tried to control their trembling. "His upper class family disowned him. It sounds terrible, but our early years were happy. There was love and laughter in our house, in the early days. Eventually my father ran through his small independence at the gaming tables. He staked everything on the last throw of the dice. He lost. The next morning he killed himself. A hunting accident, supposedly, but everyone knew the truth.

"When we returned from the funeral the bailiffs were already in our house. We were turned out of it, with nothing but the clothes upon our backs. My mother went to my father's father and begged him to take us in. He refused, blaming her for his son's death. He said he would take me, but that she would not stay a single night beneath his roof. There was only one condition. She must never attempt to see me again. And so she left me. Her fall from grace was swift. With nothing to fall back upon, she accepted the protection of a wealthy man, who set her up as his mistress."

She saw his face harden, heard his sharp intake of breath. Flora's chin lifted defiantly. "Do not judge her! She did what she had to in order to survive. Or perhaps, like my grandfather, you think she should have jumped off a bridge into the Thames, to spare the family embarrassment!"

"I am making no judgments," Blaise said quietly. "Not yet."

"When her protector died, she soon found another. You can imagine the rest. Her descent in the demimonde was inevitable. When drink and illness ruined her beauty, her last lover cast her off. For several years I did not know what happened to her. Then one day she showed up at my grandfather's door, dying. And was turned away." Flora's voice wavered. "I left with her and never set foot in that house again. It was too late to save her: she died in a charity hospital and was buried in potter's field."

She was shaking now, as if buffeted by a windstorm. Blaise's heart was wrung. He wanted to go to her, to comfort her, but he knew it would be the wrong thing. Not now. Not yet.

"My poor Flora! It is a tragic story," he said. "But why you think I would turn you out for this is beyond my understanding."

Flora lifted her chin in that proud way she had. "My confession is only beginning."

It was difficult for Blaise to stand by and watch, as Flora relived past traumas. And, he realized, with sinking heart, that there was much worse to come. "You need not go on, Flora. This is all old history."

"Oh, yes. I must! For what I have to say is very much in the present." She walked up and down the chamber a few times, trying to compose herself. It was very important to her that he understand. She was having difficulty organizing her scattered thoughts. Her thinking was increasingly muzzy.

"After my mother's death, I sold my trinkets and hers. All except for the locket my father had given her. The little bit of money I obtained for them was soon gone. I answered an advertisement in the paper, for a position as companion to an elderly woman. Miss Hansen was a considerable heiress, with a weakness for rich food and richer jewels. She was foolish and kind and I loved her dearly."

Her hands knotted at her sides. Reliving the events was terrible. Having to relate them to Blaise made it so much worse.

"In her company I met a man named Robin Harding. He was handsome and charming and witty, the heir to a small property in Hertfordshire, he said. I was young and gullible and romantically inclined—another way of saying giddy and foolish, I suppose. He swept me off my feet."

Blaise frowned. This was what he'd been expecting to hear. He hadn't been prepared for the violent surge of jealousy that made his hackles rise as she described the man.

"And you fell in love with this paragon."

"No. I only thought I did." Flora looked into the dancing flames. "Why he and my employer had a falling-out, I don't know. She ordered me not to continue my friendship with Robin, and barred him from her home. He said that she was one of those possessive, elderly women, and jealous of his attentions to me, and that this was the cause of their breach. We met in secret. He told me he had been called home to Hertfordshire and did not know how long it would be before he could return. I was devastated."

She remembered her desperation. Once again, about to be abandoned by someone she loved. "And then everything changed. Robin swore eternal love, promised marriage, and seduced me. I was . . . not totally unwilling." There. She had admitted it. "He said we would be married as soon as possible, and arranged an elopement for three nights hence. I went back to Miss Hansen's town house, walking on air."

Blaise thought he saw the end of her story. "And he never came back. Was there a child, Flora?"

She lifted her head and stared at him blindly. "Oh, no. He came back. On the appointed night I came to the park where I was to meet him, my little half-empty valise in my hand. It seemed like such a wonderful adventure! And while I waited in the moonlight, my eyes filled with stars, he entered my employer's home through the door I had of course left unlocked, and robbed the house.

"She evidently heard noises and came to investigate. He stabbed her with a brass letter opener, and left her to choke to death in her own blood. And that is when I returned to the house."

There was such horror in her voice, such bleakness in her eyes that Blaise realized she was reliving the moment of that terrible discovery. His hands curled as if they were wrapped around the throat of the despicable Robin Harding. He was filled with such rage for Flora that he couldn't speak.

Tears were streaming down her face now. "I returned when I realized I'd left my mother's locket on the bedpost in my room. I'd forgotten it in my haste. I arrived in time to hear her breathe her last. When Robin saw me he tried to persuade me that it was her fault. That *she* had attacked *him*! Then I saw her jewels spilling from his coat pocket, and he confessed his theft. He said that he would never have harmed Miss Hansen, if she hadn't threatened to call the watch. He had the gall to feel aggrieved by the turn of events, as if she had brought her death upon herself! I knew then that he was mad."

Flora wiped her eyes, but couldn't wipe out the visions in her head that reliving Miss Hansen's murder evoked. "To this day I do not know if he truly meant to elope with me, or if it was just a ruse to get me out of the house. He wanted me to flee with him then, he said. I . . . I told him there was more jewelry, hidden away, and that I would fetch it while he . . . while he hid her body behind the settee. Leaving my valise behind, I ran upstairs, then down by the servants' stairway and out through the kitchen. I was in shock. I didn't know where to go or what to do, and wandered through the streets like a madwoman.

"When I didn't return, he threw her jewels and some silver plate into my valise. He might have made his escape, but a neighbor spied him making off in the dark and cried out for the watch. He was apprehended almost immediately.

It seems that he had a history of ingratiating himself with wealthy but lonely women, whom he would bilk of their jewels on some pretense or other. If his charm failed, he would simply rob them, while a guest in their homes. Miss Hansen, however, had very strict notions, and would not have a man stay beneath the same roof as two unmarried women, so his usual routine had not succeeded with her.''

Blaise listened to her without giving his feelings away by so much as a flicker of emotion. Flora continued her narration. It was an effort. She was so incredibly weary. If she could only lie down and sleep! She forced herself to go on.

"The police, finding my valise with her goods stuffed into it atop my pitiful belongings, immediately assumed I was his accomplice, and that I had intended to flee with him. The next day all the newspapers carried the story of the murder. And I discovered that I was a wanted woman. Under the circumstances no one would have believed my story. And so Katherine McCall vanished, and Flora O'Donnell was born.''

She didn't want to look at him, had to look at him. It was one of the most difficult things she had ever done, to hold her head high and meet him gaze for gaze, when she wanted to sink into the earth. She tried to read his reaction and failed. Blaise's eyes were like obsidian, dark and utterly mysterious.

"Well, that is my story.'' Her hands were still now, clasped so tightly that the fragile bones strained against her pale skin. "So you see, the woman who accused you of so many things is far more guilty of sin than you. And you see what an ill bargain you have made. I accepted your offer to escape England, and avoid being imprisoned for a crime I did not commit. I thought I was safe as your wife.''

She was silent so long after, that a less astute man would have thought she was through. He knew better. What was she holding back?

"A tragic story indeed. And one that fills me with great pity.'' Blaise rubbed his chin. "Forgive me for wondering, but—why are you telling me now?''

Flora found her legs would no longer hold her. She sat on one of the grotto chairs, running her fingertips over the gilded carvings. "I excused myself by thinking that no one could be harmed by my concealing it, since Robin was in prison and Miss Hansen already in her grave. I was wrong.

"Fate is laughing last. For this monster, Robin Harding, escaped prison last December. He is here in Pont du Mor, masquerading as a scholar, with hopes of ingratiating himself with the De Broceliands. He is staying at the home of Loic and Yseult Kersaudy. They are in danger, and must be warned."

He looked at her for so long that she thought he'd been turned to stone. A muscle worked in his jaw. She sagged against the chair. Her confession had used up every drop of energy in her body.

Blaise stood over her, his face grim and determined. "Poor Flora. It is no wonder you were overcome." He went to the door. "Go to bed. Have your maid fetch you some sleeping drops."

"How can I sleep, when that monster is loose?"

"Leave it to me. I shall take care of this," he said roughly. "Robin Harding will not bother you again."

Flora woke gradually, from a deep and dreamless sleep. She stretched groggily. Her head felt as if it were stuffed with dirty wool, and her mouth was filled with a bitter, metallic taste. She vaguely remembered Jeanette giving her a sleeping draught. Then she remembered that Robin Harding was in Pont du Mor, and came fully awake with a start.

The room was dark with the curtains pulled, but bright light spilled around the edges. What o'clock was it? Her eyes were heavy and she squinted at the clock on her dressing table. Impossible! She couldn't have slept for sixteen hours straight! She rang for her maid. Jeanette appeared promptly with a tray and Flora's morning chocolate.

"What is the time?"

"Half past ten, madame. Monsieur left orders that you were not to be disturbed until you rang."

"I must speak with him. Has he gone down to the village yet?"

"No, madame." The maid blushed prettily, thinking they had spent an amorous night together. "His door is closed, and he has not rung for his man. He is still abed."

As she was turning toward the wardrobe, Jeanette stopped and withdrew a piece of paper from her apron pocket. "I found this on the floor, madame. I did not know if it was to keep, or to throw away."

Flora took the envelope and smoothed it out. It was inscribed in a bold, masculine hand to "Madame Blaise Cheney." Her heart stumbled to a stop, then started up again at twice the speed. She knew that handwriting all too well.

"Where did you find this?" she asked quickly.

"In the sitting room, madame. It was by the grate."

Flora slipped the paper from the envelope. It was difficult to do, because her hands were shaking so badly. It was written in English.

My very dear Katherine,
   —Or perhaps you prefer Madame Cheney, now that you have climbed so high in the world. You always were a clever girl.
   May I tell you how lovely it was to see you again, even for so short a time? My heart quite turned over when I saw you in Pont du Mor earlier today, and for more than the most obvious reason. I have thought of you more often than you know, since our abrupt parting. Indeed, I have forgotten nothing— need I say more?
   If so, I prefer to say it face-to-face.
   It would be to our mutual benefit to meet unseen by prying eyes. I am certain that you agree. I look forward with great eagerness to reanimating our friendship. There is a ruined cottage on the château grounds. Meet me there at sunrise. You have nothing to fear from me. After all, you have as much to lose as I.
   Until morning, then. I remain, dear Katherine, your most devoted servant,
   R.

Jeanette looked over at her mistress. How pale she was again. Some women were quite ill in the early months of pregnancy. It was an open secret among the servants that there would be a Cheney heir by September.

"Tcha!" she said. "I would not have given that to you if I had known it would upset you so. It is about the murder in the village, no doubt?"

Flora looked up quickly. God in heaven, had her warning come too late? "A murder you say? Not . . . not . . ." *Not one of the Kersaudys?* But the words were frozen lumps in her throat.

"No one from Pont du Mor, madame. It was a visitor from abroad. A scholar, so I am told, who was a guest of the Kersaudys. He was found strangled."

She riffled through the armoire, oblivious to the effect her revelation had had upon her mistress. "Will Madame wear the rubine silk or the blue?"

"I . . . I'll ring for you when I am ready, Jeanette. You may go now."

The maid curtsied and withdrew. The instant the door shut behind her,

Flora threw back the covers and rose unsteadily. Taking up her wrapper, she hurried into the sitting room. The door to Blaise's chamber was still shut. She tapped lightly. He didn't answer. Turning the handle quietly, she slipped inside. After the brightness of the sitting room it took a few seconds for her vision to adjust.

The room was still in shadows, the heavy curtains drawn. Flora tiptoed to the bed. Empty. The covers were smooth and undisturbed by so much as a wrinkle. He had not slept in it that night.

Flora crushed the letter in her hand, hearing Blaise's last words to her: *"Leave it to me. I shall take care of this. Robin Harding will not bother you again."*

Chapter Fourteen

Flora stood in the dim room. Where was Blaise? Where had he been all night? And, most importantly, what had he been doing?

No, she could not believe that he had disposed of her enemy. Could she?

She bit her lip. What did she truly know of him? He had fierce pride and an equal temper. He was decisive and would act quickly when necessary—just as he had when the need arose to protect Johanna. Flora was haunted by his words when he had revealed the father of his niece's baby: "Sacrebleu! *I wish I had killed him with my own two hands. I wanted to! Only the need to protect Johanna prevented me from doing so at the time.*"

And she remembered that gesture he had made as he spoke, as if his strong fingers were closing about an invisible throat.

She pulled the covers back from his bed, tousled the sheets and punched her fist into the down pillows. Standing back to examine her efforts, she was unsatisfied. It was obvious no one had slept there. Flora lay down upon Blaise's bed and let the weight of her body sink into the featherbed. His scent rose around her like a mist and she wept into his pillow. *Did you do it, Blaise? Did you do it for me? Or to protect your house and name?*

It didn't really matter. If not for her, it would never have happened. Wherever she went, she brought destruction with her.

No sooner had Flora dressed and gone downstairs, than she heard carriage wheels in the courtyard. She had completely forgotten the *fest noz,* and that they would have houseguests tonight.

Gaelle spoke from the hall behind her. "Ah, there you are. I hope you slept well? I had Claudine put some sleeping drops into your *tisane.*"

So that explained her grogginess: brandy, the doctored tisane, and the sleeping drops that Blaise had asked Jeanette to prepare! Little wonder she had slept so long.

"I slept like the dead," she said, then colored. What a poor choice of words that had been!

They arrived at the door together, just as Odile and Guy de Broceliand descended from their smart open carriage. Like everything about the two, it was elegant, expensive, and in the very height of fashion. Her gown of black and white striped silk was all the rage, and the saucy little feathered hat perched on her smoothly banded hair was from the best modiste in Paris. A thick choker of pearls ringed her swanlike throat.

She was paler than Flora remembered, but sparkling and exquisite. Stepping forward, she kissed Gaelle's cheek and took Flora's hands in her gloved ones. "How good of you to let us come to you for the festivities. It will be quite like old times! I hope you have not gone out of your way to make us comfortable, when there is so much on your mind at the moment."

Flora was taken aback. Was she that transparent? Oh, God! Where was Blaise?

"The procession and the *fest noz* preparations must be so difficult in your, ah . . . interesting situation," Odile went on brightly. "Are you surprised that I know? *Chèrie,* a woman cannot keep such secrets from another. Not in such a small place as Pont du Mor."

Gaelle greeted them. Beside the older woman's somber clothes and carriage, de Broceliand's wife had the classic beauty and nervous grace of a thoroughbred.

"I have put you in the same suite in which you stayed on your last visit to the château," Gaelle said.

"Have you?" Wicked laughter danced in Odile's eyes. "I hope Flora does not object?"

"I leave the arrangements to Gaelle's good management," Flora responded with an edge in her voice. She knew exactly what the woman was implying, but was too upset to make a good job of covering it up.

Guy joined them. The late morning sun touched his tanned skin with gold and shone on the silver streaks at his temples. He looked handsome, distinguished, a gentleman to the bone. Unless one took in the intriguing lines of dissipation bracketing his eyes, and his flashing, predatory smile.

"A fine day for the close of the *pardon*. The fishermen say the good weather will hold for several more days."

Taking Flora's hand, he bowed low over it. His lips brushed her bare skin, once again in violation of every rule of etiquette. His smile was overly intimate.

"How lovely to see you again, Madame Cheney. I sincerely hope that we shall have the opportunity to become much better acquainted during our stay."

He was as skilled at layering suggestive meanings beneath polite words as his wife. His intense gaze swept over her. "You grow more beautiful each day," he said in a low tone. "I see that marriage agrees very well with you."

"De Broceliand! Odile!" Nicolas sauntered out of the stables with Loic Kersaudy, where they had just taken their horses. "I thought I recognized your carriage."

More greetings were exchanged, and they went into the drawing room together. Flora rang for refreshments. A servant appeared like a djinn, with wine, *cidre bouché,* and brandy. Odile searched the room, her eyes lingering on the fabulous tapestries, the curios from the earth's four corners, as if taking inventory.

She has imagined herself mistress of this château before, Flora realized. *She is regretting that she is not standing here in my shoes.*

They made themselves comfortable, Odile displaying her attractions to advantage on the settee for Loic and Nicolas. Guy watched them over the top of his glass. Nicolas wandered to one of the windows, and stood there, warming his snifter of pear brandy in the sun.

Odile looked around with a pretty moue of disappointment. "But where is Blaise?"

The question Flora dreaded. It was Nicolas who came to the rescue, rousing from the reverie into which he had fallen. "He rose early and was on his way to Saint-Renan, shortly after sunrise. A matter of urgent business. He expects to be back in good time to greet the procession."

Gaelle was annoyed. "A bad time for him to leave. Surely you might have persuaded him to put it off another day, Flora?"

She looked away. "I was asleep when he left. No doubt he did not wish to disturb me."

"A man of extraordinary restraint," De Broceliand murmured for her ears alone. He raised the crystal wine glass in his hand. "To our host's early return," he said to the room at large. "No doubt he will be shocked to learn of the scandal in the village."

"Do you refer to the man who was found dead?"

"Yes," Loic said, heavily. "And he, a guest under my own roof. Yseult is distraught. I am glad she is helping Madame Rohun prepare the church this afternoon."

Gaelle did not appear interested in pursuing that avenue. "A sad event; however, I find such topics distasteful."

"As do I, Madame Morceau," de Broceliand said. "However, the magistrate has commissioned me to look into the matter for him. It is very unsettling that this has occurred in the parish close, at the height of Pont du Mor's great festival."

"The abbé is said to have almost had a fit of apoplexy." Odile leaned forward, her composure a little ruffled. "It was he who found the poor man, stretched out at the foot of the *calvaire*. It makes me shiver to think of it!"

"Do not forget there is still a murderer loose in Pont du Mor," her husband said. "The man did not strangle himself."

"A thief," Nicolas offered, "come to pick the plump pockets of wealthy pilgrims to the *grand pardon*, perhaps."

De Broceliand sipped his wine and eyed Flora over the rim of the glass intently. "Perhaps, even, a jealous husband."

Flora felt her body go rigid, and willed it to relax.

Guy twirled the stem of his glass. "Tell me, madame, did your husband take exception to that fellow's kissing your hand yesterday? Several people witnessed it. The Cheneys are a jealous line, you know. Why, the first Yvon locked his wife up in a tower and kept her there until she died. Or, in some versions, it is even said that he killed her."

Flora went white with shock. "If you are implying what you seem to be, then you are being foolish beyond permission!"

De Broceliand raised his brows. "I am implying nothing," he said smoothly. "I beg your pardon, Madame Cheney, if I have offended you. I am sure your husband was at the château with you last night."

She felt the blood rush to her face. "But of course. He was in bed beside me all night. He cannot have any knowledge of this affair."

"I was not implying that he knows anything at all about the man's murder," De Broceliand said with amusement. "Indeed, I do not know why you should think it of me." His slow smile said quite the opposite.

Loic downed his brandy. "I did not wish to say anything prematurely; however, I received an anonymous warning yesterday evening that my guest was not, in fact, Monsieur Wolfe, but an Englishman by the name of Harding. If so, he was an escaped criminal, who brutally murdered an elderly woman. A message of inquiry has been sent to the proper authorities."

Nicolas was astonished. "What a fortunate escape we have all had, if this turns out to be the case. Why, I had even urged Blaise to invite the fellow to join us at dinner this evening. As to the person who rid us of this villain—if villain he is—we should owe him a great debt of thanks."

Odile was whiter than the snowy pearls about her throat. "*Mon Dieu!* What a close call. If the dead man is indeed this English murderer, he was an evil man. He deserved to die."

"You are evidently not alone in your opinion," Nicolas said, draining the last of his brandy, "for someone else agreed most vehemently."

Flora held the wine glass so tightly she feared the fragile stem would snap between her fingers. The conversation swirled on around her but she scarcely heard a word.

It was drowned out by the questions still circling through her head like a rondelet: *Where was Blaise? Where had he been last night? And what had he been doing?*

Gaelle kept Flora almost too busy to think the rest of the day. Only three hours until the procession would set out from the church for the château, and the place was still in chaos. With such fine weather and the anticipation of the celebration to come, everyone was in good spirits.

The stablelads were helping the gardeners hang paper lanterns from the trees in the open parkland, and the house men had set up long trestles beneath the trees. Later the women would set out the huge platters of sausage and ham, cauldrons of *cotriade* rich with potatoes and white fish and of mussels in white wine sauce and herbs, butter cake and other rich desserts to be washed down with gallons of the local cider.

Even Odile got into the spirit of things, advising the gardeners on the placement of the lanterns, and complimenting the cooks on the *cotriade*. "What a shame that Claudine must miss this! I wish our hunting lodge were not so distant from the village, so that we might take part in preparing the *pardon*."

"Perhaps you could have a feast to honor one of your patron saints," Flora suggested. It was difficult to concentrate when her heart was so heavy.

"A wonderful idea! I shall tell Guy at once."

Just as Flora was congratulating herself on getting rid of Odile for a few minutes, she found Nicolas at her side. "Walk with me, Flora. I must speak to you privately."

"Now? Could it not wait until later?"

He lowered his voice. "It is about Blaise."

She looked up in alarm. "Has something happened?"

"Not yet. But he is . . . Never mind, it is best if he explains himself."

"Oh, he is here?" Fear and joy trembled in her voice.

"Hush!" Nicolas looked over his shoulder. "He is waiting for you at the house on the Druid's Isle. I will take you to him."

"I will tell Gaelle—"

"No! Tell no one." Nicolas was very grave. "He is in great danger, Flora. You must be brave. I have something to tell you."

She bit her lip. "Tell me."

"I was restless last night, and could not sleep. It was after three when I went out into the walled garden for a stroll to make me sleep. As I was returning to the house, I saw Blaise slip in through the gates, leading his horse quietly back to the stables. At the time I thought . . . well, I don't know exactly what I thought," he said hastily, flushing. "It had no great significance at the time."

Flora was stock-still. Nicolas put his hand on her shoulder. "He was not at your side last night, *pauvre petite*. You and I both know where he was."

"No!"

"It will all come out, Flora. You heard. De Broceliand is already suspicious of him. There was a time when his position and wealth would have provided Blaise all the protection he needed. Things have changed. And now he needs your help."

"Very well."

Sick at heart, she followed him inside. Not many minutes later they were hurrying through the quiet corridors of the old part of the house, heading for the Mermaid's Tower. "It is the quickest way," he said, "and time is of the essence."

They passed the pink granite with the mermaid etching and along the same way Blaise had taken her. They scrambled down the cliff path together. "Where is the boat?" Flora asked.

"Blaise has taken it there already. The tide is low. We will walk across the neck of the peninsula right out to the isle. Claudine said they used to do it as children. Once they were cut off by the rising water, and had to be rescued by his father."

It was rough going. The neck of the peninsula was a narrow tumble of broken granite blocks, split from the cliff face in centuries past. The waves lapped at it eagerly from either side, and the path was slippery with salt spray. Without Nicolas's strong arm and frequent encouragement, Flora could not have made the journey safely. By the time they reached the isle proper, her dress was ripped, her hair had come loose from its chignon, and one of her hands was badly scraped.

They came around the shelf of upthrust rock and the house of Yvon Cheney was almost dead ahead. Flora felt a terrible pang of loss. How happy she had been the last time she had seen it.

As she started toward it, Nicolas caught her arm. "No, he is in the sailboat. It is moored on the far side of the isle, where it cannot easily be seen." He studied her face. "You love him, do you not?"

"Yes, God help me!"

"And you would follow him anywhere?"

Flora gave him a wavering smile. "I would follow him to the very ends of the earth."

Nicolas beamed. "I knew that would be your answer."

The sky was blue overhead with wisps of cloud stretching out to the horizon. That made it all the more poignant for Flora. It was hard to face tragedy on such a lovely day.

Nicolas helped her down a rough patch of rocks to a cove sheltered from the wild Atlantic storms. There was a sort of beach composed of wave-worn rocks that made the going difficult in her thin slippers, but Blaise's sailboat was moored there. There was no sign of him.

"Blaise?"

There was no answer, and he did not appear. "Where can he be?"

Flora started to turn back. A shadow passed over her. She had only a glimpse of Nicolas with his arm raised high. It seemed to happen slowly, in that trapped-in-glue manner of dreams. Then something crashed against the side of her head, and the world went black.

When she came to, Flora was in the sailboat, bound to the mast. Nicolas sat in the stern, eyeing her glumly. The boat bobbed gently on the waves.

"It seems so odd. I never expected to be here with you like this," he said.

"Nor did I!" Her head ached abominably, she was terrified and confused, trying with all her might to keep hysteria at bay. "Untie me, Nicolas."

"I cannot. But I will explain, so that you may understand."

She stared at him. "I cannot conceive of any rational explanation!"

He appeared to be unchanged, the same suave and handsome Nicolas who was married to Claudine. It was his eyes, she realized—too late—that were different. Dazed, distant, as if focused on some bizarre horizon invisible to anyone but himself.

"I am doing it for Claudine."

He stopped, frowning, as if that were all he meant to say. Flora struggled against the ropes that held her wrists tied behind the mast. They dug into her skin viciously. "Surely Claudine knows nothing of this outrage!"

Nicolas was shocked. "Of course not! She knows nothing of any of it. That is what makes it all necessary. I have thought it out carefully, you see."

He was mad. She realized it with cold horror. "Where is Blaise? Oh, what have you done to him?"

"Nothing. Yet." Nicolas glanced over his shoulder. "He should be here soon, though. I left a message for him with your maid, that he was to meet you at the Druid's Isle the moment he returned from Saint-Renan."

Flora's lips were so dry she could hardly talk. A cold breeze blew in off the sea, chilling her through the thin folds of her silk gown. "You are not making sense. Let me go, Nicolas. Claudine will be very angry when she finds out what you have done."

He smiled sweetly. "She will never know, my sweet angel wife. This will be a secret for only three: you, myself, and Blaise. I will take it with me to my grave. You, of course, will be long dead then."

"For the love of God, Nicolas—*why*?"

A flush rose over his face. "For the tawdriest of reasons. For money. It shames me to say it. I suppose I must confess it all. When Claudine married me I had a modest independence, while she was a wealthy heiress. Ah, I see you didn't know that. Many people do not. They think the wealth is mine, that I parlayed my small fortune into a great one, so large that it eclipses hers."

He picked up a coil of rope from the bottom of the boat and began to unravel its ends. "The truth is, I ran through my own monies and dipped into hers. I had complete control of it. She trusts me implicitly." His face twitched with emotion.

"I threw good money after bad, trying to recoup my losses. I wanted to prove to her that I could support her in the style of a queen. But the losses continued. I sold off my properties and some of hers. The rest I mortgaged."

Lifting his head, he sent her a challenging look. "I know that I can restore everything I lost. It is only a matter of time. The investments I have in the Indies will surely prosper . . ."

Nicolas went back to unraveling the rope, while Flora watched in horrid fascination. "Tell me," she said, "how all that leads to this."

"In my own good time," he said sharply. "It is important that you understand. Claudine wanted a child desperately. She could not conceive. I tried to make it up to her in other ways. I bought her gifts, expensive gifts, to show my love. That is how I first came to speculate with her money. It was only to make her happy.

"The gifts pleased her, so I bought her more. Always trying to outdo myself. But it was not enough. Never enough! It was not jewels or exotic perfumes that she wanted. What she longed for was life itself, growing within her. And that is the one thing I am incapable of giving her. So it was all for nothing."

He buried his face in his hands. "My fault . . . all my fault!" It took him several minutes to compose himself. "I contracted malaria as a young man. I knew when I married her how much she wanted children. Knew, but did not tell her that I would never father a child."

For a moment there was silence, except for his ragged breathing and the lapping of the waves against the hull. When he lifted his head, his features were filled with anguish. "Can you guess at my torture, loving her so deeply? Knowing that I was the chief cause of her unhappiness?"

Flora took a deep breath. A cloud had passed over the sun, and she was trembling with cold and fear. The mermaid's jewel hung against her breast like a piece of ice.

"You cannot think that my death will cure her of her grief."

Nicolas gave her a long, sad look. "I am truly sorry," he said. "She loves you dearly. Indeed, I am quite fond of you myself. But there is no other way out of my predicament. I did try to keep you out of it, Flora. I was safe as long as Blaise had no heir. My creditors all know that Claudine is next in line to the Cheney fortune, and that has bought me time."

He looked up at the low cliffs again, scanning them. "I never meant to become such a villain as I have turned out to be." Nicolas gave Flora a troubled look. "That man found dead in the parish close, he was more fortunate than you, in that he never saw his death coming. He was strangled from behind, you know, with a woman's silk stocking. I doubt he even saw his executioner's face."

Relief rushed through Flora. *Oh, thank God!* It had not been Blaise, then. He would not have done something so cowardly. If he had killed Robin, it would have been in a face-to-face confrontation, with fair warning given. How could she have considered the possibility for even a moment?

She stalled for time. "Johanna is the daughter of Blaise's brother. Surely she will inherit if anything happens to him?"

"Brittany has its own ways, and the Cheneys make their own rules. The château and the Cheney wealth pass from one generation to the next through the blood, directly down the line. Male or female, it makes no difference. And if the owner dies without issue, everything goes to the next surviving descendant in the same generation. Which, in this case, is Claudine."

"How can that be of any use to you? Blaise is young and in his prime. He might well outlive Claudine."

"Do not say that! Do not *ever* speak of such a terrible thing!"

It was difficult for Flora to tell if he were enraged or terrified. Poor Claudine! To love this man, who was as mad, as much a monster as Robin Harding, in his own way.

"But surely the creditors would be aware of it."

Nicolas regained his composure. "I realized that. And I had a clever thought. I spread it about that Blaise had an incurable disease. Two years, perhaps three at most, and he would be in his grave."

His voice was so strange now, as if they were having an ordinary conversation. "They agreed to extend the loans for three years. I knew that in that time, I could bring myself about. My foreign investments would surely prosper. I would make my own fortune. I could pay off the loans and the interest, and Claudine would never know what I had done."

The wind rose suddenly and the light was changing. Flora was aware of it with one small portion of her mind, while the rest was trying to deal with the living nightmare she found herself trapped within.

The stiffening breeze ruffled Nicolas's fair hair. "I hope I have not cut the time too short. Blaise should be here soon."

"He will not come."

Nicolas shook his head and smiled. "He has no choice. He loves you."

She shook her head. "You are wrong there, too."

"Don't you think I know what a man in love is like? I have seen how he looks at you when you are not watching. As if all the world is centered in you. That is why it is so fitting that you go together. I should not want him to suffer over your death any more than is necessary."

"Your consideration is touching!" she said.

He didn't catch the irony. Nicolas turned away. "I would not want to live without Claudine. Did you know I fell in love with her while she was still practically in the schoolroom? A saucy little thing of fourteen summers, already catching men's eyes with her vivacity and beauty. I did not know she was an heiress then. I would have married her even if she hadn't a *sou* to her name."

Nicolas sighed. "It would have been so much better for everyone. Then none of this would be necessary. You and I would not be sitting here, waiting for Blaise. He would not have to die."

Flora saw movement from the corner of her eye. She tried not to look. *Please God, don't let it be Blaise. There is no use in both of us dying.*

"If you wanted to murder Blaise, there must surely be a dozen different ways to do it. You might have pushed him off the cliff, or waylaid him on his way back from the village. Why so elaborate a plot?"

He looked surprised, almost shocked. "I never wanted to 'murder' Blaise, as you put it. Circumstances force my hand. He came back to France, hale and hearty—and with his new bride in tow, just as my loans were about to come due. They refused to give me another extension on my loans. I begged and pleaded. It was humiliating. But I pointed out that there was no heir, and no proof that there would ever be one.

"Which is why, in the beginning, it wasn't Blaise I wanted to be rid of. Nor even you, Flora. But I could not let your child live."

"But . . ." She was flabbergasted. "I am not with child!"

Nicolas eyed her sadly. "Oh, yes. Everyone knows it. I suspected it was the reason for your hasty marriage. Why else would Blaise marry so suddenly, to a woman so out of his normal social sphere? But you are a lady, not some opera dancer, and he is a gentleman, so he had no choice. Gaelle spelled it all out in a letter to Claudine."

Flora was speechless. "It is not true."

"Why are you lying to me!" He leaned down until his face was almost level with hers. "I know you are expecting. Blaise told me so himself, only this morning."

He looked down on her pityingly. "If only the herbs Malin put in your food had worked! You would have miscarried, and perhaps you would not have conceived again immediately. All I need is a year's extension of the loan. In a year I will surely regain all the money I lost through my investments, and pay off all the debts. I will handle my investments differently, this time. If only I had followed Blaise's advice, it wouldn't matter if you produced an heir. We could all have gone on as before."

Her mind was reeling. "Then . . . the food poisoning. It was something Malin put in my food to make me miscarry?"

Nicolas smiled at her as if she were a clever child. "Yes. I did not mean for Johanna to be ill as well. Who could guess that she would taste something from your plate? Or that she would eat up most of the chocolates I gave you."

He frowned and shook his head. "I brought you each a box of your favorite confections. It was careless of you to leave your own chocolates lying about, Flora. Why, Claudine might have eaten one and been poisoned! I was very angry when I learned of it. Malin said Johanna was so ill she feared that she would die."

Everything was becoming horribly clear to Flora. "The food poisoning, Johanna's illness. They were attempts to make me miscarry. The seaweed I found in my room and the seashells scattered around my bed were meant to frighten me, I suppose. Tell me, how did Malin get into my room with both doors locked? Is there some sort of secret door or passageway?"

Nicolas looked confused. "I know nothing of seaweed or seashells or secret passages. And I doubt that Malin had any hand in it. If she did, she would surely have asked me for more money. As I said, she is greedy, that one." A sudden thought struck him. "I suppose I shall have to dispose of her, as well. *Mon Dieu!* Does it never end?"

Flora shook her head. He blamed everyone for his troubles but himself. His sanity was disintegrating before her eyes.

A pebble fell from the low cliff overhead. Blaise stood above the cove looking down. His face was whiter than the froth capping the waves that had suddenly sprung up.

"End it now, Nicolas. Release Flora. We will go back to the château and work this out. I will give you what you need to straighten out your finances."

"Too late! You would tell Claudine! She would know what a liar, what a failure I am . . . and now you both know that I am the cause of her supposed barrenness. She would never forgive me!"

Flora realized the tide was running out. While they had been talking, the sailboat was moving away from the cove and out to sea. And Nicolas was paying out more line.

"No," Nicolas said, shaking his head. "You both must die. In time it will become part of the legend of Château Morgaine—how the last heir and his pregnant wife were claimed by the Sea Queen's wrath."

He cut the line and the sailboat leapt forward like a live thing, eager for the open seas. The tide had turned and was running full, but eddies off the peninsula pulled the vessel seaward.

Blaise sprang down to the rocky beach, lithe as a panther, and just as dangerous. "Your plan seems to have run aground. I am safe on the shore, while you are going out to sea with Flora."

"Not for long!" They were moving rapidly away from the island now, pulled past the headland. Instead of facing the boat toward shore, it was moving at an angle that would carry it far from Brittany and eventually into the open channel. Nicolas rose, picked up a pole, and thrust it straight down. "I drilled a hole and put a cork into it. Now it is gone. How long do you think it will take before the boat fills with water and sinks, Blaise? How far, and how fast can you swim?"

Then he unfurled the sail. The wind caught it and it billowed out. With a wild peal of laughter, Nicolas jumped overboard and began swimming toward the isle's headland, helped along by the current. He would reach safety in no time at all. Meanwhile Flora was being carried briskly out to sea.

With a cry of despair, Blaise ripped off his coat and shoes and plunged into the cold water. He was fit, and a strong swimmer. He cut through the growing seas until his back and shoulders burned and his breath came in raw gasps. When he struggled for a glimpse of the sailboat he saw it was hopeless. The wind and waves were drawing it away faster than he could hope to close the distance between them.

"Flora!"

She turned her head, as if she had heard his voice. Impossible, over the sound of wave and wind. Her chin was high, in that defiant pose he knew and loved so well. The wet spray had plastered her skirts to her legs. She looked like a mermaid figurehead, incongruously lashed to the mast.

"I should have let you go," he whispered, as the waves battered him. "I should have given you your freedom."

Saltwater washed into his mouth, half choking him. He struggled mightily against the pull of the crosscurrents. His strength was lagging and his waterlogged garments weighted him down. The waves were so high he could no longer see over them when he was in the trough.

Cold knowledge iced his blood: this was the point of no return. He could head back to shore now, while he still had strength to reach it, or he could swim toward Flora and die in the hopeless attempt.

There was no question at all in his mind. While he had life and strength, he would use every last drop of them to try and save her.

Arms feeling like lead, lungs on fire, he forced his way through the water. He was mumbling prayers between his gasps for breath, until he no longer knew if he prayed for the Queen of Heaven, or the queen of the sea.

The current sucked at his legs, pulling him down. Dark shapes loomed in the mist rising off the water, but whether rocks or waves he could not tell. They seemed to leap up and then dive beneath the waves with sinuous grace. The *mari morgans*. Atavistic fears preyed upon his Breton soul.

"Queen of the Morgans!" he gasped. "If there is any of your blood in me, I call upon you now!" A wave slapped him, hard, and he went under. It was like having a stone wall collapse over him. He came up sputtering and wild with rage. "*Damn you!* You will not stop me. I *will* free her!"

The rage fueled him anew. Blaise struck out through the roiled seas. The skies were almost as dark as the water, and pellets of rain pocked the surface and stung his face. Another wall of water slammed him sideways with incredible force. He went under again, into a world all gray and opaque. Kicking with all his might, he shot back to the surface. Incredibly, unbelievably, he saw the sailboat not twenty yards ahead. It was tossed like foam on the cresting waves. Tossed closer to him with every passing minute.

A powerful wind had sprung up, as the squall scudded in toward the shore. The tide and currents were strong, but the wind overrode them. With superhuman effort Blaise closed the gap. His fingers closed on wood. The tiller! With the next sideways dip of the hull, he was over it and onto the deck. There were two inches of seawater inside the sailboat.

Flora stared at him though the driving rain. She was certain he was a hallucination. Not until she felt his body tight against hers, his mouth on her own as he fumbled with the ropes that bound her, did she believe. *"Blaise!"*

He kissed her again and wrenched himself away. The knots were too tight and slippery for him to loosen. There wasn't time. Especially now, when they were shipping water fast. He made his way across the deck, and returned with a sheathed knife. Another moment and they were slashed through.

Flora's hands were so cold and numb she couldn't feel them. Blaise led her to the best place of relative safety. "Stay here," he mouthed against the shrieks of wind. "Hang on for dear life. And pray, Flora. Pray!"

The howling of the wind was like a hundred voices, now. He could make out the Druid's Isle to his right, the headland that protected Pont du Mor to the left. Thank God he was able to get a fix on their bearings! He could try for the cove at the foot of the château's cliff path, but the way was filled with treacherous rocks. The Druid's Isle was closer but more hazardous. But they would sink long before they could reach the safe harbor of Pont du Mor.

He felt around for the hole where Nicolas had removed his plug. It was small. There must be something aboard they could plug it with. "Flora! Look about you. See if there is something that will fit this hole and keep the water from pouring in. I will try and set us a course."

Their best chance might be to cut sail and hope to ride out the storm; but Blaise knew these waters. Either way, they would surely end up dashed upon the rocks. The only choice was to let enough wind out of the sails to keep from capsizing, and pray he could guide them through the treacherous rocks to the small cove below the château.

"I've stopped the leak!" Flora called to him, but he couldn't hear her over the din.

She had taken off the necklace, and lodged the mermaid's jewel into the hole Nicolas had drilled. The egg was halfway in, but she had to lie down in the cold water and hold it in place by force. Waves broke over the bow and brackish liquid filled her mouth. She coughed and spit it out.

The next minutes were an eternity. There was a jolt and a grinding shudder, but the sailboat floated free on the next wave. Blaise lashed the tiller and came to her side. "Clever Flora!"

But he already knew that they were doomed. He gathered her up in his arms. The egg popped out of the hole and water gushed in. "Blaise!"

"It is no use," he said. "The hull is breached behind. I am so sorry, Flora. My love. My dear, forever love."

"You should not have come after me," she murmured against his mouth. "You should have let me go."

"No, this is best. Together. Two more victims of the Sea Queen's curse."

"Not the queen of the morgans, but Nicolas!"

But Blaise wasn't listening. "I should not have mocked the legends." He reached down into the water filling the hull and plucked out the fabulous necklace. "The source of all the Cheney wealth, they say. I say, the source of all our pain!"

He rose and threw back his head, looking into the crest of a mighty wave.

The stone dangled from its chain, seeming to glow against the churning waters. "Take it, but spare my wife!" he shouted. "Your daughter's soul and my life for hers!"

He hurled it into the sea. "Take it and be damned with you!"

And a strange thing happened then, which in time begat its own legend along the Breton coast. The rain ceased abruptly, the winds died, and the waves fell. Within minutes the churning sea had changed, like a bolt of rumpled silk stretched smooth by a giant's hand. And in that moment, just before the mermaid's egg hit the water, a massive flare of blue-green light illuminated the sea for miles around.

No one saw the lightning bolt, but the air shook with the mightly rumble of thunder. And in that instant, Flora and Blaise saw something strange rise from the waves: a form very like a woman's, with a spiky crown of pearl-encrusted shells and long flowing hair, breached the surface.

Flora's necklace curved through the air in a long arc. The mermaid's egg glimmered like a sea-green eye against the glare. As it passed the crest of the arc and plummeted toward the waves, a slender arm rose above the waves. Pale, gracefully feminine, and braceleted with seashells and sailor's gold, it reached out and caught the necklace.

Delicate, not-quite-human fingers closed over glowing blue-green jewel. The air shook and shimmered, and the creature sank beneath the waves, taking the mermaid's egg with it in her delicately webbed hand.

The sailboat pitched forward on a surging wave, and was dashed to splinters against the rocks.

Epilogue

The entire village of Pont du Mor had gathered in the church of St. Mari du Mor for the event. Everyone wore their best finery, and the statue of the Virgin looked down upon the worshipers with her serene smile. Whispers filled the nave. "Poor thing. So young to be widowed. And so tragically."

"At least she has the child to comfort her."

"Yes. A great blessing."

Flora approached the baptismal font with her precious burden, gowned in garnet silk. It was Blaise's favorite color. For this occasion they had all laid off their mourning clothes. It seemed fitting to celebrate life on this special day.

The baby smiled up at her, oblivious to the emotions swirling through the church about his curly blond head. The infant had no father to raise him, but his new mother would raise him well, wrap him in her love and protection.

Gently, Flora placed him into Claudine's arms.

In her black widow's weeds Claudine looked wan and frail, yet at the moment she was radiant with love. "My son," Claudine said, smiling down at little Cristophe Nicolas Le Vec, in his heirloom christening robe. She already almost believed that he was hers and Nicolas's son in truth. In time she surely would.

"How proud your father would be of you. And how proud you will be of him!" she whispered.

In time she would tell him of his father's tragic heroism. Claudine believed with all her being the story that Blaise and Flora had concocted together. A fairy-tale version, of how Nicolas had died trying to save them from drowning.

Claudine would never know that he had leapt to his death when he had seen Blaise drag Flora out of the water at the foot of the cliff path. When he had known there was no other choice left him, to protect Claudine from the disillusionment that would destroy her: and so Nicolas had destroyed himself.

His death had been his final gift to her.

The abbé came forward. "Who sponsors this child?"

Four people stepped to the font: Blaise and Flora, Loic and Johanna would speak the vows as Cristophe's godparents. Johanna would have the perfect excuse to dote upon the child to whom she had given birth in secret, to buy him gifts and play with him and spoil him. If she could not be his mother, she would be his favorite "aunt." Flora had arranged it all.

Nearby the De Brocelians sat in total amity, as if their own lives had not been brushed by wings of darkness. As if Guy had not caught Odile making love with that insufferable Englishman a few short months ago, and been forced to rid the world of Robin Harding forever.

They had both been frightened by the consequences of her infidelity and his murderous rage, and both had learned. In future, Guy de Broceliand would guard his temper well. He consoled himself with the knowledge that his victim had been a villain, a murderer masquerading under another man's identity. The body of the real Kieran Wolfe had never been found.

As for Odile, she was the very model of a doting wife— Guy slanted a look her way—at least for now.

Johanna watched the ceremony, repeated the vows after the priest with Loic at her side. She felt as if she were waking from a strange dream. As if it all—the secret pregnancy and agonizing delivery—had happened to someone else.

Flora had prepared the way for this moment, by helping Johanna to feel, through those long, uncomfortable months, that she was carrying the child for Claudine. In her heart that is how she thought of him: dear, sweet little Cristophe, Claudine's son.

Watching the ceremony, Flora hoped that Johanna would never rue her agreement to let Claudine have the baby to raise as her own. It was the only possible way. In society there was no hope at all for the future of a disgraced girl and a bastard son.

But there was a world of opportunity opening up for a young and lovely debutante, and a much-loved baby who would inherit his mother's holdings. And under Blaise's wise stewardship, Claudine's fortune was safely established once more.

Blaise closed his strong fingers over Flora's hand, thanking *le Bon Dieu* for sending this remarkable woman into his life. Every day he thought he loved her as much as was humanly possible, yet every day he loved her more.

Cristophe cried out as the abbé poured the holy water over his forehead, and Blaise smiled as Claudine comforted the baby. He knew how deeply she had loved Nicolas, and his heart ached for her.

He had known that Nicolas was in financial difficulties since arriving in Paris, but not the extent of them until he had met with his sources in Saint-Renan. The second had been an emergency meeting, with word that Nicolas's creditors were about to foreclose, or he would never have gone. He had managed to stall them with an infusion of his own resources, but it had taken longer than he'd expected.

Thank God he had returned in time to save Flora!

In the aftermath, he had done what he could, seeing to it that Nicolas's debts were paid off and that word of them would never reach Claudine's ears. It had eaten into his own fortunes considerably, but that didn't matter. All that did matter was that Johanna was safely delivered, Claudine would carry on her life with her new child and her illusions of Nicolas intact, and that Flora was safe.

And his.

A grand *fest* was held at the château after Cristophe's baptism, with all the village invited. The sky shone blue above sapphire waters, and crisp September air held a poignant note of summer's end and winter's inevitable coming. Soon Blaise and Flora would return to Paris. But first they had another duty to perform.

While the festivities went on, they slipped away to the Mermaid's Tower.

Blaise lifted out the wooden box he had hidden just inside the door that led to the cliff path. "The last of the château's secrets," he said, as they started out.

"There will be no more between us," Flora said. "Secrets have caused too much anguish to us all."

Gaelle stepped out of the shadows of the massive wall. "There is one more. Flora told me everything, Blaise. How you thought you were a bastard, because of Guy's dying words."

Her hands held her ruby cross until her bones shone white. "I have spent my life in prayer and atonement for what I thought was my greatest sin. I see that I committed another equally as damning." She looked old and suddenly fragile.

Blaise started toward her but she held up an imperious hand. "We will speak of this later, after you have had time to truly look into your heart and see if you find it there to forgive me."

She looked him squarely in the eye. "You are your father's son, Blaise. But you are not your mother's child. It was I who bore you. I who betrayed Anne with her own husband. And it was that which tipped the scales of her native despondency into terrible despair. I was with her when she died. She cursed me there, in the Mermaid's Tower, before she jumped to her death."

Although only a few feet separated Gaelle from her son, it might as well have been an ocean. They were both white-faced. Blaise's hands were knotted at his sides. He was not a bastard. He shook his head from side to side. Something had been given back to him, but something had been taken away.

Flora felt such pity for them both her heart was wrung. But this was between them. She must not speak. Not yet.

Gaelle faced her son with dignity. "I am going on a pilgrimage to Mont-Saint-Michel with Claudine and the . . . and *her* baby," she said quietly. "When I return you will tell me if you wish me to leave, or stay. Whatever your decision, I will understand."

Without waiting for a reply, she turned and went back through the door, closing it behind her.

The sailboat swooped and dipped over the blue waters of the bay. "I think it was about here," Blaise said.

He had not spoken from the time they left Gaelle until now. The foundation of his life had been built on quicksand, and Flora knew he was trying to salvage what he could. Perhaps this would help.

She shaded her eyes against the cool blues and greens, streaked and swirling like the colors in the mermaid's jewel. "Yes, this is as good a place as any."

Blaise removed the lid from the ornate box resting on the deck. It was ancient, of some aromatic wood. The carvings were surely Persian.

At Flora's insistence, he had removed the pink granite stone in the wall of the Mermaid's Tower and found it, just as she had seen it in her dreams. Inside was a pitiful collection of bones.

Flora knelt down beside Blaise. Sunlight warmed his skin, and glazed the planes and hollows of the ivoried skull he held in his hand.

"Look at those cheekbones," Flora said. "She was stunningly beautiful!"

"You speak of her as if you have seen her."

She smiled, remembering the woman with long golden hair who had come to her in so many dreams. The lapping waves echoed the mermaid's whisper: *"Yes . . . I knew you were the one. The one who would set me free!"*

Touching the fused bones that would have formed the woman's lower legs, Flora felt a shimmer of magic in the air. "Do you think she was really a mermaid? Or a woman born with a tragic defect that gave rise to the legend?"

"Perhaps the only tragedy was her great beauty. So great that her jealous husband walled her in the tower so he alone could see her. Poor creature!"

They carried the box to the stern together, and emptied it into the deep. The yellowed bones slipped beneath the waves, glimmering like shells as they vanished.

"Well, she is free now."

Blaise drew Flora into his arms. "And so are we. Free of the past and all its secrets. Free to live. And free to love."

His mouth hovered over hers. "I do love you, Flora. Love of my life. Heart of my heart! I cannot believe that I almost lost you twice, through my foolishness. I tried to seduce you into loving me because I felt unworthy of such joy—and I wanted you to stay as my wife because you loved me, not out of affection for Johanna and the child."

"You should have told me you loved me from the first moment you knew it." She nestled into his embrace. "I think my heart might burst for loving you." She thought of Nicolas and shuddered. "Sometimes it frightens me. Is there such a thing as loving too much?"

"No. Not when it is the right kind of love." Blaise's arms tightened and his mouth hovered over hers. "As I love you."

His mouth came down on hers tenderly, and then with mounting passion. They were lost to their surroundings, but if they had looked just then they might have seen something strange and wonderful.

Their boat was surrounded by a shifting net, composed of millions of tiny bubbles. Or perhaps they were really pearls floating on the stilled waters.

And if they had looked more closely yet, they might have seen a shape leaping joyously beneath the clear, cold waters, swimming with a flash of iridescent scales, down into the sapphire depths.

But while the sailboat drifted at anchor Blaise spread quilts out on the deck and they made love beneath a pure and cloudless sky, too bemused to notice much of anything but each other. Aware only of the miracle of their happiness.

Afterward they lay entwined in the shadow of the sail. "Did you hear anything earlier?" Flora asked. "When you made love to me?"

"Hear what?"

She hesitated. "Voices. Far away. Like tiny silver bells."

"You were asleep and dreaming of mermaids again," he whispered against her throat as his hands stroked her tenderly.

"I don't think it was a dream," Flora said, but she forgot about dreams and mermaids and silvery bells as Blaise kissed her again, passionately.

And all around the waves rose and fell, and the pearls vanished beneath them, and the sea gleamed and glittered, like a great blue-green jewel.

KATHLEEN KANE

"[HAS] REMARKABLE TALENT FOR UNUSUAL,
POIGNANT PLOTS AND CAPTIVATING
CHARACTERS."

—*PUBLISHERS WEEKLY*

A Pocketful of Paradise
A spirit whose job it was to usher souls into the afterlife, Zach
had angered the powers that be. Sent to Earth to live as a
human for a month, Zach never expected the beautiful Rebecca
to ignite in him such earthly emotions.
0-312-96090-5 _____ $5.99 U.S. _____ $7.99 Can.

This Time for Keeps
After eight disastrous lives, Tracy Hill is determined to get it
right. But Heaven's "Resettlement Committee" has other
plans—to send her to a 19th century cattle ranch, where a
rugged cowboy makes her wonder if the ninth time is *finally* the
charm.
0-312-96509-5 _____ $5.99 U.S. _____ $7.99 Can.

Still Close to Heaven
No man stood a ghost of a chance in Rachel Morgan's heart, for
the man she loved was an angel who she hadn't seen in fifteen
years. Jackson Tate has one more chance at heaven—if he finds
a good husband for Rachel…and makes her forget a love that
he himself still holds dear.
0-312-96268-1 _____ $5.99 U.S. _____ $7.99 Can.

ANTOINETTE STOCKENBERG

"In a league of her own."

— *RomanticTimes*

A CHARMED PLACE

In a charming town on Cape Cod, professor Maddie Regan and correspondent Dan Hawke team up to solve the mystery of Maddie's father's death. And what they discover are old secrets, long-buried lies—and an intense, altogether unexpected passion. 0-312-96597-4 ___$5.99 U.S.___$7.99 Can.

DREAM A LITTLE DREAM

Years ago, an eccentric millionaire decided to transport an old English castle—stone by stone—to America. Today his lovely heiress Elinor lives there—and so do the mansion's ghosts, intent on reclaiming their ancestral home. Now Elinor must battle a force stronger than herself—and, when a handsome nobleman enters the picture, the power of her own heart.

0-312-96168-5___$5.99 U.S.___$7.99 Can.

BEYOND MIDNIGHT

Ghosts and witches are a thing of the past for modern-day Salem, Massachusetts—but Helen Evett, single mother, is beginning to wonder if this is entirely true. A strange power surrounds the man with whom she is falling in love—is it the ghost of his dead wife trying to tell her something?

0-312-95976-1___$5.99 U.S.___$6.99 Can.